PRAISE FOR
FIRST-DEGREE FUDGE

"An action-filled story with a likable heroine and a fun setting. And, oh, that fudge! I'm swooning. I hope Ava Oosterling and her family and friends take me back to Door County, Wisconsin, for another nibble soon."
—JoAnna Carl, national bestselling author of
the Chocoholic Mysteries

"The first in a new series set in the 'Cape Cod of the Midwest,' *First-Degree Fudge* is a lighthearted confection that cozy mystery readers will devour."
—Lucy Burdette, author of *Topped Chef*

"As palatable as a fresh pan of Belgian fudge, this debut will delight candy aficionados and mystery lovers with its fast pace, quirky cast, and twist after twist. A must read!"
—Liz Mugavero, author of *Kneading to Die*

"Christine DeSmet has whipped up a melt-in-your-mouth gem of a tale. One is definitely not going to be enough!"
—Hannah Reed, national bestselling author of
Beeline to Trouble

First-Degree Fudge

A FUDGE SHOP MYSTERY

Christine DeSmet

AN OBSIDIAN MYSTERY

OBSIDIAN
Published by the Penguin Group
Penguin Group (USA), 375 Hudson Street,
New York, New York 10014, USA

USA | Canada | UK | Ireland | Australia | New Zealand | India | South Africa | China

Penguin Books Ltd., Registered Offices: 80 Strand, London WC2R 0RL, England
For more information about the Penguin Group visit penguin.com.

First published by Obsidian, an imprint of New American Library,
a division of Penguin Group (USA)

First Printing, September 2013

ISBN 978-0-451-41647-6

Printed in the United States of America
10 9 8 7 6 5 4 3 2 1

PUBLISHER'S NOTE
This is a work of fiction. Names, characters, places, and incidents either are the product of the author's imagination or are used fictitiously, and any resemblance to actual persons, living or dead, business establishments, events, or locales is entirely coincidental.

The recipes contained in this book are to be followed exactly as written. The publisher is not responsible for your specific health or allergy needs that may require medical supervision. The publisher is not responsible for any adverse reactions to the recipes contained in this book.

The publisher does not have any control over and does not assume any responsibility for author or third-party Web sites or their content.

ALWAYS LEARNING   PEARSON

To those who love Door County, Wisconsin

Chapter 1

I was cutting a pan of Cinderella Pink Fudge into twenty-four bite-sized squares on the white marble-slab table near the window that fronted the docks when my friend Pauline Mertens burst through the door, rattling the cowbell hooked to the knob. Snow flurries and cold air rushed in to stir the chocolate-scented air.

"Ava, she's here!" Pauline said, not bothering to take off her coat. "Can you believe it? Oh my gosh golly giddy-ups, I saw Hollywood's voluptuous, *von vivant* vixen vamp!" She whipped her long black hair back over her shoulders, acting the part herself.

Pauline is a kindergarten teacher, so over-the-top alliteration and other word games often spilled into our conversations.

But an excited tickle was running through me, too, because this was the day my fudge would debut for a celebrity. "You saw *the* Rainetta Johnson? Where?"

"At the Blue Heron Inn. Isabelle said she stayed overnight. Oh, that looks luscious."

I slapped her hand away before she stole a piece of pale pink, cherry-vanilla fudge, which had my own mouth watering. The gustable air in the shop smelled like cotton candy and freshly made vanilla waffle ice cream cones combined. My little shop had already seen a dozen fishers and early-season tourists duck out of the unusual May cold because of the smell they said hit them yards away along the Lake Michigan docks of Fishers' Harbor in Door County, Wisconsin.

"This fudge is for the party," I said, "but here, I'll give you a taste from the new batch. Tell me if it's creamy enough."

I moved to the next area of my six-foot marble table, where I'd poured warm but cooling creamy pink fudge straight from the copper kettle nearby. I'd whipped the pink confection fast for the last fifteen minutes with four-foot walnut wood paddles. My shoulders were still aching.

The next step was working the white chocolate with my small wood spatulas until it stiffened enough for my hands to take over in a process called "loafing." I would then knead the pink pile of sugar crystals until they transformed like magic into just the right consistency for slicing. Fudge was all about chemistry—and the aromas emanating from melting sugar, butter, and Belgian chocolate. I found a clean spoon and carved into the pale pink cloud of fudge, handing the treat to Pauline.

Pauline set the smidgen of pink cherry-vanilla fudge on her tongue.

Her eyes melted like dark chocolate as an ambrosial smile curved onto her face.

I hopped on my feet like one of her kindergarteners. "Well?"

She blossomed in rapture, looking down on me. She was six feet tall—two inches taller than me, which bugged me when we played hoops over at the school.

"This is yummy, better than cherries jubilee!" She dipped the spoon into the fudge loaf again before I could catch her. "Once they taste this at Isabelle's fund-raiser, they're all going to descend on this place. Did you make enough? What if Rainetta wants to mail some right away to all her Hollywood friends?"

My head spun with sugarplum visions of grandeur and glamour for myself. "Can you stay and help? I've never made this much fudge so fast in my life."

"I'm sorry. I have to get over to the school." It was Sunday, and Pauline frequently prepped her classroom for the week on Sundays. "Isabelle was wondering why you weren't at the inn yet with the fudge."

"I'm waiting for Gilpa to get here. He took some of the inn's guests on the lighthouse tour. And then this storm came up." Gilpa was what I called my grandpa Gil Oosterling. He was the co-owner of my shop.

"He's too crusty to let anything happen."

I hoped Pauline was right. I returned to cutting the hardened Cinderella Pink Fudge into one-inch squares. "What's Rainetta look like?"

"Aging well. Big boobs and bodacious at sixty-five. Rainetta's already holding court like the movie star she is—or was. And after one bite of this, she'll be recommending your pink treat for all the swag bags given away at next year's Oscars."

My hands shook with anticipation, so much that I thought for a second I'd cut off a finger in the pink fudge, but it was only a cherry popping up under the blade.

For Cinderella Pink Fudge, I'd married the best white Belgian chocolate with tart, red cherries that grow in the orchards surrounding our little town of two hundred or so permanent residents.

Rainetta Johnson now lived in Chicago, having retired from films years ago, but everybody my parents'
age remembered her movies with Elvis and Cary Grant.
I'd spent a few years in Los Angeles before moving back
to Door County recently, and I knew that Rainetta put
money behind plenty of upstart indie filmmakers. So
why not my Fairy Tale Fudge line? I'd never met her, but
I'd heard she liked vacationing in quaint Door County,
called the Cape Cod of the Midwest.

I felt bad about our inhospitable weather welcome
for Rainetta. On this first Sunday in May, the day had
started in the fifties. Trust me, it really did. Now, nearly
noon, snow spit past my fudge shop windows. Tulips
alongside buildings bent under the frozen betrayal. The
sudden storm on Lake Michigan was churning our bay
with wind gusts up to forty knots, enough to shred the
flags outside on their posts. Whitecaps splashed foam
and spray over the dock in front of my fudge shop.

My just-opened fudge shop was the last stop on the
docks of Fishers' Harbor before you boarded a boat or
your first stop after you disembarked following a day
spent sightseeing among the ten lighthouses dotting the
shorelines of our peninsula county. Lighthouses attracted people who loved to buy souvenirs, including
homemade, handmade fudge. I figured my location
would give me a pretty good chance of success.

My place used to be called Oosterling's Live Bait,
Bobbers & Beer. In Wisconsin everything ends with "&
beer." But when I moved home a couple of weeks back,
my grandpa let me tack up a temporary sign and share
his space. He moved both his live minnow tank and the
apostrophe on "Oosterling's." We're now Oosterlings'
Live Bait, Bobbers & Belgian Fudge. There wasn't

enough room on the building to keep "& Beer." In these parts, beer is assumed to be on the shelves and in the coolers.

I said good-bye to Pauline, then tried Grandpa Gil's number again. Still no answer. My stomach bottomed out. I took out my worry on the pink fudge cloud, working it with the wood paddles, watching for just the right sheen and mirrorlike look before the final loafing.

It was my fault Gilpa had taken the chance to go out today. He wanted to be out of the way so that I could have my fudge debut all on my own. I'm thirty-two, and he feels sorry for me not finding my "thing" in life yet. He was the first to warn me about my ex-husband, too. To say he doesn't have faith in my fudge fantasies and judgment is an understatement.

My assistant, Cody Fjelstad, startled me by calling from across the small room, "Miss Oosterling, hurry up. We got only ten minutes! This isn't La-La Land!"

Cody always called me "Miss," which made me feel old or like my schoolmarm friend, Pauline, who was forced to wear thrift shop dregs that kindergarten kids could throw up on with impunity. I didn't think I looked particularly like an old-maid "Miss." Or did I? My brown ponytail put up in a twist with a wood chopstick hung half undone over one shoulder of my faded yellow blouse and my long apron. My jeans were ripped from the real wear and tear of fixing up my shop and not the fake tears you buy in the store. I always wore work shoes now—boots, really—with lug soles for safety's sake, in case I needed to step out onto the wet docks or help Gilpa haul equipment onto a boat. And then there were my copper kettles—don't dare drop them on bare feet!

Cody was eighteen and challenged with a mild form of Asperger's and obsessive-compulsive disorder, according to what Pauline knew. He'd worked long and hard on his speech patterns, eye contact, and his sense of humor and sarcasm. Calling me "Miss" made him happy, so though it made me feel old, I also knew it was a sign of him working on his goal to be a happy and well-adjusted adult someday. He was sweet and sincere and ten times as good as any intern I'd had to deal with in Los Angeles, or La-La Land.

Cody had red hair and freckles and liked to be called "Ranger" because he dreamed of being a ranger at a local park, particularly at the Chambers Island Lighthouse, where Gilpa was supposed to have taken those four guests of the Blue Heron Inn. That lighthouse was seven miles into the bay, smack-dab in the middle of the shipping lanes and this upstart storm.

"Sorry, Ranger. My mind is racing today."

"You should race faster or you'll miss your party and we won't be famous after all."

I sped up my fudge loafing operation. "How's the wrapping going?"

Pink cellophane crinkled and squeaked.

He said, "I'm catchin' up to ya. Hurry up, Miss Oosterling."

He came over to take the pan of fudge I'd cut into pieces and moved it to the register counter, where he was wrapping. "I'm gonna make it beautiful for you. Fairy Tale Fudge is the best!" he crowed. "Divine, delectable, delicious!"

"Pauline would love those D's. Go easy on the fairy dust."

"You got it."

He did a fist pump in the air to make an invisible exclamation point.

Fairy Tale Fudge was my girlie brand of fudge. I was also developing ideas for a Fisherman's Catch Tall Tale Fudge line—male fudge (fudge with nuts!).

For the Cinderella Pink Fudge, I made tiny bite-sized and edible marzipan fairy wings and glass slippers, which Ranger and I placed atop each piece. Ranger loved sprinkling on the fairy dust—edible pink sugar glitter—before wrapping each piece.

I reached for my lightweight red spring jacket, already feeling chilly. I should've watched the weather earlier that morning and brought my winter coat and gloves, but that's how I was about too many things—spontaneous. It's not good advice for getting married, by the way.

Snow flew thicker now outside the big glass windows, obliterating the docks and bay. I called the Coast Guard; the guys assured me they'd look for Gilpa. The fishing season had officially opened yesterday in Wisconsin. Every year we had people overboard on the first weekend. They didn't always come back alive. At this time of year, hypothermia developed in a person within minutes.

I forced such thoughts away as Ranger flipped the lid shut on the big box that held Cinderella Pink Fudge for fifty. He offered to carry it up the hill to the Blue Heron Inn.

After declining his offer, I said, "When Gilpa comes in, you take the people by the hand to help them off the boat. Wait until each one is steady before assisting the next one."

I had to be exact and literal with Ranger. Sometimes he hurried too much with his tasks; a guest could end up being flung by him from one side of a pier into the water on the other side.

When I burst into the blustery outdoors, the wind nearly whipped the heavy fudge box right out of my hands. The coat I'd put on but failed to button flapped all over the place. Snowflakes stung my cheeks and pecked at my eyes, making me bend my head as I walked blindly up the narrow blacktopped street that threaded up the steep hill. The Blue Heron Inn was only a couple of blocks away, but with it sitting on a small bluff, the street had a pitch that made me step half sideways like a skier travailing up a snowy slope.

As I drew closer, my heart began to pump faster. Besides Pauling and Ranger, no grown-up had yet seen or tasted my Fairy Tale Fudge, each sumptuous, sugary piece dressed with slippers or wings and glitter. Was it too silly? Was it tasty enough? Would it impress Rainetta?

I had hopes after Isabelle Boone—owner of the Blue Heron Inn—had stopped by earlier.

"I can smell the vanilla all the way up the hill to my inn!" she'd declared.

I had shooed Isabelle to the back room, where she'd picked up her usual supplies for the next week of cooking at the inn for her guests. We shared the same delivery service, which brought bulk sugar, flour, and other ingredients to the bars and restaurants in the area. The drivers didn't always like going up the steep, narrow, winding street to the inn when conditions were slippery. Even rain freaked out some drivers.

Ranger's social worker, Sam Peterson, had also come by earlier, offering to help. Sam and I went way back; Ranger didn't understand why we weren't married. Sam had never liked my ex-husband, and I was still embarrassed from the experience even though eight years have passed since the debacle.

I had intended to marry Sam eight years ago, at the end of the summer, but the day before my wedding, I got cold feet and ended up with another guy I'd met in college. He was like a prince whisking me off to a castle. We did the Vegas wedding thing and settled in Las Vegas, where he pursued his career as a stand-up comic. I worked as a waitress at a casino, then got a job making the desserts for its buffet. It wasn't but a month after our wedding when two women informed me that they believed they were also married to Mr. Dillon Rivers. Bigamy puts a damper on a marriage. I got a divorce and an annulment soon after. I had become enamored enough of the bright lights that I went to Los Angeles, where I worked as a waitress and then a baker in Jerry's Deli while writing my experience with Dillon into scripts. After a year, I submitted a couple of scripts to a new TV series on a little-watched cable channel. I toiled at my writing craft, hoping for fame, but I worked for an anxiety-ridden executive producer. I wasn't his favorite writer on the staff. Mostly he favored the guys and their ideas. I hung on to pay my college debt and to pay back everybody here for the wedding expenses, including Sam for his tuxedo rental.

Sam was going to be at the party. I had to expect people to talk. In small towns, people tried to pair you off with the same vigor they used for betting on Packers-Bears games.

The Blue Heron Inn's lights were particularly inviting by the time I reached it. My fingers had become frozen wires bent around the edges of the cardboard box.

Isabelle Boone's cream brick and powder blue–trimmed B and B was two and a half stories of history. The original wood boarding house had burned in 1871 in a great fire that ravaged the peninsula, killing more than a thousand people. The inn was rebuilt of Cream City brick hauled here by ships from Milwaukee. The brick comes from the clay soils in that area of Wisconsin. The high levels of lime and sulfur in the soil turn creamy colored when fired. The firing of bricks interested me as much as the chemical formula for fudge; I'd taken chemistry classes in college just for the fun of it.

I'd been in the house only once since I'd left town eight years ago in a hurry, but that visit had been a quick nighttime errand in low light. I'd heard customers rave about the collection of Steuben glass Isabelle had assembled. The famous Steuben glass artists out in New York had ceased operations in 2011, so I knew the value must have gone up considerably for Isabelle's collection. I was eager to see it all under bright lights.

As I reached to ring the doorbell, I heard heated debating from within.

When Isabelle opened the door, her normally sophisticated gamine looks were pinched and she was out of breath.

I asked, "What's going on?"

"Rainetta." She took the box. "I leave for a minute to go upstairs to turn down her bed and put chocolates on her pillow and come back down to find Rainetta has everybody arguing over what needs money first in Fishers' Harbor."

I stripped off my jacket and shook off the snowflakes before hanging it on the coat tree. "How about you put my fudge on their pillows from now on? And how about she invest in my fudge?"

"She'll love your idea. Fairy tales and Hollywood? A perfect match. And I'm tired of hearing Al Kvalheim talk about spending Ms. Johnson's money on new storm sewers and grates."

I laughed. I eagerly sent my gaze searching for the famous actress. I didn't see her at first amid the throng of at least a hundred townspeople wearing their Sunday church clothes and enough aftershave and perfume to scare even a skunk. Panic set in. I couldn't breathe.

I whispered, "I didn't bring enough fudge, and the new batch isn't quite done."

Isabelle whispered back, "We'll make sure Rainetta gets the first piece. Others will just have to bid for the rest. I'll tell everybody it's part of the fund-raiser."

"You're a genius, Izzy. Thanks!"

I still couldn't breathe much, but now it had to do with the beauty around me. The two-story-high reception hall was packed with displays of expensive glass. Everybody kept their elbows tucked in and barely moved while talking.

Glass is made of amorphous crystals, which means they're random molecules and light can go through them. Glass sparkled from every surface high and low, with rainbow chips of light in flight under the overhead chandeliers. There were crystal birds and animals—many life-sized, including a seagull. Other items were smaller abstracts or vases, swirls of fire-roasted molecules of sand that bent the light into colorful beams splashing on the cream-and-blue wallpaper. Making glass was probably like making fudge—only a few thousand degrees hotter.

But my appreciation of Isabelle's collection was interrupted by the loud discussion near the magnificent blue-carpeted staircase dead center in the house.

"That's Rainetta Johnson," whispered Isabelle, nodding with raised eyebrows toward an impeccably coiffed blond woman of a regal age wearing an expensive lavender pantsuit.

To my surprise, the object of Ms. Johnson's animated discussion was Sam Peterson.

I asked Isabelle, "What're they arguing about? Seems like Sam's taking the wrong tack to get his donations."

This party wasn't just the opening of the refurbished inn or my fudge debut; it was a fund-raiser to help purchase and redo another historic home in town. It would become a group home for people like Ranger who wanted to live independently. So Sam's being here was logical, seeing as how he was a social worker. I'd never known Sam to raise his voice. I could see that the arguing was mostly one-sided, though. Rainetta was smiling and embracing others with some funny asides even as Sam kept pressing some point with the actress.

"Let's not worry about it," Isabelle said. "Sam's overly eager, perhaps, to sell her on the group home."

"Poor Rainetta. Sam should relax. You told me she loved Door County."

"She does, but she's a shrewd business lady. Come with me and I'll show you."

Isabelle and I skirted the edge of the fray to the round serving table that Isabelle had reserved for the Cinderella Pink Fudge. After she put the box of fudge down gingerly, she lovingly picked up a six-inch glass unicorn from the back of the table.

"My favorite piece," she said with glistening eyes. "I wanted it here on the table with your fudge. Fairies and unicorns go together in tales. I thought maybe it would bring good luck to your Cinderella debut."

"Thank you, Isabelle. That's a lovely thing to say." I

gave her a hug, though a careful one so as not to break the unicorn.

"Rainetta loves this piece," Isabelle said.

"She has good taste." The unicorn had the exquisite definition of a horse with a horn. Little girls could easily imagine fairies riding on its back.

"That's the problem. She wants to buy it."

"Then sell it to her," I said, feeling a speck of jealousy as I stood among Isabelle's riches.

"I can't. She wants to buy it for half what it's worth. That lady isn't rich because she gives money away. She drives a hard bargain. And she's making that known to everybody."

"And doing it with a smile. She looks radiant. As if she's truly come home here in Door County and Fishers' Harbor."

"Indeed. But some of the locals don't trust her. They think she's got to have a hidden reason to help us."

The odd thing about it was I'd heard that Rainetta was always generous. So something wasn't jibing here, particularly with Sam's behavior. If he was getting her upset over a group home investment, it didn't bode well for selling her something as silly as fudge, even though I was determined to elevate it to an art.

Isabelle set the unicorn back down. "And Ms. Johnson was perfectly charming to our new village board president, but I overheard Erik say he thinks she's a stuffy old lady."

Through a slim fissure in the crowd, I caught a glimpse of our new president—Erik Gustafson, a wunderkind of nineteen who'd shocked the town in April by deposing the fiftysomething Mercy Fogg. Mercy, who was milling about, voicing her opinion to Erik about our lack of a stoplight, had reigned supreme here for more than twenty years. I groaned, turning back to Isabelle. "Mercy wants the great Rainetta Johnson to buy us a stoplight?"

Isabelle nodded. "Decidedly boring."

"Hmm, but suddenly Sam doesn't look bored," I noted. "If anything, it looks like he's given Rainetta some kind of green light."

Rainetta had a hand cupping his chin. The legendary dame looked like she was about to kiss Sam! I squelched a gasp.

Sam was only a couple of years older than me. Sure, he was good-looking. He was six foot, still had his football player's physique, and had Adonis blond hair in crisp, thick waves. What woman of any age wouldn't want to be on the guy's arm and set her fingers to walking through that hair? But Rainetta? She was more than thirty years older than Sam.

I asked Isabelle in a quiet voice, "Where's the reporter when we need him?"

Isabelle had told me earlier that Jeremy Stone was staying at the inn. I wondered why he was still upstairs when the action was down here. Stone worked for the *Madison Herald*, a daily morning newspaper out of the capital. He roved the state reviewing everything from A to Z: arts to zoos. He loved "quirky." I had high hopes for him finding pink cherry fudge with fairy wings on top "quirky."

Isabelle said, "He's probably sending in a story already about how hideous my party is. Sam is ruining it by hogging Rainetta's attention."

"I won't let him."

I flipped open my fudge box sitting on the table, grabbed a pink cellophane–wrapped and winged bite-sized morsel of Cinderella Pink Fudge, then wended my way through the throng. I was getting looks, and only then realized I'd forgotten to change clothes. I still wore my messy, long baker's apron dotted with pink cherry juice that looked like bloody finger smudges.

I held out my hand with the fudge in it and delivered my memorized Oscar-winning speech to Rainetta. "Hello, Ms. Johnson. I'm Ava Oosterling, from Oosterlings' Live Bait, Bobbers & Belgian Fudge. I'd love it if the guest of honor would have the first bite of Fairy Tale Fudge. This flavor is the Cinderella Pink Fudge. I hope it lets you feel like you're Cinderella at the ball, Ms. Johnson."

My eyes were sucked out of their sockets by the circle of purple amethysts the size of dollar coins that she wore about her neck. They were inlaid in a museum-quality setting of gold leaves. Certainly she could afford to endorse my fudge fantasies.

"Fudge?" she said, her blue eyes soaking up the purple in the amethysts. "How quaint and perfectly wonderful, but I'm allergic to chocolate."

The blood drained from my head. She hadn't even tasted my fudge.

I prayed like any sane Cinderella would and tried again. "This isn't dark chocolate. This is white, made from sugar and soybean oil. No caffeine either. The texture is creamy and smooth . . . like your skin."

The woman raised her eyebrows at my inane and all-too-spontaneous words. She stared at the pink confection in crinkly cellophane I was placing in one of her hands.

Sam huffed at me and said, "Excuse me while I find the little boys' room." He marched up the staircase.

Sam obviously was miffed I'd interrupted him and

Rainetta. He wasn't normally brusque with me, except about my boyfriend choices in the past.

Isabelle rushed up with a crystal goblet of pink wine made from Door County cherries, which Rainetta didn't take. Isabelle persevered. "Ms. Johnson, please come with us to the dining room, where we can toast you."

"I recommend the cherry wine," I said, indicating the proffered glass in Isabelle's hands. "My fudge is made from cherries from that same orchard."

Rainetta tossed her head back in a genuine laugh, relaxing me a little. Her helmet of blond waves didn't move a speck. "I'm impressed by your homework. I love the orchards here in spring."

Then she ripped off the pink sparkly string and opened the pink cellophane to reveal the tiny sugared fairy wings. The crowd was so quiet I heard the furnace kick in.

Rainetta nibbled a corner of my pink confection. Then to my horror, she winced. "Perhaps I'll finish this in my room. I'm not feeling well."

She spit the fudge back into the crinkly, pink cellophane. Then, with my fudge still in one hand, she hurried up the stairs, disappearing into the upper hallway that ran down the center of the B and B.

My mouth went dry.

People began to murmur. And stare at me. With ugly frowns, the kind we use around here when somebody spills a beer or the Packers miss the Super Bowl.

Isabelle had gone so pale I could see blue veins under the winter white skin of her temples.

The chandelier above us bombarded the Steuben glass figurines and all of us with rainbow darts. Rainetta's lingering perfume billowed into an invisible cloud that was suffocating me. My dream of talking with her about actors' swag bags evaporated.

I muttered to Isabelle, "She hates my fudge."

Isabelle laid a hand on my arm. "Of course not. This is Sam's fault."

"How so?"

"Whatever they were talking about upset her. I better go see to her. But first, egads, we need music, don't we?"

She flipped a switch on the wall beneath the staircase before hurrying up the stairs. Hot jazz jolted us. Even the glass figurines on the shelves and tables vibrated.

The crowd kept staring at me.

Our wunderkind board president, Erik Gustafson, said, "This isn't going the way I expected."

From the outer edges of the crowd, Mercy Fogg croaked, "You can still resign if you like, Erik. It takes a grown-up to handle the likes of Ms. Johnson."

Mercy bullied her way around a couple of men in suits and lumbered up the stairs.

I felt sorry for Erik. A year ago he was playing football with the high school team, and now he was in the middle of this groveling for money that small towns have to do in order to survive.

I told Erik, "Maybe you could serve wine and stall a little by talking about new things you want to do for the village."

"Like the new playground equipment we need?"

"Perfect idea," I said. I silently prayed Gilpa would be coming soon with the other four guests to resuscitate the party and charm Rainetta Johnson.

Erik called out, "Who wants cherry wine? I'll pour."

"I'll help," I said, wanting to slam back a glass fast.

Erik and I had passed along only a few glasses of wine when Isabelle's scream sliced through the jazzy sax riffs.

I charged up the powder blue carpeted stairs with several people in tow.

In contrast to the glittering brilliance downstairs, the upstairs hallway was dimly lit with only two blue glass globe sconces. But doors popped open from the guest rooms, their lamplights helping to illuminate Isabelle standing in horror at the other end of the hallway.

Rainetta was laid flat on her back on the carpet, half in and half out of her room.

I rushed down the hallway. A woman screamed behind me. A door slammed.

Isabelle trembled. She shook her phone in her hand. "I called nine-onc-onc."

"What happened?" I asked, going immediately into action to pump at Rainetta's rib cage.

Isabelle said, "I used the bathroom; then I knocked on her door, and she staggered out, choking. On your fudge."

Chapter 2

Rainetta's lips were indeed smudged pink from my fudge, but before I could pry her mouth open to clear the passageway, the local volunteer paramedics were there, with Sheriff Jordy Tollefson right behind. He'd likely been just blocks away from here directing the traffic coming through town because of the party.

"Get back, folks," Jordy said. "What do we have here?"

I was huffing and puffing from the palpitations, relieved to have the paramedics rush in. "She's not breathing," I screeched in panic. "I started CPR immediately."

Jordy was a thin, tall guy, a runner in his forties with a boy-next-door face, brown eyes, and shorn hair showing from under his official hat. He got down on the floor with the paramedics—Nancy and Ronny Jenks, a middle-aged married couple who ran a bar on the edge of town.

Nancy and Ronny slapped on the defibrillator, making us all gasp when nothing happened except Rainetta bouncing. To my horror, the pink fudge fell out of her mouth; it appeared that in death she spit out my fudge in disdain.

"What happened?" Jordy asked, his eyes probing all of us, but landing back on me for some reason.

Isabelle said, "Ms. Johnson said she fell ill after taking a bite of the fudge; then she came up here. I found her coming out her door choking and then she collapsed."

I wanted to fall dead myself on the spot. I feared what was coming.

"Where's the fudge?" Jordy asked.

"Downstairs," Isabelle replied.

"Nobody touch it. Where'd it come from?"

Everybody looked my way.

The reporter, Jeremy Stone, snapped a cell phone picture of me, saying, "A fudge fatality."

Headline speak. Kindergarten-level alliteration. Which could ruin me. I cleared my throat, my mind racing for fancy answers, but all that came out was "It's just fudge."

Jeremy noted, "Not 'just.' It's pink. Whoever heard of pink fudge? What flavor is it?"

"Cherry and vanilla," I stammered, not sure why I felt compelled to tell him anything.

Jordy cut in. "Ava, you'll have to come with me."

"Why?"

"Because a woman has expired with your pink fudge in her mouth."

Isabelle said, "It's called Cinderella Pink Fudge."

Jeremy Stone wrote that down.

Jordy had a grip on my elbow that made my arm ache.

"Jordy, come on," I said. "You know my family. You know me."

"Not really. You ran away eight years ago. That was a mess, too, created by you."

"The poor woman may have just had a heart attack. It's nothing more than that."

Somebody behind me coughed; it sounded like they were stifling a nervous chuckle. Jeremy Stone had a small recorder in his hand, which he held up. A door opened next to us and a young couple stared out, looking like frightened possums, their dark eyes darting about in fear.

The paramedics weren't having any success in resuscitating Rainetta. My Cinderella Pink Fudge lay in an unhealthy wad looking more like spent bubble gum than the artwork I'd created earlier. It'd taken me approximately four hours to make that fudge. As a murder weapon, it had needed only about ten minutes.

Jordy made everybody go downstairs so the paramedics could remove the body.

Isabelle scooted fast in front of everybody to lead them down. I suspected she was concerned about the figurines being knocked off her tables in the hubbub. She turned off the jazz music she'd put on minutes before the horror began.

Jordy escorted me down the stairs, his hand manacling my elbow.

For some reason, I tried to act normal, as if this weren't real, as if it were only one of Rainetta's movies, though it'd be called *Fatal Fudge* and badly reviewed by Jeremy Stone. As we descended the long staircase, I said, "Did you hear anything about my grandfather? I probably should get back to the shop right away."

"I don't think you're going anywhere," Jordy said.

We were back on the oak floors of the grand foyer area and Jordy wasn't letting go of me.

He asked, "Where's the fudge?"

I led him to my Cinderella Pink Fudge with its marzipan fairy wings and slippers atop the pieces.

Isabelle lifted the Steuben unicorn off the table. The sheriff shook a quart-sized Baggie out of his pocket, then chucked several pieces of pink fudge into it, squishing them down, ruining the wings and slippers so that he could zipper the bag shut. My fudge looked like a mass of pink mud.

He nodded to the table with the rest of the pieces. "They'll need to come with me, too."

"Why?" I asked.

Erik Gustafson said, "You think there's poison in the fudge?"

"Poison?" shrieked the woman who was half of the honeymoon couple who'd peeked out at us upstairs. "Oh my God. Get me out of here. We should never have come to this backwoods place."

Jeremy Stone pushed forward to snap pictures of the fudge with one hand, his other hand stuffing his recorder in our faces. He was my height, had dark brown hair, like most of the populace, but he had a crooked nose that looked like it'd been broken a couple of times. I was tempted to give it a punch, too.

When I moved toward the table to box up the fudge, the sheriff threw an arm down in front of me. "Not you," he said.

The marrow inside my bones went liquid with the realization that Jordy considered me a serious suspect. "You can't really think that my fudge is a murder weapon?"

Isabelle handed me the unicorn to hold while she boxed up the rest of my pink cellophane–covered treats. I trembled, afraid I'd drop the precious glass. My luck had run out today.

Jordy announced in a loud voice, "All of you should stay available until I've had a chance to talk with each you."

A great howl went up, but the locals cleared out fast,

leaving me alone with Isabelle, Jeremy Stone, and the honeymooners from New York. They introduced themselves reluctantly to the sheriff as Hannah and Will Reed. They were in their early twenties, both with dark hair chopped into the latest oddball hairstyles I'd seen in magazines at the store. They wore expensive-looking, city-chic black attire mostly; Hannah shivered under a red shawl draped just so around her shoulders.

"We're not under arrest, are we?" she asked.

"No, ma'am," Jordy said. "But if you leave town now, I might have to consider issuing a warrant for your arrest. Are you in a hurry to leave?"

Will said, "That's bullshit. Come on, Hannah."

They fled back up the stairs. I almost felt sorry for Jordy. Almost. He said to me, "You're coming with me."

"I'm under arrest? For real? Officially?"

"No," he said, "I need somebody to help carry the fudge to the car." He grinned, but I didn't find his little joke funny. He added, "I'd rather take your statement in private at the office."

Isabelle relieved me of her precious Steuben statue.

Feeling battered and scared, I went with Sheriff Tollefson for a ride down to Sturgeon Bay. We passed fields being plowed and planted even on a Sunday, Holstein cows grazing in grass pastures, sturdy redbrick houses built by Belgians back in the 1870s, and cherry orchards flaring with pink buds. Everything appeared innocent and normal. I still didn't see how poor Rainetta could've choked on or been poisoned by my fudge. I was sure they'd discover she'd died of a sudden, massive heart attack after all that pressure on her for money for playground slides, stoplights, and storm sewers.

A flash came to me then. She'd been arguing with

Sam. He'd run upstairs, and then poof, he'd disappeared. Isabelle had been the only one to come out of the rest-room. But Sam couldn't have done in Rainetta; I couldn't believe a social worker would do such a thing. Maybe he thought he caused the heart attack and hid because of his shock.

Shock was what slammed through me once I got to the sheriff's department in Sturgeon Bay and was told that Ranger had been hauled in by a deputy for questioning, too.

"You can't do that," I railed at Jordy. "Ranger can't handle being told he did anything wrong." I itched all over with worry for Ranger.

"Cody Fjelstad helped you make the fudge. We have to question him."

"About what? He's not capable of being questioned."

"He's quite capable. You're not suggesting I discriminate because he has certain challenges?"

We were sitting in an interrogation office on blue plastic chairs with metal legs, with just a coffee-stained table between us. The walls were beige with maroon trim around the door. I let my head sink momentarily into my hands and lap in disbelief and despair. "You don't understand. Cody is sensitive, and he prides himself on doing a perfect job. He's very, very proud of his ability to wrap fudge. This is going to upset him in ways that aren't good at all, Sheriff."

"We have skilled people with him."

"But you're asking Ranger questions about things like poison getting into the fudge, and he won't understand that. He'll think he killed that woman. Holy cow, what a mess." Tears stung my eyes in my frustration.

Jordy handed over a box of tissues.

I got off the chair to snatch a tissue, then headed to the door. Earlier in the squad car I'd called Pauline to come pick me up. I figured she had to be waiting outside by now. "I'll take Ranger home."

"We'll handle that." The sheriff came around the table to hand me a clipboard with a blank piece of paper on it.

"Now what?" I asked, not caring that I sounded belligerent.

He showed me to my chair. "Write down the ingredients you put in the fudge."

"I'm not revealing my recipe."

"Are you saying you're refusing to cooperate?" He leaned over his knuckles and got right in my face. I could smell his coffee breath.

"No, I'm just saying I'm not telling you my trade secrets. Food artists don't reveal their recipes." I suspected he wanted me to break down in sobs about the poison.

Jordy sat down on his side of the table, nodding toward the clipboard in my hands. "Write down what you recall putting in the fudge."

"Fairy glitter? Wings of spun sugar? Is that what you want me to write?"

"Whatever you claim is in the fudge, I want to know about it."

Darned if I was going to give him any trade secrets. Nobody but Ranger knew what I put in my Cinderella Pink Fudge. I thought for a moment, then wrote.

I handed the clipboard across the table.

Jordy squinted at it. "What's this gibberish?"

"The chemical formula for the reaction of sugar boiled in milk. It's boiled at two hundred thirty-eight degrees, which is above the normal boiling point of two-hundred twelve degrees for water. This high temperature boils off enough water to bring the sucrose and fructose into alignment for proper crystallization of the fudge. If there was poison present, it would have interfered with the crystallization, and I would have noticed."

"Poison can be added to anything after it's done boiling," he said in a deadpan way. "This silliness just makes you look guilty, Ava."

I signed my statement and sketches of chemical formulas with a shaky hand.

He said, "You can go now, Miss Oosterling, but you'll have to stay out of your fudge shop until I say it's okay."

"You can't do that. For what reason? I haven't been arrested."

"Do you want to be?"

"Cut it out, Jordy. My grandfather's bait shop needs to stay open for the fishermen. It's fishing season. This affects my grandfather, too."

Jordy shrugged. "I'm sorry. I'm sure the deputy will take only a couple of days to swab down that tiny bait and bonbon shop."

He was making me mad. Fortunately he let me go at that point.

Pauline and I got back to Fishers' Harbor a little after four that afternoon. And sure enough, there was yellow tape unspooled around Oosterlings' Live Bait, Bobbers & Belgian Fudge. The graying wood building looked pitiful, as if it wore a prison uniform now. I sank into my own miasma rising from the sudden decay of my life.

I must have said that out loud because Pauline said, "Quit being so dramatic. You didn't kill anybody."

The snow had stopped, but a cold wind flapped the tape against the weathered wood and the windowpanes.

My stomach juices surged with disgust. I walked right up to the tape and ripped it down. "You're right, Pauline."

Pauline charged up to me, whipping her black hair over a shoulder like she meant business. With her height and that hair she can be intimidating when she looks down at me. "You can't do that," she said. "That's real tape, not the fake Halloween type of tape."

"I don't care."

"You'll get in trouble. Arrested or something."

"Or something. I can't let Ranger or Gilpa see this."

We went inside to a mess. The only thing on Grandpa's side not out of place was the minnow tank bubbling away.

My side? I started with the two center aisles in my half of the building and groaned. The deputy had confiscated the just-delivered pink fairy tale items for girls, including locally hand-crafted Cinderella-at-the-ball dolls and fairy godmothers with wings in pink that matched my fudge. The deputy had probably assumed I hid poison in their bodies.

With a sigh I also noticed that the loaf of pink fudge had disappeared off my marble table. I rushed to my copper kettles; all the dry fudge ingredients there were gone. The wall shelves were empty. On them I featured the standard fudges to just give me a reason to open my business— double chocolate, caramel, peanut butter, butterscotch, maple, and cookies and cream. I had also made a couple of male varieties. The deputy had cleaned me out.

He'd also rubbed some chemical on my marble slab and in the copper pans I used to make my fudge. A whiff of something akin to nose-burning solvents ruined the air and obliterating the smells of chocolate and vanilla. Everything would have to be cleaned and sterilized.

I pushed up my sleeves. I still wore my cherry-stained apron that I'd had on all day. I untied it and balled it up, tossing it aside. I grabbed a fresh apron from a closet behind the cash register.

Pauline said, "What are you doing?"

"Making more fudge. Wanna help?"

"I don't want to be arrested, so no. Besides, I'm tired."

She'd missed the party because it took her three hours to hang book titles and character names from the ceilings of her classroom.

"How could teaching reading be more important than the debut of my Cinderella Pink Fudge and Cinderella being under suspicion for murder?"

"Stop it, Ava. There's no need to take my head off."

"All right. Sorry, but . . ." Belgians are stubborn. We hate losing. Pauline was Belgian, too, so our squabbles could go on for days just on principle.

I finished tying on the fresh apron. "Sorry, Pauline, but this always happens to me. You know it does. As soon as something good comes to me in my life, I'm guaranteed to have something bad happen."

"Nothing bad happened to you. The only 'bad' thing is the bad heart that woman evidently had."

"No, my fudge is gone. That's very bad. I'm making fudge this instant to bring back good karma. Eating fudge is all about having good karma. Besides, I can't let Gilpa see these empty shelves and copper kettles. He'll lose all faith in me and plunk fishing lures in the space."

"Tell him you sold all the fudge."

"Lies are mortal sins. I don't have time to go to confession."

Pauline muttered something that wasn't fit for kindergarteners, but she followed me to the back room.

My cleaning and cooking supplies had been pawed through. Plus, to my chagrin, whoever had been poking around for poison had taken my bottles of vanilla extract. "Crap. That was the expensive stuff."

A quick glance in the refrigerator revealed they'd taken my milk, sour cream, and buttermilk—ingredients for my fudge and all fresh from my parents' farm down near Brussels in the county. I checked my chocolate bins; the imported Belgian bulk dark chocolate was gone, too. That cost a fortune.

"Why would they take that? Do they believe I sent all the way to Belgium for poison?"

"They were likely hungry. Better for their hearts than doughnuts."

"I can't make my fudge until I reorder supplies and my Belgian chocolate. The sign outside says 'Belgian' fudge, not 'ordinary'! I'm ruined, done for, cut down in my prime!"

Pauline grabbed me, flipping me around to face her. I expected her to slap me, but she didn't. She said in a soothing voice, "Hey, let it go for tonight. Let's go to your place to regroup. I'll make you hot cocoa. We'll wait there to hear from your grandfather."

For a startling moment I realized that in my selfish need to rail at the world I'd forgotten about Gilpa's plight. I forced myself to breathe. "Wow. Sorry. That's why I needed to move back here from Los Angeles. I just sounded like the producer I worked for on that crappy TV show."

My dream of becoming a writer had become one of my infamous spontaneous combustions, like my marriage. The experience of working in TV production was still too raw to talk about, and a wish that I'd done better lingered inside of me; nobody but Pauline knew I was basically licking my wounds. When my grandmother Sophie Oosterling had broken her leg three weeks ago, my dad had called me to say she and Gilpa needed somebody to help them and would I consider coming home?

Of course I leaped at the chance to help my beloved grandparents, but only Pauline knew I was probably going to be fired from the half-hour TV comedy *The Topsy-Turvy Girls* after this season's low ratings. The show starred two young women like me and Pauline, trying to find love and success. The script that got me on the show was based on my very odd divorce circumstances. By the fifth year working for the show, I was beginning to run out of ideas based on my experiences or lack thereof in the realms of romance and success. The only good thing about the TV experience was that as my writing assignments decreased, the executive producer had put me in charge of buying the treats for the cast table. They thought I got the stuff from fancy chefs. I pocketed the cash and made what made me hunger for home— homemade fudge. At least the fudge was a hit.

Then, last Christmas, when I was home and making fudge from my grandma Sophie's recipe, she and Gilpa offhandedly said that I should start my own business making candy. When I came home two weeks ago, I was surprised to find out that my grandparents and my parents had been scouring the county and beyond for secondhand equipment for my business—should I ever end up moving back to the Midwest. Between the time I'd said yes to coming back and my arrival in Fishers' Harbor just days later, my grandfather and dad had remade the bait shop.

Pauline and I went to my rental place in the small enclave of fishers' cottages behind the bait shop to share my misery over cocoa. Gilpa and Grandma Sophie owned one of the cottages across the narrow street and west from me. My rental sat right behind my fudge shop. The cottages were log cabins that had been built in the 1800s by the Belgians, Finns, and Swedes who came to Wisconsin for a new life based on fishing and lumbering.

"Have you called your parents?" Pauline asked.

"No way. This will blow over like that storm outside."

My parents, Pete and Florine, were dairy farmers down in Brussels, a town in the southern area of the county. My parents supplied all the dairy products that made my Belgian fudge unique and tasty. Mom and Dad were salt-of-the-earth folks, expert farmers and proud of what they did. They had not liked me running off to Vegas and then to Los Angeles after the divorce. They'd felt I was abandoning them and my heritage. They had expected me to join them to milk cows, raise calves and my own kids. And here I was, back for only two weeks — working alongside Grandpa and helping Grandma, which was all good — then bam, something bad happens and I'm accused of murder. My same old pattern. Good, then bad.

"I doubt a murder will blow over," Pauline said. "Jeremy Stone will issue his 'Fatal Fudge Flames out Forgotten Film Star' front-page headline tomorrow all over the Web."

"Thanks for making me feel even worse." I set my cup of cocoa down in disgust on the table by my chair. We were in the living room area with the fireplace roaring.

Pauline said, "You should call or e-mail Stone. Give

him your side to the story right away. Tell him how sorry you are she died of a heart attack."

"We don't know yet how she died," I said, tapping my fingers on the chair arms, feeling increasingly on edge.

"Tomorrow's Monday. The medical examiner will be back in the office then, and he'll have it all solved. However, Stone will have already run his 'FFFFF' story in the morning paper, which will be too late for you if you wait to talk with him. You'll be drowning in your 'miasma.' You always do things spontaneously, so talk to him now."

That brightened my mood a smidgen. "You're right. I can remind him to wait for the medical examiner's report. My family's name will be saved from the muck."

"I just said that."

"You said 'miasma,' not 'muck.'" Stubborn Belgian.

I dragged my laptop onto my lap, punched myself online, found his e-mail address at the newspaper Web site, then shot off an e-mail to Mr. Stone. I could almost visualize him in the Blue Heron Inn, just above us on the bluff, reading my message. I felt better already.

But he shot back a message instantly that said, "Some years ago arsenic was found in well water in an area of Door County. You were here at that time. What area was that?"

I almost threw my laptop into the fire. But instead I snapped it shut, then set it aside.

Pauline asked, "What's wrong? What'd he say?"

"Damn man thinks I used arsenic in my fudge!"

"So maybe we should go up to the inn and talk to him in person."

"No, Pauline. Everything I touch right now turns out unlucky. He had a crooked nose that looked as if he'd been a boxer. He's used to fighting. He'll punch out my lights." I got up, though, and said, "The person we need to see is Ranger. I need to go apologize and make sure he's all right."

"And maybe find out if he accidentally put something in the fudge?" Pauline shot me a plaintive look.

My heart ached. If Ranger was responsible for Rainetta Johnson's death, I wasn't sure what I was going to do. Ranger, or Cody Fjelstad, had been hanging around the bait shop off and on for a couple of winters, anytime he and his dad came in for bait for ice fishing. I'd met him a couple of times when I'd come home for holidays. Ranger liked the bait shop. And like me, he liked a little sparkle in life and fun. We'd become fast friends almost the instant Sam Peterson fixed him up with the job working for me.

"Come on," I said to Pauline, grabbing my red jacket. "I'll need your support."

The clouds parted as we wended our way in my recently acquired, used, yellow Chevy pickup truck through the back streets to get to the Fjelstads. I'd loved the cheery, bright color of the truck when I'd bought it; now I was self-conscious about its flashiness. I expected people to line the streets to point fingers. *Look at the fudge murderer!* But it was five o'clock, dinner hour for a lot of people around here, so the streets were nearly empty.

Arlene Fjelstad met us at the door. She had puffy eyelids and shiny wet cheeks. I smelled hamburgers frying on a stove.

"Hi, Arlene," I managed. "Is Ranger here? I'd like to talk with him."

"No, he's not." She swiped at her tears.

"He'll be at work tomorrow?"

"I don't know. My husband had to pick him up at the sheriff's department and then pick up some new medications for him."

I felt ill. Evidently Ranger's time at the jail didn't go well. Pauline just stood there beside me, looking down at us, no help at all.

I said, "I'm sorry. Ranger makes good fudge. He's a great wrapper, too. Everything will be okay tomorrow when he gets back to work." That sounded lame. Nothing would be okay. I had no idea what to do, though, to make things better. "He can take a day off. He doesn't have to come by in the morning. He can just sleep in and go to school instead. I don't have any supplies, and it'll take me a day to go get those or have them delivered."

"He won't want to go to school to be laughed at." Her entire face wrinkled up like cracked glass that would break into a thousand pieces at any second. "He was doing so well."

My anger with the sheriff rushed back into me with the force of a Lake Michigan storm tide. "Everything will be normal tomorrow. They'll find out that there's nothing wrong with the fudge. It was a horrible thing, but sometimes people . . . expire. And the sheriff made a mistake taking Ranger down to Sturgeon Bay. A simple mistake. Ranger will come to understand."

"Understand what?" Arlene cried out. "That he can't trust anybody? He trusted you. I trusted you because you're an Oosterling. That was my mistake." Arlene closed the door.

Pauline was biting her lower lip, looking as lost as I felt.

I said, "Ranger hates his medications, Pauline. Says

he's not normal when he has to take pills. He was thinking he could get off his meds."

"But the medications help him."

"He wants to be normal." A whimper drifted off my lips. "I have to fix this."

"Everything will be back to normal tomorrow. You said so. Believe in that."

But it wasn't. Ranger didn't show up in the shop on Monday. Pauline called me during her kindergarten class's nap break to report that Ranger hadn't shown up at school, as predicted by his mother.

I snuck into my shop to clean up things, defying the sheriff's orders to stay out. I started on Gilpa's side, putting packaged snacks back on their hooks. Gilpa and the four guests had been rescued by the Coast Guard in the wee early-morning hours. They'd drifted over to the protection of the Chambers Island Lighthouse, which was the good part.

A ruddy-faced Gilpa, with his uncombed silver thatch of hair making him look like he had horns, passed through the shop growling about it being closed, growling over getting no sleep, growling at the poor fishing weather. He didn't even look at me. That sucked something out of my soul. I suspected he was totally embarrassed and his pride hurt from his old boat's engines giving out on him, but most of all he was disappointed in me.

My parents found out about everything, too, and they ragged at me over the phone as if I were one of Pauline's kindergarten kids. I hadn't yet talked with Grandma Sophie but would have to face her judgment later when I went over to tidy up and wash dishes for her.

Gilpa hurried outside and down the dock with a cup of the strong, black coffee I'd made. He was on a mission to find a mechanic. What he really needed was a new boat and engines, but there was no way he could afford such things. And I doubted a banker would loan the "Fatal Fudge Family" any money.

Then the sheriff showed up at nine. He rudely left his red and blue bubble lights on to strafe me and the walls through the fudge shop's big bay windows. Jordy walked in with the yellow tape that I'd taken off the fudge shop in his fist.

I managed a fake hearty, "Good morning."

Jordy set the ball of tape on the cash register counter, where I was cutting cellophane into pieces as if all were normal. I wanted them ready for Ranger when he came back tomorrow; I was trying to stay positive about that. I was determined to be making more flavors of Fairy Tale Fudge by then, maybe Snow White Fudge since I now had experience with killing people off with morsels in their mouths.

Jordy said, "I'm afraid I have to put you under arrest."

I almost wet my pants. "What for?" Had they found poison after all? Had Ranger somehow done something like find rat poison and think it was flour?

Jordy's deputy walked in behind Jordy then. Now I knew this was serious.

Jordy waved the deputy to come forward as he said, "The medical examiner says in his preliminary exam that the woman died choking on your fudge."

"That can't be." I gulped. I could almost feel the lump of fudge.

"You were standing right there when you saw it pop out of her mouth."

"But if she choked, that's not my fault. It's awful, but I didn't force it down her throat. I have witnesses."

"And do they know about your diamond smuggling?"

"What diamonds?"

"The ones you put in your fudge. Your fudge was filled with hot diamonds. It was hot fudge. I'd like you to explain why you're putting diamonds in your fudge."

Chapter 3

"Hot diamonds?" My screech was so loud it made the cowbell on the door vibrate. Or maybe that was from the wind. When the dull bell clank made the sheriff and his deputy turn around, I ran for my life the other way through the doorway to the back hall, past my kitchen, and was at the back door when Jordy's deputy caught up with me. He yanked me to a stop, then parked himself at the back door and smiled back at me.

I hauled my butt back into the fudge and bait shop customer area to face Jordy.

"Jordy, you're not going to arrest me, are you?"

"It depends. I seem to keep collecting evidence that points to you."

"This is nonsense. I know nothing about diamonds. Just chocolate. And I'd like to know what you did with all my supplies." I took my cell phone out of my pocket.

"Who're you calling?" Jordy asked.

"My mother. I need chocolate."

Mom's voice on the phone calmed me. She was a sane, rational woman at all times. I wasn't going to tell her I was in the process of being questioned for stealing diamonds and hiding them in my fudge. Even I couldn't believe it. I'd be able to get rid of Jordy just by stalling. But my voice was quavering while Sheriff Jordy Tollefson stood across from me in front of my cash register, his hands resting on his holster and a pair of steel handcuffs.

"Uh, hi, Mom. I was, uh, wondering if you had ideas for finding Belgian-grade bulk chocolate. I really don't want to wait a week for a shipment."

"Honey, are you all right?"

"I'm, uh, fine."

Jordy rolled his eyes at me.

Mom said, "That woman's death is awful, but probably more awful for your friend Isabelle. The poor thing. Imagine holding a party for the spring opening of your business and somebody dies from your food."

"Mom, I can imagine. That was my fudge, remember?"

Jordy twirled a hand at me to indicate I needed to wrap things up with Mom. But that might mean I could be wearing those handcuffs, so I kept talking to her.

"Does that lady in Namur still get those bulk chocolates from Belgium?"

"I don't think so," Mom said, "but we deliver to that small country store in Brussels. Do you want me to drive up to your shop today with some of our new cheddar? At least you'd have something to sell."

My parents had started making their own brand of cheddar and other cheeses right on the farm just a couple of years ago. They'd worked several years to get to the point of selling their own Oosterling organic brand dairy products—a very good reason not to have a daughter besmirching their name by going to jail for heists and murder. "Buy Your Fatal Fudge and *Fromage* from the Oosterlings" likely wouldn't make Mom's list of billboard slogans.

Jordy ripped my cell out of my hand to speak to my mother. "Florine, this is Sheriff Tollefson. Your daughter will need to talk with you later." He hit the disconnect button.

"That was rude," I said, keeping the counter between me and Jordy. I imagined us having a game of tag around the counter, with me winning and running out the door.

But as soon as I reached forward to put my phone down on the counter, Jordy grabbed my outstretched arm and dangled the shiny bracelets. "Where'd you come up with the diamonds, Ava?" he practically barked.

"You can't be serious. I know nothing about diamonds except their chemical formula."

"Don't start with that mumbo jumbo again."

"They're not made from coal. Let me draw you a picture."

"Dammit, no more pictures."

"Eruptions in the earth a hundred miles down in the mantle bring them up in xenoliths. Those are rocks to you."

"I don't want to hear about rocks."

"But you should. An asteroid could've plopped those diamonds here. This could solve your case somehow. When asteroids crashed into the earth with the force of a hundred thousand atomic bombs millions of years ago, that impact created diamonds that got shoved down into the earth."

"Like they got shoved down Rainetta Johnson's throat?"

I shuddered. "Not quite like that. Sooner or later the continental plate coughed up rocks with the diamonds inside them. Maybe the person you're looking for is a geologist."

Jordy came around the counter, ready to hustle me out. "An asteroid? A geologist did it?"

I nodded, totally believing my own story, but also moving my feet backward a couple of steps, getting ready to run. "Maybe one of Isabelle's guests is a geologist. Have you checked?"

Jordy's brown eyes were like asteroids themselves— fiery orbs of glassy rock. In one lurching motion, he planted a firm hand on my back, then began marching me toward the door. "We're going to have to shut down this shop. I have to ask you to leave, Ava. And if you give me grief about this, I'll have to arrest you."

"I really have to go to the bathroom." I stiffened my legs to dig my work boots into the wood floor.

"No, you don't." Jordy pulled me along now by the arm, my feet sliding in protest. The feet routine made him change his tactic. He slung an arm around my shoulders, smashing me up against his lean body to haul me out.

The door flapped open, startling us. The cowbell slammed with a *clunkedy-clunk* against the wall. Isabelle Boone and Pauline Mertens stood there aghast, out of breath and windblown.

Isabelle, her gamine face white and short dark hair sticking up all over, said, "I saw the squad car lights and called Pauline at school."

Pauline flipped her long black hair over a shoulder as she stared at me and Jordy and my potential shiny wrist accessories. "What now?"

Pauline said that as if I'd gotten into a whole string of trouble in my life, and that's true. But her words still stung.

"My fudge sparkled for a good reason yesterday—it had diamonds in it."

Isabelle shrieked, "Diamonds? How did diamonds get in your fudge?"

"Did Rainetta swallow diamonds? Is that why she died?" Pauline asked. "Ick. Maybe diamonds don't pass through like pop beads? My kids at school are always swallowing beads or crayons or something. One mom wanted me to save her little boy's poop because the beads were actually real pearls. His poop was worth two hundred dollars, she said."

We were saved from more of Pauline's story when Grandpa Gil shoved in the doorway covered head to toe with black grease from working on his engines. He even had a black swipe up his forehead that ran into his thick silver hair. A skunk in reverse. The sharp, nauseating smell of gasoline and oil flooded the air. "What in the double-H-E-L-L is going on here?"

Pauline and Isabelle stepped aside—way to the side—to let Gilpa through. He took one look at me in Jordy's armlock before stomping in his boots into his bait shop, where he grabbed a foot-long metal tool from behind the counter and then came back over to my fudge shop.

Jordy said, "You threatening a law officer, Gil? Let's not get silly."

Gilpa said, "If you try anything fancy like cuffing her, I'll be ready." Gilpa's hands held out his wire cutters.

Jordy stepped between us. "She's not under arrest, Gil. I was just asking her to leave. You can't interfere with the law."

"The double hockey sticks, you say."

Not quite as tall as Jordy but as wiry, my grandpa faked to the left, which tricked the sheriff into stepping that way to block him; then Gilpa popped back to the right, reached around Jordy, and snatched me, whirling again to stand protectively in front of me. Slick as a whistle. I beamed with pride. At seventy-three, Gilpa had outmaneuvered the sheriff with the kind of moves Pauline and I used to perform on the basketball courts in high school and college.

Clapping erupted in the doorway and from outside. Five fishermen and two boys of maybe ten years old were cheering for our team as they came in. Right behind them but not cheering were Mercy Fogg and a few other curious fishermen. Through the big shop windows on either side of the door, I could also see other townspeople and strangers gathering on the dock, obviously drawn by the squad car's red and blue strobes. I wished like all get-out that I were whipping fudge in my copper pots right now. Surely I'd sell it all with a crowd like this. I almost wished the crooked-nose reporter were here snapping pictures of me to post on the Web.

The stout, roly-poly Mercy Fogg huffed about, taking in the shambles of my fudge shop with its empty shelves as well as Gilpa's bait, bobbers, and beer. "Did I hear something about shutting this down? Good idea. None of this is code. You can't be selling fudge next to open-water tanks of minnows. It's not sanitary."

I groaned. Mercy, her blond hair poufed around her face with too much hair spray, needed something to do since she'd lost the recent election. It looked like shutting me down was on her to-do list.

My grandpa marched over to his side of our messy, mutual store to return his wire cutters to the shelf under his register counter. He waved the customers in. "Welcome to Oosterlings'. We have a special on everything today. Buy two bobbers or baits, get the third item of your choice for half price. Minnows at half price. Beer, too. And buy some of my real worms and I'll toss in the gummy worm candies for free."

The little boys squealed, instantly grabbing for the gummy worms, then swarming the minnow tanks over in the corner by the coolers that held soda pop, beer, and some cartons of worms in dirt. A couple of the guys were on their phones, obviously calling buddies to tell them about the beer deals. My grandpa was amazing when it came to money. And me. He'd ignored Mercy and now squared off with the sheriff, pointing him toward the door.

"Nobody's being arrested here. Get those cuffs off my granddaughter."

Jordy stood his ground. "We found loose diamonds, Gil. The quantity and type fit a description from a heist in New York last week."

"Who cares about a robbery in New York? This is the Midwest, son."

"Gil, the authorities out there have been following a paper trail on them. They think there's a possibility of diamonds being shipped to Chicago. I'm on the lookout up here because Door County is Chicago's playground."

My grandpa stretched his wiry frame up to meet Jordy's wiry frame. Jordy was half a head taller, but he backed off a smidge to avoid getting grease on his tan uniform.

My grandpa said, "Did you test these diamonds? What if they're fake? It's spring, and the high school kids are always playing pranks in spring. They could have snuck in the back door and dumped a bunch of baubles in the cocoa or somethin' for the heck of it."

Pauline spoke up. "Just like my kids eating those pearls. For the fun of it. My little girls come to school with fake sparkles stuck in their hair all the time. Maybe that's what was in the fudge."

Isabelle offered, "The jeweler would be able to tell you if they're fake or not."

"Great idea," I said.

Gilpa poked a finger at Jordy. "See? Listen to A.M. and P.M. plus I.B."

My grandpa had affectionately nicknamed Pauline Mertens "P.M." and me "A.M." for my first and middle names, Ava Mathilde, when we were kids, saying, "You two are a bunch of trouble and sunshine all day long, a.m. and p.m." It was nice of him to include Isabelle Boone, or "I.B.," in the club. I added, "But the jewelry store isn't open until tomorrow. Maybe we can talk about this then." Many shops were shuttered on Mondays until the tourist season started full force after Memorial Day.

Jordy said through gritted teeth, "I'll take the gems to Green Bay today if I have to. The mall stores are open. And your store needs to be closed. Now."

My grandpa waved a hand around. "Give us a few minutes to serve the customers. What is it you have to do anyway?"

"Search the place again."

"Search what?" my grandpa asked, true to his stubborn Belgian ways.

"Anyplace that could hide diamonds."

"But you did a search already. Are you saying your deputy wasn't doing his job?"

Jordy's countenance darkened. I intervened before my grandfather got arrested for obstructing justice or something. "Listen, Jordy, go ahead. Look around. And if you want us to close after you're done doing that, we'll close."

When he'd reached the small hallway behind the cash register, I hurried after him, stopping him just outside the kitchen door. "I recall you said that the medical examiner's findings were 'preliminary.' When will he give you the *final* report on Rainetta Johnson's cause of death? That will clear my fudge of any wrongdoing."

Gilpa and my girlfriends gathered around.

Jordy squared his shoulders in a last-ditch effort to look threatening. "He said he'd have something official by Friday. And I suppose it'll take the state crime lab that long to dig around for the poisons in your fudge."

The sheriff marched into the kitchen to begin poking around.

When we returned to the main floor area of the shop, a wide-eyed Mercy toddled out the door, smug with determination on her face. I had a feeling we hadn't heard the last of her about our so-called code violations. And who knew what the rumor mills would now say about fudge and diamonds?

Isabelle and Pauline crushed around me in a three-way hug and human sandwich.

Isabelle said, "You're off the hook. It's not like you keep diamonds around here in sugar tins or anything."

"The sheriff is all bluster and bluff, a big bully and buffoon," Pauline said, the alliteration habit signaling that she was relaxing along with the rest of us.

My grandpa, though, wore a frown, his oil-stained forehead creased, his silver eyebrows knitted together while his mouth was twitching.

"What's wrong, Gilpa?"

Despite his oily duds, he stepped over and hugged me tight. Now I knew something seriously was wrong. "Gilpa?"

Behind us, the sheriff was rattling through pans and dishes in my kitchen. He couldn't be finding anything because his people had already stripped me clean in there. The refrigerator door popped open.

"Ava," Gilpa said, stepping back but keeping his hands on both my shoulders, "as much as I'd love to think this is all a big mistake, the fact is a woman died. And the sheriff thinks it's murder. And he thinks there's a connection to these so-called New York diamonds; that's plain to see." Gilpa gave me one of his soul-searching looks that make my heart sputter and my knees knock together from paralyzing fear. "You've got only four days of freedom unless we do something."

Pauline and Isabelle squelched cries of disbelief. Isabelle said, "Four days? To prove your innocence?"

"That's silly. I *am* innocent," I said, but the look on Gilpa's face was funereal.

Pauline muttered, "I think they could arrest you, Ava, just to be safe."

"Safe?" I yelped. "I make fudge. I'm harmless. It's all circumstantial evidence, nothing more than that."

Gilpa said, "I'll call your father before this hits the Internet." With a greasy hand, he pulled his phone out of his shirt pocket.

My heartbeat paused in panic.

Isabelle said, "This is awful. What can I do?"

I hadn't a clue. I stared at them. The customers behind us in the bait shop were clamoring for my grandfather to ring up their purchases. He clicked off his phone before letting it ring through to my parents, a tiny reprieve for my heart. The oil and gasoline smells on Gilpa mixed oddly with the vague hint of vanilla and chocolate still lingering in my empty half of the shop.

The whiff of aromas revived me. I looked into my Gilpa's worried eyes and offered as bravely as I could, "You always say that when the going gets tough, the tough get going. We just have to solve the case somehow."

"In four days?" Isabelle asked again.

She was new to my social circle. I'd known her for only the two weeks I'd been back. Her being new challenged me to dig somewhere deep, to show her my stuff. My fear began to melt like chocolate and turn into determination as strong as chili pepper–infused fudge. I said to Isabelle, "We start now. We have to go over the list of people staying at the Blue Heron Inn."

"The couple from New York is certainly suspect," Isabelle said, her pale cheeks turning pink with excitement. "They've been agitated the entire time they've been at my inn. They're forever arguing. Maybe they're professional thieves."

Pauline said, "Maybe they were trying to sell the stolen ice to Rainetta, but she didn't like the idea of swallowing them in order to hide them."

Isabelle quipped, "And maybe Rainetta was going to turn in the New York couple, so they killed her."

I crowed for my grandpa's sake, "Woo-hoo! See? The case is solved already."

Gilpa shook his head at us as if we were all Pauline's kindergartners making up stories. "I'll get us a good lawyer," he said. "And I'll call your father and mother."

We went silent as Jordy passed us in a hurry. He wasn't carrying anything that I could see. But I got the feeling he'd gotten an answer to some question just by being in my kitchen.

*   *   *

We girlfriends agreed to meet after Pauline was done with school at two thirty to go over the Blue Heron Inn guest list. Meanwhile, it was almost ten o'clock and Isabelle had to prepare lunch for her guests. I rushed past the kitchen of my shop, flung open the back door, then charged across the quiet back street to my grandparents' house. But not before my phone rang. It was Mom.

Mom cried every word. "We'll"—blubber, blubber—"sell the"—blubber, blubber—"farm. We'll sell all the"—louder blubbering—"cows. We'll do"—sniffling snorts—"what it takes."

"No," I said. "You won't do any of that. Gilpa's hiring a lawyer and this will all blow over. You're not losing the farm because of me. I'll pay Gilpa back for the lawyer."

"I should call Father Van den Broeck."

"Why?"

"He can dedicate the next Mass to you. And we can announce it for the prayer chain groups for all the sister churches in Door County."

Egads! Now Mom was going to have the whole county praying for my soul. But then I thought, maybe I needed that kind of help. Everybody would be hearing about my mortal sins soon enough anyway. "Mom, thanks. I guess the only time I envisioned having a Mass said for me would be my funeral, so having it said now before I go to jail gives me a warm feeling."

She wailed louder.

My grandparents weren't criers, thank goodness. I barely knocked before going inside their home across the street from mine. The core of Grandma Sophie's and Gilpa's cottage was identical to mine and all the rest along this street. In the 1800s, the immigrant Belgians, Finns, and Swedes felled trees fast to build shelters from the brutal winter weather that sets in here come November. My grandparents used to live on our farm down by Brussels, about a forty-five-minute drive from here, but when I was born they moved up to Fishers' Harbor, I guess to give my family room to grow. Unfortunately, my parents had me and then nobody else. They were hoping when I married eight odd years ago that I'd fill the farmstead house's four bedrooms with kids, but that was another disappointment involving my ex. My grandparents added two bedrooms to the back of their cottage, turned the old bedroom into a dining room by knocking down those walls, and also enclosed the front porch for a year-round sunroom. It's a lot of space to clean and keep up when you're in your seventies and have a broken leg like my Grandma Sophie.

The house smelled of strong coffee, cinnamon toast, and fried eggs from breakfast.

Grandma Sophie — her thick mass of white, cascading hair looking fairylike and as if it had been sculpted from the whitecaps of Lake Michigan — was sitting in the living room area by the fireplace watching a cooking show. "Hey, Grandma."

"Double hey back, Ava honey."

The softened sparkle in her deep brown eyes told me Grandpa had reached her with the news.

I took her hands in mine, then gave her a cheek-to-cheek hug that grew into one of those where your grandma encircled you with her arms, pulled you in tight, and then refused to let go. Greetings were important to Belgians. We smiled and chuckled a lot just saying "Hi," and it's not uncommon for Gilpa or my dad to shake your hand but forget he was still hanging on to it as he launched into a conversation.

They say that if you hug a person for at least twenty seconds you both release the calming and friendship-making hormone oxytocin. In other words, a hug means a tiny "I love you." Grandma says that the home country was overrun a lot in wars because the Belgians were lovers and not fighters. If world leaders hugged my grandma, her soft cheeks would soften their intentions immediately. She didn't have much for wrinkles, having never smoked, and always washed her face with her home-made soaps. She was also young yet, barely in her seventies. She had gotten pregnant with my father when she was only sixteen. Yeah, a big oops. She said that Gilpa's love never wavered and his hugs made her cheeks glow, so she knew everything would be all right. And it was for her. I dreamed of being as beautiful—and as wise and useful—as Grandma Sophie when I hit seventy-one.

She said with a toss of a hand toward the TV, "Ava, they're making a stew with snakes today. Can you imagine serving snakes here in Door County?"

"No. I can't imagine changing over our fish boils for snake boils," I said, enjoying the relief of laughing after the past hour at the fudge shop. "I'll make up your bed and do the dishes. What do you want me to cook for lunch?"

"Oh, Ava honey, I can manage on my crutches to lean against the counter and use the microwave. Now, tell me about this hubbub over your film star. They say you killed her."

I nearly fell down. "They?" I sat down gingerly on her couch so as not to bounce the leg with the cast on it. "Where did you hear that?"

She reached to the table next to her to pat her laptop. "On the Internet."

"Jeremy Stone?"

"His online newspaper headline said, 'Film Flower Finished by Fudge.'"

I let go with another laugh, despite the situation. "Not quite Pauline's guess, but close. She predicted 'Fatal Fudge Flames Out Forgotten Film Star.'"

"Too long for a headline."

"I guess. At least he was nice enough to call her a 'flower.'"

"Rainetta Johnson was a knockout in her day. Gil and I drove all the way to Madison one time for one of her movies."

"You did?"

"We stayed overnight at the Park Motor Inn and walked down State Street to the Orpheum. Rainetta was an ingenue then, and she wore Tiffany jewels in every scene." Grandma Sophie sighed with a faraway look. "I talked about the jewelry so much after that, that your grandpa bought me a diamond necklace for Christmas that year."

"But I never see you wear jewelry much."

"I got out of the habit on the farm. Do you want to see the necklace?"

I did, but I felt an urgency to take care of my big problem so begged off for now. I filled in Grandma Sophie on our plans to solve the case in four days and Grandpa's quest to find a lawyer.

She puckered her face. "That's all you've got? A lawyer and a guest list?"

Worry slammed back into me. I told her about Cody Fjelstad being a suspect, too, and his social worker Sam

Peterson disappearing upstairs at the inn just prior to Rainetta being found.

"Your friend Sam must have his reasons. He really raised his voice?"

"I don't want to believe it either," I said, getting up to go to the kitchen to begin washing their dishes. I didn't want to talk about the rift between Sam and me that had begun back when I decided to date Dillon Rivers during college. The only two times I'd ever heard Sam raise his voice was with Rainetta and with me all those years ago. Sam was protective of me, and maybe jealous of Dillon, who was just about as nice and charming as any guy could be with my parents or anybody. He'd driven up from school in Madison several times to visit me during summer vacations or other times. Dillon was six years older than I was and had interrupted his schooling a few times to pursue his love of being a comedian, but he was back studying to be an engineer when we met. He was smart, and his family was well-to-do. His parents lived in Milwaukee then, in a big home on the lake. But Sam said Dillon was too charming and spoiled. I felt like Sam was calling me spoiled, too. The sting of that contributed to my need to leave Door County, though I'd never admit that to Sam. Whenever we had met by accident on the street during my holiday visits home, we were always civil, but the edge between us had always remained, like some piece of nut stuck between your teeth and you can't dislodge it.

"You have to talk with him right away," Grandma called from the living room. "Sam always liked you."

Maybe too much, I wanted to say. "I suppose."

"There's no 'suppose.' He and that Ranger boy can help you figure all this out in a jiffy."

I doubted that, what with Ranger avoiding me, too.

She hobbled up on her crutches, but when she headed my way in too much of a hurry, she teetered too far forward.

"Grandma!" I rushed to her, grabbing her and the crutches with a sweep of my arms. "Please be careful. Sit down. Watch your cooking show about snakes. I don't need your help."

"But I think you do. We have to make fudge like crazy. A boatload of fudge."

"Why?" I helped her to the kitchen with my hands firmly clasped on her birdlike limbs. After leaning her crutches on the back of the chair, I eased her into the seat, then poured her a cup of coffee from a simmering pot. The lingering aromas of cinnamon toast and eggs filled my lungs full force, making me hungry and making me want to hide out right here with Grandma Sophie and not face the world.

She said, "You have to get back on the horse, as we say, and make your wonderful fudge."

I slid into the chair opposite her at her squeaky oak table to tell her about the ingredients being confiscated and my quest later today to find Belgian chocolate to start over with more Cinderella Pink Fudge. It required the sometimes hard-to-find white chocolate chunks. In addition, I wanted to experiment with Belgian couverture chocolate, which had cocoa butter solids well over fifty percent for a creamy texture. Sometimes that type of chocolate needed tempering and the recipes needed last-minute adjustments. Making fudge with Old World ingredients wasn't for amateurs and it couldn't be a rushed process.

"That's very fine," Grandma said, "but making even one loaf of fudge is going to be too slow with you taking all that time to stir your heart out in those copper kettles. That'll make good pictures if Jeremy Stone drops by, but you need to fill those shelves with an onslaught of fudge to show people you can't be kept down and that you didn't do in poor Miss Johnson. You could be getting crowds of people coming here overnight. This is a big story, Ava."

I hadn't thought about that aspect. What good are a lot of customers if you have nothing to sell? But there was the fact of how long it took to make real fudge. "I don't know, Grandma. I can make only what fits in my copper kettles." I had six, but I could stir only one at a time myself. "As it is, I have to start work at seven in the morning to make a batch that's ready for the following day, at the earliest. I have to mix, heat, cool, loaf. It's a long process."

"I can make microwave fudge right now within an hour, start to finish."

I wrinkled my nose. "That's quickie melting of chips basically. That's not the kind of fudge I want in my shop, Grandma. Sorry. Nothing personal."

"Who will care? People are going to be flocking to your shop to stare at the woman accused of murder, and you need fudge to sell."

"But a lot of them are going to believe I put poison in my fudge. That rumor caught fire yesterday already, I'm sure."

"Yes, but others will hear about the diamonds soon enough, and they'll think you hide gems in all your fudge. They put plastic toy babies inside cakes for Mardi

Gras. Maybe we can find things to stick inside your fudge. People will flock to the shop. You're going to be famous. And make a boatload of money."

"You think so?" Maybe I'd attain the fame I had missed out on when working for *The Topsy-Turvy Girls*. I thought about Jordy threatening to close us down. If the murder had happened at the shop, we would be closed and out of business. I still worried, though. Jordy could order it closed for another search on a whim. I sat down across from Grandma. "But I don't have time to microwave batches of fudge, and neither do you." The truth was, I was shivering still at the thought of foisting fake fudge onto the public.

Grandma Sophie reached over to pat my hand, her warm fingers and palms clasping mine and not letting go. Like infusing my fudge with flavors, she was infusing me with her warmth and wisdom. She made my soul lighter and purer. I supposed all grandmas do that for their grandchildren; these moments gave me fleeting yearnings to have children just so they could know Sophie Oosterling.

With a smile creasing the faint wrinkles around her brown eyes, she said, "I'll get on Facebook and e-mail and call the ladies from church. We'll clear our cupboards of chocolate chips this very afternoon. We'll fill your shelves. You can still make your fancy stuff, too. Sell our version for cheap but put a premium price on yours."

That plan felt acceptable to my honor code. Excitement tickled my innards. "This'll be just like putting props on our stage sets for the show."

She squeezed my hands. "This is what you have to do to save yourself, honey. Just what I said. You have to put on a show to make sure you look innocent."

"But I *am* innocent."

"You know what I mean. You're in charge of your destiny. The producer of your own show!"

Me? In charge of my own "show"? A fairy-tale wish for it swelled inside me like a time-lapse video of a spring tulip budding and unfurling into full bloom under the sun. And I would make money to repay Gilpa and Grandma for hiring the lawyer. And my parents would be proud of me finally.

Grandma's plan seemed foolproof. What could go wrong with church ladies praying for me and making fudge?

Chapter 4

Grandma's idea had given me permission to think of creating a fudge shop extraordinaire that would surpass anything the Disney corporation could create. When a customer entered the shop from now on, I'd overwhelm all five senses with rainbows of colors, contrasting taste sensations, textures of sugar crystals, the scents of ingredients like warm caramel and butterscotch but also lavender and roses infused into my fudge, and customers would hear the pleasant canoodling of wooden paddles within my copper kettles. I had faith that the church ladies would be the spark of a holy fudge revolution in Door County.

A little past eleven, with Grandma Sophie fully engaged in contacting her friends, I turned my thoughts to the list of suspects. If I worked fast enough—as fast as my grandma seemed to think I should—this case could be solved and out of our hair by tomorrow. The phrase, "If it's Tuesday, it must be Belgium," struck me. That old phrase was about those obnoxiously fast bus tours of Europe, but now I was fairly humming, "If it's Tuesday, it must be Belgian fudge." Tomorrow was Tuesday. All would be well.

It struck me that Isabelle Boone would be serving lunch at the Blue Heron Inn right now, which meant her eight guests — oops, seven now — would be in the dining room and not upstairs. Which meant I could poke around at the crime scene.

Somebody had put my fudge in Rainetta Johnson's mouth to make it look like I'd killed her, but who? And why had I been targeted? Why would somebody put diamonds in my fudge? How had they done it, exactly? Did Rainetta have any connection to the diamonds? Or that New York heist? And where had Sam disappeared to after he'd gone upstairs before Rainetta? Was Sam part of some plot to target me? Was this his cruel payback for what I'd done to him eight years ago? All those years ago, during college, I'd been dating Dillon off and on, but when Dillon hit the road for months at a time, Sam and I struck up a closer relationship. It blossomed into something I didn't expect. I thought it was love. It looked like Dillon was out of my life for good, and Sam felt comfortable, safe, and he'd always watched out for me. Things proceeded too fast toward a wedding, though, and I got cold feet. On the night of my rehearsal at the church, the week before our wedding, Dillon came back. My heart panicked like some poor deer standing in the middle of the road in the headlights with a car coming from both directions. And I leaped into Dillon's car. Vegas was our next stop. Could Sam still hold a grudge for my jilting him?

Goose bumps rippled over my flesh. Anger flickered to life inside of me. It wasn't anger with Sam at all. Being accused of murder made me mad.

The sun was out, filtering its spring beams through the reddish first leaves and whirligig seed pods of the maples on my street, which helped me shake off the gooseflesh. I dropped off my jacket at my house, rolled up the sleeves of my sweatshirt, then exchanged my heavy and noisy work boots for quiet rubber-soled jogging shoes.

I hiked fast up the steep hill to the Blue Heron Inn, gasping for breath by the time I reached it. After creeping across Isabelle's wood porch, I waited to see if I'd been spotted. But nobody came to the door. Eerie déjà vu drenched me in a cold sweat. I'd been here alone once before. Not even Pauline knew about it because I was so embarrassed. On Friday night, on impulse, I had scrawled a quick note to Rainetta Johnson, inviting her to visit my shop. Then I'd rushed up to the inn when I'd seen everybody, including Isabelle, leave for the fish boil. I'd left the note in the room Isabelle had previously told me she'd cleaned and readied for Rainetta. Since the sheriff hadn't said anything about the note, it must have been thrown in the trash and taken out before he and his crew inspected the room. I almost felt disappointed for Jordy Tollefson not finding it; he seemed determined to arrest me.

I eased into the grand front hallway with its blue-carpeted staircase opposite me. Yet again the mass of crystal and glass Steuben figurines filling the enormous hall mesmerized me. The refracted light from the chandeliers played about the room like fairies flitting.

Most of the collection was clear glass, though for the first time I noticed a shelf on a wall to my left with a row of glass paperweights swirling with colors. I must not have noticed them last night because they were above the table where my fudge had sat in its ill-fated pink glory. *The deadly debacle of my debut.* Pauline would be proud of the alliteration.

I looked about the area for Izzy's favorite piece, the unicorn, but didn't see it. Perhaps a guest had bought it. Izzy had said Rainetta Johnson offered her a pittance for it. Maybe the snooty Reeds snapped it up as a souvenir of the murder.

Voices in the dining room reminded me of my mission, so I hurried on stealth feet up the carpeted stairs.

The dark hallway gave me chills. I paused at the head of the stairs to let my eyes adjust. I could still visualize where Rainetta had sprawled across the hallway by her door.

As I sneaked along the carpet, wary of the old wood possibly creaking underneath, I noticed some of the doors hung ajar. The doorknobs and locks were antiques. The guests likely had to use old-fashioned, big keys to secure their doors, if the keys or locks even worked. We had doors of that sort back on the farm when I was a kid. You could jiggle those darn keys in the locks for five minutes and still not get the lock to engage.

Rainetta's door had police tape across it jamb to jamb. My heartbeat sped up as I stood in the hallway, my hand on the cool, brass doorknob to her room. The voices babbled downstairs from the back of the house somewhere; utensils pinged against steel bowls and pans. They were fixing the meal together. But one of them could hike up here at any moment. I ducked under the tape, then slipped inside Rainetta's room, closing the door silently behind me.

The sweet, innocent smell of carnations hit me. A huge bouquet of at least two dozen pink carnations with a purple bow around the vase sat on a small side table straight ahead but slightly left of a window. It made me sad to see them abandoned. I had left my note on that table for Rainetta. I lifted the vase to check for it; the note wasn't there.

There was a blue-and-cream-colored flowered chair that matched the blue-and-cream flocked walls. The polished dark wood floor had scatter rugs in front of the chair and bed.

The bed, to the right, was rumpled, a mess really. Sheriff Jordy Tollefson and his crew likely looked high and low for my poison fudge or for hairs missing from my head to test for DNA. My hands fluttered up to run through my brown hair, which I'd left loose. No hairs came off.

A hefty, antique walnut five-drawer dresser with an ornate mirror hugged the wall to my immediate left. Straight ahead and next to the chair and flowers was the window overlooking the Lake Michigan bay and docks. To the right of the window, an antique walnut desk held a flat-screen TV on one end. The TV was unusual; the inns around here assumed you stayed at a B and B to get away from such trappings. Izzy had mentioned Rainetta being demanding, though. I looked around for the chocolates Izzy said she'd come up to put on the pillows but didn't see them. Jordy's deputy probably ate the darn things.

The desk had a five-by-seven white pad of paper and pen next to the TV. Curious that it hadn't been taken in the evidence gathering, I tiptoed over, and to my surprise saw that it was a small pad with the logo for a Hollywood studio. The pen had the same insignia. These were Rainetta's personal items! The police likely didn't take it because there wasn't anything written on the pad; the family would need to pick up her personal effects later.

Family? Who were they? I needed to read Jeremy Stone's stories to see if any family members had been quoted or referred to. I wondered who would be visiting Fishers' Harbor. And my fudge shop. Thinking of Jeremy and his sleazy attitude and photo taking yesterday made me pick up the notepad. I didn't want him having it. I wanted to hand it back personally to Rainetta's relatives and tell them how sorry I was about everything, maybe tell them that I was in the same business as Rainetta—show business—and that my grandmother loved her movies. I twisted my hair into a ponytail, then slipped the Hollywood studio pen through it. I didn't have a pocket big enough for the pad, so I stuffed it under my sweatshirt and tucked it into my jeans.

The dresser drawers called to me next. The two small drawers at the top didn't yield anything. But when I opened the first big drawer below, I found a pair of white panties, a woman's half-slip, and a pink chiffon scarf of the kind elderly ladies like to tie over their hair to keep their hairdo in place against the wind. Women didn't usually mix their scarves with their underwear. Maybe Rainetta had been laying out clothing for the following day, taking items out of her luggage and plopping them into the drawer as she sorted through things.

Her luggage was gone. Either Jordy had it or Izzy had put the luggage away for the relatives to pick up. I looked about for the closet door. It was only a couple of steps past the TV.

To my surprise, the closet was jam-packed with a couple dozen different designer outfits, from dresses to skirts, blouses, and suits. Many things were pink or lavender, Rainetta Johnson's signature colors. There were silks, satins, sparkly beading on some things.

The clothes suddenly vibrated, moving on their hangers.

I leaped back, my breathing on hold.

Somebody was hiding in the closet!

I ran for the door.

A hoarse whisper rasped the air behind me. "Miss Oosterling, it's me."

"Ranger?"

Cody Fjelstad's red-haired head poked out from the mass of clothing lined up on the hangers. His freckled face bore a mask of distrust for me, which broke my heart.

I sat on the corner of the bed farthest away from him. "What're you doing in Rainetta Johnson's closet?"

"Are you going to report me, Miss Oosterling?"

"No, unless you don't talk to me. Why aren't you in school?" I knew the answer and felt bad instantly for being stupid enough to ask. "Never mind. The kids will tease you about the fudge. Ranger, nobody really knows how the lady was killed. And it's not your fault."

"But I made the fudge she ate and she choked on it, the sheriff said."

"The sheriff also said there were diamonds in the fudge."

"Diamonds? There were? How many?" He popped from the closet. "Is that your new recipe?"

He was practicing his sarcasm again with me. But he obviously had known nothing about the diamonds. At least not consciously. Somebody else had to have slipped them into the fudge ingredients that had been confiscated yesterday by the sheriff's department.

"No. We're sticking to fairy tales and fisherman ideas

for our fudge recipes," I assured him. "Now tell me why you're here. And how did you get up here without somebody seeing you?"

"The back stairs." He pointed toward the hallway.

But I didn't recall seeing any back stairs. I opened the door a tiny crack to look out. All I saw was the room across the hall and the shared public bathroom door to the right. "Cody, I don't see any stairs."

"They're in the room across the hall. I snuck up the back way when I climbed in the window in the back porch this morning. It was cold out."

This was no time to scold him for breaking into a house. Especially since I'd done the same. The Blue Heron Inn had an enormous screened porch replete with gliders that overlooked a lawn, flower beds, a vegetable garden, and beyond it all—Lake Michigan. I'd been on that porch once in my whole life and recalled a couple of closed doors on the house wall. Perhaps the room across the hall was originally a servant's quarters, with the stairs giving the help easy access to the back of the old inn for doing chores, gardening, or, well, serving. Whatever the case, those stairs explained how Sam Peterson had disappeared so fast yesterday from the crime scene.

"Whose room is that across the hall?"

Cody shrugged. He had the thumb of one hand hooked in a front belt loop of his jeans, but the other was hidden behind his back.

I ventured around him for a good look, but he stealthily turned and hid his hand. I focused on the closet. "She sure loved pink and purple."

"It's sad for you. She would've bought all your Cinderella Pink Fudge. Especially if it had diamonds in it. Your fudge is the best."

When I turned around, I found him grinning at me. The old Ranger was back. "That's nice of you to say, Ranger." Or was he buttering me up to hide something?

"She was a nice lady. We have to find who killed her."

"Is that why you're here in her room instead of in school or at my shop?"

He sat hard on the bed, bouncing up and down a couple of times, his one hand clearly around some object. The poor kid looked ready to cry. "Bethany liked me when I was making fudge for the movie star. She doesn't want to go to prom with the killer of the movie star. There's a difference, you know."

"Oh, Ranger," I cooed, sitting down next to him. Sam had told me Cody didn't like being touched, so I kept my hands on my jeans-clad thighs. "Bethany won't think you killed anybody."

"You're right, Miss Oosterling. That's why I made notes. You want to see what I heard this morning?"

He headed for the desk, stuffing something into a pocket before looking for the notepad I'd picked up.

"Here it is." I sheepishly brought the notepad out from under my sweatshirt.

Cody took it, flipped up a few pages, then showed me several notes he'd made on a hidden page, including: *Hannah and Will don't care if fudge lady goes to jail. Sooner the better.* ☺

"There's a funny face, Ranger. Does that mean you laughed or they laughed?"

"They did."

"And when did you hear these words?"

"When I was in the room across the hall this morning, I heard them through the wall. They talk loud. Do you think they want you in jail because they killed the movie star? Can they get away with murder? If you're arrested, does that mean they get to leave here?"

I swallowed hard. It suddenly felt creepy to be sitting in this room with the possibility of Will and Hannah Reed barging through the door at any moment. Time had slipped away on me.

"We have to go, Ranger. Now. Show me the back stairs."

We wended our way through what had to be Jeremy Stone's room. It was filled with bags and books, notes scattered like spring apple blossoms on the wind, a laptop recharging. His room was bigger than Rainetta's, a suite really, but it lacked the view of the lake. In front of a love seat was a sofa table with an expensive bottle of white wine from a local winery and two glasses. The wine bottle looked empty. My curiosity was piqued. Who had he been entertaining in his room? Who would put up with him?

But we had to hurry. The stairs split in two at the bottom, with a short passage to the kitchen and another to the porch. We chose the porch and our escape.

As soon as Ranger and I got down the steep hill and onto level ground near the docks, Ranger strutted ahead of me, clearly not heading down the street toward the school. Once we hit the dock area, he passed the pier where my shop sat. I called to him. He paused long enough for me to catch up, but his hazel eyes held a stormy look that matched the wind-whipped lake.

"Ranger, what's wrong? Aren't you coming to help me make fudge?"

He shook his head.

"But I thought you just said you wanted to help me."

"I am helping you. I'm going to solve the murder so Bethany respects me. Don't you remember?"

"Is that why you have something from the movie star's room in your pocket? What did you find?"

His mouth flinched.

"Ranger, you can't take things from that room. You have to give it to me or take it back there. Or give it to the sheriff."

"Not until I solve the mystery."

I'd known Cody Fjelstad only a little over two weeks, since Sam had set him up for the part-time job. Although Cody and I had become close enough, sometimes I was at a loss as to how to respond to him. "But the sheriff will solve it. It might be best if you come back to my fudge shop and look for clues there to help him. We can look for more diamonds."

He shook his head vigorously. "I can't go back to your shop, Miss Oosterling. I can't help the sheriff, either. He thinks I messed with your fudge. He won't be letting me wear a badge until I prove I'm innocent."

So that was what this was about. Cody's sole goal in life was to become a man who wore a badge. He wanted people looking up to him. "Ranger, I'll get you a badge to wear. You can be my deputy of fudge."

My attempt at lightheartedness died when he looked off toward the water with a sad twist to his mouth. The wind ruffled his curly red hair. "I'm a man, Miss Oosterling. Giving me a toy badge to wear is insulting. I expect a lot more from you. Sam said you were a nice person. I trusted you. But now you're treating me like a baby."

He strutted away down the docks, ignoring the lakewater spray bashing him. A few fishermen waved at him from their moored boats, but I could tell he ignored them.

My heart felt as empty as those fishermen's nets. I had no choice but to call Sam Peterson.

"You sure have a way with men," Sam said, after marching into Oosterlings' Live Bait, Bobbers & Belgian Fudge. The cowbell voiced a violent *cling-clang*.

My grandpa, who had been on the phone for the past half hour begging for parts for his boat motors, seemed to sense that a storm squall had overtaken the inside of the shop. He got off his phone, mumbled something about being gone for an hour, waved offhandedly as he passed Sam, then set the cowbell to banging again. My shoulders hunched up at the sound.

Sam, every short blond hair on his head in place, his blue eyes ablaze, looked particularly tall and menacing when he sauntered over to where I was screwing a new shelving unit together in anticipation of fudge glory by later today or tomorrow. His tread on the wood floor was heavy, like damning exclamation marks. He wore cowboy boots, denim jeans, and a light blue shirt stretched across his broad chest and shoulders. He still sported all the muscles he'd built playing football in college and then on the Green Bay Packers practice squad for a couple of years.

I mumbled a "Howdy." My heart hopped about inside my chest like a bunny's when faced with a fox. This is how it was every time Sam came to the shop to check on Ranger. I wondered if Sam liked making me nervous; it was his way of torturing me for what I'd done to him in the past.

I focused on the screw I was trying to work into place in a steel plate on the back of two pieces of scrap plywood Dad had given me, left over from building a calf shed on the farm. My shelving unit would be four feet wide and about as tall with four shelves. It would hold a lot of microwaved, no-fail fudge.

Sam said, "I didn't catch up with Cody. Which way did you say he was going?"

"East on the docks. Maybe he circled back around to the school?"

"I ran over there and didn't find him. I'm going to have to call his parents if I don't find him soon."

His words sounded accusatory, compounding my guilt for handling Cody so badly. "I'm sorry," I said, not looking up but unable to do anything with the screwdriver with my shaking fingers. "He'll be all right, I'm sure. This town isn't that big and everybody knows him."

"What did you say to him?"

That made me stand up and face him head-on. But still in my sweatshirt, my hair up in a messy twist, and sweat trickling down the sides of my face, I felt like a frump in comparison to Sam. After swiping my sleeve across my forehead, I spat out, "I said all the wrong things, obviously. So sue me, Sam."

After repeating what I'd said to Cody about the badge—which had sent Cody stalking away, I followed that with the news of finding Cody hiding in the closet at the Blue Heron Inn. "He found something he was hiding from me, Sam. I think he thinks he found evidence of the murderer."

A muscle jerked along Sam's jawline. "He shouldn't be barging into places. I'll have to talk to him."

"Go easy," I said, finishing putting the screw in place in the shelving joint. "He wants to impress Bethany so they can go to prom together."

"A lot of us do crazy things for a woman now and then."

The words dropped like bombs in the fudge shop. After hoping fruitlessly that somebody would walk in and save me from this conversation, on impulse I said, "What was that crazy thing you were doing with Rainetta Johnson yesterday at the party?"

"There was nothing crazy."

But his face flushed. His scalp moved his hair in front a smidge in a nervous tic I remembered he'd had since childhood.

Pointing my screwdriver at him, I countered, "She was touching you in a way that looked like you two were just this side of a pretty spectacular kiss."

"You were in Hollywood too long."

"I saw what I saw, Sam."

"You're jealous."

He had the audacity to advance into my personal space. I picked up a four-foot piece of plywood shelving off the floor and held it between us. "Jealous of Rainetta? I suppose you think I'd murder her because she stole my man? That's *your* soap opera fairy tale, Sam."

"But I'd like to think it could be true."

I blinked hard up at him. "You can't be serious."

"It's no secret I still have feelings for you."

"Sam, please. I chose the other guy over you. Get over it."

"But you said yes to me. Who knew I'd be jilted on the same day you ran away with the other guy?"

I wanted to explode. I shoved the shelf into his arms. "We have more important things to do than talk about what happened eight years ago. We've changed since then, Sam."

He stood for the longest time looking down at the four-foot piece of plywood. "We have changed, haven't we? Your show's pretty good."

"You watch *The Topsy-Turvy Girls*?" The incredulity of such a claim calmed me down.

"Well, sure."

I took the board back from him. "It sucked this season."

"You've always been too self-deprecating."

"For good reason," I said, shoving the board into place inside the shelving cavity. "Nothing in my life has ever turned out the way I've wanted it to. And please leave my marriage out of this."

"Maybe this fudge shop is finally going to be your thing. Your copper kettles are cool. And I bet guys don't say that out loud to you every day."

Darn but he'd made me smile. Why was he being so nice to me? "You think I can make a go of this place?"

"I know so. Look how hard you're working on those shelves and on this place. You're determined. Determination breeds success."

His blue eyes were like lighthouse beacons on me. Could I trust him? I felt both safe and scared simultaneously, as if my heart were in a tipsy rowboat.

My throat had slaked dry; it took effort to form words. "Listen, maybe you could help me put this up against the wall. I've got to hurry and change clothes still and meet Isabelle and Pauline in about an hour."

Together we dragged the shelving unit against the wall behind the copper pots. I'd paint it tonight.

Sam headed for the door. "Call me if you hear from Cody."

"Will do."

I followed him to the door. After he left, my legs crumpled under me. I sagged against the white marble-topped loafing table, pressing my palms on its cool surface. The air filter across the way in the minnow tank fizzed. My insides felt the same way, but then a thought bubbled up in my brain: Sam had just tricked me.

He'd evaded my questions about his relationship with Rainetta Johnson. And what he said about my determination and success was just some social worker slogan he probably spewed to all the kids and people he counseled. Sam wasn't being nice at all; Sam was being his old wily self, trying to control me by being nice. Because why? Because he'd had a relationship with a murdered movie star?

Chapter 5

By two thirty, when Pauline's kindergarten class was done, the three of us headed up toward Sister Bay in the Door County peninsula in my yellow Chevy pickup to catch Highway 57 to Koepsel's Farm Market. The big barn building houses every product made in Door County. I'd called ahead and they had a modest amount of Belgian chocolate in stock for candy making, enough for a couple of batches of fudge. My stomach was churning already about what tomorrow would bring for my shop with the church ladies descending on me.

Pauline rode in the shotgun seat in my yellow Chevy pickup; pint-sized Isabelle took the slim bench seat in back.

Isabelle cleared her throat behind me. "I know you want to hurry, but you're going to get pulled over."

"Oh, sorry," I said, letting up on the pedal. "Thanks, Izzy. Jordy would love an excuse to put me behind bars."

Pauline said, "Let's not give him one." She pulled a ruled pad from her big schoolbag, then clicked her pen. "We know the list of suspects has to include Hannah and Will Reed. We have the New York diamond connection, as loose as it may be."

So as not to damage my fledgling friendship with Isabelle, I didn't dare mention sneaking into her inn, where Cody Fjelstad had told me that the Reeds were hoping the murder would get pinned on me. I also didn't want to hurt Cody in all this mess by revealing he'd broken into the inn. I hoped he returned home tonight.

Isabelle said, "Jeremy Stone worries me. He's never around."

"But he's a reporter, out interviewing, doing his job," I said.

"He's creepy," she insisted. "He was helping at lunch today; then he was gone before we ate. And last night, I suspect he had a woman in his room until late."

Pauline said, "Having an overnight guest is allowed, isn't it?"

"Of course," Isabelle said, "but it's the way he does it. He sneaks the person in and out the back staircase. His room used to be the cook's room. There are stairs from his room to the kitchen and the back verandah."

I knew about the stairs, too, and had to bite my tongue, which was killing me, but the information about Stone was new and had to be pursued. I remembered the two wineglasses and empty bottle in his room. "Who do you think he's interviewing in his room? Or seeing?"

"I suspected at first it was Taylor. She's a guest."

I groaned. "She's one of them that went out on my grandpa's boat Sunday and had to be rescued off Chambers Island. Jeremy's probably writing a story that's not going to portray my grandpa in a good light."

Pauline clicked her pen again. "So what do I write down about her on our list? Full name?"

Isabelle obliged. "Taylor Chin-Chavez. Cute girl, in her twenties, fairly new out of college. She's from Miami."

"So why's she here?" I asked, slowing down for a couple of deer that poked their heads out of the roadside sumac bushes.

"She's an artist—a sculptor, she told me—and had heard about my Steuben glass collection. She said she wants to do what I'm doing, run an inn with an artistic bent, but she's interested in finding an old lighthouse to live in instead as well as use the lighthouse as her shop."

The deer leaped across the road, then evaporated into a copse of maples and cedars. I sped up again.

"She certainly came to the right place," I said. Some of Door County's ten lighthouses were run by volunteers, and maybe there was a chance one of the lighthouses was looking for a new caretaker. "She doesn't sound like Jeremy Stone's type. Or a murderer."

Isabelle said, "I agree, but maybe she knows something about Stone or his investigation that we need to know."

The thought of cozying up to the crooked-nosed reporter left me cold. Pauline glanced my way and surely sensed the "ick factor" as I appealed to her with a smile. She said, "No way am I even having the best Belgian beer with that guy to get information out of him."

I gave Isabelle a look in my rearview mirror. "Who else is staying at the inn?"

Isabelle told us about Boyd and Ryann Earlywine, in their forties, from Madison, Wisconsin, the state capital and a four-hour drive south from us. He was a history professor and she taught music. I didn't see how they might want to murder an aging movie star. The other person on Gilpa's boat had been John Schultz, fiftyish, from Milwaukee, who was visiting wineries and breweries and other Door County places prior to setting up tours for travel companies and college alumni associations. The wine aspect intrigued me.

I told Isabelle about the bottle I'd seen in Jeremy's room. "Maybe John was the one enjoying wine with him."

"I hadn't thought of that," Isabelle said from the back. "Now that I think of it, John didn't stay long for lunch today, either."

"Aha!" Pauline said. "They had agreed to a rendez-vous. But where? Maybe we'll stumble across them today trying to sell diamonds out of the back of a car."

We had a good laugh; then silence settled around us. I suspected my gal pals were wondering, too, if one of the guests were indeed part of some diamond heist, maybe fencing the diamonds. But it seemed totally unbelievable that such a thing could happen in Fishers' Harbor, population two hundred. Or was our quiet, quaint locale exactly why diamonds showed up here? Did somebody hope to make a connection without being noticed? Was that somebody Rainetta Johnson? Certainly no phalanx of photographers followed Rainetta Johnson here as they might do in Chicago, where she likely got pictures taken of her just for going for coffee. Escaping to Door County had to feel good; it allowed her to be a private person. She could meet up with anybody she chose here and nobody would notice; there'd be no cell phone pictures ending up on the Internet.

By the time we got to Koepsel's Farm Market, we'd gone through the list of people at the party, too. As far as we could remember, the only other people who'd gone upstairs ahead of me that day were Sam Peterson and Mercy Fogg. But knowing there was a back stairwell now put a different spin on everything. Somebody could have gone through the kitchen and up the back staircase, through Jeremy Stone's room, and then across the hall into Rainetta Johnson's room, where they murdered her. And then shoved my lovely Cinderella Pink Fudge down her throat to make it look like she choked to death. If only Cody had sneaked up then and overheard what had gone on in that room.

None of it really made sense, but I shivered a little for Isabelle. One of her guests could be the killer, and she had to live in the Blue Heron Inn with that killer until somebody solved this crime.

In my rearview mirror, she looked morose, fearful perhaps, her face paler than usual.

I bought her a gift at Koepsel's—cherry barbecue sauce that came from the same orchard that made the cherries used in my fudge. I reminded her, "It's that time of year when we have our first cookouts. It'll get everybody out of your inn and change their mood."

"Thanks." Her cheeks pinked a little as she smiled finally. "The atmosphere inside has been a little tense."

"Because everybody's scared of turning around and breaking some of your glass figurines worth a fortune!" I said, laughing.

She gasped in a way that told me that was exactly her concern.

I added, "Then my idea is a great one. The guys will love cooking out. I bet even Will Reed will stop arguing with his wife long enough to eat something with cherry barbecue sauce on it."

Pauline recommended the bison burgers from Koepsel's for the grill. Door County raised a lot of buffaloes now, which I always thought funny since Belgians called themselves buffaloes, too. Some say Belgians got that name because when there's trouble, they put down their heads and forge straight into the storm just like a buffalo. Isabelle also picked up sweet potato butter and other exotic items for her guests, all meant to quell fury over being held captive in Fishers' Harbor.

I purchased all the Belgian bulk chocolate the market had, but it was all dark chocolate; somebody had beat me to the white chunk chocolate. Pauline had an idea then. She'd taken her kindergarten class once to the Luscious Ladle in Sister Bay. "It's a new bakery and cooking school that focuses on baked goods."

We called, and the owner had white chocolate! We had to drop off Isabelle, though, so she could make dinner for her guests. As she got out with her big bag of goodies in hand from Koepsel's, she invited us to come for a cookout tomorrow night at six o'clock in her backyard. I knew the Reeds hated me, and that fueled my answer. "Of course. I'd love to come."

When Pauline and I got back in the truck, she hissed at me, "What are you thinking? Everybody thinks you're a suspect. They don't want you around. You're going to cause a food fight worse than any I've seen in our school cafeteria."

"But what if something pops out of Will's or Hannah's mouth—like a confession?"

"I can't argue with that logic."

"And it certainly isn't a tactic Jordy Tollefson would use to shake a confession out of his perps."

"We have lists now of possible perps from all the peeps we previewed in this pickup truck. Perfect." She patted her big bag sitting on her lap, proud of her alliteration. She never quit. That was what I liked about her. It was why her kids loved her, too.

On the way back up Highway 42 to Sister Bay, we had to first pass through the village of Ephraim, where the main street wound closely to the waterfront. The slow twenty-five-mile-per-hour speed gave us plenty of time to talk. Most of the shops were still closed, even Wilson's Ice Cream Parlor, where I was always tempted to stop in summertime for their "Cherry Berry Delight," made with Wisconsin blueberries, strawberries, and our Door County cherries on French vanilla ice cream. My mouth was watering while I told Pauline about what I'd found in Rainetta's room at the Blue Heron Inn—namely Cody with something he'd found.

"What do you think it is?" Pauline asked. "More diamonds?"

"No." Then I thought about it. "Maybe?" It was a definite question. "He found something mighty precious to him."

"He was in the closet. Maybe Rainetta kept her jewels hidden in the pockets of her clothes."

"I've never heard of such a thing."

"Did the room have a safe?"

"No, not that I remember seeing."

"Then maybe her clothes are filled with jewels," Pauline said. "I used to hide my stuff from my little sister that way all the time. She never caught on."

"Holy cow. I have to get back into that room and rifle through Rainetta's clothes."

"Nice R's. Some kids have problems pronouncing R's. Then there's the whole rolling R thing they have to learn for Spanish words. We start with growls, though. You can learn how to say a rolling R if you pretend you're tigers eating each other."

"You have kindergarten kids pretending they eat one another?"

"Oh yeah. They love gross stuff. Maybe Jordy should hire them to solve this murder."

I shook my head, but she had made me smile.

Sister Bay was bigger than Ephraim and more people were about. The Luscious Ladle was in an old one-room schoolhouse on the main drag that had been refurbished. The wonderful aroma of freshly baking bread lured us up the walkway.

The chef of the cooking school, Laura Rousseau, was a head shorter than I was, with clear blue eyes and messy curly blond hair cut in a short bob. She was about my age and very pregnant. The condition didn't hinder her energy. Several fragrant bread loaves sat in rows on her butcher-block counters, and she was pulling more from the industrial-sized stoves. She was pleased to give me her white chocolate. She refused to take my money.

"It's extra I had from a class that made white bark candy with walnuts in it."

"You saved me!" I tried to hug her, but then we laughed when her belly got in the way. "When are you due?"

"Two months. We know we're having twins, but that's all. We want to be surprised when they're born."

She offered us each a loaf of cheese bread as a gift. I tore off a corner right there to try it. My mouth felt like it had rainbows in it made of cheddar cheese, butter, wheat, and oats. I was ravenous; it was all I could do to close up the wrapper and resist eating more.

Laura said, "If you want to experience a great taste sensation with my bread, just go up the street to Al Johnson's. I'm on my way there now with these fresh loaves."

Al Johnson's Swedish Restaurant was a classic old place with an extensive menu and gift shop. In the summer, goats grazed on the grass roof, which made it a de rigueur spot for tourists. I was surprised it was open for dinner at this time of year. Laura said they were doing a run-through for new staff and menu items, like her cheese bread. I offered to ferry the yummy-smelling bread for Laura in my pickup truck. I also promised to bring her some of my new Cinderella Pink Fudge made from her chocolate.

A smile spiked onto her flushed face. "Please do! We could do some cross-promotion in the future. I'll give people a taste of your fudge and send them your way, and maybe I could drop off samples of my baked goods at Oosterlings."

I'd do anything for the smell of the bread in my arms. We had a pact immediately.

My pleasant, warm feeling evaporated, however, when we got to Al Johnson's. I delivered Laura's bread at the hostess stand where I was met by a kitchen staffer, but then I turned around and got a surprise. In the middle of the dining room with all its beautiful, cobalt blue glassware, there sat Cody Fjelstad with Mercy Fogg, of all people! Pauline and I backed up into the entry hall near the gift shop area to stay hidden from view.

"What is Mercy up to?" I asked, spitting the words out as if I'd just bit into a bug. "She threatened me, and now she's questioning Cody?"

"You don't know what she's doing," Pauline said, in an all-too-rational voice. "You said he ran away from you. Maybe she was kind enough to see him on the street and pick him up."

"She should have dropped him off at his parents' place. This isn't good, Pauline." I peeked around the hostess stand. "She's looking at something. A watch? It looks like some big expensive thing. It's sparkling."

Pauline edged around beside me for a look. "Looks like a man's watch. A big, elegant, expensive, excellent one."

"And she's giving it to him."

Something didn't compute. Why was the has-been village president of Fishers' Harbor out for dinner with a high school kid? Then I recalled that Cody said he was going to solve the murder on his own. Maybe *he* had invited Mercy Fogg to dinner? To question her? That seemed bizarre, but then, I kept underestimating Cody. But Cody was only eighteen and nervous as heck about dating Bethany Bjorklund, a cheerleader; asking women out wasn't his forte. Mercy was fifty-nine, according to the election stories in our weekly newspaper.

It would be disastrous to interrupt Mercy and Cody in this popular and crowded restaurant. Both of them had no use for me at the moment. So Pauline and I left before we were discovered. But my stomach was growling. Smelling the delectable Swedish pancakes and wonderful perch and walleye specials—with almost everything served with lingonberries—had my mouth watering yet again.

Pauline and I ended up at Nancy and Ronny Jenks's bar, the Troubled Trout, on the east edge of Fishers' Harbor, for fried cheese curds and a local dark brew that had a smooth chocolate finish. My parents made the fresh cheese curds that went into these bite-sized treats that Pauline and I dunked in homemade ketchup. Fresh cheese curds squeak in your teeth; when dunked in bat-

ter and a deep fryer, they become puffs of gooey goodness that taste like miniature toasted cheese sandwiches.
I can't begin to tell you how much I missed fried cheese
curds while in Los Angeles. The other thing I missed was
freshly brewed Wisconsin beer. It was an art form here,
and the Troubled Trout was a place where a woman
could get a real sipping beer or beer cocktail. Door
County's wheat and cherries and Belgian chocolates
made heady flavorings for beer. Wisconsin's German and
Belgian brewmasters were the best in the world, most of
them trained in the home countries. When you added in
world-renowned cheeses—or someday soon my new
fudge to nibble on with your beer—Door County was a
Garden of Eden for sinful eating.

As much as that meal helped me get drowsy later, I
could barely sleep. My head was muddled with the
strange conglomeration of murderous things I had to
sort out, not to mention hoping I could scare up a living
from pink fudge.

At six a.m. on Tuesday morning, somebody was rap-
ping at my front door. Groggy, a robe slung over my
T-shirt, I opened the door. "Hello?"

A plump lady with short, fluffy white hair and a bright
white smile stood there. She was only a couple of inches
shorter than me. She wore a longish, pink sweatshirt with
sequined flowers over pink leggings. All in all, she looked
like a giant order of cotton candy.

She said, "You must be Ava Mathilde. Your grandpa's
been flappin' off his mouth all morning already about
A.M. and P.M. bein' in such trouble trying to figure out
this movie star dyin' right here."

"All morning?" I shook my head to clear it. Who was

this woman who knew Gilpa's pet initials for me and Pauline Mertens?

"Oh yeah. You betchya. The other ladies and I got here at five. That's what the message from your grandmother said, to be at Oosterlings' Live Bait, Bobbers and Belgian Fudge in Fishers' Harbor by five." She stuck out her hand. "I'm Dotty Klubertanz. I'm from Saint Ann's Parish in Egg Harbor."

The church ladies! I'd forgotten about them.

We shook hands. I was more awake now. "What can I do for you, Dotty?"

"Well, we're doing just fine rearranging everything in your little shop—"

"Rearranging?" The blood in my veins stopped flowing.

"With everything we brought for sale, it's kind of hard fitting things in with those copper kettles in the way. So we put them out on the dock for now—"

"The dock?" My heart plunged into my stomach.

"And we thought we might put up a sign for donations of copper pennies. Lois thought that'd be cute. Copper in copper."

"Lois?"

"Lois Forbes. She's from Saint Bernie's in Jacksonport. Nice lady. You know those pennies add up. But your grandpa said we needed your permission to move the marble table."

Jacksonport? Egg Harbor? How many parishes had sent church ladies? There was something like half a dozen Catholic parishes in Door County, plus the Baptists, Lutherans, Episcopalians, Moravians, Evangelicals, the Jewish congregation, and even a Lighthouse Mission.

Had they all responded to my grandma Sophie's social networking?

What other disasters was I going to find at my fudge shop? I tossed on clothes but didn't take time to put on my work boots. Carrying them, I raced barefoot across the dewy wet, cold grass behind my cottage to get to my fudge shop.

Chapter 6

At six a.m. on a Tuesday, Fishers' Harbor is usually dead. Weekenders have gone home, and the next long weekenders don't arrive until Thursday. During the summer tourist season, a Tuesday might be flush with visitors, but not in May. Except today. This Tuesday our little bait and fudge shop was packed. With women.

After entering through the back door, I was hit in the noggin' by the aromas of peanut butter, maple, and butterscotch. The women were melting all kinds of chips to make fudge. That baby-powdery scent that older women always seem to have also laced the air. The women were all shapes and with hair mostly the color of pewter candlesticks, though a dyed redhead dotted the room here and there. They squeezed past one another in my small galley kitchen with bellies and butts rubbing as they made coffee and drizzled warm icing onto cinnamon buns. Others were using the counters to cut into pans of lemon bars and microwaved fudge made last night in kitchens all over Door County.

I was dressed in my serviceable and dull blue jeans, boots, and a long-sleeved white blouse. They looked like a flock of colorful birds in their various sweatshirts and

sweaters adorned with wildlife scenes or Green Bay
Packers logos. Here and there a gold necklace or a strand
of pearls accented their outfits.

The women ignored me, giving orders to one another
while sipping coffee in between gossiping about people
I didn't know. I felt foreign, like a gauzy ghost passing
through a dream.

When I left the kitchen and made it into the main part
of the store, more shock slammed me. They'd turned the
bait and fudge shop into a . . . church bazaar!

Where my copper kettles used to sit, the women had
set up four six-foot folding tables, likely brought from a
church basement. The tables nearest me were mounded
with homemade clothing—like beer can hats made from
slicing up the logo portions of cans and then knitting
them together with yarn to form the shape of fishermen's
hats. There were also piles of crocheted doilies, table-
cloths, and pillowcases, including ones with Green Bay
Packer green-and-gold logos. Another table held homemade felt flower pins, hair combs with yarn doodads on
them, and crocheted crosses used as Bible bookmarks.
And, yes, there was fudge, but not nearly as much as the
plates of cookies, including chocolate chip, peanut butter, and oatmeal with raisins. I saw pies, too, and smelled
them, including fresh-baked rice pie—a local specialty
made with thick cream and lots of eggs. The end of one
table held seedling tomato plants that one of these ladies
had likely started in her house for spring planting.

Women scurried about folding things; then other
women slipped in behind the first ones to refold the
same things and fuss with the stack so it was just so.

My sales counter had been taken over by three
women putting prices on colored paper dots. Three other

ladies hurried to place those dots on the goods on the tables.

Rising on tiptoe, I saw my grandfather over at his register on his phone. He was pale, shell-shocked, too, obviously. Tables had also been set up in his portion of the place. I made my way over to him. He put down the phone to scowl at me.

"Gilpa, I'll get rid of them. Don't worry. And please don't blame Grandma. I take full responsibility for this, this"—I looked around—"whatever it is."

"Call it a starstruck party. They're here because of that movie star. They were waiting on the dock when I opened at five, all asking questions about what she was like. I wasn't even at the damn party."

The curse word jolted me. Gilpa swore only when something got serious. He slapped through the pages of a tattered phone book we rarely used.

I flinched, but then I thought about Grandma Sophie calling on these women as a big favor to help me. "Maybe you'll sell out of everything today."

"These women aren't here to buy bobbers to put in their hair."

He had a point, but I persisted. "We'll just have to coax the men in the door somehow."

Gilpa growled, his oily fingers smudging the yellow pages.

"Who are you looking up?" I asked.

"Attorneys. I'm not sure what kind I'm supposed to get for our situation. Criminal attorneys? Probably criminally expensive. Or maybe we need a business or municipal attorney who can help us fight off Mercy Fogg if she comes sniffing around again wanting to shut us down."

"Maybe there's such a thing as a fudge attorney?"

Gilpa looked up with pinched, silver eyebrows, but then he let loose with the biggest grin. "Ah, Ava honey, your fudge needs no defense. It's pure magic."

We hugged. He smelled of bacon from breakfast along with a tonic of gasoline and crankcase oil. I asked, "You've been working on the boat already this morning?"

"If I don't get it working by this coming weekend for the outings for Mother's Day, my heinie's in a sling for sure."

I knew he didn't want to say he couldn't afford a new boat, so I said, "Maybe it's time to think about partnering with Moose Lindstrom."

"That young punk of a Swede? He's not even of Social Security age yet."

Moose was Carl Lindstrom, a tall, barrel-chested guy, and he'd just turned sixty, two years shy of qualifying for his first Social Security check. Not that Moose needed money. He'd had a birthday party on his new charter fishing boat last week, the *Super Catch I*, which sat at the far end of the harbor. You can see his boat through our windows, its riggings and captain's crow's nest sitting high and pretty. Although Gilpa had refused to set foot on the *Super Catch I*, I had. It's a thirty-two-foot Grady-White with autopilot, with real-time weather and sea conditions delivered by satellite, air-conditioning, and even an iPod stereo system. It made Gilpa's old boat, *Sophie's Journey*, look like a Conestoga wagon out of an old Western movie.

Things were rough enough at the moment with all the women taking over his bait shop, so I steered us back to safe ground. "We're going to make magic in the shop today, Gilpa. I'm making more Cinderella Pink Fudge today. Grandma said I have to put on a show, and she's right. We'll sell tons of fudge and start our season together flush with cash."

His brown eyes twinkled with hazel green highlights in their irises. "We Oosterlings are fighters."

He tousled my hair, which I'd forgotten to comb or put up; I promptly whipped it into a twist atop my head. I hauled myself across the store to swipe a hair comb with a yellow felt flower in it to hold my hair in place.

Next, I took charge. I flung a long apron over my head. With the ladies' help, I made room for a copper kettle and my double boiler near the window north of the door to the docks. Passersby would see the show and thus be enticed in to buy fudge and beer can hats and maybe even bobbers and beer from Gilpa.

By seven thirty, the giant double boiler was cooking with twelve pounds of sugar, more than two whole quarts of cream from my parents' cows, and all the white chocolate I'd bought yesterday at the farmer's market and the Luscious Ladle. With vanilla and red cherry juice added, the ingredients soon infused the shop with a savory bouquet. I felt official when I rolled up my sleeves, put the chef's hat on my head, then stirred with my four-foot walnut wood paddle.

Several of the women clapped.

Sam showed up then, wending his way from the back toward me. He'd obviously come in the back door thinking he'd avoid the crowd. A mistake. He wore a tie, which was already askew and it wasn't even eight o'clock. He was wiggling a finger for me to join him outside. I knew right away something awful had happened to Cody Fjelstad. A couple of ladies were happy to take over stirring the bubbling fudge potion.

Out front, in a refreshing, misty fog and the hint of a warmer day, I took off my hat as Sam led me several yards down the wood plank pier that jutted out over the water where Gilpa's crippled charter boat sat.

With dread, I asked Sam, "What did Mercy do now?"

"Mercy?" Sam asked, perplexed.

"I saw her having dinner last night with Cody up in Sister Bay at Al Johnson's."

Sam straightened his tie, his mouth agape as he digested the odd news. He wore a white shirt and tan pants. Everything about him was neat except the troubled look in his blue eyes. "Cody never went home last night. His parents called me a half hour ago. When he was late getting up for school, Arlene went in to wake him up and found his bed hadn't been slept in."

My mouth went dry. "You have to call Mercy. Maybe he stayed at her house."

He called her, then pocketed his phone with a sour face. "He's not there. She said he was very upset with you. What happened?"

"Nothing. But maybe he saw me spying on him at the restaurant." I felt horrible. I worried my hat with my hands.

Sam whirled on his heels in clear disgust. "I have to make a report about this, you know."

"Leave my name out of your report."

"You want me to lie."

"Yes."

His eyelids flared and his blue eyes took on the intensity of a mad bull. But I had the oddest reaction; heat galloped across my body. It was a little sexy the way Sam Peterson had just made my heart race. I didn't want to feel this way toward him.

I pleaded, "You have to speak with Mercy again. I think she was giving Cody a gift last night for all the wrong reasons, and it was an expensive watch. Maybe something with diamonds."

"What?"

"It sparkled way too much to be an ordinary watch. Mercy had gone up those stairs with Rainetta on Sunday and then Mercy disappeared. She might have stolen things from Rainetta and gone down the back stairs."

Sam paled, backing up just enough to scare me, but he didn't fall into the water. The mist feathered around us in gray, gossamer strips. He said, "I have to talk to Mercy."

He trotted back up the pier, making it bounce under my feet. Sam never panicked, but he was clearly upset now. I couldn't shake the feeling that he wasn't telling me everything he'd seen or done that afternoon with Rainetta when he was upstairs with her. Had Sam and Mercy witnessed something together? For some reason, in my head I'd been imagining each of them alone with Rainetta. But now I wondered about that.

A woman's voice called to me through the mist, "Your fudge keeps wanting to boil over!"

Oh shoot. I'd forgotten the church-lady invasion. I ran as fast as I could, slapping my chef's hat back on.

Church ladies were all about prayer and money. Don't let them fool you about being humble and charitable. They liked the *ka-ching* of pennies in copper kettles, the smell of folding money, and the zippery sound of a credit card sliding through a card reader. More of them arrived while my fudge ingredients were cooling for a few minutes in the copper kettle. The sea of gray heads and fancy sweatshirts soon had red hats bobbing in it when a bus-load of the Red Hat Society arrived from Sturgeon Bay for a sojourn in Fishers' Harbor.

My grandfather slipped out unseen, probably after a drop-and-roll maneuver to avoid all the hats, hair combs, and henna rinses that could rub off on his clothes and stain worse than the crankcase oil already under his fin-gernails. A couple of fishermen stepped into Oosterlings' looking thirsty, then pivoted, about to slink out. I rushed over with a six-pack of beer, took their money; then they left. The next man we saw was Jeremy Stone.

When a broad smile curved up under his crooked nose, I wanted to kick him in his derriere, but I'd already tied on a long apron and was whipping my fudge mix-ture with what amounts to a long-handled metal spat-ula. It was flexible on the end so that it could scrape every bit of delicious chocolate off the sides of the cop-per kettle.

Once you started whipping in the copper kettles, you couldn't stop for fear of ruining the fudge crystals. I was missing my apprentice in a big way. Cody could easily take over the whipping; I couldn't trust any of these older ladies to do the task. They'd surely stop willy-nilly to sip coffee and gossip, wasting my money and time spent gathering the ingredients for Cinderella Pink Fudge.

Jeremy Stone took photos of the whole hullabaloo, finally focusing on my whipping procedure. Sweat trick-led down my back. I was forced to smile for him, which pained me.

"Can I taste it?" he asked.

"No," I said, purposely short with him.

"Quite a crowd. What's your estimate?"

"We might be able to hold a couple dozen people usually; this has to be twice that."

"I counted more than sixty. You're to be congratulated on the idea."

His compliment—which I didn't deserve because this was Grandma Sophie's idea—almost made me stop stirring, but I couldn't. My shoulders ached. I glanced at the old clock over the door. I had ten more minutes to go. I pulled the stirring spatula into the air to check the consistency. A long, three-foot column of pure pink chocolate—like a stalagmite meeting a stalactite—whirled in front of me. Again and again, up into the air I lifted the drizzle of pale pink perfection. The air grew so thick with the aroma of the chocolate-cherry confection that you could taste it by breathing. I explained to Jeremy the close relationship between breathing in aromas and the ten thousand taste buds that each of us has. Taste is the weakest of the five senses, but what we smell enhances the taste. I threw in the fact that fish can taste with their fins and tails, which the crowd seemed to enjoy learning.

Jeremy scribbled it all down. The room had gone quiet while everybody watched me.

Finally, the consistency was right and a little more than fifteen minutes had gone by. I stopped for a breather.

"Can I taste it now?" Jeremy asked again.

This time I couldn't be tart with him. There were sixty women staring at me, all my potential fudge shop social networkers whose gossip could bring me customers. "Who wants the honor of helping me lift the copper pot onto the marble table to pour it out and begin loafing this delectable fare?"

The pride in my voice sounded foreign to me. The realization that I could be *that* proud of something as silly as fudge making stunned me.

Dotty Klubertanz strutted forward. "It matches my outfit, so it has to be me."

The women giggled and clapped. Jeremy photographed us lifting the kettle in front of the picture window. I ladled out half the batch. I'd knead or "loaf" that batch for the amusement of customers and Jeremy's camera. The other half we poured into pans.

"This will take until late tomorrow before it's ready to cut and eat," I explained.

They groaned.

"Okay. Another plan. I'll teach you how to loaf fudge and you can take as many tastes as you like while you do it."

That mollified them. My shop became an instant fudge-making school. I handed over my short, knifelike walnut blades to let them scrape across the white marble until the fudge "set."

As the women converged toward the front of the shop, Isabelle rushed in from the back. "Our delivery is here. I saw all the cars, so I thought I'd come down to help the guy unload while getting a look at what was going on. Wow. Look at the crowd."

I stood taller. "Did he bring any chocolate this trip?" I'd ordered some online last night from a Green Bay wholesaler who regularly received imports from Belgium.

"Sorry. Just more bags of sugar, some flavorings, and my flour. The driver and I already restocked your shelves for you."

"Thanks, Izzy."

We moved over behind Gilpa's cash register to stay

out of the fray. Three women in red hats were doing a fine enough job at my own register, ringing up sales of crocheted pillowcases and felt doodads. Jeremy Stone was interviewing a couple of church ladies.

I must have muttered some doubts because Izzy surprised me by taking my hand closest to her and squeezing it briefly. "It's going to be all right."

But sadness niggled me, oddly enough. "It looks mighty fun, but this isn't what I envisioned for a fudge shop. And Gilpa's given up."

That was what made me the saddest. I missed the quiet mornings with just my grandpa and me puttering around selling to one customer at a time. We had time to offer them a cup of coffee. And most of all, Gilpa and I were getting reacquainted. It was like old times, when he and Grandma Sophie had worked on the farm when I was a little. He was always there when I was four and five, ready to eat cupcakes with me or take me fishing.

I realized in this moment that my upbringing was why I wanted our shop to work and why I wanted to share it with Gilpa. This was my soul. And Gilpa had shaped or "loafed" my soul just as surely as I could loaf fudge. I couldn't lose the shop or his trust and respect. Yet I was in danger of doing just that.

After a deep breath, I gave Izzy a hug. "Thanks for all your help. We've known each other for only a couple of weeks or so, but already you've been a lifesaver. Thank you."

"And thanks to you and Pauline for the idea of a cookout. I did a trial run last night outside on the grill with the cherry sauce. It helped to get those people outside. There was less bickering last night."

"Did Jeremy Stone disappear early again?"

"No. In fact, he and Boyd and Ryann Earlywine became entranced with the history of glass and my Steuben collection. Boyd knows a lot about the history of glassmaking."

My brain turned on with that fact. "Did you know that when he first arrived?"

"No. I thought he and his wife were merely vacationing when they came last Friday night. And I saw them only briefly for coffee on Saturday and Sunday mornings before they set off for sightseeing, so it wasn't until last night we had a chance to chat. With the fire pit going outside, we all gathered around and a lot of information came out."

"Did you talk about the murder?" I was already thinking of a way to sneak back into Rainetta's and Jeremy's rooms for a closer look into their things.

Isabelle said, "I steered clear of murder, and so did they. We needed to relax."

"Well, I can't afford to relax. I have until Friday before Jordy gets all hot and bothered about putting me in jail after that medical examiner's report comes out. Maybe I'll find out something at your barbecue party tonight. What should I bring?"

"I hadn't really thought about all the dishes yet."

"I'll cook something and bring a dish-to-pass."

"I thought you only knew how to make fudge."

"True, but don't tell your guests that. I'll figure out something."

"I'm not sure this is a good idea." Isabelle seemed to shrink to elfin size, as if she were trying to shrink away from me.

"Please, Isabelle. I need you to do this for me. Don't tell them I'm coming. Invite some other shop owners from around town and their families for your guests to talk with. That way they won't run away on us before-hand. I'll sneak in behind the crowd with my contribution." I tapped my white chef's hat I still had on.

"Okay," she said, skepticism on her face. She excused herself to head through my back door and then hike up the hill to prepare a small lunch for her guests at the Blue Heron Inn.

It struck me as odd that on a nice day she'd even have guests staying for lunch instead of exploring. Jordy hadn't said they were confined to the inn itself. He'd said they couldn't leave Fishers' Harbor. That meant they could still explore the couple of bars and restaurants along the main street. Better yet, they could visit my "church bazaar" and buy microwaved peanut butter fudge and lemon bars, along with a beer hat. What more could a person want while on vacation?

My curiosity sent me over to Jeremy Stone, though I was squeamish about engaging him. "Jeremy, are you going back up to the inn for lunch?"

"No. Why?"

"It seems most everybody stays there for lunch, except you. Why don't they all get out more?"

He bent his head back in a big guffaw. "Because they're afraid somebody will go through their rooms."

I felt caught, though he had no idea I'd traipsed through his room and had plans to do it again. "You mean they all feel guilty?"

"Could be."

"Except you."

"I had nothing to do with murdering the lady across the hall from me. I'm trying to figure it out myself. Here's what I saw that night."

He showed me photos on his cell phone. There was

me in my dirty apron looking freaked out. He had photos of the pink fudge on the table with the marzipan fairy wings. The glass unicorn was in the background.

I asked, "Where's Isabelle's unicorn now?"

"I don't know. I haven't seen it." He gave me a cockeyed look of appraisal, and I knew I'd just scored a point with him. "I'll look around for it. You think somebody stole it?"

"I do. Maybe somebody involved with the diamonds. Maybe somebody is here to steal some of Izzy's glass collection, too."

He gave a low whistle, then handed me his phone for the few seconds it took him to make a note in his pocket-sized notebook.

I asked him, "Why don't you just use voice activation on your phone to make notes?"

"Because this is a work phone and anybody involved in this murder case—like your lawyer—could try to subpoena what's on it."

"I don't have a lawyer."

He scrawled another note. "You're that sure *you're* innocent?"

"Of course. And you're that sure you're innocent?"

After shaking his head in amusement, he showed me pictures taken in the hallway that fateful afternoon. Rainetta Johnson was splayed across the floor on her back. There was a pose of Isabelle gasping and looking down. He had no pictures of the Reeds, who had hidden inside their room. But as the paramedics and Jordy had hauled Rainetta's body out of the hallway, Jeremy had snapped a picture that showed a door with an empty wine bottle sitting outside it.

"Whose room is that?" I asked.

"John Schultz, the travel agent from Milwaukee."

"He was on the boat while it happened."

The way Jeremy blinked gave me pause.

I asked to confirm it, "He was on the boat, right?"

"I think so."

"Then why'd you blink?"

"I remember there were noises coming from his room. Or maybe it was the room next to him. But that doesn't make sense. That was Taylor's room, and she was out on the boat, too."

"Taylor Chin-Chavez."

"Yeah. A looker." He scrolled through more pictures, and one popped up of Taylor in the dining room and another with John Schultz holding on to a wine bottle as he emerged from his doorway near the stairwell; the picture made it look like he'd been drinking straight from the bottle. A prickle zipped up the back of my neck. It was the same kind of wine bottle I'd seen in Jeremy's room. I didn't dare ask because that would surely ruin any chances I might have of rifling through Jeremy Stone's room later. But I wondered what John and Jeremy might have talked about following the murder. I certainly had to talk with John Schultz.

I asked, "Have you concluded anything yet?"

"You mean, do I have a suspect in mind? I think it was somebody from the outside, not the guests."

That gave me dread. Did he mean Sam? "Who do you have in mind?"

"That kid who works for you."

His words impaled me like an arrow into my chest. I sputtered, "I left Cody Fjelstad in charge of my fudge shop while I delivered the Cinderella Pink Fudge."

Jeremy showed me another photo taken from upstairs

and looking down on the back lawn—with Cody striding away from the Blue Heron Inn.

"How did you get this?" I asked.

"As I got upstairs, Isabelle came out of the bathroom. My room has a stairwell to the kitchen and back porch, so on a hunch I hurried around her and into the bathroom for a look out the window, and sure enough, Cody was running away."

"But you can't prove that he was running from anything or had even been in the inn."

"You're right. Maybe he just wished he'd been invited to the party and came up the hill to look through the windows. But I don't believe that."

I didn't either. Cody prided himself on being organized and sure of himself. "Let me look at those pictures again."

I thumbed to the photos with Rainetta on the floor. The third picture of her made me stop. I had to swallow some bile coming into my throat.

Jeremy asked, "Something wrong?"

I didn't dare tell him. "Nothing. It's just all so awful."

After excusing myself, I hurried out back of Oosterlings' and away from the prying ears of the church ladies to use my phone. I punched in the sheriff's number.

"Jordy, I need to know something very simple. What did you find on Rainetta Johnson's person?"

"I can't tell you that, Ava."

"You don't really need to tell me because I know. I was just calling to confirm it. She wasn't wearing her amethyst necklace."

"Uh, I don't know anything about a necklace," he said. "Tell me more. Did you steal it?"

I hung up on Jordy. His big oops of a hesitation with

"uh" confirmed for me that the necklace was missing and I was way ahead of Jordy in this investigation. Somebody had stolen Rainetta's amethyst necklace right off her body. The murderer? Or just a plain old thief?

My heart felt heavy as a bowling ball as it descended into my stomach. Had Cody come up the stairs and into her room to steal her jewels? Or borrow them? Had he been on some misguided mission to please his girlfriend, Bethany, with an expensive gift? Was that why he'd been back in the room when I'd found him? Had he come back to steal other things? Had he taken things right out of her suitcases and hidden them in her closet? And had he taken the very fudge he'd helped me make and stuffed it into her mouth to keep her quiet? Maybe she'd tried to stop him and they'd tussled? Cody would never murder anybody, but maybe Rainetta's death was a tragic accident.

Or was it? What if I was wrong about Cody?

Truth nettled my skin, making me itch all over. I knew one very good reason Cody might do harm to another person.

And I knew where Cody was hiding.

Chapter 7

Knowing I might have solved the murder had my stomach acid hopping. Cody had played into the killer's scheme quite handily.

I didn't dare meet up with Jeremy Stone back in my shop because he'd pump me for more information and ruin all our lives. And I couldn't bear to see Sam yet either; I was sure he had a connection to the stolen necklace and he'd want to stop me from finding it. My best strategy was to make more fudge and wait until Pauline and I could go together to retrieve the stolen necklace. We'd go incognito in her gray, nondescript car that looked like it belonged to a teacher on a yearly salary that amounted to what we had paid stars for one day's appearance on *The Topsy-Turvy Girls*. A tiny little window inside my heart still remained open to the possibility of my fudge ending up inside the Emmy or Oscars swag bags.

I had to cast aside my fear of Jeremy Stone. Amid the fray of sequined sweatshirts, silver hair, and gossip, I finished helping the church ladies loaf the Cinderella Pink Fudge. It wasn't my best batch, but the foot-long, six-inch-wide mound of pink on the white marble slab in front of the window was enticing anyway. Maybe I had the touch for success at something in life, finally.

I said to the ladies, "It looks and feels like Cinderella's cheeks!"

Dotty Klubertanz called it, "The cheeks of Mary, the Holy Virgin, Mother of God."

Hmm. *Okay, Dotty, a bit over the top, but I'll go with it if that'll help sell fudge.*

And it did. The sixty church ladies with a speed-dial button on their cell phones to heaven turned my place into the place to be in Fishers' Harbor by noon. At least for women. Ladies, some with children on a hip or in hand toddling next to them, came in to buy the pillow-cases, doilies, beer hats, and hair doodads, but they also insisted on buying all the home-baked cookies and microwaved fudge.

I glimpsed the oddest sight while I was at the marble table at the front window—Hannah Reed's distinctive choppy black hair across the crowded room. She was at the cash register, making a purchase. I hadn't seen her pass by me at the front door, so she must have slipped in the back door. Many people used the back door, but she was so out of her element in my little fudge shop and amid homemade doodads that I was immediately suspicious. And a touch triumphant. She was a prime suspect. Did she know that I thought that of her? Was she keeping an eye on me? Probably. She scurried off through the back hallway before I could disengage from my fudge loafing to follow her.

Then I got distracted when Dotty and her friend Lois Forbes took it upon themselves to give away tasty samples of the new loaf of Cinderella Pink Fudge to kids, who promptly fed it to Gilpa's guppies in the minnow tank.

"Dotty," I pleaded, "it's not done yet. Fudge is all about a chemical process. It has to cure for a couple of days, and twenty-four hours at a bare minimum. Even as fish food."

Lois, her hair dyed red as fox fur and looking wily as a fox, said, "Cure like what? Cement? I hate watching cement dry and I'm not about to watch fudge dry." She stood on tiptoe and called out, "Anybody who buys something today in the shop gets another and bigger free sample of the movie star's fudge. Take it home and use it as ice cream topping."

Topping? My incredible fudge? Given away as if it were equal to that high-fructose syrup used at carnivals? So much for my feeling of success.

Just like that, Lois and Dotty brushed me aside to hand out nibble-sized samples of my unfinished, gooier-than-normal Cinderella Pink Fudge. Some took a feathery glob on paper napkins to taste or feed the fish; others tucked samples in zippered plastic quart bags into their purses for home.

My whole being seized with failure.

But my old-fashioned cash register handle was pumping up and down steadily. Soon the ladies had to move over to use Gilpa's cash register, too. Unfortunately, my grandpa didn't return, which worried me. He'd lost his boat and now his shop, the latter because of me. My only saving grace in all this was that maybe I'd made enough in sales this Tuesday to pay for a couple hours' time of the lawyer he was scaring up for me.

Then Pauline called me to say she had a flat tire at school. Kids liked putting nails under tires or just letting the air out. So instead of driving incognito in her gray car, we ended up in my dandelion yellow Chevy pickup.

As we headed south of Fishers' Harbor on Highway 42, I told her about my theory of who had killed Rainetta Johnson.

"You can't be right about Cody killing that woman," Pauline said, filching about in her big black purse the size of a heifer calf while we hurried down the highway. She came up with her phone.

I panicked. "What're you doing with that? We can't call the sheriff. It had to be an accident. I didn't say Cody killed her. I said he had a part in it, unwittingly set up by the likes of Hannah Reed or her husband."

"I'm calling Sam Peterson. He'll know what to do."

"Sam might be involved in it."

Her phone spurted out of her hand, hit the dashboard, then landed on the floor under my feet. Pauline scooped it up, then put it away. She was shaking. "I could lose my job. We're covering up evidence and protecting murderers."

"Not us. But the person we're going to see is likely doing just that," I said.

Neither one of us wanted to say the name. If you say a name, it makes things real. Could the sweetest people in the world really have a hand in murdering somebody? For sparkly diamonds?

My hands held on to the steering wheel so tightly they were numb already.

We continued south on Highway 42 about five miles, heading to doom, though it would resolve the mystery behind Rainetta's death. I made a left turn onto a narrow, winding, two-lane blacktop road and sped up. My yellow truck pinged and bucked on its springs. I felt a kinship with the tension of being dangerous.

"We're going to end up in the ditch if you don't slow down," Pauline said.

"I just want to be sure we're not being followed."

"Why do we care if anybody follows us? If we solve this, won't that be something to shout to the world?"

"I don't want Jeremy Stone or any other of the reporters who are sneaking into town plastering Cody's picture across newspapers and computer screens. He's a kid."

"He's eighteen. An adult. You can't pretend he's not."

"I don't know everything about him. What if this sets him back in his development? I can't let him go to prison. I doubt they offer free mental health plans there." I could still hear Cody's angry voice excoriating me on the docks near Oosterlings' Live Bait, Bobbers & Belgian Fudge. He hated me for all the wrong reasons. He thought I was a bad person.

"What does Sam say about Cody's current progress and condition?" Pauline asked. "Sam's been his social worker all through school."

"Sam's acting strange toward me, like everything's my fault, so he won't reveal much about Cody's condition."

The road flattened out again as we sped under the dark overhang of oak branches.

"Well, Sam Peterson has a right to think things are your fault," Pauline said. "He wanted to marry you once, after all, and you left him standing at the altar while you hitched a ride with Dillon Rivers to scratch an itch you had."

A shiver went up my spine at the name "Dillon Rivers." Not even the spring sunshine coming through the windshield could warm me. Dillon Rivers had been everything a woman could possibly want. But now I would definitely go out of my way to run him down. As a manner of speaking only.

Pauline screamed.

Brown cattail stalks hit one side of the truck. I'd veered too close to the ditch.

Pauline said, "So this is how it is? You're not over him? After eight years?"

"Oh, I'm over him. He probably made new friends in prison, anyway."

"I heard they let him out early for good behavior."

My shoulders flinched. "He was a comedian and a good talker. Figures he'd find a way to charm them out of Waupun." That was the state correctional facility in Waupun, Wisconsin, a community maybe halfway between Door County and the capital of Madison. Despite myself, I wondered what he was up to these days.

Dillon Rivers had been a civil engineering student when I met him at the university in Madison. Or at least he said he was. I had never verified that, come to think of it. He'd said he was my age when I first met him; he turned out to be six years older, something I found out when he had to tell the truth in front of a judge who was different from the one who'd married us. I had met him one night at a local comedy club on State Street. He was good. I laughed hard. I fell hard for him, too. I was tall, and he was taller. He had thick, wavy chestnut hair and wore a black cowboy hat. That color should've been a clue. But it wasn't. He nurtured the cowboy mystique. He even walked with a swagger. His eyes were so brown they were almost black to match his hat. When he smiled, his eyes glittered like, well, diamonds tossed across a freshly plowed field.

I flung the steering wheel fast toward the left.

Pauline screamed again. "Stop the truck. I'm driving."

"I'm fine." I'd just missed putting us into a pond that ran close to the road.

"You're not fine. You're worried that Dillon will come looking for you, now that you're back."

"He won't."

"He might. That's what Isabelle thinks."

This shook me. "You told Izzy about Dillon?" We were almost to our destination. I slowed down.

"Sorry, but I thought you'd told her. She asked who you were dating, and we just got into a little of your history. Gosh, we're all friends. Don't be so prickly."

I didn't know anything about Isabelle's dating habits, though we'd become friends in the past couple of weeks, which was natural with us running businesses so close to each other and being about the same age. She'd moved into the Blue Heron Inn last fall and had spent the winter sprucing it up before moving in her Steuben collection. I'd met her during the Christmas break when I was home, but that had been in passing on the street when I'd come up from Brussels with my parents to go with my grandparents to a party at the senior center. She had mentioned coming from Arkansas, where it was a lot warmer than Wisconsin in the winter, but neither of us had time for long conversations then, or even now, for that matter; setting up businesses and getting ready for the summer tourist season in Door County had consumed us.

"I'm sorry for biting your head off," I said. "What is it about love that twists us all up? Poor Cody. Look what he did for love."

We fell into silence. Could Cody have really been a party to killing Rainetta? I feared so.

Pauline said, "Maybe Bethany will have a different story. Maybe we're connecting the wrong dots."

"I hope you're right."

As we swung into the Bjorklunds' gravel driveway, my body tensed. If Bethany had that stolen necklace in her possession, I didn't know what I was going to do next.

The Bjorklunds lived on a hobby farm. Their big white farmhouse had a welcoming verandah with rockers on it. The house was flanked with pastures holding horses and alpacas, with a big red barn to the right and an animal shed on the left. The Bjorklunds' dog, a white Great Pyrenees the size of a polar bear, wagged his tail as it walked up to sniff our legs. Cody loved animals. I imagined him gladly hiding here.

Bethany's father, Hans, came out the front door, letting the screen door slap on its hinges as he met us at the verandah steps. My tongue pasted itself to the roof of my mouth. I hadn't thought this far ahead. I wasn't ready to get Bethany involved in Cody's or my troubles. I hugged my arms, rubbing up and down the sleeves of my white blouse.

Pauline knew Hans from school events. "Hi, Hans. Listen, we're here to talk to Bethany about the senior prom activities. Is she around?"

"Oh sure." He turned back to open the inner door, then yelled, "Beth! Prom stuff!"

A faint "I'm coming" echoed from inside the house. Hans excused himself to do chores in the barn. Did he have a role in hiding Cody out here?

While we waited in the front yard for a moment, I whispered to Pauline, "Thanks. I wasn't sure what to say."

"I lied for you. So you owe me one. How about tickets to a Packers game together?"

The Green Bay Packers were just about the only football team in America that sold out their stadium for years to come. Needless to say, any available tickets would cost me plenty.

When Bethany joined us, I teared up because I knew what she meant to Cody. She was sweet, all girlie-girl, petite, and short enough to do acrobatic cheerleader tricks. She had long blond hair that hung loose past her shoulders and eyes the color of bluebird feathers. She was everything I wasn't. She was the young woman Cody wanted to go to prom with. And more. Had he asked her? Did she know?

"Bethany, this isn't about the prom. It's about Cody."

She bit the corner of her lower lip while her eyes dulled to a wary gray.

I pressed on. "You know something, don't you? Is he here?"

She shook her head.

"But you saw him recently. When?"

She shrugged, her eyes downcast.

"This is serious, Bethany." I took a fortifying breath. "He didn't go home last night. He's run away. Did he give you a necklace?"

Bethany tossed her hair back, a look of confusion on her face. "No."

"Did he give you diamonds?"

"Huh? Like you mean, like, we were getting engaged or something?"

Pauline intervened. "Honey, that can't be a surprise to you. I see the way he hangs around you in the school halls whenever he can." We had a consolidated school, with kindergarten through twelfth grades under one roof, so Pauline knew everybody's business.

"He's always following me, but that's okay. I know he doesn't mean anything weird by it. He's got problems."

I said, "He likes shiny things. We're wondering if he's been stealing jewelry to give to you."

Bethany winced, then sat on the verandah's steps. "Oh wow. You think maybe he stole diamonds from that actress who got killed? You think maybe he had something to do with . . ."

She was tearing up, and so was I again. I nodded, then swiped away my tears for the last time. I had to stay strong. "It was probably an accident. We have to find him. He doesn't understand that we can help him. He doesn't have to go to prison. Are you sure he's not here somewhere?"

"He's probably at the house."

"What house?"

"In town. Where he wants to live. After . . ." She rolled her eyes. "After we get married."

"So he's asked you?"

"Not in those words. But he told me in the hallway we have to go to prom together because that's where he wants to ask me something. I knew what he meant right away."

Pauline and I took off for Fishers' Harbor. The house Bethany had referred to was the old, abandoned historical one that Sam and others hoped would become the group home for people like Cody. The fateful party at Isabelle's last Sunday should have raised a few thousand dollars, if not ten thousand or more from Rainetta Johnson. The fate of the abandoned house was up in the air now, right up there with the fates of my fudge shop and Cody.

I wished Jeremy Stone hadn't said he'd seen Cody rac-

ing from the Blue Heron Inn. That had been the missing
piece to the puzzle—which reminded me that Pauline
and I would be attending a cookout at the inn later. My
truck's clock said it was four o'clock already; I had two
hours before Isabelle would fire up the grill for the backyard barbecue. What was I going to tell those guests in
order to draw out the truth? Could I shame somebody
into a confession by talking about how low it was to use
somebody like Cody to steal jewels or diamonds? Or
blame him for the murder? I wondered what would happen, though, if I pretended that I thought Cody did it.
Who among those at the party might look the most relieved? The Reeds from New York? Jeremy Stone? Sam
would be hoppin' mad at me, but I wondered if that
would help him think about anybody he'd seen slip into
Jeremy's room and use the staircase. Maybe we'd all
blanked out on somebody's presence. This party was
sounding like work for me.

As we inched along Main Street in Fishers' Harbor
toward the house, I noticed several news vans from
Green Bay, Madison, Milwaukee, and Chicago. A tickle
zipped through my belly, making me laugh with glee.

Pauline asked, "Now what?"

"Pauline, this is my chance!"

"Chance for what? To marry a reporter? We're crawl-
ing with them. Sheesh."

"No, silly. My chance to make Oosterlings' Live Bait,
Bobbers and Belgian Fudge famous. And you're going to
help."

"I don't like the sound of this."

"After we find Cody, we're going back to my shop. I'm
sure the church ladies have gone home by now to make
supper." Supper around here—and it was called "sup-

per" more often than "dinner"—was five o'clock for the farmers and older people who went to bed at eight to get up at five. I was headed in that direction; being a businesswoman demanded I start the day with the chirping robins and fishers—both looking for worms early in the morning. I said to Pauline, "I have a plan for my fudge sitting in those pans, the stuff that the church ladies didn't give away or feed to the fish."

Pauline groaned. But we had no time to talk about that plan. I stopped the truck in front of the grand old historical home on the north end of town. This was where Cody had to be hiding out with his stash of lavender gemstones, maybe diamonds, a diamond watch, and maybe—in a sudden flash of memory—Isabelle's missing Steuben glass unicorn.

The old mansion with peeling yellow paint sat back on a large, shabby lawn across from the bay and just before the road curved before going out of town. The house had matching, three-story turrets at both front corners, with their lower windows covered by plywood. One of the bay windows flanking a double front door also sported plywood. During my childhood, the place had been lived in by some family with kids, but somewhere lost in time they'd left, probably incapable of paying the heating bills. The mansion had been built by a Great Lakes shipping captain in the late 1800s. That was all I knew.

I wanted to shout at the haggard, one-eyed mansion for Cody to come out. But I didn't want to attract any more attention than my yellow truck probably did already. The news crews were only a few blocks away, casing Isabelle's inn and my shop.

As we ventured up the uneven stone sidewalk, Pauline

said, "Maybe we should ask Sheriff Tollefson to join us. Breaking and entering will get me fired."

"You can stay out here. I'll go in."

The front door was locked, as I'd expected. But I'd also expected to bully the rusted doorknob and handle and bust my way in. Nothing doing. I knocked on the door and waited. I called softly, "Cody?"

Nothing. We walked around one side of the house. Overgrown bushes hid basement windows, most of them boarded up. The one window not boarded was filmy and showed no sign of disturbance.

Pauline suggested we leave. "People might see us. Let's go."

I glanced toward the back, where I spotted thick pyramidal evergreens and ratty lilac bushes about to burst into bloom.

Once behind the house, we were well hidden and I saw how Cody was getting into the mansion. An old trellis led from the ground up to a second-floor balcony over a porch. It looked like a window up there had been busted.

"Come on," I said to Pauline.

"That trellis won't hold us."

"It held Cody."

"I weigh more than him. How much do you weigh?"

After two weeks of eating cheese curds with wild abandon, I would have to buy a swimsuit with a tummy hider. "Just boost me up. I'll grab the floor of that balcony. Come on. Pretend I'm a basketball. Throw me up to the hoop."

"This is stupid. You're going to get hurt and I'm going to throw out my back and not be able to finish the school year."

Stubborn Belgian. I sighed. "P.M., please, less yack and more action."

She crouched down, laced her hands, I stuck in my booted foot, and then in a flash was standing on the balcony.

I didn't want to crawl through the broken window with its jagged glass. My white blouse wasn't about to protect me. Fortunately, the door was unlocked. I told Pauline to meet me at the front door.

The door from the balcony opened onto a wide, dark oak plank floor and yellow wallpapered hallway. I stood for a moment, listening. I could see a far door on the other end, which likely opened into a large room between the turrets.

"Cody?" I called, staying rooted to my spot for the moment. There were several doors along the hallway. "It's me, Miss Oosterling. Miss Mertens is outside. But that's all."

I got no response. The breeze whistled through the broken window next to me, but that was all I could hear besides the occasional car or truck lumbering by on Main Street.

A shuffling jerked my instincts awake. "Cody?" I braced myself, ready to run after him if he burst from one of the doors.

The far-off rattle of the front door handle let me relax my shoulders. Pauline was trying to get in.

As I crept along. I noticed footprints in the dust. They had to be recent. They led straight down the hallway to the big room at the front of the house. Pauline rattled the downstairs door handle again. I figured I'd better hurry and let her in; then both of us could coax Cody out.

Pauline would have more sway with him than I would anyway, since Cody didn't like me at the moment.

I hustled through the dusty hallway, spotting the stairway to the left built into one of the turrets. Just as I started down the circular stairs, my feet were ripped out from under me, pitching me forward. I sailed headlong into the maw of the curving, wood staircase.

Chapter 8

My body banged into one wall of the staircase; then I pitched forward with arms flailing into thin air.

I hit hard into the other wall, a sharp pain radiating up an arm as I spun downward onto the stairs on my belly.

From there I slid and bumped belly down on the slippery wood steps with arms covering my face as I bobsledded around a final curve to the finish.

At the bottom, I landed spread-eagle on the flat floor. Shaken to my core, I tried to roll over. I screamed. My vision spun with a person hovering over me with a tree branch.

"Thank God you're alive," Pauline said. She tossed aside the branch and her big purse, then helped me sit up. "Your nose is bleeding. Is anything broken? Don't move. I'll call nine-one-one."

"No. I'm okay." But I wasn't. My left wrist throbbed. The sleeves of my white blouse had been pushed back during the fall and were spotted with blood. My arms were scraped and bleeding on their undersides where I'd used them to brace myself as I slid down the stairs. My belly hurt from the surfing, and one hip bone ached. "And to think we used to surf the stairs at home as kids for the fun of it," I said. "How did we do that without getting hurt?"

"We were five. Never mind that. What happened?"

"Cody must have tripped me from behind and run. Did you see him?"

"No. I was still outside. I heard the horrible noises and had to bash in the window to get in."

She started to help me up, but I yelped. A pain sharper than anything I'd ever known lanced up my arm from my wrist.

"Is it broken?" Pauline asked.

I stared at my throbbing left wrist. "I hope not."

She switched to the other side to help me up. "This is getting out of hand. We have to call the sheriff."

"Not yet. I have to talk with Cody, give him a chance to come clean on his own."

"But why? He needs help. He needs Sam. Oh, so that's it." Her face got close to mine, and she looked down her nose at me. I hated that and she knew it.

"It's not about Sam," I said.

"Sam reminds you of your mistakes, so you're avoiding him, even if it means Cody's on his own. Someday you're going to have to face up to what you did and why you chose Dillon over Sam."

"Someday. But not now."

A cool breeze drifted in from the broken bay window. I hobbled over to see if Cody could be seen running away. The only thing I saw out front was my yellow pickup truck at the curb and the view of Lake Michigan across the street.

I insisted we look around upstairs for the jewelry and anything else Cody might have stashed. My wrist hurt so much I had to hold my breath every few seconds. But adrenaline helped me push along. I was shocked that the laughing kid I'd known in my shop would do this to me. Which led me to the sudden realization that somebody else might have been here just now instead of Cody. Who knew we might be here, though? Bethany. But that cute cheerleader wouldn't hurt a fly.

We found nothing but mouse droppings in most of the empty rooms. The dust was disturbed in the big room along the front of the house, so Cody—or whoever it was—had to have been hiding there before he flipped me and ran to escape via the trellis.

Pauline insisted on driving my truck. "If you're not going to call the sheriff, at least get Sam to help you. Sam should have been here. He could've talked Cody into surrendering."

I got a chill from that. "I don't need Sam's help. He already thinks I'm a hopeless, helpless woman who needs his advice on how to live."

She *tsk*ed at me while we headed back to my quiet, treelined street and rental cottage behind the fudge shop. While Pauline washed up at my kitchen sink, I showered off my blood one-handed. Needlelike pain stabbed my left wrist. Bruises were forming up and down my arms. I still couldn't believe Cody had done this to me. Could Jeremy Stone have been following us? Or could he have been snooping around in the empty house on a hunch, too, and not wanted to be seen? After all, he clearly suspected Cody of sneaking around the Blue Heron Inn on Sunday.

With my damp hair left loose over my shoulders to dry, I dressed up in a fresh pair of jeans, flip-flops, and a long-sleeved red T-shirt to hide the stairwell rash and bruises. I wasn't about to have to explain what had happened to all the guests at Izzy's barbecue. It was less than an hour away. I switched my brain to fudge.

By a little after five, Pauline and I were in my fudge shop—or what was left of it. It was practically empty. The church ladies had cleared the tables of all the goods—or sold everything—and had dragged the copper kettles inside the door. The pennies were gone. The cash registers were empty. I checked Grandpa's, too. He wasn't around. The place was wide open, the front door unlocked. I wondered if we'd been robbed.

"Maybe your grandpa took all the cash home with him," Pauline offered. "The whole thing was your grandma's idea, after all. And he needs the money to pay for your attorney."

"I don't need an attorney."

"He thinks you need one. Though, if Cody did it . . ."

The sadness tingeing Pauline's voice made me think, too, about Cody. I wondered how much he missed making my fancy fudge. Could he end up in prison? Maybe Cody wasn't a murderer, but Jeremy Stone seemed to think he was involved. Do they let you make fudge in prison? Using just one arm mostly, I set marzipan out on the marble slab where we could carve fairy wings. But a yelp escaped me when my left hand bumped too hard against the white marble.

"Are you sure we shouldn't take you to the clinic to have that wrist looked at?" Pauline asked.

"Give it a day. I'm sure I'll be fine."

But fear as hoary as a spring tornado spun inside me. What if I couldn't use my wrist by tomorrow? How was I going to make fudge? I shoved the panicked thought aside.

Pauline helped me carve and place marzipan wings

atop individual pieces of the pale pink vanilla fudge with cherries in it. Cody had always loved this part. He imagined the fudge flying to people's mouths, which wasn't a bad image. Just after I shook pink luster dust—called fairy glitter by Cody—over a winged piece of fudge, Pauline snapped it into her mouth.

"Pauline! We need every piece!"

She was smiling like she'd gone to heaven, which elated me. I asked, "So the flavor's okay? The texture? I usually let the fudge sit longer."

She swooned, licking the ends of her fingers. "Tart with tawdry sweetness, cherry cheekiness becoming all vanilla vampy. Your fudge makes me feel like I'm dancing with a handsome prince at a ball and I've just been kissed!"

"You're horny." I handed her pink cellophane and multicolored ribbons. My wrist couldn't handle wrapping anything. "Let's hope it charms the newspeople. Camera people can't resist color. I want to look good on the news at six and ten."

"They're going to be at the party?"

"I doubt Isabelle invited them, but you can bet they're going to be there once they find out several shops are closed early for the evening for the barbecue. The aroma alone of that cherry barbecue sauce will draw them in. And they're going to want to know all about how I put diamonds in the fudge."

"Which you didn't. Maybe we shouldn't go. Didn't we get into enough trouble already today? And we have to go back to that house now and repair that window I broke so squirrels and raccoons don't get inside."

"No, Pauline. Our focus now is the party and my fudge."

"So this is all about you getting free advertising?"

I confessed that earlier I had been thinking such self-ish thoughts. Now I had something more important on my mind, and it all came about because Pauline and I were making my fudge into bite-sized gifts with glitter and pink wrapping. "If Cody sees the fudge on the news, he might come out of hiding. Cody was really proud of his part in making Cinderella Pink Fudge."

"But if he's run away, doesn't that mean he doesn't care about the fudge?"

"He cares deep down, but I doubt Cody is watching TV at all."

"I'm not following you."

"My pleading for him to give himself up is what matters. The people at the party will think that I believe Cody really killed Rainetta if I put on a good show for the cameras. Jeremy Stone will certainly corroborate my theory; he believes Cody did it. I want to see who's happiest about Cody being blamed."

"But Cody just tried to harm you. He *is* to blame."

But I'd just had several revelations. First, I had this odd feeling now that anytime I wanted to conjure a solution to something I needed only to get near my fudge. Its aromas, texture, and taste helped me think more clearly. And here was my new revelation: Cody wasn't mad at me. He had to be frustrated, in a deep way, that he couldn't be helping me make the sparkly Cinderella fudge that he loved to wrap. The only way he'd be kept away from wrapping pink fudge would be if he'd been *threatened* to stay away. Which meant somebody else was involved. Somebody was using Cody. I told Pauline it was Mercy Fogg.

Pauline said, "We saw them together in Sister Bay,

which is suspicious. She's certainly angry enough over losing the election to want revenge. And she doesn't make much money driving the school bus and being a relief driver in the winter for the snowplowing."

"And she's stout and strong enough to have knocked off Rainetta Johnson and stuffed my fudge in her mouth in one swift move."

We had just put the bite-sized fudge gifts into a flat cake box when Gilpa walked through the door covered in oil. The oil dripped off one side of his silver hair and down across an ear. His white T-shirt and denim bib overalls were brown and covered in oil. He headed over to his bait shop with a wave of a hand that meant "Don't ask."

"Gilpa, what happened?"

The rank smell of oil made my nose burn and my eyes water. Pauline coughed. Thank goodness we'd just wrapped the fudge because chocolate tended to soak in surrounding odors.

Gilpa filched about in a cabinet below a wall of bobbers and lures. After much racket and tossing aside supplies, he came up with a drill, holding it like a gun. "Now that engine's going to behave. Or else!"

"Gilpa, have you done anything else today besides work on your boat's engines?"

He ran a hand through his hair. I cringed as the oil embedded further. He didn't appear to care. "I have one engine running. She just seems to be spittin' too much oil. I've got a theory about how to relieve the pressure."

"With a drill? Gilpa, you could blow something up. Let's buy new engines. We'll use my credit card."

"Which you maxed out for this place. No, no, no. A.M. and P.M., you go on about your business. I've got it handled."

That was what I was afraid of. I suspected the hunt for our lawyer had been put on hold, mostly because he couldn't afford one and didn't want to admit it to me. "We're up at the Blue Heron Inn if you need us," I said. "And please, Gilpa, it's almost suppertime. Go home. Grandma must be worried. I'll be over later to fix dinner."

"I'll get dinner. This'll take no time at all." He raised the drill in the air as he hurried out, the cowbell going *clinkety-clank* in his wake.

I looked at Pauline. "This isn't good. A drill? Around all that oil and gasoline?"

"He's an experienced fixer-upper, Ava."

"No, he's cheap. He cobbles things together. It's why he can't find a lawyer. He's too cheap to really say yes to hiring one."

"Okay, but what could we do right now to help him with the engines besides get covered with oil and make him mad by talking too much?"

She was right. Neither of us was dressed for engine work. We were dressed for delicious deviousness and making a murderer confess.

Newspeople and cameras peppered the lawn and the front porch of the Blue Heron Inn. The spring day had warmed nicely into the sixties and still hovered there. Many people at the party had shed winter clothing in exchange for summer-weight clothes and sandals, as if they had molted. As we neared, I heard the soft but clear voice of Isabelle Boone explaining the history of Steuben glass coming from inside.

The babble of a crowd in the backyard drew us along with the aromas of grilled corn, salmon, and steaks slathered in the cherry barbecue sauce I'd bought Izzy at Koepsel's. This picnic was an even bigger event than Sunday's fund-raiser. When a party is held outdoors in a backyard in this small town, neighbors and even strangers don't have to be invited; they just drop by and are welcomed. Clouds moving in, and the threat of rain didn't seem to bother anybody. Poor Izzy. What she'd hoped to be a small party for her house-bound guests had turned into a county fair. A buffet table overflowed with my favorites, though, including lime green gelatin molds filled with our local apples, three-bean salad with cheese cubes added, and jut—a Belgian dish popular here that was essentially mashed potatoes made with cooked and chopped cabbage and freshly fried bacon.

A round table sat empty, so Pauline and I commandeered it for my individually wrapped pink perfections. I also scattered pieces as table decorations on the buffet table and the wine and beer bar featuring local ingredients including honey. Some people might hesitate to eat the fudge if they thought it had killed Rainetta, but I wanted to get conversations started about the murder.

Pauline slowed me down to whisper, "I'm surprised you haven't tackled a TV cameraperson and stuffed a piece of your fudge in his mouth. This is your chance to be a star."

The thrilling hope of being a success sparkled like diamonds inside of me, but it was as fragile as all the glass inside Isabelle's B and B. "I want my fudge to be the best in the world. Do you think it is?"

She waved off my self-doubt. "I'm helping myself to that cherry wine. Want a glass?"

I was about to say "no" when I spotted John Schultz across the lawn with a glass of red wine. The memory of the wine bottle in the photo on Jeremy Stone's cell phone made me change my mind. "Yeah, I'd love one."

With the glass of wine in my good hand and Pauline in tow with a piece of my fudge, I proceeded across the lawn.

"Hello," I said, nodding for Pauline to hand John the piece of pink cellophane-wrapped confection. "I don't believe we've met. I'm Ava Oosterling, of Oosterlings' Live Bait, Bobbers and Belgian Fudge just down the hill here at the docks. Please accept a sample of my new Cinderella Pink Fudge."

With trepidation, I waited for him to react to the gift in his big palm. He was a man my height and stocky but in athletic shape under the soft edges. He had thinning brown hair graying at the temples and wore a Hawaiian shirt, sturdy sandals, and fashionable tan men's shorts with several pockets. He had the look of a tour guide.

To my surprise, his brown eyes lit up at the fudge. He handed his wine to Pauline, then pulled off the ribbon to reveal the pale pink prize inside. The cellophane blossomed like the petals of a flower.

He chuckled. "This is a downright beautiful presentation. The ladies'll love this. You say you're just down the way?"

"Yes, on the docks. We used to be Oosterling's Live Bait, Bobbers and Beer, and we still have plenty of beer there, but now we also have fudge."

A scowl planted on his face. "You're related to that Oosterling who got us stranded for a day out at the lighthouse?"

"I'm so sorry." My stomach did a flip-flop. "That was my grandfather."

Pauline edged forward to touch his arm. "It's great

fudge. The greatest. Don't blame Ava at all for the broken boat engines. She and her grandfather actually don't get along."

I gave her a look, but it didn't matter.

John addressed only her and with a big smile. "And what do you do there? Just look pretty like you're doing now?"

I held back from rolling my eyes at his almost-sleazy behavior. Pauline was still dressed in her school clothes of chinos and black blouse covered with stains from kids, with her jet-black hair in a braid.

Pauline giggled with an odd twinkle in her eyes and said, "I'm the taste tester. I'm still here, so you know it's not poison!"

He leaned forward toward her, lip-lock close. "Is this another lucky batch of fudge? Filled with diamonds?"

"No," I interceded between them. "I have no idea how the diamonds got in there. The sheriff is still figuring that out. We assume somebody hid them in some of my ingredients."

John looked about. "He's here somewhere. Let's ask him what he's found out."

Pauline must have seen me turn white. She said to John, "Try the fudge. The vanilla flavoring creates a villainous vector of vivaciousness on the tongue. Your vote, too?"

John stuffed the small piece into his mouth, smacking his lips. Pauline handed him his wineglass. He sipped, making an art of savoring the flavor cocktail in his mouth. Then he wiggled his lips, like a bunny sniffing a carrot. Finally, he held up his half-empty wineglass in a toast to me and Pauline. "Cataclysmic creation! The cherry wine cleaves to the cherry-vanilla fudge. Exquisite, exciting, enchanting!"

Pauline, practically panting over his C's and E's, reached out again to tenderly touch his forearm. She smiled in a comely way I hadn't seen since college when she'd flirted, half-buzzed, in a campus bar.

She said, "You must add the winery and the Oosterlings' shop to a tour. You could be paid extra for this tour because there's a show involved. Ava makes fudge by hand in copper kettles. Nobody else does that in all of Door County. Your tour ladies could stomp grapes with their own feet and then stir the fudge goop with their own hands."

Fudge *goop*? I was offended but kept quiet.

John chortled. "I love it. You're in tour sales, right?"

"I teach kindergarten, which makes me an expert in field trips and tours on a different level. There's less drinking on my tours."

John laughed heartily again.

I flashed Pauline a sideways and meaningful glance. She was never this impulsive; I had always been the impulsive one. Before she had tour buses of tipsy women stopping by to stomp fudge instead of grapes and stir grape juice in my copper kettles, I said, "John, what did you see and hear Sunday morning before you left for the boat tour? You were in your room, right? Your room is ... which one?"

He sobered fast. "Next to that old actress's when I first got here. I had to move."

"Why?"

"I laugh too loud. Can you imagine somebody complaining about laughing?" He spewed a bawdy guffaw before shaking his head.

I was wondering if his disagreements with Rainetta ran deeper. "Rainetta Johnson complained that you laughed that Sunday morning? You two weren't arguing about a bottle of wine, let's say?"

Pauline threw me a daggers look, then smiled for John. "You have a good laugh. The world needs more laughter."

"Not my kind," he said. "She told the owner to get rid of me. Isabelle Boone just shook her head but asked me to trade with Taylor."

Isabelle had said Taylor Chin-Chavez was a twenty-something artist looking for a lighthouse to live in and use for displaying artwork. Probably not John's type. Maybe she was somebody in need of money, though.

I asked, "Is Taylor here?" I'd never met her, and though I'd seen her in a photo, I wanted her pointed out to me in case she'd changed her looks for the party.

John looked around. "Oh yeah. I see her over with the sheriff."

Which meant I wasn't going to talk with her right now. She had on heavy eyeliner. Her black hair flowed over one shoulder and she wore a caftan, creating an exotic appearance—like someone who would never fit in here. Was hunting for lighthouses merely a euphemism for hunting for diamonds? I was going to ask John more about her, but the TV camera people were coming through the back porch area led by Isabelle on their tour. They'd be chowing down on the grilled food and my Cinderella Pink Fudge within a minute, and thus occupied.

"Excuse me. I need to use the ladies' room," I said. "Pauline, would you like to come with me?"

John said, "And leave me? Stay here and tell me where teachers like to go on their summer tours."

I gave Pauline a look that said, *If you don't want me to kick you in the shin, you better come with me now.*

She excused herself with an annoying touch again on the man's arm. "I'll be right back, John."

A few feet from him, as we were heading fast around the side of the Blue Heron Inn for the front, Pauline huffed at me. "You don't like him."

"Pauline Mertens, what are you doing flirting with somebody who doesn't like my grandfather?"

"He was on the tour with your grandfather, though."

"He was probably swilling wine the whole time. He didn't say a word about the harrowing trip."

"He was being polite in front of you."

"I tell you, Pauline, he knows something pertinent to the murder. That was nervous laughter."

"Well, he was out on the boat. He didn't do it."

"Then why is he acting guilty? He's drinking too much. And you better not be falling for him."

"Sheesh, Ava. Can't I at least use him to practice my rusty skills? You know, it's been eight years since you washed yourself of Dillon Rivers. Isn't it time to get back in the waters again yourself?"

"Just now you made dating again sound unsavory."

We reached the front porch. I looked about to see who might be watching. "Jeremy Stone and John Schultz shared wine together in Jeremy's room. I'm thinking that John is too much of a party animal to go out on that boat. Besides, wouldn't he have had a hangover on Sunday morning?"

"What are you getting at? Your grandfather can verify if he was on the boat. So can others."

"What if he had been here on Sunday and has been lying about it all this time and nobody's bothered to verify who was on that boat?"

"Call your grandpa."

"Indeed. I'll call him later. Something about John doesn't add up."

"He gave you a dirty look and now you don't like him. That's your grandfather's fault for having a crappy boat that broke down."

"All right. But Jeremy Stone said he heard sounds coming from John's room, or maybe Taylor's. What if the killer struck, then hid in that room? Listening? And trying not to laugh at all of us in the hallway?"

"Now you're giving me the creeps. So the killer ducked into Taylor's room when all hell broke loose. I refuse to believe it was John. He's just too nice."

"I saw the Reeds pop their heads out of their room, but it was quiet on Rainetta's side of the hall, except for what Jeremy says he heard."

"Maybe the Reeds had been in John's room before and that's what Jeremy heard."

"Hmm. So maybe there was a game of musical chairs going on upstairs on Sunday. But who was there?"

Pauline shook her head vigorously. "There's no way John Schultz killed a woman even if he was there."

I gave her the fierce look I used when I was about to steal the basketball from her on the court. "You were drooling. Pauline. The guy is maybe twenty years older than you. And he's shorter than you. What are you thinking?"

"That nobody's flirted with me like that for at least five years."

I pulled her inside the inn, closing the front door behind us. My eyes had to adjust to an onslaught of crystal-refracted light. The glass Steubens sparkled with extra vibrancy. For the tour and TV cameras, Isabelle had turned on all the chandeliers, sconces, and lamps. Sequins seemed to float through the air. I couldn't get over how grains of sand could create such beauty.

Pauline murmured, "I bet some of these pieces are worth more than my annual salary."

"No time for thinking about it. Our job is to sneak upstairs into those rooms and see what we find."

Just then Isabelle walked in through the large dining room. "I thought I heard voices."

I gulped and said, "Hi, Izzy. We thought we'd use the ladies' room while the lines were long at the buffet but not in here."

Pauline and I shared a nervous laugh.

"Smart thinking," Izzy said. She hugged us both. "Can you believe all the cameras? My collection's going to be famous. One of the guys mentioned it'll probably end up on a network morning show."

"That's wonderful! Any word from Rainetta Johnson's relatives?"

"Well, no. She'd been estranged from her family for quite some time, according to her manager. He called to say he'll be coming soon to collect her things and make arrangements for the body to be transported for the funeral."

"Where is that going to be?"

"Some small town in New York."

"New York? An amazing and unfortunate coincidence with that diamond heist being there, too. Has the sheriff said anything more to you about that?"

"I asked. He says that maybe her body will be released by tomorrow, and then he'll issue more details."

Tomorrow? Wednesday instead of Friday? Jordy had said he'd be making arrests by Friday, but would he be doing that sooner? My left wrist pulsated with sharper pain as my heart raced. "Has he said anything more about how she died? Who he suspects murdered her?"

"No." Isabelle teared up. "It's so unfair. She was a lovely lady."

A lovely lady who hated laughter. I could tell Pauline was ready to lay that alliteration on us, so I stepped forward to give Izzy another hug. "It's unfair to you to have a death happen here amid all these beautiful things. How did you ever amass all these pieces? Did you inherit them?"

Her tears flowed like rivers down her cheeks. Pauline and I stood like statues at first. I offered Izzy a tissue I ripped from a box on a table near the entryway.

"I'm sorry." She sobbed.

"It's okay. The Steubens obviously mean a lot to you. And the death upstairs was a shock to all of us, but you especially."

She nodded, finally sighing as she looked about the grand hall with its glass menagerie. "I feel close to my mother here. That helps."

"You inherited these things from her?"

"No. We were way too poor for that. But when I was little, back in Arkansas, she took me once to a field where you can mine diamonds."

"Like mining gold?" I was incredulous.

"Yeah," she said, wiping at her eyes with the tissue. "Near Murfreesboro, there's a place where tourists can go. You get to keep anything you find in the fields."

Pauline said, "And you found some?"

"One tiny one is all, but it meant everything to me. I kept it under my pillow. Until my mom took it."

I asked, "She stole it?"

Izzy laughed. "No. We needed a car. Our old one

broke down. She sold it to a jeweler for a couple hundred dollars to buy an old junker. We went back to the diamond field a couple more times, but never found anything. I wanted to go back more, but my mom said we couldn't afford the gas and time to do that."

I still didn't "get" how Izzy could afford this extensive Steuben collection we were standing amid. "How did you come to own your first piece? Which one is your first?"

She pointed to an egg-shaped vase about eight inches tall. "It was a gift to my mom from her employer when she first went into the hospital. I was in high school. She died of cancer."

"Oh, Izzy, I'm sorry," I said, realizing I called her a friend and hadn't taken the time to learn much about her at all. I was shamed by it. "Let's make a date for dinner sometime and talk. Okay?"

"I'd love that." She kneaded the tissue between her hands. "You asked how I got my collection. Several pieces came from my mother's employer as payment for cleaning her house. It took me a while to catch on that rich people stay rich by keeping their cash and giving gifts instead, but that was okay. She told me to save the Steubens because they'd be worth a lot someday. What mattered was that I saw how much my mother loved looking at the glass vase in the hospital, with the light coming in through the window. The glass gave her joy. I guess each piece in here," Izzy said, casting about in wonder, "gives me joy, too."

Someone called her from the kitchen and she hurried away.

Pauline's face held confusion and maybe some of the guilt I felt, too. She said, "Can we really sneak upstairs after that? I feel terrible just thinking about it."

"We have to look, Pauline. For Izzy's sake. And Cody's. And mine. If the sheriff is announcing something by tomorrow, I could be in jail because of those diamonds in my fudge."

We hurried up the blue-carpeted staircase, pausing at the top to let our eyes adjust to the dim light.

The low muttering of a husky voice came to us. My skin itched with excitement. Who was in what room? John and Taylor were outside, and I presumed Jeremy was, too. That left the Reeds and the Earlywines. Or somebody in the throes of a theft.

The voices came again, from the room to our left, the first one near the top of the stairs. Boyd and Ryann Earlywine. I tiptoed up to their door.

Boyd's muttering grew louder. "We can't just take the diamonds with us."

"Why not?" His wife's voice feathered through the door. "We're not suspects, really. That kid did it. That's what we'll tell anybody who asks. Nobody's going to miss a few diamonds anyway."

Pauline had stayed back. I waved her to come listen. She refused. She stood near the stairwell clinging to her big black bag as if it were a life preserver.

From inside the room Boyd said to his wife, "I saw the kid in that room. He has to know these diamonds were in there. He'll be coming back for them."

"Exactly. He killed that woman for the diamonds."

"He put them in that lady's fudge to hide them."

"He's not that bright," Ryann said.

I crouched down to put my ear against the keyhole.

Ryann said, "I bet there's some fudge somewhere that was supposed to be at the party that didn't have diamonds in it and there was some mix-up. There has to be somebody who thought he or she was picking up the diamonds and got only fudge for their trouble. I'm not even sure the fudge was all that good. Did you see the color? Pink? I've never seen pink fudge. Ick."

I almost barged in right there to give them a piece of my mind but held back.

"Mix-up or not, he killed her," Boyd said. "But I don't want to get involved. We're leaving the diamonds here so we can get the hell out of here. Just leave them across the hall in that loudmouth's room. He deserves to be arrested. I'm through with being told I have to stay here at this B and B and in this town. I've got my research to do."

"But we came for a lot more than your research. I don't want to leave empty-handed."

The door popped open, and I tumbled onto the rug at the Earlywines' feet.

Chapter 9

The Earlywines stared at me writhing on the floor and holding my left wrist.

"Ow, ow, ow," I muttered up at them instead of the curse words I really wanted to say. I was inches from their designer loafers.

Pauline rushed over, slamming her big black school-bag next to me. While picking me up, she said, "I'm so sorry, everybody. It was this purse. It's so heavy, and it slipped off my shoulder and tripped her. So sorry. We were coming up to use the bathroom."

The Earlywines moved into the hallway, then shut their door. Boyd was my height, with short sandy-colored hair and a boy-next-door look. His wife, Ryann, the one I'd overheard wanting to keep diamonds they'd found in Rainetta's room, was cover-girl pretty with a heart-shaped face framed by a blond bob. Both were fortyish and dressed in sporty leather jackets over blue jeans. Expensive, spicy scents shifted the air around me like an approaching storm.

I held out my hand. "I'm Ava Oosterling."

Boyd quickly withdrew the hand he'd put out. "The hot fudge lady."

"It was hot, but I have no idea how the diamonds got in my fudge."

"Neither do we. Now if you'll excuse us—"

With Pauline next to me, I easily blocked their path to the staircase. "I heard you talking about diamonds you found."

Pauline gasped.

For a moment the couple stared at me like two mice caught in a corner by a cat.

Then Boyd sighed, holding out a palm to his wife. "I told you these were trouble."

From out of her purse, Ryann retrieved a red velvet drawstring bag the size of a deck of cards. Boyd handed the bag to me.

The soft velvet in my right palm weighed hardly anything. After my pleading look, Pauline obliged and untied the drawstring. Nestled in the darkness were tiny crystals, maybe a dozen.

I asked the couple, "You're sure these are diamonds?"

Boyd shrugged. "I'm here doing research on Talbot Chambers and the lighthouse named after him. We stumbled across the diamonds."

"By snooping in Rainetta's room." I pursed my lips at them.

They both shrugged. Boyd said, "You can keep them."

Pauline said, "No way." She backed away.

Boyd took that as his chance to duck through the gap between us with his wife.

As I was being tear-gassed by their spicy perfume, I said to Boyd on the staircase, "I'm going to have to show these to the sheriff and tell him you had them."

"Actually, you have them now. And I'll tell the sheriff I saw you sneak into Rainetta's room with Cody

Fjelstad—your conspirator to a murder and diamond heist."

The couple hurried down the stairs while my mouth hung open. The diamonds in my hand felt like a hot potato. "Here," I said to Pauline, "put these in your purse."

"Not in my bag. I'll be arrested!"

"No, you won't. I'm the one who will get frisked by the sheriff if he's suspicious."

"We'll leave them up here somewhere."

"We can't do that," I said, shoving them in her bag amid the crayons and Sharpie markers. "Somebody's going to come back for these."

"Like the killer? You've got to be kidding if you think I'm going to wait around for the headline 'Killer Kicks Off Kindergarten Keeper.' That's not my kind of alliteration."

"But we know somebody's going to return to Rainetta's room for these and whatever else she hid there."

"How do we know that?"

"Because these diamonds were there after the sheriff inspected her room. Which means they were well hidden. Which means Rainetta knew enough to protect herself from somebody around here who she knew might snoop in her room."

"You sound crazy from that fall down the stairs."

"No, Pauline. Cody wouldn't have been in her room, either, unless somebody put him up to that because they knew the diamonds were there. As in, they still had to pick up the diamonds from Rainetta."

"Or these are merely her diamonds and she hid them to prevent people from stealing them."

I relented with a huff. "Perhaps. But my theory was sounding a whole lot sexier."

"A plot fit for your situation comedy, maybe." With a sigh, Pauline put her big bag down at my feet on the carpeted hallway. "You take it. It's no longer my bag. It's my gift to you. I am not a detective. I'm a teacher."

"Don't be silly." A groan escaped me when I picked up the heavy bag with only my right arm. "What do you have in here? Hidden kindergartners?" I groaned a second time with much drama, holding out my impaired left wrist.

"All right," Pauline said in a huff, yanking the bag back onto her shoulder. "I've got the diamonds. Now what do we do with them?"

"Just don't let your kindergartners eat them or you'll be following them into the restrooms with plastic Baggies."

"Very funny."

"You'll be fine. Let's get back down to that party and see who might sneak back inside."

"But what about the Earlywines? They had the diamonds. Aren't we letting them get away with something?"

Pauline was right. As I crept down the hall to Rainetta's room with Pauline on lookout back at the staircase, I told her what I'd heard Boyd and Ryann say about Cody and about Ryann saying something about coming to Fishers' Harbor to get something valuable. I countered our suspicions with a lingering reality. "But what if they were merely taking advantage of the situation of Rainetta's unlocked room and happened to find the diamonds?"

When I opened the door, Rainetta's room still looked ordinary. I flipped over the scatter rugs by the bed and chair. The floor didn't appear to have any scratches or loose boards for hiding things. I contemplated the bed and looked under it. Nothing.

I mused out loud, "They didn't actually kill her, but the Earlywines definitely took those diamonds and were talking like there was something more to it all."

"What if they're part of some ring of thieves and murderers?" Pauline asked from the doorway, her face still pale with fear. "I'm used to catching my kindergartners in lies, and the Earlywines were lying."

"Meaning what?" I tried to lift the mattress with one hand, but couldn't.

Pauline came over to help. "Isn't it odd they'd be here at this time of year to research a lighthouse? It's darn cold out on the water. Nobody visits lighthouses at this time of year. They wait until after Memorial Day."

There was nothing under the mattress.

I defended the Earlywines again. "He's a university professor and she teaches music. Why would they risk their careers? And don't you teachers have codes of honor?"

"He's young enough yet that his salary probably isn't all that much more than mine, and did you see the clothes they were wearing? That leather isn't cheap."

"Neither was their perfume." A hint of Ryann's expensive fragrance lingered in Rainetta's room. "But if what you're saying is true, and they were here to pick up diamonds from that heist, that still lets them off the hook for Rainetta's death. They were out on the boat with my grandfather on Sunday, stuck in Lake Michigan."

"True. Maybe they and the Reeds were working together. The Reeds were here. Maybe the Reeds and Earlywines know one another and it was all part of some plan."

I had to give Pauline credit for that supposition.

"But this means we have to talk to Jordy about the heist and get the details," I said. "By now he might know if these diamonds really are from that case."

Talking to Sheriff Jordy Tollefson was the last thing I wanted to do, but if the Reeds and Earlywines were connected somehow, that information might be of vital interest to Jordy. Perhaps the murder case could be solved and Cody and I would be off the hook.

Pauline tapped her fingers on the doorjamb. "We should get out of here before we're caught."

"I just need to look in the closet. Maybe there's something hidden in the hems of the clothes. I saw that done in an old movie."

Pauline said, "That's even better than hiding stuff in pockets."

But opening the closet gave me a surprise. The clothes were gone. Had the Earlywines stolen them? Or maybe Isabelle had merely collected them for the manager who was coming for Rainetta's body and personal effects? That was logical. Yet nothing about this hot-fudge case had been logical so far.

When we returned to the backyard party, cameras were rolling on the sheriff. It was frustrating not being able to talk to him right away, and yet, amid a crowd of maybe a hundred people, counting all the journalists, was not the place to try to explain my theories about the murder. I'd be questioned in unflattering ways. But then I smiled. They were doing the interviewing right in front of the round dessert table with my Cinderella Pink Fudge. And half the pieces were gone. I hoped that meant people were eating it and not just stuffing it in a pocket as some weird souvenir.

A flash of pink caught the corner of my eye. Over at the bar area, Mercy Fogg was picking at my fudge in front of a news camera manned by a male reporter. Panic set in. I rushed over in time to hear Mercy say, "And we'll be closing down the Oosterlings soon. The inspectors will be there tomorrow."

My heart fell into my stomach. Closing me down? Why? I didn't dare jump in front of the camera. The reporter asked the question for me.

Mercy lifted up the piece of fudge in its pink cellophane. "It's totally unhealthy there. She had all manner of people bringing food to sell to the public, and who knows what the conditions of their kitchens were. You have to have a commercial kitchen license, and certain health standards must be met. I'm amazed that more people haven't gotten sick and died."

"They were church ladies," I ranted. "The food was blessed!"

The camera swung my way. The male reporter rushed at me.

And I ran.

At least I stumbled as fast as I could in flip-flops and holding on to my wrist. Now a hipbone was aching again, too. I slowed to an uneven limping gait as I rounded the front of the house, then headed down the steep street, finally taking the shortcut past my house to get to Oosterlings' Live Bait, Bobbers & Belgian Fudge.

Out of breath, I leaned for a moment against my counter.

Whistling startled me.

It was my grandpa, restocking a lower shelf over on his side of the shop. "I thought you and P.M. were at that big party at the Blue Heron."

After another puff of air, I said, "We were. Gilpa, Mercy Fogg's sending inspectors here tomorrow."

"Yeah? What for now?"

"She wants to shut us down. Or me, at least."

He was humming.

"Grandpa, didn't you hear what I said?"

"Oh yeah, but I got my motors running again, so if she shuts us down, we'll just sell bait in here and fudge right off the boat."

That sounded cool at first blush, but I needed a place for my kettles, the boiler, and the gifts I wanted to sell with the fudge. Not to mention needing space for my white marble table for loafing, plus my supplies.

Gilpa was shaking fish food into the minnow tank. "I'm going home to your grandma. You stickin' around?"

"Yeah." My breath was finally returning to normal, but the bruises on my arms felt stiff now, and one knee was ballooned tight against my jeans, as if a bruise there had swollen. "I'm going to whip up a batch of fudge. I might as well use all the ingredients in the place now before I'm shut down. Why can't Mercy stick to her fight for a stoplight?"

Gilpa gave me a hug that hurt, though I couldn't let on. He'd be disappointed in me if he found out about my foolish adventures at the old mansion. "You get to sleep early tonight, A.M. I'm fired up about heading out with the boat in the morning. With all the publicity this town's getting, I'm bettin' on more fishers than Moose can handle."

I had to smile. "Maybe there's an upside to my hot fudge."

Gilpa laughed as he grabbed his Green Bay Packer cap and slapped it on over his thick, silver hair. "Think you could mind the place by six a.m.?"

"Yeah, sure. I'm glad you got the engines back up."

"Me too. All's right with the world. And don't you worry about that mess with your fudge and that actress. I've got some leads on good lawyers, but we won't need them."

His confidence buoyed me. The round clock with fish for numbers above the door said it was past "trout" or seven in the evening now. I asked, "Did you happen to catch any news?"

He paused before heading into the back hallway. "You mean did I hear what the sheriff said about tomorrow? Yup. Don't worry about being arrested."

I felt heavy as an anchor plunging fast through deep waters. "You heard I was going to be arrested?" Guilt slithered up my back like a snake itching to bite me. Had Jordy found my note in Rainetta's room after all? Did he know about her diamonds and think I stole them? Did the Earlywines rush right out of the inn to report me?

"Now, now, Ava. Newspeople embellish things. They said the body's going to be released tomorrow and there'll be warrants for arrests, but there's no proof you had anything to do with those diamonds."

"Except that they were in my sugar sacks." And Pauline had a sack of diamonds in her purse, which the Earlywines would say we stole from Rainetta's room, if they hadn't done so already.

"That was Cody's doing, is all." With a wave of his hand, Grandpa Gil disappeared. The back door banged softly.

My grandpa was obviously in his own bliss about his boat working. Our troubles weren't about to disappear with a wave of my hand. And I'd forgotten to ask him about John Schultz being on his boat or not. I'd do that tomorrow first thing.

Alone, looking about my nearly empty fudge shop, I almost cried. The sheriff had obviously been busy or he wouldn't be talking about arresting somebody. He'd confiscated my goods and had been going through them. He also had sophisticated equipment and procedures to analyze everything and to gather facts, and I didn't. His list of circumstantial or real evidence was likely mighty long while my list was a mere supposition or two.

It would be easy to give up. How could making fudge turn into this much trouble? But being a cheap Belgian myself, I just couldn't let the ingredients go to waste or be confiscated tomorrow by Mercy Fogg and her gang of inspectors.

In the galley kitchen, pain in my wrist brought tears to my eyes, but I flipped my hair into a twist on top of my head, then slipped on a white apron, fumbling with the tie in back. Next, cream and butter came out of the refrigerator and vanilla off the shelf. Butter went into the microwave. So far, with one hand, I was doing okay and feeling energized.

In the main shop, I scooted a copper kettle next to the boiling apparatus, which I settled next to my register counter and the new shelving unit behind it. My walnut paddles and steel spatulas were at the ready. Everything was pristine clean. Mercy's inspectors would congratulate me instead of shut me down. The more I worked, the better I felt in my head, though my bruises hurt under my long red sleeves and jeans. I dared not look at any part of my anatomy; I'd be green and yellow by now— Green Bay Packer colors! I chuckled. I was hurting and happy. Indeed, making fudge was a freeing feeling for me; there was no doubting that. I could trust in fudge if nothing and nobody else.

When it was time to gather the sugar, I had to bring the six ten-pound bags off the shelves in the kitchen pantry one at a time. The empty shelf saddened me. Would I ever be open again for another delivery after tomorrow? Every Wednesday was my and Izzy's last major delivery of each week. In only about three weeks I'd gotten into a routine of sharing the deliveries with Isabelle. I'd miss our camaraderie. I still felt bad about knowing nothing about her mother or her upbringing before today. And I'd miss Cody yelling "Miss Oosterling!" I worried about him, too, even if he had thrown me down the stairs earlier today.

I lugged each sack to the main floor, then opened the first with a fumbling right hand. Using a knee to steady the bag, I poured it into the vat. With the second sugar sack, I had already created a snow-capped mountain of sparkly white crystals.

I froze.

Some of those crystals were rather fat.

Like diamonds.

A few were colored, too, a tinge of amber, even light brown. Chocolate diamonds? The famous Harry Winston jewelry store in Beverly Hills had loaned some to one of our show's characters for the Emmy Awards. You'd never be able to discern these diamonds if they ended up in dark chocolate fudge.

After taking a step back, I shook my head, thinking I had to be wrong. But when I put my hand in my boiler to sift through the sugar, I came up with several crystal-clear diamonds along with colored ones. What little I knew about diamonds didn't matter; all women know that colored diamonds are worth a boatload of dough.

I shut off the burner so the sugar wouldn't start melt-

ing into the cream. With a small scoop and a sifter retrieved from the kitchen, I worked with mostly one hand
to return the diamonds to an empty paper sugar package
sitting on my counter. Now I knew for sure how the diamonds had gotten into my fudge earlier. Somebody had
put them into a sugar sack, then carefully glued the sack
shut again. Not all my sugar sacks had been filled with
diamonds; Jordy would have found those early in his investigation. But somebody had again used the same trick
to hide diamonds. Clever, really. Jordy probably wouldn't
come back again checking my sugar sacks after he'd
done that once and found nothing.

Now what? What if someone walked in? Like Mercy
Fogg or the Earlywines or Jeremy Stone? Or some other
suspect? Would they kill me for the diamonds? If they'd
killed Rainetta, the answer was yes. With my bad wrist
and stiff legs, I was no match. I shuddered, going cold all
over.

Rushing to the kitchen, I perused my shelves. Where
to hide diamonds? I had no safe, and neither did my
grandpa. I didn't have any of those fake lettuce heads
people used in their refrigerators to hide things. All I had
was a ceramic cookie jar that looked like a black-and-
white Holstein cow. My mother had given it to me. I
grabbed it, opened it—and discovered Rainetta Johnson's lavender necklace!

That was how it always went for me—something good
happened, then something bad. I was happily making my
fudge when, bam, I was a disaster. Cuddling the cow
cookie jar in my arms, I ventured back to the front of the
shop. It was getting darker now, so I flipped on the lights.
I could leave the cookie jar in plain sight, but with the

way my luck was rolling, somebody would break in and steal the diamonds and amethyst necklace. But I didn't want to take them home to my rental cottage and carry my bad luck there. If Jordy were getting close to some arrest, such as Cody's, he might decide to widen his search for evidence and scour my cottage.

After putting the cookie jar down next to my cash register, I withdrew my phone from my pocket. A voice in my head said I should call Jordy Tollefson. But if he were going to arrest Cody or me tomorrow anyway, why tempt him tonight? I'd rather sleep in my own bed than on the cot in a jail cell down in Sturgeon Bay.

Harsh raps at the front door startled me. My heart kicked in double speed, creating a fizz in my veins down to my fingertips.

But it was only Sam Peterson. I relaxed. Only a little.

"I saw your light come on," he said after I let him in. "I was walking along the docks to see if Cody might be moping around."

"He's not here."

"Baking cookies now? Or is that filled with fudge?"

"Cookies."

"I'm starving. Chocolate chip? Let me have one." He took a step to go around me for the cookie jar.

"No." I stepped in front of him; then, feeling like a fool, I turned away from him to pick up the ceramic cow. I let out a small yelp because of my wrist.

Sam gave me a strange look, his blue eyes darkening a smidge. "Are you all right?"

Words failed me. I needed Pauline with me. I didn't trust myself to even talk anymore. "I'm fine. These cookies are a surprise."

"For who?"

"A surprise for . . . Gilpa. Did you hear he got his boat running?" I headed to the front door. "I was just about to put these on his boat so he had them in the morning when he took his first customer out fishing."

"I'll go with you. We can talk." Sam took the black-and-white cow out of my hands. Carrying it in one arm, he pushed the door open with the other. The cowbell jangled.

The air had become danker with evening coming on. The cold waters of Lake Michigan sloshed under the docks. I still wore my flip-flops, so my toes and feet became icicles as we walked down the wood planks toward *Sophie's Journey*. Indistinguishable voices from Isabelle's party feathered around us.

In the evening's half-light and the shadow of the hill, my grandpa's boat looked decrepit. It smelled of the oil and gas I'd sniffed and seen on Gilpa earlier in the day. It was also pretty much a mess, the open seat area in the back near the engines filled with oily rags, sullied newspapers used to catch dripping oil, tools, a bucket of bolts, and crushed beer cans.

Sam said, "Huh. You sure this tub runs?"

It came to me then that this would be the perfect place to hide the diamonds and amethyst necklace because nobody in their right mind would want to board this boat. I felt sorry for Gilpa, though. He wanted to be proud of me, but I also wanted to be proud of him. And it was hard to be proud of somebody who was foolishly hanging on to an old junker of a boat because he was too cheap to invest in a good one.

I climbed aboard gingerly in my flip-flops, then turned around to take the cookie jar from Sam, who stayed on the dock. I went inside the cabin. Sam was watching from outside, so I couldn't shove the cookie jar down inside the space where the life preservers were kept and where my grandpa wouldn't find it. I had to set the jar right on the table in plain sight, making a mental note to come out later to hide it better after Sam left.

Unfortunately, Sam wanted to hang around. He followed me back to the shop, where I was forced to tell him about my need to make up batches of fudge tonight.

He slipped off his jacket, then rolled up his white shirtsleeves. "Put me to work. If Cody sees us both in here making fudge, maybe it'll entice him to come in out of the cold."

I didn't seem to have a choice, so I handed him an apron. "I think he's scared of Mercy Fogg. So am I."

"I doubt you really need to worry about Mercy. She's more interested in fame, but there's no way she can shut you down. Her bluster is for the cameras. She's jealous of you and everybody getting more attention than her and her stoplight."

I trained my eyes on the mixture in the boiler to look for diamonds I might have missed. "Sam, could it be possible that Rainetta Johnson was part of a ring of thieves who stole those diamonds the sheriff mentioned?"

Sam ruminated, his gaze avoiding mine as I handed him the spatula to continue stirring the cream, sugar, and vanilla. I had intended to pop back into the kitchen for the white chocolate, but Sam's behavior made me pause.

"Sam? You know something, don't you?"

"I promised Rainetta not to say anything."

"Like what? She stole the diamonds?"

"No, that much I know. She didn't steal anything."

"But . . . ?"

"I met her a year ago, when she vacationed here and stayed at a condo. Mercy introduced us."

"Mercy was the board president then. How'd it come about that you were introduced?"

"Mercy wanted to get Rainetta more involved here, instead of just vacationing from Chicago. Mercy suggested to me that Rainetta would like giving to a good cause."

"Like the group home. So Mercy knew Rainetta before last year?"

"I assumed so. Rainetta was a regular visitor here for years, though rarely seen by us ordinary folks. But I'm sure Mercy had seen her now and then, because of her official status."

"Mercy would want to get close to a movie star. I can imagine it bothered her a lot to lose this spring's election and not have a proper reason to cozy up to Rainetta."

I ducked into the kitchen for my remaining bulk chocolate. Fortunately, the bags were small enough to carry with one hand. But when it came time to stir the fudge ingredients as it rose to a rolling boil, I realized in a panic I couldn't do it. I couldn't hold the long spatula and stir the thick cream and sugar and melted chocolate with only one hand.

"Sam, can you stir for me? I did something to my wrist today."

"What happened?"

I wrestled with what to tell him, then decided I couldn't tell him what Cody might have done to me. Sam would feel like a failure, for sure, if he knew Cody had acted in that manner. Something felt wrong about the whole episode anyway. I still didn't want to believe Cody could do that. So I simply said, "I ran off my front porch too fast and tripped."

"Maybe you should have it looked at tomorrow. Your wrist, not the porch."

"Very funny. Yeah, maybe I should."

Sam and I focused on the rolling boil in front of us. Making fudge was like making old-fashioned, hand-cranked ice cream; you couldn't stop cranking or you ruined the ice cream—or in this case, my fudge. I expected perspiration to pop out on Sam's forehead as he kept stirring, but he was still as fit as his football days.

I asked, "Just a few minutes ago you said you promised Rainetta not to say anything. About what? And who couldn't you say it to?"

Sam stopped stirring. He stepped back from the steaming pot, then ran a finger across his chin, as if weighing his trust in me. "She brought some diamonds with her that she wanted to give to me."

A lightning bolt zapped my body. "Holy cow. Diamonds? When? Sam, my gosh, but you're not involved in the murder, are you?"

"Of course not. But I saw her this past weekend. When she arrived."

"She arrived Saturday night. You saw her before the party?"

His face turned red. My insides felt like a compass with a needle quivering questioningly for a direction to follow. I could tell they'd had some kind of intimate interlude, and I was hoping like crazy it wasn't sex. But I wanted to ask. My brain felt like one of those teaser commercials for a sleazy talk show.

"You have to keep stirring, Sam, or the fudge'll be

ruined." He resumed. The aroma was making my mouth water, and Sam's information was doing the same to my brain. "So she brought you a gift? How large?"

"Oh, just a few. They were in a red pouch."

The diamonds now secured in Pauline's purse. "Sam, what's going on?"

"I don't want you getting into trouble." He stepped back again from the boiling vat.

"Can you pour it for me into that copper kettle to cool?" I pointed to the nearest one.

Sam poured the hot mixture into the huge metal bowl, then meandered in an agitated state around the shop in the white apron. I leaned my butt against my cash register counter.

"Sam, you better just confess to what's going on."

With hands poked into his pockets, he came over to stand in front of me with a grimace wrinkling his face. "I think Rainetta was in love with me."

My butt came away from the counter. "You 'think'? If she's giving you diamonds . . . Were you in love with her?"

His hesitation made me feel like a cold, stone statue waiting and hoping for sunlight to warm me. Or a little truth.

Finally, he said, "She was eccentric, okay? She had the diamonds and wanted me to come up to her room later that day. That would have been last Sunday night."

"After you saw her Saturday night, too."

"I didn't stay long Saturday night. I was getting in over my head."

"That's what you were arguing about at Sunday's party, wasn't it? When I saw her touching you in an intimate way? She wanted more from you?" I raised an eyebrow.

"Yes." He flushed redder this time, which made him appear honest and boyish and oddly more handsome than normal.

I tried to imagine Sam kissing the sixtysomething Rainetta. It was disconcerting. I slid away from him to grab the metal spatula for whipping the fudge. "So she had diamonds she wanted to give you. You went into her room—"

"No, I didn't. I was about to go in, but thought how foolish I would be doing that. Believe me, Ava, I didn't kill her."

"I believe you, Sam."

His shoulders heaved in relief. It touched me to know he cared about what I thought of him.

I stuck the spatula into the creamy, pale pink fudge mixture in the copper kettle. With one hand, I couldn't budge it. "You think Mercy knew about Rainetta's feelings for you? And the diamond gift?"

"Are you saying Mercy killed her?"

"Mercy always wants the limelight. Maybe she was jealous of you being close to Rainetta. Maybe they got in some fight over you."

"Pretty ridiculous."

I shrugged. "I worked in Hollywood. That's a common crime show plot."

"Yeah, Hollywood. I've said too much." Sam pulled off the apron, then threw his jacket back on. "I better head out and look for Cody some more."

The air inside my shop had shifted to frigid. Sam obviously still didn't completely forgive me for taking off for La-La Land after my marriage ended. But I had to ask Sam before he slipped out the door, "Did you see Mercy go into Rainetta's room?"

"I saw her at Rainetta's door, but I was already heading through Jeremy Stone's room to leave down the back way."

"Did you see Cody anywhere then?"

"No."

But Jeremy Stone had seen Cody from the upstairs bathroom window walking across the lawn. That meant Sam left first, and Cody had to be hiding up there somewhere while Mercy Fogg stood at Rainetta's door or went inside her room. Was Cody who Jeremy had heard in John's or Taylor's room? I feared that my earlier hunch was right: Cody had seen more than he should that day and now Mercy was using him—blackmailing him or paying him for information, or paying him to steal things for her.

After Sam left, I locked the door again. I couldn't wait to call Pauline. The diamonds in her purse had to be the ones Rainetta had tried to give Sam. Mercy found out about them and was jealous. But if Mercy worshipped Rainetta, why would she kill her? I recalled Rainetta's sudden illness after her nibble on my fudge. Perhaps that was a faked reaction to help please Mercy? The two women were the proverbial two peas in a pod. Or something else? Lovers?

I shuddered. Maybe our former board president was desperate to keep a secret. Had the women been breaking up because of Sam? That was beginning to feel like a motive.

But why had I found more diamonds in my sugar? And Rainetta's necklace in the cookie jar? The necklace had been removed before she died; I had been too panicked about trying to get her breathing restarted to notice details. Obviously Mercy had taken the necklace.

But when and how had she convinced Cody to go in with her? Moreover, how could I possibly prove she was the murderer? That woman was like Teflon, as my mother used to say. Nothing stuck.

I had to talk with Sheriff Tollefson about Mercy Fogg. And find Cody "Ranger" Fjelstad.

Chapter 10

A light drizzle was good for the daffodils and tulips in back of the fudge shop, but not so good for engines or murder suspects.

Gilpa's swearing made it all the way down the wooden pier to the inside of our shop, where I stood rearranging the pans of pink fudge I'd made last night with Sam's help.

As promised to my grandfather, I had hurried in just past dawn on Wednesday. Feeling almost giddy with my theories, I had dressed in a fancier, pale pink, long-sleeved blouse. With the sheriff's announcement today about the ME's findings, there'd be cameras. My chestnut hair hung loose about my shoulders, and I looked good in pale pink. And innocent. I hoped.

Grandpa came in after seven for hot coffee, grumbling about the rain getting inside his engines where it didn't belong. By that time I'd spotted Moose Lindstrom's big behemoth boat at the other end of the docks taking off with six guys who had likely paid him handsomely to fish for trout, bass, and coho salmon on Lake Michigan. It must have irritated Gilpa to no end to watch that sleek, big new *Super Catch I* purr out of its slip, then haul butt into Lake Michigan with those state-of-the-art engines. I wondered how much boat we could buy with the diamonds and amethyst necklace I'd hidden last night in the bowels of Gilpa's boat. And if we added in what was in Pauline's purse, maybe we could even include air-conditioning.

The thoughts made my hands shake. I had to do something about that cow cookie jar filled with jewels on his boat, but what? I wasn't sure yet how to approach Sheriff Jordy Tollefson with everything I knew—and had in my possession.

And would there really be a big announcement today? What had the medical examiner found through the autopsy? They hadn't found poison here in my shop, but what if somebody had slipped something in the fudge at my shop when Cody and I weren't looking? Cody and I came and went while we worked. Or what if somebody— like Mercy Fogg—had slipped something vile in it while it was upstairs with Rainetta at the Blue Heron Inn? A part of me couldn't wait to hear what the sheriff had found out; another part of me knew this wasn't going to end well.

Why did I know that?

Because the fudge I'd made last night with Sam looked like my best batch yet. Sam had strong arms. But with something good, I always seemed to attract something bad next. And this bad thing was going to be super bad because this batch of fudge was super good. It was the color of cherry blossoms. And the vanilla-cherry fragrance married well with the heavenly coffee perking in the bait shop.

Gilpa's side of the shop was still discombobulated from the church ladies rearranging things to their liking, so I spent time doing him a favor and cleaning up the displays of bobbers, rubber worms, spinners, and flies. The fishing lures with their beautiful feathers in rainbow colors nudged my inner artistic muse. I'd love to do something with them and my fudge, but the final idea hadn't yet popped into my head.

It was almost eight o'clock when I turned to cutting pink cellophane into the squares I needed to wrap each piece of fudge. I missed Cody's help. I hoped he'd finally returned home last night. We could mend our relationship with Sam's help, and maybe Cody would have an idea about a new Fisherman's Catch Tall Tale Fudge flavor.

Crescendoing voices grabbed my hearing. My mouth went dry.

I hurried to the front window. A mob was storming up the boardwalk, umbrellas over their heads, their shoes and boots clomping on the damp wood. The parking lot was filling with news vans, and reporters tagged along behind Sheriff Jordy Tollefson and his deputy—heading my way!

The village board president—young Erik Gustafson— was scrambling right behind the sheriff, talking into a microphone shoved in his baby face. And dang, behind him was stout Mercy Fogg with two guys in suits carrying clipboards. Jeremy Stone, sans umbrella, was snapping photos with his phone. In the distance, more townspeople were showing up; more umbrellas burst open like spring flowers.

Armageddon was upon me!

I locked the front door, for whatever good that would do.

Isabelle swept in from behind me, making me leap out

of my own skin. She'd come in through the back door, which I'd stupidly left unlocked. "Izzy, you don't want to be here."

"I have to be here," she said, breathing hard. "I'm your friend, and Rainetta was my guest."

"Do you think Jordy's taking me to jail?"

"For having diamonds in your fudge? No." Izzy's hopeful smile on her gamine face drooped. "I don't know. Maybe if they found them in her stomach contents and they did horrible things and she bled to death?"

"Izzy! I never thought about her bleeding to death. Well, I did at first, briefly, but not seriously."

"I'm sorry I said that." She flung her arms around me.

I flinched from all my bruises. I'd have to fill her in later on what had happened at the mansion. After all, the party at the Blue Heron Inn was supposed to have been a fund-raiser to refurbish the place. The first thing they needed to do was put rubber treads on those old wooden stairs.

Faces and cameras filled my front bay windows. I was a fish in an aquarium being watched. It made me wonder if I was properly dressed. Yup, white bib apron on over my pink, long-sleeved shirt to hide my horrible bruises. My hair hung in loose waves.

Jordy jostled the front door latch so hard that the cowbell gave a plaintive *clang*.

I asked Izzy, "How do I look?"

"Good. Pretty. The usual. Why?"

"Do I look innocent?"

"Of course. The cameras are going to love you. This'll be good for your fudge."

Maybe some good could come out of the bad this time instead of the other way around.

"Open up, Ava!" Jordy called, staring hard at me through the glass.

When I flipped the bolt, he burst in, holding back the crowd. "Looking guilty isn't going to help your case," he said. Then he blinked several times, sniffing. "Man, it really smells good in here."

"I'll wrap up fresh fudge for you right now," I said, hoping to avoid the real reason for his visit. I grabbed a pan from the nearest glass-fronted display case.

"No time for that."

"It's a free sample."

His countenance darkened. "You're trying to bribe me?"

"Yes, of course," I said with bright cheer, though defeat was deflating my insides.

Isabelle pulled me aside to step between me and Jordy. "Sheriff, we just want to hear the autopsy results. My guests would like to leave town if they could. So what'd you find? She died of a heart attack?"

By then, news cameras had shoved in around us, along with what seemed like half the town. Although after the church ladies' bazaar, I knew that approximately only sixty people could squish into Gilpa's and my shop.

The guys in suits slithered past me in the wake of Mercy barging her way through, pointing. "The kitchen's back that way. And the minnow tank is right over there, not but a few yards from where she makes fudge."

A rain-soaked, already-sweaty cameraman scooted after them.

Just outside my door, which had been propped open, wunderkind Erik Gustafson was saying something into a microphone about my building being historic and "it could be that arsenic was used to treat the wood and the ancient wood rafters could be flaking into the fudge and that's how Miss Johnson was poisoned."

Oh Lordy. I was toast. Erik had just graduated from high school last year; what kid his age knew anything about history or what was used to treat wood? But something in my memory said arsenic once was used to treat lumber.

"Izzy," I whispered, "could he be right? Is this old building an arsenic trap? What has your research shown about the history of the buildings in Fishers' Harbor?"

She whispered back, "I haven't done research. I've been too busy."

Fortunately, Mercy was in my kitchen and couldn't hear Erik or she'd have leaped on the arsenic thing.

Jordy, smashed up against my sales counter now, finally held up his hands to the crush of cameras and people. "Folks, please. I'm afraid we've disappointed you if you think we're going to arrest Miss Oosterling for murder. Yet."

"You're not?" I screamed out my relief, then impulsively leaped at Jordy, my arms engulfing his neck as I hugged him cheek to cheek. He smelled clean and manly, like the rain outside mingled with some of that springtime-smelling green soap. "Thank you!"

"Not so fast," he said, unfastening me from around his neck. "Do you want to hear the autopsy results or not?"

Jeremy Stone called out, "You said 'yet.'" Does that mean she's still a suspect?"

Izzy and I clung to each other, waiting. Mercy and her henchmen emerged from the kitchen. Sam's head jutted up from the back of the crowd near the door. Then, through the windows, I saw my parents in the rain, waving, their faces wrinkled in terror for me. My nerves crackled under my skin like an electrical storm.

The cameras rolled with blazing white lights shining on the sheriff and me and Izzy.

Looking about at the crowd, Jordy said, "Rainetta Johnson, a sixty-five-year-old resident of Chicago—"

Jeremy Stone muttered, "Her manager said she was sixty-two."

"Was strangled to death."

Gasps echoed.

Mercy asked, "She wasn't choked to death by the fudge?"

Jordy said, "The official autopsy shows marks on her neck. She was strangled from behind. The fudge might have been used to make it look like she choked to death. We suspect that two people were involved, one choking her and another silencing her with the fudge."

Two people? I hadn't thought of that scenario.

A news reporter asked, "Was there poison in the fudge?"

All of the cameras and lights flipped to my face.

"No," Jordy answered for me, to my relief. The lights flipped back to Jordy. "We found no poisons. Just diamonds."

Jeremy Stone asked, "Has a connection to the New York heist been confirmed?"

"We're working on that."

Another reporter asked, "So there is a connection between the murder and the diamonds? If two people were involved, are we talking about a ring operating here in Door County?"

"We don't know."

Jeremy Stone asked, "What about the missing man, Cody Fjelstad?"

Crap, I thought. That darn Jeremy was determined to blame Cody.

The sheriff said, "We have to put Cody Fjelstad, also known as Ranger, under suspicion now because he's been missing for two days, according to his parents. Until recently Mr. Fjelstad worked here in the fudge shop with Miss Oosterling, where we assume diamonds were put in a sugar sack."

Eek. The hot cameras swung my way again. I smiled; then Izzy poked me into a sobering countenance.

"You don't think he's been harmed, do you?" the reporter asked the sheriff.

I hadn't thought of that! My stomach was now churning.

"We can't know that. We hope not. Now, everybody, that's all I have today."

Mercy was miffed. Her henchmen in suits didn't help her mood. They handed me a clean health inspection report. I waved it around, mostly under Mercy's nose. "Cinderella Pink Fudge is on special today! Mercy, wanna help wrap?"

The Green Bay woman reporter wedged between us with a microphone. "What's the origin of this fudge idea?"

"Indeed," Mercy said, practically spitting at me. "Why does one dream up fudge, of all things, if one wants to be taken seriously?"

"Well," I huffed, feeling invisible boxing gloves slipping onto my hands, "a college sorority type such as yourself, Mercy, should know that fudge was invented here in the States by the girls at Vassar College in the 1880s as a fund-raiser. And copper kettles have a fine tradition going back to making candies in England and Belgium before that."

Mercy puffed up, even madder now, turning beet red in the face. "You're involved with the killing of Rainetta. I know you are."

"I wasn't even near her when she died, Mercy. But you, now—"

Her beady eyes went wide with warning—almost as if I'd caught a skunk in my headlights at night. "That's slander. I'm suing you." She pivoted away, elbowing past the cameras and bowling everybody out of the way until she burst into the rain, where she almost hit a strike with Erik Gustafson and the reporter. They leaped sideways.

Izzy said, "I'll wrap the fudge for you."

"Huh?"

"Everybody's here. Hurry up. This is your big chance."

Mercy's threat had clouded my brain for a moment. "Thanks, Izzy. You're a good friend."

After hugging my relieved parents, who both said this would all blow over now, Izzy and I cut, wrapped, and sold pink fudge. Cameras moved in as I demonstrated carving fairy wings out of marzipan and then made them glitter with luster dust.

The Green Bay woman reporter said, "You're not just a fudge maker. You're a fudge sculptor."

I hadn't ever thought of myself as an artist. I just made fudge. No big deal. Until now.

Because my parents had been thoughtful enough to bring more cream from the farm, along with retail bags of sugar and chocolate bits Mom had been given by a neighbor in Brussels, I began making a new batch of fudge for the crowd. As I was heating the materials in the boiler, Sam charged in, banging the cowbell hard against the wall. "Your grandfather's just been arrested."

It was as if a tornado sucked all the reporters and cameras outside. As well as the oxygen.

Izzy asked, "Why?"

But I knew. Sam pierced me with an angry look that matched the one during our encounter after I'd married Dillon. My knees went weak, and not in a good way, not like when I was watching him make fudge last night.

Sam said between clenched teeth, "Gil had a boatload of diamonds and Rainetta's amethyst necklace hidden on his boat. Inside a cookie jar. He's being arrested for murder."

"Murder?" I screamed, racing out the door with Sam in tow.

"You have the right to remain silent . . ."

The paparazzi shoved one another to get next to me and Gilpa.

Sheriff Tollefson had my grandfather in handcuffs and was pushing him along the crowded wood planks of the dock area past our bait and fudge shop.

"Jordy," I called out, "this is a mistake."

His firm hand on my Gilpa's upper arm showed no wavering. He was marching my grandfather lockstep to the squad car.

"Stop! I did it!" I trailed behind them, bumping into people and cameramen as they halted to turn to me. "That's my cookie jar—"

"I borrowed it," my grandfather said, "to put the jewels in for safekeeping."

"He's lying," I said. "He's trying to protect me."

"No, I'm not," Gilpa said.

"Gilpa! I put the cookie jar in your boat last night!"

"And I put the diamonds and the necklace in it."

"No, you didn't."

Jordy intervened. "All right, you two. Gil, get in the car. I have to take you in based on the evidence found on your boat."

While Jordy sighed at me, Sam showed up with another one of his blistering looks. His forehead wrinkled, making his hairline shift, as if his hair were taunting me, too.

The reporters were eating this up. Jeremy Stone wore a big grin as he snapped cell phone photos with one hand while carrying a recorder in the other.

By now my parents had heard the hubbub and had driven back in their van. They were trotting up the boardwalk toward us at this end of the parking lot. My father, all farm muscle and tanned, and tall and wiry like me and Gilpa, said, "Sheriff, this is insane. You can't connect a cookie jar to a murder. Anybody could've left it there. What about Cody Fjelstad? This is something a stupid punk would do."

Sam muttered out the side of his mouth, "Stupid somebody, anyway."

Not even the misty rain could cool the heat splashing across my face. I chewed on my lips. Breathing became hard, as if I'd sunk underwater.

My mother was crying now. My father was yelling, "My dad did not murder that woman. You're making a huge mistake. My family is not involved in any murder or diamond heist."

But, Dad, I wanted to say, *we are. Deeper than you know.*

And the worst thing of all? I'd have to confess my stupidity to Grandma Sophie. That conversation was not going to go well. Already my stomach felt strangled and knotted like a bunch of bad fishing line.

Chapter 11

The caravan down to Sturgeon Bay to the county sheriff's department on Wednesday morning included me in my yellow truck with Sam driving, at his insistence, and my parents ahead of me in their beat-up farm van painted black and white like a Holstein cow. I suspected they still had a full load to deliver—if their customers still wanted to deal with them. My parents carried cream, butter, and cheese in ice chests, so the food was safe for a while.

So many transgressions were piling up behind the Oosterling name, I was afraid that any day now we'd be banished from Door County by Sheriff Tollefson. The county budget went only so far, and I could hear the *ka-ching* of expenses spent on the Oosterlings already.

Passing the farmland and Holsteins reminded me of the cookie jar Mom had given me.

"Go ahead and say it again. I'm stupid," I muttered to Sam. He'd been unnaturally quiet on the ride.

"You're not stupid. At least not all the time."

"Don't you dare bring my marriage or ex into this."

"You take actions without consulting me first, without consulting anybody first."

"I'm a grown-up. I'm supposed to be able to make my own decisions."

"You're thirty-two going on twelve sometimes, Ava."

"That was a mean thing to say. If I wasn't wounded, I'd sock you in the chops."

"Just what a twelve-year-old does. I was right."

"You see. That's why I couldn't marry you. You always have to be right."

Sam chuckled. "It's my job. And being right isn't a bad thing. Why can't you ever trust me? Or trust anybody who has good advice for you?"

I rolled down the window for air. The mist had gone away by the time we cruised through Egg Harbor. A bracing, crisp air met us as we climbed hills overlooking Lake Michigan in the distance. I tried to clear my head by taking deep breaths. I didn't know why I couldn't trust Sam completely. To trust meant you gave all of yourself over to another person. At least that was how I felt it should be. I know that's how Grandma Sophie and Gilpa felt about trust, and it was what my parents believed. But their trust was all balled up with love. Maybe I was afraid of love.

After thinking I could trust—and love—Dillon Rivers, my trust-o-meter was shot. I was a worn-out oven when it came to trusting men; I couldn't trust the temperature I was feeling. Even if I felt something warm toward a man now, like I felt sometimes for Sam, I assumed that heat wouldn't stay steady or last. Looking back on things, I had probably been in love with the thought of marrying a football player, which was Sam. I trusted him eight years ago when he said he loved me, too. Sam and I had talked about traveling, getting jobs away from Door County after we got married. That summer before our wedding, I'd been applying for all kinds of jobs in big cities, thinking Sam was doing the same.

Then, at my bridal shower, Sam gave me a gift—the key to a house. He'd bought a house in Fishers' Harbor. Everybody at the shower—most especially my mother—thought it was the sweetest, most wonderful, loving gift a man could give his bride-to-be. But I hadn't helped pick it out. I felt rotten, though, once I saw the house. It's a beautiful one-story brick cottage, with original stained glass in parts of the front bay windows overlooking an open porch with a porch swing. There were even a few heirloom roses in bloom at each corner of the porch. How could I not love the house? But then Dillon had come along . . .

I had to trust and love that man. Don't laugh. If you ever met Dillon Rivers, you'd understand why women have to have him. He was like, well, like a piece of my best fudge—an intense, pleasurable experience. And you craved more of it—him—all the time. Addicting. Dillon was about adventure and freedom and the feeling that I had control of my choices.

My brain didn't want to revisit all the reasons I had ditched Sam for Dillon, who ultimately broke my trust-o-meter.

As we rode along, I couldn't answer Sam Peterson. I didn't know why I messed up with trust all the time. I was saddened about that, and my heart and soul were like cold and empty copper kettles at the moment. I knew I wanted to try to trust. But how could I start when I was scared of more painful failure?

We slipped into the parking lot at the justice building just south of the canal that split Sturgeon Bay. The solid, serious look of the red bricks and tan rock of the new and modern building gave me shivers.

My grandfather was processed like a common criminal, fingerprinted and given jail clothes and a pillow, of all things. It was like they were merely putting him down for a nap. We weren't allowed more than a brief visit, and since we had no lawyer to intercede, we left him with promises of coming back tomorrow. They wouldn't even let me hug Gilpa good-bye. They probably thought I'd slip him a fudge cutter.

Sam had the presence of mind to ask when we could see him tomorrow; the woman in uniform at the desk said that visiting hours for males were on Thursdays only and in the evening only. Sam asked about getting permission from the lieutenant for other visits and for getting a public defender. The woman crisply said that Gilpa could make those requests. She handed Sam some forms.

My dad was muttering, "Mother isn't going to take this well."

He meant my grandma Sophie, of course.

"Dad, I'm sorry. It's all my fault."

"No, honey, it's not. Your grandpa lied for some reason."

"To protect me."

"I know. He loves you. We all do." Dad engulfed me in a hug that was totally Belgian. It lasted and lasted and lasted. If that hug were a fudge flavor, it would have the world beating that proverbial path to my door on the dock in Fishers' Harbor.

We stood next to my truck and their black-and-white Holstein van. A breeze gusted about, flapping the flag flying above us. Dad opened his driver's door, then paused to shake his head. At times he looked startlingly like Grandpa, except his hair, which was now whipping about, was brown instead of silver. "Honey, maybe we need to close that fudge and bait shop for now."

"No!" My sharp retort embarrassed me. "Sorry for yelling, but no, Dad. We can't. We need the money now more than ever."

Dad winced. "But you're going to kill yourself trying to keep it running. And you seem to be a target for whoever's involved in this murder. It scares me. That's the real reason I want you to close it. Close it and come home. We love you."

I gulped. Tears pushed at the backs of my eyes. "Thanks," I mumbled. "I appreciate that."

Mom had gotten in the van on the other side, but she leaned toward us and called out, "This person is dangerous. Don't mess around with this, Ava. This isn't like your silly TV show."

Mom couldn't know how that hurt me. Okay, the stupid show *was* silly. But that was because the executive producer never let me write enough of the episodes! I could write better than any of those guys. I had a vision for the show, but the executive producer had another. I know Mom didn't mean to slight my time in Los Angeles. Or did she? I guessed I'd spent eight years out there for what? To learn how to make fudge in my spare time? What my parents really wanted was for their only child to be happy, married, and having grandchildren. And to be safe.

We got in our vehicles. Mom and Dad peeled south of Sturgeon Bay to head toward Brussels and the farm, while Sam and I headed the other way across the bridge for Fishers' Harbor.

"Thanks, Sam, for coming along. And asking all those questions we were too shaken up to ask."

"Buy me a beer sometime."

That was what guys said when they didn't want you to make a big deal out of a favor they'd done for you. Sam had made me smile just now. Maybe someday people would say after a kindness was done for them, "Buy me some Oosterling fudge sometime."

The notion brought back the reporter calling me a "fudge sculptor." That made me smile, too.

I let out a sigh as the landscape of redbrick farmhouses with white trim and fields of alfalfa awakening from winter slid by. A green-and-yellow John Deere tractor and corn planter crawled along a field in a sure and steady way.

"What am I going to do about the shop, Sam? I sure wish we could find Ranger. He'd love taking over the bait shop for Gilpa."

"Then we'll have to find him."

I collected my courage to tell him about the mishap at the mansion yesterday.

Sam eased up on the gas pedal to look at me. "I'm glad you're okay. And I'm glad you told me about him sneaking into the Blue Heron Inn and then getting mad at you. Maybe that information will help the sheriff find him."

"How so?"

"He's been gone since Monday night, two nights now. He's had to sleep somewhere, and he's had to have gotten food somewhere. Maybe he's established a pattern already. We can call all the businesses in Fishers' Harbor."

"That won't take long." We had a smattering of tourist

gift shops, a few small galleries, a jeweler, a couple of restaurants and bars, but then you were out of town and heading for Sister Bay and sights like Al Johnson's Restaurant roof with its goats. Where Ranger had ended up with Mercy.

"But Ranger could have stolen a car that hasn't been reported yet for whatever reason."

I thought about the curtained windows of the house behind the historic mansion. Those owners were out of town perhaps. I told Sam we had to check to see if one of their vehicles had been stolen.

Sam agreed. "He could be anywhere in Door County. If he's broken into places, there might be a pattern of break-ins we can check on with the sheriff."

"He likes shiny things," I said. "Sorry if that makes him sound childish."

"Well, he's only eighteen and still in high school. High school kids of any type do foolish things sometimes. That's a good clue. We just have to think of a place with something shiny he likes and then we'll find him."

"Ugh, like shiny watches. Given to him by Mercy Fogg. Mercy might know where he is, Sam. I wanted to talk to Jordy about Mercy, too. He should keep an eye on her. She was clearly trying to pin the murder on me today in my shop in front of all those cameras. First she tries to shut me down, and today she threatened to sue me. She's gone over the edge. Sam, is it too 'out there' of me if I say I'm pretty sure Mercy murdered Rainetta and involved Cody in it?"

"Sounds like you're trusting your gut. That's not a bad thing to trust," Sam said.

His words opened a tiny window of my heart. I confessed more of my thoughts about the situation with

Mercy, about how she might have been jealous of Sam's relationship with Rainetta Johnson.

Sam whistled a note of concern. "She's starting to scare me. We need to talk to the sheriff about this right away." He slowed the truck as if to turn around.

"I was about to do that when Gilpa got arrested by mistake. And I'm a little scared of her, too. She's unpredictable and desperate, obviously."

"Ava, please don't be in your shop alone anymore. If there's nobody around to help you, call me."

The warmth of his offer zipped through the open windows in my heart. "That's kind of you. Thanks. But you're too busy to be at my shop all the time."

"I meant that my office knows people looking for part-time jobs. We can send people over."

So much for the flash of warmth toward Sam. The thought of strangers working in Oosterlings' Live Bait, Bobbers & Belgian Fudge didn't sit right with me, but I didn't say anything to Sam as he sped up again and we drove back into Fishers' Harbor. I needed a plan, but I had nothing. What I had to do next was obvious—make a new batch of Cinderella Pink Fudge. By now I knew that immersing all five of my senses into my special fudge was like going to a clairvoyant and having my cards and tea leaves read.

Sam tried to drop me off at my cottage so I could freshen up, but my small side street was clogged with vehicles. I knew I wasn't ready to face Grandma Sophie with a bunch of her church-lady friends all gathered around wringing their hands or praying, so I had Sam drive to the next block.

Oosterlings' Live Bait, Bobbers & Belgian Fudge had

a fair amount of fishermen hanging around, as if waiting for me. Sam came inside with me on the off chance Cody had returned, but he hadn't. Sam took over the bait shop cash register to ring up customers wanting live minnows while I trotted into the back and washed up in my kitchen. Pain still pulsed in my left wrist. But I managed to shuffle around my shelves and refrigerator with the other hand. I had enough ingredients to make another batch of fudge. Sam helped me pour everything into the double boiler at the front of the shop next to the copper kettles. He had to leave then for an appointment with a client, so to pour the mixture into the kettles would require a new recruit. Ironically, I was saved by Carl "Moose" Lindstrom—Gilpa's archenemy.

The tall, robust, ruddy-faced Swede, who was closer to my dad's age than Gilpa's, burst through the door, the cowbell clanging to announce him.

"Hey," he said, stomping in his rubber boots and running a hand over the thin, graying stubble on his big head. "Is it true? Gil knocked over the lady for the jewels? Gil catchin' a little nooky with a movie star makes quite a story."

My whole body burst with indignation until I saw his smile. "Moose, don't joke, please." The lovely white chocolate was bubbling just right. "Can you stir this for a few minutes? I hurt my arm. I'll set the timer. Just fifteen minutes."

He went wide-eyed, then saw that nobody was left in the shop. He took over with the long wood spatula. "Just fifteen. I gotta get on down to Sturgeon Bay and pick up a new skiff before my next fishing tour later today."

"You're doing a lot of investing in new boats lately."

"Oh, this isn't an investment. Insurance'll pay for this.

The darn thing unhitched somehow, and I didn't notice it was plumb gone before it was too late."

The skiff was a tiny lifeboat with a motor, usually tied to the side of his big cruiser and used if the big boat's motors went out. Which had to be never on his new boat. Gilpa didn't have an auxiliary boat, so I couldn't offer to help Moose.

"Somebody will find it out in the bay and bring it back for you, Moose. Maybe you should look for it again. The currents might have shifted."

"I looked enough. Nothing."

"It'll turn up."

"Not soon enough for business. Can't be out there without one, not with customers. Might get stuck if the motors die, like . . ."

My face flushed hot. He was referring to my grandpa getting stuck out at the Chambers Island Lighthouse with the four residents of the inn on Sunday. Instead of waiting half the night for a Coast Guard rescue, they could have motored back in the skiff. If Gilpa had had a skiff. Sunday's mishap seemed like an eternity ago to me, though it was only Wednesday.

"Damn this smells good," Moose said. "My mouth is watering."

To my surprise, he was grinning like a kid at the white chocolate fudge mixture bubbling away. His nose was twitching as he snorted in the vapors while he stirred.

"When the fudge is done and ready tomorrow, I'll bring you some pieces to sell on your boat."

"Too girly. No, thanks." He wrinkled his nose.

"But don't you get women on the boat?"

"Not much. They don't like all the fish guts and sea gulls flapping around when we bring in a catch."

I still had my grandpa's idea swimming in my head, though, about selling fudge on the boats. "So what would help me sell more fudge to the fishermen?"

"In the morning? I make 'em eggs and bacon and pancakes on my boat at seven a.m. A few guys pop their first beer of the day then. Men aren't really a fudge crowd. Maybe you'd do better over on Main Street somewhere. Especially now, what with you probably closin' down."

"I'm not closing. I'm expanding." The words spurted out. I surprised myself. But I also knew if I didn't nip rumors in the bud, they'd not only flourish in Fishers' Harbor but condemn me by becoming real. My mother and father wanted me to shut down. And all it would take to ruin my fudge venture was for the whole town to side with Mercy Fogg. It was me versus Mercy's push to get a stoplight.

"You got your grandpa's stubbornness." Moose dipped a beefy finger into the hot fudge mixture before I could stop him. He didn't even flinch from the boiling temperature, but he had a workingman's hands that never wore gloves to do much in icy winter weather, either. Gilpa's hands were the same way—strong and impervious to pain. Moose popped the finger into his mouth. His eyes lit up like firecrackers. "Damn, that's good stuff. Floaty in my mouth like heady foam on a hoppy beer."

"Wait until I add the cherry juice and tart cherries. Want to help me pour it into the copper kettle?"

He obliged, sneaking a finger into it again. He snorted at the air one last time, enjoying the perfume of the shop before he scooted on his way.

I sighed, watching his broad back go on down the

dock toward the *Super Catch I.* There had to be a way to sell more fudge to fishermen. If I was going to stick it out here with my grandpa, I had to find a different way of selling fudge. Cody had been excited about our Fisherman's Catch Tall Tale line of fudge that we hadn't even begun yet. What flavors might entice fishermen? How I wished Cody were back. I had to find him.

I dipped a finger into the creamy white confection. Indeed, it was "floaty, foamy" soft, fit for an Oscar party. I put in the touch of cherry juice to turn it pink, then realized I wasn't capable of stirring it with my one good hand. Maybe I had broken the wrist and should have it checked, but I just didn't have the time. But how would I save this batch of fudge? Panic set in. Until I remembered the church ladies were probably still at my grandma Sophie's.

Stuffing my nerves down into my stomach, I ventured over to Grandma's house, where I found Dotty Klubertanz and Lois Forbes more than happy to come over again—if I'd do a favor in return.

Dotty, dressed in pink as usual and wearing some flower clip in her short, white hair, said, "We want to feature your fudge at the Brussels Booyah Bash in two weeks. It's set for that Sunday after Mass."

Since I hadn't been around for eight years and I'd been at college down in Madison before that for a few years, I needed a refresher course. "What exactly are you talking about?"

The ladies reminded me that booyah was like the story of stone soup. Everybody brings an ingredient, like onions, celery, potatoes, cabbage, and stewing chickens, and then the church volunteers stir up batches of delectable soup in fifty-five-gallon drums over an outdoor fire.

Everybody then buys booyah to support the fund-raising effort. They take the thick soup home in plastic ice cream buckets. It's a Belgian tradition.

Grandma Sophie spoke up from her perch on the couch in the living room. "Honey, this is a high honor. Every year we ask somebody who's especially well known for excellence in baking to be featured at the Booyah Bash. We raffle off the desserts to help support the free community dinners we hold. Cinderella Pink Fudge will be raffled off to the highest bidders."

I wanted to cry and laugh at the same time at this ridiculousness. But their faces said they were serious. And I could see that Grandma Sophie needed to think about this rather than Gilpa being in jail because of me. This lady was built of stern stuff, but she also had a tender spot in her heart for her man. I so wanted to be like her. But didn't she and these ladies know that pink fudge was likely not going to get very high bids? I couldn't imagine that a man like Moose Lindstrom, for example, would want to be seen bidding on pink fudge. But one look at Grandma Sophie's beseeching eyes—on the verge of tears from her stress—and I knew what I had to do.

"I'm in." Then I stupidly blurted out, "And we'll introduce my secret new flavor of Fisherman's Catch Tall Tale Fudge."

The women glowed with eager smiles. Lois Forbes asked, "What is it?"

I flashed a fake, crafty smile. "Now, it wouldn't be a secret if I told. But those who help me in my shop will, of course, be part of the secret society of fudge that learns the recipe." My lying reminded me of how I bluffed my way through my TV show meetings in Hollywood.

Dotty, Lois, and the other women purged from my grandma's house in a blink, pleased and excited about my offer.

Awkwardness set in as I stood there looking down at Grandma Sophie on the couch, her broken leg stretched out.

"I'm sorry," I said. "I lied to them. I've been lying a lot lately. I'm the reason Grandpa's in jail. I'm truly sorry."

She heaved a heavy sigh. "You better be."

Gulp. "I'll get Gilpa out of jail."

"How?"

The look she flashed me could freeze fudge from forty paces. And I felt even sicker knowing I was alliterating in my thoughts like Pauline. It had to be a sign I was in trouble.

I said, "I'm pretty sure I know who murdered Rainetta Johnson. I just have to put the pieces together."

"Then what are you standing here for? Get going and find those pieces." She thumped the arm of the couch next to her. "Come here, dear, and give me a hug."

Gladly, I sank next to her on the couch. We hugged long enough for her love to pour from her into me, almost like I was a baby bird being fed by a mother bird.

I left Grandma Sophie's house knowing I had to hurry and do something to clean up my messy life, which was harming everybody around me. Grandpa was in jail, Cody had run away, Sam thought I needed to grow up, and my parents were disappointed and scared for me. Heck, I was scared for me. Somebody had planted the jewelry in my shop, and somebody had tossed me down the stairs. Was it Cody? I just couldn't believe he'd do those things. And yet a lot of evidence pointed to him. But I must be missing some clue. I had the feeling you get when you know somebody is right behind you, watching you. But who? Jeremy Stone? Sam? Mercy? I shivered.

As I stood under the maples listening to raucous robins fighting over territory, I phoned Pauline. It was the school's lunch hour.

She answered amid the racket of the cafeteria.

I yelled, "What time do you get out of school today?"

"In a half hour. Early release for a big track meet. The whole school gets to go. We might make State this year."

"Perfect. You and I are going to crash the lunch at the Blue Heron Inn. Bring the diamonds."

"This sounds like trouble, Ava."

"Everything I touch turns to terrible trouble. Alliteration to entice you, Pauline. Now, please get your tush over to my house with the diamonds. We catch mice with cheese, but murderers with diamonds."

Chapter 12

Pauline and I had walked inside the foyer of the Blue Heron Inn before I realized my mistake in bringing her. She was craning her neck every which way and doing so with a glint in her eyes.

I had to remind her, "We're not here so you can flirt with John Schultz. He could be a party to a diamond heist or worse."

"Fat chance. He was out in the boat that day, and the man is a tour guide and travel agent. You'll be jealous when he offers to take me to Paris during my summer break."

I'd called Izzy as we'd walked up the hill, so she was expecting us. She entered the sparkling reception hall looking especially elegant. Her petite frame was wrapped in a long lavender shirt cinched at the waist with a black leather belt that matched black denims and ballerina flats.

Pauline had dressed up for John of course. Because she was a kindergarten teacher and had to deal with mishaps before important meetings, she always had a change of clothes at school and in the car. She wore tan chinos, new matching pumps, and a long-sleeved aqua T-shirt that, with her long, glossy and loose black hair, gave her an alluring look that threw a twinge of jealousy into me. I had on my usual boring work boots and blue jeans with specks of fudge on them, but had changed into a clean white shirt. "Izzy, is there a special occasion?" I asked, indicating her attire.

Her dark eyes grew brighter, sparkling with the reflection of the Steuben statues. "The sheriff called to say that he'll allow everybody to go home tomorrow. My guests are ecstatic, so I thought I'd dress up for their bon voyage day."

Panic threatened to close my throat. "But he can't let them go. We haven't revealed who the murderer is. Or who stole the diamonds."

Izzy bit her lower lip. She glanced over at Pauline.

Pauline nudged me. "Ava, I think this means . . ."

"Gilpa is not guilty. The sheriff can't possibly think he's solved the crime." Or maybe he could, if the look on Izzy's face was to be believed.

Izzy gave me a hug, an extralong one. She smelled of expensive perfume, like carnations and gardenias and exotic spices stirred together. It bothered me that she was accepting what the sheriff had said, but then, what choice did she have? Her guests wanted to leave. Was the killer and diamond thief about to leave town? My gut said so.

"Izzy, I have to talk to Jeremy Stone. Is he here?"

"Unusual for him, but yes. I guess he stayed inside today so he can pack."

"Where is he? Are you eating in the kitchen?"

"Yes, but he went upstairs to his room already."

"Perfect."

I hurried up the blue-carpeted staircase with Pauline

in tow. We paused at the head of the stairs in the dark hallway. We were next to the Earlywines' room to the left.

"You have the diamonds with you, right?" I asked.

"Yes."

"Let's look for a good place to put them."

"What are you talking about?"

"To catch our murderer, we're going to leave the diamonds in a room, then ask Jeremy Stone to come with us as we search the rooms right now. We'll find the diamonds and the case will be reopened and the person arrested."

"Are you nuts?"

"Yes, but at least that will get my grandfather out of jail. Which room should we put them in?"

"Not John's."

His room was to our immediate right. "Fine. What if we put them in the room next to Rainetta's? That's Taylor Chin-Chavez's room."

Pauline grabbed my left arm too hard. I muttered an "ouch."

She whispered, "She's in her twenties, just a kid. You can't do this to her. I'm leaving right now, and you better do the same."

I grabbed the strap on her purse as she tried to head back down the stairs. "You heard Izzy. Sheriff Tollefson has let them all go as of tomorrow, so we have to act fast. We have to talk with Jeremy Stone to see what he knows, so while I distract him with my questions, you dump the diamonds in his room. Then, while I'm still talking with him, you leave and call Jordy to tell him what we've found. He'll arrest Jeremy Stone. You don't like him, either, so what's the harm in that? My grandfather will be freed, and Jeremy has a whole newspaper enterprise that can hire a lawyer to free him. And none of this will have cost me or my family a dime."

Pauline stared down her nose at me in her annoying way. She thought being taller than me meant she was smarter.

She finally muttered, "You're starting to sound like a cheap buffalo, like your grandfather, in fact."

Since a "buffalo" was a Belgian, I wasn't too offended. The cheap part stung, but right now I was okay being like my grandfather. He'd risked everything to set me up in business. He let me take the "Beer" word off the building, after all, and put up "Fudge." If he could make room in his life for me, I could make room in my life to save him.

I took a quick peek into all the rooms before we got to Jeremy's at the end of the hall. Nobody was around. Voices were coming through his door. I couldn't place the other voice, a man's. Pauline made motions to leave, so before she could, I knocked on the door.

"Jeremy? It's Ava Oosterling and Pauline Mertens. We'd like to talk with you."

When the door opened, to my surprise, the man was Hans Bjorklund, Bethany's father.

"I'm sorry to interrupt," I said. "Hi, Hans. Bethany's okay?"

Pauline said, "We can come back another time."

Jeremy stepped up beside Hans. "No, that's okay. We were just finishing an interview."

The men shook hands; then Hans sauntered down the hallway.

Jeremy wrinkled his crooked nose at me. "Bringing me poison fudge for a good-bye gift?"

"Not this time." Frustration heated my insides already. "We're here because, with your help, we're going to solve the murder. The wrong man is in jail, but you know that. And obviously you don't care."

His countenance shifted from slimy to something approaching indignation. "I'm a journalist. Of course I care about the truth."

I'd found his Achilles' heel. Who knew a reporter valued the truth? They certainly didn't in Hollywood, not the ones I'd seen in action mobbing the stars of our show. But I was back in Wisconsin; little things like the truth mattered to folks here, maybe even to Jeremy Stone.

I sat down on one of the small cream-and-blue couches that surrounded the table where I'd seen the wine the other day. Jeremy sat opposite me. Pauline stood clutching her bag—and the diamonds—in the doorway.

"What do you know about the diamond heist in New York, Jeremy?" I had to get right to it since he'd be leaving by tomorrow probably. "Are the diamonds connected? And what do you know about Rainetta Johnson's family? Any connection?"

"Wow. Want a job at the *Madison Herald*?"

"No. But you want to keep your job. So spill. You and I have to solve a murder case in about twenty-four hours, I figure."

His mouth gaped for only two seconds before his brain seemed to engage. His eyes grew darker. His crooked nose twitched. He dug out his notepad from the pocket of his shirt and flipped through it. "The heist happened a week ago today in upstate New York in Corning."

"Corning?" I'd heard of Corning glass, of course.

"There are summer homes of the rich in the area, many at local vineyards or wineries. One of those homes belongs to a man by the name of Kruppenmeier. The diamonds were stolen from the safe in his home."

"These are the same diamonds that were found here?"

"It looks like it," he said. "My colleagues out there tell me the Kruppenmeiers were in a feud over the rocks with a cousin's son by the name of Benton Alpanelp. Benton had purchased the raw diamonds from a blood-mine situation in an African country."

"You're talking about a dictatorship, slavery, that sort of thing?"

"Yeah. But it seems Benton bought the diamonds with the intent of giving them back to the workers of the mine. He's a philanthropist and an activist."

I moved to the edge of my seat, fascinated. "And the Kruppenmeiers didn't like that? They wanted the diamonds, I bet, because many are colored diamonds, worth much more than usual."

"How did you know that?" He smiled sheepishly. "You saw them, of course."

"So the Kruppenmeiers had them stolen from Benton Alpanelp?"

"No," Jeremy said, to my surprise. "It seems a third party was aware of the flap and hired a professional to steal them, and I suspect they thought that the feud between the families might help cover up who really did it."

"And you know who did it?"

Jeremy flopped back on the sofa in defeat. "No."

"Could it be the Reeds? They're from New York."

"I'm looking into that possibility, of course. But because of the diamonds showing up here at the same time as Rainetta Johnson, I paid a genealogist to see if there was a connection between Rainetta and these families. And there was."

I leaned forward in my seat with glee. "There is? Oh my gosh. Jeremy, why haven't you told us this before?"

"I just found it out today. These things take time. But she's only a shirttail relation, way off the grid really. But I did find out her last name used to be Kruppenmeier."

My brain went into overdrive with possibilities. "Had Rainetta visited them recently?"

"No. I've traced her steps, and she was in Chicago until she came here on late Saturday afternoon to stay over for the fund-raiser party on Sunday. I spoke with Isabelle already, thinking maybe security people had come ahead of time to check out the place and maybe be the connection to the thieves, but that didn't happen either."

"But it's weird that Rainetta is a relation and the diamonds end up here. She likely knew about the feud between the families."

"I have an idea," Pauline said, making Jeremy and me jerk. I'd forgotten she was in the room. She stood behind the kitchenette counter. "What if somebody knew either the Alpanelps or Kruppenmeiers intimately and was sick of their feuding, so decided to teach them a lesson?"

Pauline sounded like a teacher. Everything in life was about learning lessons.

Jeremy sat forward, worrying his hands. His nose wiggled. "I'm pretty sure that by now all the maids, mechanics, gardeners, vineyard workers, and whoever else they employ have been questioned."

Pauline looked slapped down by Jeremy's dismissal. I felt sorry for her, so I said, "But maybe there are former employees of those estates who should be questioned. Were they, Jeremy?"

"Hmm." He made notes in his notepad. "I'll see what I can dig up."

"That still leaves us with this question: Why me? Why hide the diamonds in my sugar? Why was Rainetta's necklace in my cookie jar?"

Jeremy wrote down those questions, too, which felt good because I felt validated, as if he took me seriously now.

Then he looked me square in the eyes. "It has to mean that someone around here knew the diamonds were coming to town but was smart enough not to keep them at their place."

"Jeremy, they were smart enough not to keep them here at the Blue Heron. Have you noticed that none of the doors have locks? Izzy has kept the place historically accurate. So that has to mean the thief is somebody staying here. At least that's my theory."

"I like it." He made another note. "And the nearest place that seemed innocent enough for a cover would be a bait and fudge shop. Nobody would suspect an all-American, true-blue establishment like Oosterlings."

"I appreciate the compliment, Jeremy, about our shop, but maybe we've been an easy target because the shop is hidden behind Main Street and the bustle there, not to mention the lights at night. It's pretty dark on the docks at night and after we shut off our shop's lights."

"And so the guilty person or persons also had somewhat easy access in and out of your shop and knew they could pick up the jewels anytime."

"Except Ranger and I made fudge with the wrong sack and the diamond thief didn't expect that."

Pauline said, "We've known that all along. What we don't know is who was expecting the diamonds." She helped herself to a glass of water at Jeremy's sink.

The lighting in the room caught Pauline's water glass just right and reminded me of Isabelle's party and how disgusted she'd been with Rainetta's cheap offer for the unicorn figurine. If Rainetta was loaded—or was about to become filthy rich from the sale of stolen diamonds—I didn't think she'd want to bother with a mere glass unicorn. Or would she? Just as I'd been about to let Rainetta off the hook, I wondered if she were casing Isabelle's collection, trying to buy—or steal—pieces and then sell them for profit? I'd had that thought previously concerning somebody after Isabelle's collection. What about Rainetta's manager?

"Rainetta's career was definitely on the wane. Would her manager be behind this?"

Jeremy said, "I don't know the guy. Refuses to talk with reporters."

But the manager had talked with Isabelle about collecting Rainetta's luggage and clothes, Izzy had said. Which meant we had to check on those things before the luggage and clothes disappeared.

I hurried from Jeremy's room.

Pauline caught up with me halfway down the staircase. "What's the rush?"

"Rainetta's manager has to be the key. He might even have murdered her."

"I don't follow you."

"I'm betting he came to town sometime over the years that Rainetta has been visiting Door County and vacationing here. Egads, this place is known worldwide for its nice spas and the cruises from here on the Great

Lakes. I haven't met him yet, but others in town, including Isabelle, probably have. And thus the guy comes and goes unnoticed by now."

"So he wears denims and something with a Green Bay Packer logo on it and everybody just waves hi to him like he's a local or a normal tourist. You think he snuck into your shop?"

"Easy enough. Gilpa would've just called out 'Can I get ya a beer?' and accepted him, maybe even thought he was a delivery guy."

"Oh my. You might be right. This manager had to have known the New York family flap. Managers know everything about their clients. What does yours know about you that's a secret he keeps from the tabloids?"

My manager, Marc Hayward, was nice, an eager guy who worked hard to encourage me to stay on the show. I'd also had an agent, but we'd parted ways when she learned I was heading back to Wisconsin. Agents specialized in doing your contracts, so if no contract was in the offing, they moved on. My manager, on the other hand, still hung in there. He sent me text messages and e-mail messages about possible shows I should think about writing spec scripts for. I thought a moment as we looked about at the Steuben glassware scattering light like fairy glitter into the air. With odd disappointment, I said, "What does my manager know that's juicy about me? Not a darn thing. Am I really that dull, Pauline?"

"No, my friend, you are not dull. Just Belgian. You can build on that, though."

"Thanks." The glow was back inside me. "What we have to do next is show the diamonds to Isabelle and see what she says about Rainetta's manager."

"I don't think we can do that."

"Why not—? Oh no. You didn't leave the diamonds behind in Jeremy Stone's room, did you?"

Pauline whipped her dark hair off a shoulder. "You told me to."

"But Jeremy turned out to be friendlier than I thought."

"You're going back to his room to get those diamonds, not me."

"Okay. After we find Izzy." We headed through the dining room for the kitchen.

She wasn't there, nor in the backyard, so we came back through the foyer and headed through the other half of the old boarding house to her private suite.

When Izzy let us in, I was mesmerized by how beautiful her suite was. She'd done it all in creams with black accents and touches of peacock blue. The furnishings were antiques, but comfortable and of the lived-in variety. Two creamy striped couches with dark walnut clawfooted legs flanked a fireplace, its bricks painted white. And now I knew where her unicorn had gone. It sat on the mantel, next to a gorgeous bouquet of pink carnations.

The carnations rang a bell in my head. "Are those—?"

"Yes," Izzy said, "from Rainetta's room. I couldn't let them go to waste. Do you think I should've left them there?"

I laughed. "No. I almost took them myself." Then I flushed, admitting, "When I was snooping in the room."

"That's okay. All my guests have taken their turn, I'm sure. I was just about to make some hot cocoa. It's cold out again today."

I hadn't noticed the weather because of my horrid morning. There had been rain, I recalled, and the usual fog and mist that Door County got in May, but I hadn't even bothered with my rain jacket. It was cloudy again, though, and the temperature was probably around sixty now, not cold for locals. But it would likely dip later, and we'd have frosty streets tonight, not uncommon at this time of year. "Thanks, Izzy. Cocoa sounds wonderful."

We made cocoa together, me finding her marshmallows in her cupboard and Pauline the cups and saucers.

"Izzy, I hate to ask you this, but Jeremy Stone told us things that make us think that Rainetta's manager might be somebody of interest in her murder."

"You're kidding?" Her diminutive size appeared to shrink even more where she stood stirring cocoa over her stovetop.

"Did the manager come and pick up Rainetta's things yet?"

"Yes. This morning."

Disappointment at not getting to meet him made me ask, "Did you watch him? I mean, was he acting suspicious?"

Her stirring slowed as she pondered. "How do you mean?"

"You weren't watching him when he gathered up her things? You have valuable things here, Izzy. He could've stolen something."

"I—I—oh crap. Okay, I confess. I didn't watch him because I didn't want him seeing my guilty face. I kept some of Rainetta's things."

Pauline said, "That could get you in trouble."

I fluttered a hand at her. "Not unless it's something really valuable. What did you take, Izzy?"

She sheepishly eyeballed her long, lavender shirt. "It's hers. And this." She went to an antique dresser that served as a cabinet for her television set next to the fire-place and then came back with a scarf covered with pink flowers, very much like carnations. "I admired it the af-ternoon she arrived." Izzy began to puddle up. "My mother had one very similar. I couldn't help myself. It was just stupid to take the shirt and the scarf, I know, but for some reason having Rainetta here was like having my mother around. And my mother liked these colors, too." She let out a sob. "I feel so stupid now, telling you this. Excuse me. I'll change clothes and make sure I send these things to her manager tomorrow."

She was heading off toward her bedroom, but Pauline and I looked at each other and then we both said, "Stop."

I said, "Izzy, it's just a scarf and a blouse. Rainetta would have loved giving those to you if you'd told her about missing your mother." I recalled Rainetta's lovely laughter in the foyer that day and the way my grand-mother later swooned about Rainetta's movies. Rainetta had been a popular actress in her day, and frankly, in looking her up on the Internet, I had only found inter-views that showed her to be gracious, though direct, in her opinions about her male costars. I shook off a brief thought of Sam's involvement with her.

Pauline said, "Many of my kindergarten kids sneak something from Mom with them to school, like Mom's necklace or her lipstick. It's soothing for them. And we never outgrow it. The teenage girls in school who get along with their moms are always wearing their clothes these days. It's like they're sisters. If you feel a sisterhood with Rainetta, so be it. It's nobody's business. It's not like you found diamonds that you're keeping."

I flashed Pauline a warning to keep quiet about our stash of hot ice. I added, "I doubt that manager cares about a scarf and blouse, even if they're from some fancy designer. He's probably more concerned about what became of all the diamonds and why he doesn't have them in his hot hands."

Isabelle gave us the manager's name, Conrad Webb. I didn't know him, but I could call my own manager and likely get something on him. The only problem was I didn't want to call Marc Hayward because he'd ask me yet again what I was writing. He got paid only if I wrote something that sold. I also didn't want to hear that I was fired from my show. Staff changes usually came in May, at the end of the spring television season. I hadn't formally quit the show yet when I had left Los Angeles this spring. But why did it matter to me? Wasn't I ready to stay in Door County? It was funny how I needed safety nets in my life. In a way, I was already planning my failure here and was counting on keeping my job in Los Angeles. My own life had gone topsy-turvy, just like the lives of the girls on the show. But then Sam's chiding words about me being a twelve-year-old echoed in my head. I had to prove I was worthy to somebody. Like my grandfather.

We were finishing our cocoa and standing around the counter when I asked Isabelle about Cody. "Did you ever see him sneaking into your inn?"

"No. Why?"

"Jeremy Stone saw him running from the back door the day of the murder. Jeremy was in the bathroom upstairs and looked out the window."

Isabelle gasped. "Was Cody up there? Maybe he saw the murder? And that's why he's run away?"

For some odd reason I hadn't thought of that. I thought he'd run away because of me. How stupid I felt now. "It all happened so fast. Maybe he saw all sorts of things. You ran up to see about Rainetta. What did you see?" She'd told me once, but I needed to hear it again.

Isabelle set down the cocoa cup she'd been holding aloft in front of her lips. "Her door was closed. I went into the restroom at the end of the hall to use it; then I heard her door open and close. I washed my hands and came out. I knocked on her door. She came out and fell over."

"Did you notice that her necklace was gone?"

Isabelle held a hand over her chest, as if she couldn't breathe. "Oh my gosh, no."

"Meaning you saw it? Or not?"

"I don't remember it. If it was gone, does that mean somebody was in her room hiding while we were in the hallway?"

"The sheriff looked in the room, but . . ."

Isabelle tapped her fingers to her cup in thought. "Her clothes were still there. Maybe they hid behind the clothes."

"Like Cody did." I told her about finding him hiding in the closet. "Did Rainetta have a shiny, expensive man's watch?"

"I never saw anything like that when she arrived. But it's not like she would show me her jewelry."

Pauline asked, "Maybe the watch was a gift for her manager?"

Or a gift for Sam, I was thinking. But Cody stole it from the room and showed it to Mercy at the restaurant. Pauline and I filled in Izzy on the restaurant visit.

Izzy said, "Do you think that Conrad might have engaged Cody and Mercy in the diamond scheme?"

"Hard to say. Mercy went upstairs, too. Then seemed to disappear. Did you see her?"

"No, but maybe she slipped into John's room. He was likely sleeping pretty soundly and didn't notice."

Pauline plunked down her cup with a *clink*. "Wait a minute. He was out in Gil's boat, stranded on Chambers Island, I thought."

"No," Izzy said. "I found out from Taylor that he'd gotten seasick after they started out, so they had to bring him back in. He slipped into his room to sleep off the seasickness."

My shoulders sank with a new realization. "So that's why they got caught in the bad weather and the engines couldn't handle it. Grandpa would have known about the storm clouds brewing, but with the hubbub of bringing John back in, Gilpa got flustered and just kept going." I shared a look of surprise with Pauline. I asked Izzy, "So John Schultz was actually upstairs when Rainetta was murdered and he lied about it?"

Pauline groaned. Her face had a sickly hue.

Isabelle nodded.

"Where's John now? We need to talk with him."

"He chartered a fishing trip with Moose Lindstrom for this afternoon. He's probably down at the docks."

Pauline and I raced out of the Blue Heron Inn, then down the steep street. As we tried not to fall forward on our faces in the steep pitch, Pauline said, "What about the diamonds in Jeremy's room?"

"They're safe for now. If we call him and tell him about them, that'll just cause us trouble with Jordy Tollefson because Jeremy's got his journalism code of honor and he'll have to tell the truth about the diamonds."

"And you'll be arrested and fixed up with a jail cell next to your grandpa," Pauline said, puffing.

"Exactly. With you," I puffed back.

"I could lose my teaching license because of you."

"Be grateful I helped you find out what a sneaky, lying guy John Schultz is before it was too late."

We galloped down the final twisty turn into the level street below the inn. As we neared the docks, the *Super Catch I* was heading into the expanse of Lake Michigan.

We sagged in defeat. As the fishing rig charged up its engines and rode higher on the water, I noticed the new skiff slung on one side.

"Oh my gosh." A realization bloomed in me. "I know where Cody is."

"Where?" Pauline was still breathing hard. That purse she carried weighed too much, or else we were way out of shape. Probably both.

"Come with me."

I raced down the dock past Oosterlings' Live Bait, Bobbers & Belgian Fudge, rattling the boards underfoot as I clomped in my boots to *Sophie's Journey*. I climbed in, finding the hidden keys under one of the seat cushions.

Pauline stood on the pier, shaking her head. "This tub is dangerous."

"I think I know where Cody is. Toss in your purse, Pauline, and untie us."

The engines sputtered to life, though they coughed like an old man trying in vain to clear himself of phlegm. The boat vibrated against the rubber tires serving as bumpers on the pier.

Pauline untied the ropes. The boat swung wide of the pier as Pauline leaped to come aboard. She missed the boat and splashed into the water up to her waist. I let go of the wheel to help pull her up with one hand. She struggled over the side rail. If Cody had been here, this wouldn't have happened. He would have rushed out of my shop to help us board.

"I'm freezing! I'm suing you," Pauline yelled. "Look at my shoes. They're ruined."

They were go-to-church-style tan pumps, now soaked to a dirty brown hue from icy Lake Michigan water. I tossed her a towel, which unfortunately had grease on it. She wiped at her clothes before noticing and now had a grease streak down the front of her wet, tan pants.

She ranted, "Skip my suing you. Just get us out in the water and I'll toss you overboard. You're totally freakin' unbelievable, Ava Mathilde Oosterling."

Pauline could go on forever like that. Figurative smoke poured off Pauline while the blue-black stuff shot off the engines as I steered us out into the gray waters churning under the overcast sky.

Chapter 13

I piloted *Sophie's Journey* northwesterly, unfortunately into stiff winds this Wednesday afternoon. I looked for my grandpa's anemometer—a foot-tall windmill contraption—which usually sat secured outside the windshield on the boat, but it was gone, probably broken off in his mishap on Sunday.

Pauline was already worried. She was good only in calm water. Wrapped in a wool blanket, she was standing huddled behind my captain's chair inside the small cabin.

"We're going the wrong way," she said, her teeth chattering. "Doesn't this thing have a heater?"

I flipped the knob for the heat, but the knob fell off. Since I had to keep my good hand on the wheel, I tossed the knob back at her and returned to concentrating on piloting. Spray came up over the front deck and smacked the windshield. Pauline screamed into my ear and ducked beside me.

"P.M., it's just foam off the waves. Now, go sit down."

"Big foam off big waves that are getting bigger." She scrambled into the cocaptain's seat to my right. "It's too windy. We shouldn't be out here. It's calmer along the shore. Go back there."

We were only a hundred yards out. She was right about the calmer waters, though I suspected her real reason for wanting to go in that other direction was to catch up with John Schultz. The *Super Catch I* was off to the east, following the shoreline, where they typically caught coho salmon, steelheads, and brown trout at this time of year. It burned me that John was such a liar. Pauline didn't deserve the same fate I'd suffered with Dillon Rivers.

The wind bashed our boat, tipping us toward the water on Pauline's side. She screamed again. She's been a screamer ever since our childhood. Swings and slides terrorized her. She was tall but hated heights; she was agile on a basketball court but hated feeling her body out of control. Like on a boat. But maybe she was right to be scared. I needed to check the wind and wave conditions before we chugged too far. Lake Michigan was unforgiving to small craft if you didn't play it smart.

"Pauline, take the helm. I'm checking on the weather."

"Thank goodness. Want me to turn back now?"

"Just head us straight on."

"Straight on what?"

"Toward Chambers Island." We couldn't see the land yet, but we'd been there a couple of times before, so we knew the way along a watery path strewn with orange buoys of commercial fishermen.

"That's seven miles away! You really think Cody's out there?"

"Yes."

The boat rocked again. Spray splashed across the windows. Pauline ducked needlessly, but to her credit, she didn't let go of the wheel. "How the heck would he get out there? Okay, a boat. But what boat? He doesn't own one, and nobody would rent to him."

"Maybe they should begin to trust him and treat him like a man." His tongue-lashing for me on that score still made me ache with shame. "I think he stole Moose's skiff a couple of days ago. Moose didn't notice it until today, when somebody on his tours probably pointed it out."

"But that's just a tiny motorized rowboat. Cody couldn't possibly make it all the way in these choppy waters to Chambers Island."

"Let's hope he did, Pauline. He's likely stranded without his cell or he would have called by now. That small boat motor likely ran out of juice, too."

"Let's call the Coast Guard."

"We will if we have to, but let's let Cody save face. My rescuing him is better than it being broadcast over public airwaves."

"I suppose. He'd never live it down at school."

"Worse than that, he'd hate disappointing Bethany," I said, calling up the Lake Michigan weather on my cell phone.

We could get wind speeds right off the buoys and other devices planted in the water and from the massive cargo ships passing through. My cell showed wind velocity at around nineteen knots, or maybe twenty-two miles per hour, enough to whip up white-crested waves and aggravating spray. The forecast said cumulus-nimbus clouds were hanging around to the west, but no lightning. Yet.

Gilpa's boat coughed, spewing smoke. It took us almost an hour to bring Chambers Island fully within view.

We didn't see Moose's skiff or any boat along the two miles of east shore and the occasional pebbly beach. We kept motoring north to go around the northeast thumb of the island. The lighthouse was about a mile southwest of the thumb tip on another jutting piece of land.

Pauline still had both hands frozen on the wheel, but she'd done a decent job of steering. She screamed less when I kept her busy like that.

Through the binoculars, I didn't see anybody on the island walking around or signaling us. My heart went into my stomach. What if Cody hadn't made it? Plenty of boaters hit hidden rocks and capsized in these areas. The museum in Sturgeon Bay was full of history about shipwrecks here, and the Coast Guard was stationed here for good reason. Fear slithered up my spine. Cody Fjelstad had run away because of me. I couldn't bear the thought of harm coming to him because of my stupidity—no, my lack of trust in him. The realization hit hard that Sam was right about me not being able to trust anyone fully. I had to get over that somehow.

Pauline said, "Maybe he ended up in the marina."

She was just trying to cheer me up, but I said, "Good idea. Cut back on the engines and we'll take the tour."

"I don't think there's anything to cut back on."

I wanted to laugh, but it was sad that Gilpa wouldn't give up this decrepit boat.

We managed to slow, though, which made the engine grind even louder. The floor underfoot shook. If Cody were nearby on Chambers Island, he'd have to hear us. But as we headed up the east coast past the area of the Catholic Holy Name Retreat House and then came in close to the small, private marina, we saw nobody. The island was thirty-two hundred acres of dense forest and a small inland lake; I hoped he hadn't wandered far. But had he been hurt? If Cody had made it to any of the fifty or so cottages scattered here and somebody was about, we'd have heard about that. The island had a cell phone tower. There was also a tiny airstrip behind the lighthouse, which accommodated the Coast Guard plane, but we hadn't heard from them. My stomach sloshed like the lake with its worry. Was Cody a pile of broken bones among the shoreline rocks?

After passing by the marina and going around the thumb of land, the lighthouse came fully into view, a mile west of us. Being the ranger of this small, historical spot was Cody's dream.

I took over piloting us closer to the shoreline in front of the lighthouse. Grandpa had taught me how to pilot when I was a kid. A warm feeling sprang up inside of me as I sat now in his captain's chair and heard his voice telling me to ease up on the throttle and reverse the engines to keep us from getting hung up in the shallows. I veered the boat to place us parallel to shore. Beyond the rocks and sandy shoreline, the Chambers Island Lighthouse sat atop a grassy knoll with pine trees behind it. Maples were still trying to leaf out.

Pauline said, "I don't see anybody."

"We'll go back to the marina and tie up, then walk over."

I could have anchored here if we were willing to swim to shore, but at this time of year the water felt like ice cubes against your body. Minutes later, we'd tied up at the marina, then hiked the mile or so down a lake path to the forty-acre site of the lighthouse.

"Cody?" I called out, then caught myself. "Ranger?"

Only the lap of the water and a blue jay cawing answered me.

The house and tower were built in 1868 and named

after Talbot Chambers, a colonel who passed by the area on his way to build a military presence in Green Bay. The small house was a story and a half high with the three-story lighthouse tower on its northeast corner, all built of Cream City brick from Milwaukee. An octagonal room atop the tower had a light run by solar panels. Nobody appeared to be around. A lighthouse caretaker—a volunteer from Fishers' Harbor usually—would come here some days June through Labor Day, when it was open for tours.

When Pauline and I approached the door, we found it open.

"He has to be here," I said. "I'm sure they lock this up." I called out again, "Ranger?"

There was no response, but we smelled fried fish and eggs. My hopes rose. The first floor had only a few small, sparse rooms, including a closet and a pantry. We saw no evidence of anybody sleeping here, though. The pantry was stocked with only a handful of canned goods.

Following the smells, we ventured into the kitchen, which was in an attached room built at a lower level than the rest of the house. I gave a pan a good whiff. "Fresh. He cooked today."

Suspecting we'd found him, I eagerly tromped in my loud work shoes up the cast-iron, circular steps to the second floor. He wasn't there, so I hiked up the tight staircase to the top of the tower. Where he wasn't, either. I sagged against the railing, peering about the terrain of water, trees, and a narrow inland road. When I returned my gaze to the shoreline, I spotted the skiff half-hidden west of us among berry brambles and rocks.

We rushed from the lighthouse. After we got to the area near the skiff, we stopped to get our bearings. A trail from the lake led us to what looked like a modest, ranch-style log cabin.

The front door was locked. I rapped my knuckles several times on the wood. "Ranger, answer this door right now or I'm calling the Coast Guard to haul you out."

For a minute, we didn't hear anything. My knuckles were on the door again when it opened fast. I didn't recognize Cody at first. He sported a buzz cut. He'd shaved off his red hair. Lacerations on his face and arms looked wicked and raw. He wore a torn T-shirt that had a Harley motorcycle slogan on it; I suspected it wasn't his. His pants looked borrowed, too. They were baggy and held up by a belt notched so far in that a foot of leather hung off the front.

"Ranger? Is that you?" I didn't know if I should hug him or what.

He grabbed me, though, into both his arms and squeezed. "I'm so sorry, Miss Oosterling."

"Ouch." He'd crimped my bad arm in the hug.

"Miss Oosterling, you're hurt. What happened?"

His innocent concern appeared genuine, which confirmed that he hadn't been the one to toss me down the stairs at the mansion.

"A sprain. I fell down."

"Maybe I should wrap that for you. They have all kinds of good first-aid stuff here in the bathroom. Just like at school."

He led us down a short hallway to a bathroom, where one of those shelving units that hangs over the back of the stool was filled with first-aid stuff, including ACE bandages. I spotted a pet hair clippers sitting next to the sink; he'd obviously used that to shave his head. Which meant he knew how to run a generator—the only way to get electricity on the island. I sat on the stool lid while he wrapped my left wrist. He told us he'd taken off at night after stealing Moose's small rowboat.

"The light in the tower really works at night, Miss Oosterling. I found my way."

I suspected the lake current was more responsible for his landing than he was, but said instead, "You did find your way, thank goodness. And I apologize for treating you like a kid. I need you back at the fudge shop, Ranger Fjelstad."

Pauline said, "We need you to help us figure out who stole the diamonds."

His face soured.

"I know you didn't do it," I said in a hurry. "You were in Rainetta Johnson's room on Sunday trying to figure out the mystery, too, weren't you?"

"Not really. I was there to steal stuff."

That took me aback. Pauline winced, too, speechless for once.

He led us back down the hallway and through a lovely living room with black leather furniture and braided rag rugs on maple wood floors—a nice hideout. I smelled coffee perking. I asked, "Is somebody else here?"

"Just me. May I get you a cup of coffee, Miss Oosterling?" He smiled at us as if he owned the place. "There wasn't any coffee at the lighthouse, so after I ate my noon meal there, I came back here to make the coffee like your grandfather likes. Two extra scoops no matter what, he says."

Now I knew why the coffee always tasted so good when Gilpa made it instead of me. "Where'd you get the fish?"

"I used one of the fishing poles I found in the garage.

It was a small brown trout. I cooked him at the lighthouse so the house didn't get stunk up."

"That was nice of you."

Pauline asked, "So you've been living at both places?"

"Just like La-La Land. I'm rich enough to have two houses." He laughed like the old Cody with loud, quirky guffaws. He was a John Schultz in the making.

He retrieved cups off a cup tree on the counter. In the stainless-steel dream of a kitchen, he poured us coffee. He wore a huge smile, as if every little thing he did tickled him. This was his nirvana. Pauline could see it, too; she grinned at me. I still couldn't get over his haircut, though. He looked grown-up. Adult.

Pauline and I sat down on stools at a kitchen island bar that separated the room from the living room. Cody settled on a stool opposite us on the kitchen side.

I asked, "Why did you shave off your hair?"

"It was too curly, like a baby. And it was red. I don't think Bethany likes red hair."

"Bethany's been worried about you."

Pauline jabbed me discreetly with her elbow. We both knew Bethany wasn't worried except for being fearful of a marriage proposal. But it looked like Cody was trying to create a nest right here on Chambers Island.

Cody asked, "When you take me back, will I have to see her?"

He had just surprised me again. "I thought you'd want to see Bethany."

He shook his head. "I stole stuff. She won't like that."

"You stole a watch, but you were all mixed up because Mercy Fogg asked you to do that, didn't she? We saw you at Al Johnson's with her. But you saw us, too, didn't you?"

Cody averted his gaze. I reached out to touch his arm, though I was careful because it was so scratched up from his adventures in getting here a couple of nights ago. "Listen, Ranger. Whatever Mercy told you, we'll fix it. It's not nice if she used you to steal stuff from that room."

"But she's nice."

Pauline and I exchanged a few blinks. I asked him, "How has she been nice?"

He got up to pour us more coffee, though we didn't need it. While topping off our cups, Cody said, "Miss Fogg said that Mr. and Mrs. Reed killed the movie star, and she was going to prove it. Miss Fogg said if I could find stuff in Miss Johnson's room with fingerprints on it, she was going to prove the Reeds killed her."

Like a computer with a virus, my brain scrabbled to make sense of that. Mercy was playing detective? And she wanted to pin everything on the Reeds? Not me? Did she know more than Pauline and me about the murder? The thought of combining forces with Mercy came to me; then I dashed the thought. Mercy didn't like me, for some reason. I still couldn't trust her.

"Why didn't you tell me this earlier?" I asked.

"Because I didn't want you to get arrested again like we did last Sunday." He shuddered.

"We weren't really arrested," I said. "You were questioned, is all. The sheriff is a thorough guy. He wanted to know what you know."

"I know the jail was not a good place."

Pauline said, "Honey, it's not good for anybody, but you might have to tell all this new information to the sheriff."

"No way."

I said, "We'll go with you, Ranger. Look, my grandfather's in jail and you can save him."

"Why's he there?" Cody went wide-eyed.

"He was arrested this morning for allegedly stealing jewels from Miss Johnson and murdering her. At least, they'll see if there's a connection to murder."

Cody whirled off his stool. "I can't go back. You can get him free, Miss Oosterling. You're smart. I like it here. I'm staying."

"You can't stay here."

"I'm going to be the ranger at the lighthouse and for the park here. I already started."

"Doing what?" I asked, leery of the answer.

"I raked the winter leaves off the bushes around this house. Did you know there are rose bushes here? Bethany loves roses. She won't be mad at me when she sees the roses. I'm staying until I have roses to bring Bethany."

Oh boy. Roses. I recalled how the roses around Sam's house had charmed me those years ago. I really needed Sam at this moment to help advise me on how to handle Cody's special brand of reasoning and lack of impulse control. All I had for skills was truth. "Ranger, this isn't your house. You can't live here. Bethany doesn't want to live here, either. And maybe she prefers other flowers. She needs a choice in the matter."

He gave me a quizzical look that said he hadn't fully considered that possibility. My heart went out to him. I added, "When we get home, you can help clean up the big yellow house in Fishers' Harbor, the old mansion. I thought you wanted to live there."

"Not anymore. I went there the other day and somebody was in the basement."

"Who?"

"I don't know. I got scared and ran."

Pauline asked, "Why were you there? And what day was that?"

"Uh, Monday afternoon sometime. After I got mad at Miss Oosterling. I went there because it's my special place. It's where I want to hold my prom party. My mom and dad said I couldn't have a party, but I think they just meant that our house is too small. The mansion is way big."

"Not everybody has a prom party," I said, though my heart was aching again for him.

"But I want one. And the prom is a week from Saturday night. I have to get crackin', Miss Oosterling. Would you make more of your Cinderella Pink Fudge for my party? Maybe I can borrow Miss Johnson's pink carnations and make a corsage for Bethany so it'll match the fudge. Please?"

He was grinning so broadly that I felt myself falling down the proverbial rabbit hole. I recalled Rainetta Johnson's carnations now sitting in Izzy's suite at the Blue Heron Inn. "If you come with me now and promise to go to the sheriff with me and make Bethany proud of you, I'll do more than make the fudge for you. I'll even chaperone your party. And that pink corsage idea is do-able, too."

Pauline gave me a cross-eyed look, but I persevered because Cody was now hopping up and down in the kitchen. He swiveled to me for a high-five.

He crowed, "I'm going to have a prom party! Thank you, Miss Oosterling! Our party will be bigger and better than anything you ever had in La-La Land, I bet."

That was a sure bet.

We were boarding *Sophie's Journey* when Cody said, "Miss Fogg should come to my party, too. And we should invite Mr. Schultz, too."

Pauline asked, "Why Mr. Schultz?"

"Because the watch I took from Miss Johnson's room belonged to him. Miss Fogg says that Mr. Schultz probably left the watch there to pay for the diamonds he took from Miss Johnson."

Pauline nearly fainted. She sat down hard on one of the bench seats inside the boat's cabin.

Cody took charge of the cocaptain's seat just as rain started to tap on the cabin roof.

I asked from my captain's chair, "John 'took' them or he 'stole' them? What did Mercy say exactly?"

"She said 'took.' But he took them from the room next door, because the girl staying there stole them. John took the diamonds from her."

I thought about the diamonds Pauline had hidden earlier today in Jeremy Stone's room, diamonds we'd retrieved from the guilty Earlywines. "Did you see the diamonds?"

"No, but Miss Fogg said they were in a red velvet pouch."

I looked back at Pauline, who flashed me a knowing hike of an eyebrow. She was shivering under the blanket again.

Cody said, "Did you know Miss Chin-Chavez wants to buy a lighthouse? That's why she stole the diamonds, Miss Fogg said. But she didn't kill Miss Johnson. Miss Fogg says the Reeds did that. The Reeds are rude. I believe that they could murder somebody."

"When did you see them be rude?" This intrigued me.

"They tried to push me down the back stairs at the

Blue Heron Inn. I snuck in on Sunday because I wanted to see the party and how our pink fudge with the pink glitter sparkled, but the Reeds chased me through somebody's room and they pushed me hard."

Pauline and I exchanged a look of horror. Had one or both of the Reeds tripped me in the old mansion, too?

"You sure it was the Reeds?"

"Sure. Miss Johnson came up the stairs right past me; then the Reeds looked out of their room. I turned and ran, and a door was open and I found the stairs and then I felt a push. I tripped but slid mostly down the stairs on my butt and then ran."

It was clear we had to sort this out with Sheriff Jordy Tollefson. I couldn't tell what could be merely Mercy's theories versus fact in any of Cody's stories. It could have been Mercy shoving him down the stairs; she'd gone up the stairs and had disappeared, after all. Despite the confusing stories, one thing was clear: Cody wasn't going to enjoy what was about to happen next for him.

Chapter 14

Rain and wind lashed at *Sophie's Journey* all the way home, keeping Pauline suffocating herself under a blanket. The decrepit boat got us back to the dock in front of Oosterlings' Live Bait, Bobbers & Belgian Fudge by around four on Wednesday afternoon. Black smoke continued pouring out of the engines, not a good sign. Cody leaped out first to help Pauline. This time she didn't land in the water, but she was still soaked from her earlier dunking, and without an umbrella, she was getting even wetter. I handed over her big purse. She snatched it and ran in her ruined pumps to her car in the parking lot.

Sam Peterson was waiting for us inside the fudge shop, along with Dotty and Lois and several church ladies who had commandeered my shop again. The place felt gloriously warm and dry. My olfactory senses were pleasantly assaulted by the aromas of sugar, butter, cream, vanilla, cherries, chocolate, butterscotch, peanut butter, and maple syrup.

Cody wrinkled up his nose. "They're not cutting the fudge right," he said. "They're not cutting the pink cellophane right. And the fairy glitter is all over the place. They don't know how to put magic in fudge."

It sounded like he was reciting *Goldilocks and the Three Bears* and the "somebody's been eating my porridge" routine.

Sam's blue eyes went wide at Cody's new look as he shook his hand. "Glad you're okay, but we better call your parents."

"I'll call 'em later," Cody said with a commanding voice as he marched over to grab an apron out of the closet behind the cash register. "I have to make sure Miss Oosterling's fudge is done right. This glitter takes special skills."

In a nice way, he shoved red-haired Lois aside, but she took umbrage with him telling her to cut new cellophane squares. He told her she'd cut the old squares too small. "You have to have enough cellophane for a handle so your hand doesn't warm the fudge. And so you can make crinkly noises. Our fudge makes noise."

This was the first I'd realized that noisy fudge was an asset, but I liked it.

Lois and Dotty and the half dozen other ladies had plenty keeping them busy. They'd used the afternoon to create more microwaved fudge in the several flavors I'd smelled walking in. Delectable-looking fudge morsels filled the glass case next to the register. More batches cooled on the new shelving unit I'd put together earlier in the week with Sam's help. What was more, a shipment of naked fairy dolls had come in, along with several other items that I'd been missing since the sheriff confiscated everything. The women were stocking shelves, and white-haired Dotty Klubertanz was stuffing several naked dolls into a sack.

She said, "I've texted all the gals at Saint Ann's. We'll have the fairy doll clothes crotched and sewed by Saturday. Lois's parish gals over at Saint Bernie's are in charge of making the fairy wings. She just sewed for two weddings and has lots of lace and netting left over that'll be perfect for starching and making into wings. Your shelves will be brimming and ready for gift-buying for Mother's Day."

Mother's Day? I'd forgotten it was coming up this Sunday. I hugged Dotty. "Thanks. Now, if I can just find customers without news cameras attached to them."

The bait side of the shop where the minnow tank bubbled was empty. I hoped my grandfather would be home soon.

"I need your help," I told Sam. "Cody has agreed to talk with the sheriff about things that will require a guardian with him, I'm pretty sure, and I think he wants to do it without his parents along. He's an adult now."

Sam ran a hand through his blond hair, his blue eyes surrounded by wary squinting. "What kind of trouble did you get him into?"

"Me?" I couldn't keep up my pretense of indignation. Sam knew me too well. I took him aside over to the minnow tank and away from the church ladies' ears. "Mercy and Cody have been playing detective. They allegedly have some proof that the Reeds killed Rainetta. Cody thinks they tried to hide it by pushing him down the stairs at the Blue Heron Inn on Sunday."

"What?"

Heads swiveled our way, but soon returned to cutting and wrapping fudge and divvying up naked dolls to dress later.

"I know it sounds ridiculous, but it's plausible."

Sam shook his head, leaning closer to my ear, so close that I enjoyed the manly scent of his neck. He whispered, "I never saw Cody there on Sunday."

"I believe you, but Cody admits to being there, and

Jeremy Stone says he saw him. He has a picture of Cody. The upstairs at the inn was evidently like a college dorm party, with everybody changing rooms and stealing diamonds from one another."

"What?"

When all the heads turned to us a second time, I said, "Shhh. Stop saying that. Please, let's just take Cody down to Sturgeon Bay now and talk with Jordy while Cody's in the mood and Jordy's in the office. It's getting late. I don't want him leaving before I can convince him to keep Isabelle's guests in town for a couple more days. If they leave, the murderers leave."

"You believe the Reeds did it? I don't think Cody's all that reliable. What happened to your theory that Mercy did it? Heck, she's probably convinced Cody of a whole bunch of lies." He rearranged the frustration on his face with a swipe of his hand, then said, "Never mind. I'll go with you. Let's get this over with."

"Don't say it like that, Sam. I thought maybe you'd trust me, or at least trust Cody."

"Don't pull the trust card on me now. I don't trust you. That's why I'm going with you. The next thing I know, you'll have *me* arrested for murder."

"Well, you *were* at the inn. That's not a bad idea."

I smiled, but he sighed before going over to collect Cody. I supposed Sam's sometimes lack of humor was what had attracted me to Dillon Rivers, who was a stand-up comic, after all. It made me wonder: What would I do if Dillon walked through the door right now? What would he make of all this mess I'm in?

While Sam went into a different private interrogation room with Cody and his parents, who Cody wanted with him after all, I asked to see my grandfather and was surprised to be escorted to a larger meeting room near the jail cells.

My parents and Grandma Sophie were there with Gilpa, all sitting in blue plastic chairs around a six-foot table. Evidently they'd tried calling me, but I hadn't looked at my messages for a while. My dad was muttering about how they had to get home to start the milking. Grandma Sophie was biting her lip. Gilpa peered at me with a crimp in his ruddy face.

My throat closed in terror. I had to swallow to breathe again. "Did something happen?"

Gilpa said, "I found Destiny."

This had to be a dream. I shook my head to clear it. "Okay, Gilpa, that's nice. Your destiny is to run your bait shop. And maybe buy a new boat?"

Gilpa's wrinkled face clouded. "Not that destiny." Then he smiled around the table at us, his eyes sparkling like stars. "I found us a lawyer. Her name is Destiny."

Obviously, this had to be *some* lawyer. Gilpa appeared *that* happy.

He said, "She'll be here any minute."

We waited. And waited. My father hemmed and hawed about needing to leave for the cows. My mother sniffled, muttering about how afraid she was for me. Grandma Sophie said she liked how well Cody had wrapped my left wrist with the bandages.

Another half hour of small talk went by. Gilpa kept saying to us, "We have a lawyer now; everything will be fine."

Finally, the door to the small tan room opened. We turned; our plastic and metal-legged chairs pinged and popped.

A petite, short girl stepped forward. She looked sixteen, with too much makeup on flawless cocoa skin and a sleek cap of black hair. Her eyelashes were brooms sweeping up and down when she blinked; I was instantly jealous because they looked real. She wore a black suit, making her look like a high school kid playing a librarian in a school play.

Gilpa said, "This is Destiny Hubbard. She just graduated from law school in Madison. She'll be defending me on the murder charge."

"But, Gilpa," I said, interrupting the girl-woman's grand entrance, "you're getting freed today. That's why we brought Cody Fjelstad down here."

"Not so fast, y'all," said Destiny in a chirpy voice. "That's why I'm late. Had to talk over some things with the DA's office and the sheriff."

Destiny stepped forward on her high heels—red ones—and held out her hand. "Ma'am, it sure is good to meet y'all. You're my first case. But don't worry. I know all about Belgians. Our Memphis in May celebration coupla years back honored Belgium. We pick a new country every year to celebrate while we hold our barbecue contests. You guys are stubborn. But so am I. I'm from Memphis, and living along the Mississippi takes strong people. We endure. I hear you cook up a mean batch of fudge. We like good food in Memphis, in case you haven't heard, so I think we'll get along just fine."

All of us stared back at her with a look that said: *We are in trouble*.

She talked on with her exquisitely polished lips, luring us with her big eyelashes. "I always did well in practice court. I defended two murder cases and got the highest scores. I took acting classes, too. So I'm prepared."

Practice court? An actress? Yup, we were in trouble.

My parents shook her hand and then excused themselves after hugging me. No matter what was happening in life, even a tornado bearing down on you, you had to tend to the cows. Cows would knock the doors down to get in a barn to be fed and milked on time. I was left alone with my grandparents and our new actress lawyer.

Destiny had been appointed by the public defender's office to take my grandfather's case. In other words, my family was officially too poor to afford a criminal attorney. But I sensed we were in deep poo here because if my grandfather were getting freed today we wouldn't need a lawyer. But he was smiling, still positive in his outlook. Or insane.

"Isn't she wonderful?" he said to me. "And she's free."

It was a good thing Pauline Mertens wasn't here because she'd be calling us "cheap Belgians."

Destiny didn't look uncomfortable with my grandfather's remark. She sat down next to him on his side of the table. Her head barely came up to his shoulder. She took a sheaf of papers out of her briefcase, fanning them out in front of my grandfather. Grandma Sophie and I had to read them upside down. It didn't matter. I could tell the news was bad.

Destiny pointed out, "The amethyst necklace was in your possession, and you insisted on confessing to the theft of a necklace taken off a murdered woman, and even though that alleged theft might be a false confession to save your granddaughter, it gives the sheriff's department and the DA enough cause to keep you for questioning just a bit longer because there's a murder involved."

"But I found the necklace and put it in his boat. It's my fault," I said.

Grandma Sophie patted my hand, careful not to touch

my bandaged wrist. "Honey, let Destiny talk. I suspect the less we say, the better."

"You're so right, Mrs. Oosterling," Destiny said. "But I'm going to see about bail." Her smile broadened. "I've never said that for real before."

I couldn't help but wiggle in my plastic chair. "Are we really your first case?"

"Yes, but I was valedictorian of my high school class, graduating early at age sixteen; then I graduated *cum laude* in three years instead of four, with a degree in human resources, before going to law school, where I finished top of my class. I am simply the best at what I do."

Even Gilpa flushed at the speech. Grandma Sophie bit her lip again; I couldn't tell if she was impressed or confused.

"So," I said, "how old are you?"

Destiny laughed. "I get that all the time. I look sixteen, but I just turned twenty-three."

"She's legal!" Gilpa crowed. "And free," he repeated. "A twofer." Meaning two for one price.

I asked, "When can my grandfather get out of here?"

"I was hoping Mr. Fjelstad might admit to something, which would mean immediately, but the sheriff tells me Mr. Fjelstad has some convoluted story that pins the murder on everybody staying at the Blue Heron Inn. We all know that not 'everybody' can be guilty."

"Why not?" popped out of my mouth. I recalled my earlier thought about the college dorm party, with the inn's guests all joining in the fun together and maybe covering up for one another. But I wasn't sure I could speak up about the diamonds in the pouch since Pauline and I had stolen them, too. My perch on my chair in the jail felt precarious at best.

Destiny cocked her pretty head at me. "Do you know something I should know?"

"No," I lied. "It's just that, well, yes. You should talk with Mercy Fogg. And Sam Peterson."

Sam's name flew out before I could stop myself. My face burned and my stomach soured with panic. Had I just betrayed Sam?

Destiny said, gathering her papers, "Sam's with the Fjelstad boy now. What should I be talking to him about?"

"I don't know." It was hard to talk with my grandparents staring at me. There was no way I wanted to tell them that the guy I was once engaged to had a "thing" for the dead movie star, who might have had a "thing" going on with Mercy Fogg, the recent past president of the village board of Fishers' Harbor. My grandparents would accuse me of making up stories befitting my soap-operaish *The Topsy-Turvy Girls*.

Destiny apparently read my mind, because she got up, clearly ready to leave. As she came around to our side of the table, she said, "Listen, y'all. We have a lot of work ahead of us. You're all gonna get sick of me, but that's how it is. Mr. Oosterling, I promise to get you out of jail soon. Now, here's your homework until we meet again."

She proceeded to give us several questions to work on overnight. One of the questions was: Is anybody jealous of your good fortune?

After Grandma and I got into Sam's car to return to Fishers' Harbor, I asked, "What good fortune? We seem to be the most hexed family on the planet. Nobody would be jealous enough of us to want to frame us for murder."

Grandma Sophie piped up from the backseat. "We

have each other and lots of love. A lot of people don't have that, honey."

Sam agreed. "You're lucky." Sam didn't talk about his own family all that much. His parents were divorced and his siblings were scattered around the globe. I knew it affected him. Maybe part of the reason I hadn't married him was because I suspected he might have fallen in love with my family more than with me.

As we were zooming northward up Highway 42 toward Egg Harbor, he said, "And maybe Destiny is smart about people. Didn't she say she majored in human resources? She probably took psychology classes."

"Just yesterday," I sniped. "She hasn't lived life. How is she going to defend us against a murder charge and for stealing jewelry? The DA is going to eat us alive."

Grandma piped up from the back, "I'm hungry. What's for dinner? You two want to come over?"

"No," Sam and I said in unison, flashing each other a look that said, "It's not good to look like we're a couple in front of a grandmother."

I added, "No, thanks, Grandma. I've got to get back to close up the fudge shop. But I'll be over to cook dinner within the hour, if that's okay."

"I'm bored staying inside all the time with this leg. It felt good to go to the jail just now, so you know how bored I am."

We all laughed.

She said, "Let's go over to the Troubled Trout for some greasy food. My treat."

She was determined that Sam and I would be eating together and with her. I had the feeling she was plotting something. Intrigued, I agreed to go. "I'm in the mood for cheese curds and a good beer. Sam?"

"Why not?" he said. "It's probably best I keep an eye on you, anyway. Every time I leave you, something bad happens. Mostly to me."

For a smidgen of a moment I thought he meant my marriage to Dillon Rivers. Then I hoped he'd only meant Cody. I'd forgotten to ask. "What's going to happen to Cody? He's not going to be arrested or anything, is he?"

"He's cooperating. So far. But he's impulsive."

"I noticed."

"It's his parents who worry me. Cody let slip something about you okaying some party for him at the empty mansion."

"Prom," I said, sagging inside my seat belt. "I promised him he could hold the party there."

"What the heck were you thinking? That scrap heap of old lumber is nowhere near code."

"What would it take to get it up to code?"

"Tens of thousands of dollars. Rainetta Johnson's pledge."

"Hollow pledge now," I said. "It's tough to write a check when you're dead. But there has to be a way to make Cody's dream come true."

"Get real, Ava. This is how you are. Your head in the clouds. Or stars. Hollywood stars. It's why you left. Every time I give you a reality check, you check out and run."

From the back, my grandmother said, "Now, now, you two sound like an old married couple."

Scalding embarrassment came to my face. I'd forgotten she was there. I was getting distracted a lot lately.

Sam flexed his fingers around the steering wheel. He was grinning.

*   *   *

After we ate cheese curds, burgers stacked tall with slices of Swiss and cheddar cheeses, and wafted a cherry-laced beer from a local brewery, Sam dropped off Grandma and me at her house. It was past eight, dusk, and chilly and damp. The rain had stopped, but the wind outside was fierce and howled past the windows. Nothing mysterious transpired at the Troubled Trout, but I could feel Grandma Sophie aching to tell me something.

"Grandma, what's up?" I asked, after I helped her get to the living room couch in front of her television set. She settled into her corner next to the arm and little table where she kept magazines.

"Plenty," she said. "We Oosterlings are in a pickle."

"I'm so sorry. I feel like all of this happened because I came back and opened a fudge shop."

"Well, maybe it did." She said it in a matter-of-fact way, not accusatory.

I sat down next to her. She patted my knee, then said, "Just keep doing what you're doing."

I scoffed. "I haven't a clue what I'm doing, Grandma. Except I'm here to help you, which I thoroughly enjoy." I hugged her, then kissed her soft cheek.

"But you're all over the place, trying to do too much at once. Each of us can be successful at only one thing at a time. We build our lives in that way. You put down a foundation, then you build a wall, and that wall holds up the next wall and the next."

"I guess I don't know your point."

"What's your foundation? Is it your fudge shop? If it is, take care of that first. Or is it Sam? Or helping Cody? Or maybe you yearn to go back to Los Angeles?"

"Are you afraid I want to leave already?"

Grandma Sophie reached for her remote and turned

on the television. A sitcom was on, one that had great ratings. Grandma said, "I sense that you're scared and don't know what you want exactly."

"Maybe I am. But I'm only thirty-two."

"Destiny Hubbard is twenty-three, and she knows exactly what she wants from life and she's going to get it by twenty-five, I have a feeling."

Oh dear. This was starting to sound like Sam's lecture about me acting like I was twelve. "Grandma, I'm okay. Don't worry about me. And don't try to fix me up with Sam."

"Don't try to tell your grandmother what to do. And you needn't be so rude to him."

That hurt. She was thinking about us arguing in the car. "Sam and I disagree a lot. It's why it's lucky we never married."

"Honey, that man has nothing in his life, nobody. He hasn't loved anybody since you left."

She didn't know about his dalliance with Rainetta Johnson, though that was probably mostly Rainetta making a pass at Sam, a handsome and still-in-shape former football player. I had a twinge of jealousy over the thought of the two of them alone in the Blue Heron Inn.

I gave her a quick hug again and stood. "I gotta go. I'm exhausted."

"Not so fast. Would you please bring me my jewelry box, honey?"

This could get into territory where I didn't want to tread. But she shooed me away to the bedroom. I brought the big cherry wood jewelry box back to the room and set it on the table beside her.

She opened it, then looked up at me. "You can have it all. Including the necklace your grandfather bought me that Christmas after we saw Rainetta Johnson in the movie down in Madison."

The box was filled with bona-fide antique gold jewelry, sparkly earrings and broaches, and pearl strands that Pauline wouldn't let anywhere near kindergarten kids.

My jaw went slack. "You're being silly. I can't take your jewelry."

"Honey, it'll help pay for doing what you have to do next in your life. It'll help you make choices. There's enough in here that you can double the size of your fudge shop or buy a ticket back to Los Angeles. What's your heart's desire?"

I stared blankly down at her jewelry. This was the oddest moment in my life. A shameful part of me wanted her jewelry because money was freedom in a way, but there was even more shame in the truth revealed in this moment: I wasn't sure what I wanted from life. She was right.

I closed the lid, picked up box, and then marched it back to her bedroom. When I returned, I said, "Grandma, I see your point. I wanted to set up a fudge shop, and yet I've been letting the church ladies take it over. I've been worrying about my old show, but I don't know why I care. And Sam's been trying to be a friend, and I could at least let him be just that instead of fearing he wants more. Does any of that make sense?"

She beamed. "It's a start. You've got a long way to go on setting priorities, but that's a start. Now come here."

We did one of those Belgian hugs that felt so good it could cure sprained or broken bones. My wrist was feeling a lot better already. I hoped I was helping her leg heal, too.

*　　*　　*

On Thursday morning Cody showed up at the shop with something akin to a cinnamon bear but with a tail that wagged. I was cleaning my copper kettles with one arm when the shaggy dog loped over to leap up at me and lick my face.

"Cody! Help!" I had kneeled down to meet the dog closer to his height, and I was laughing in between my shrieks. The dog's tongue was lapping all over my chin, where I'd likely swiped with a hand covered with the essence of cream and sugar.

Cody said, "Down, Harbor!"

The dog had big, perky flaps for ears, a long nose, and a huge swish of a tail. He was all puppy from the gangly look and big paws. He appeared assembled from parts of collie, curly poodle, and golden retriever with Dodge Ram truck for good measure. He was full of cockleburs and looked damp.

"Where did you get this thing?"

Cody had his arms firmly around the dog's neck now, though the attention seemed to have sped up the wag in the tail. "He was trotting down the middle of the street, lost. Sit, Harbor."

The dog plunked his hindquarters on the floor. The tail now thumped on the wood floor.

"He's obviously trained. Not bad for a puppy. Don't get attached," I chided.

"Harbor likes you. See how he stares at you? He's talking to you. He's smiling."

"He's panting. And how do you know he's called Harbor? Does he have a tag?"

"Nope. No collar. He jumped in the harbor, though, and looks like a Fishers' Harbor mascot, so I called him Harbor."

The dog's big brown eyes wouldn't leave me, which was disconcerting. "We have to call the Humane Society to see if anybody's missing him." Just what I needed this morning, a dog in my shop, a clear violation of the health code. Mercy Fogg could easily shut me down with this.

When Cody let go of Harbor, he rushed up to me again. I stuck my good arm out in time. "Harbor, no."

He complied, snuffling loudly along the glass-enclosed fudge shelves as if picking out his favorites. His panting tongue and nose smeared the glass.

Seeing Cody happy with the dog made me wonder about Cody and yesterday. "You're not mad at the sheriff questioning you again?"

"I'm mad. But he said I didn't have to be in jail right now."

"Why did he want you in jail?" I paused over the kettle I was wiping dry with a towel.

"He says my stories don't add up. My dad was really pissed about that. He thinks I want the attention to impress Bethany."

I was afraid to ask, but did anyway. "Do you want to impress her?"

"Sure."

"Did you lie? You know that murder is a serious issue."

"I don't know if I lied, Miss Oosterling. If Miss Fogg lied to me, how would I know? I'd repeat her lie, but I wouldn't be lying because I wouldn't know."

"Good point." I could see that sorting this out would require Sam's expertise, so I changed the subject. "Ranger, we can't have that pup over on our side. You'll have to tie him in the bait shop somewhere."

It was only six thirty in the morning, and the humane

shelter didn't open until ten o'clock, so I'd have to put up with the big gangly pup for a while. Harbor flounced in front of me and sat, as if begging me not to report him. His brown eyes beseeched me.

"All right," I said to the dog, feeling myself being sucked in like an idiot. "If you can behave, you don't need to be tied up."

I led Harbor over to the bait shop area, pulled a package of beef jerky off a wire and handed it to Cody to open. Harbor whirled about with excitement, his tail whopping bobbers off a shelf and onto the floor. They popped about like Ping-Pong balls all over the place. They were too small to be safe for him to mouth them as toys, so Cody and I had to pick them all up and retrieve one out of the dog's mouth. Harbor hopped up to lick my face again. We got more tail wags. I was exhausted already and it wasn't even seven in the morning.

Cody grabbed some towels and put them on the floor, then pointed to them. "Harbor, lie down."

And Harbor did. Go figure.

"Whew. Thanks, Ranger. You want to start a new fudge batch boiling for me? I have a hard time yet because of my wrist."

"Sure thing, Miss Oosterling. How long before your arm'll be healed?"

"With the way you bandaged it, soon. It feels better this morning already."

The back door banged. Isabelle walked in, looking oddly horrid, as if she'd had no sleep. Her pale skin was ashen. She'd tossed on a gray sweatshirt and sweatpants; it was uncharacteristic of her to be seen in public this way. And of all things, she was cradling her precious Steuben glass unicorn statue in her arms.

"What's wrong, Izzy?" I asked, unlocking the cash registers for the day.

"I can't believe you did that."

"Did what?" My gut lurched at her tone.

"Everybody was ready to go home today, and this morning the sheriff stops by—getting me out of bed at six, no less—to tell me and my guests they have to stay longer, that they're 'persons of interest.' You told the sheriff they're all suspects for murder and they all stole diamonds. The sheriff and his deputy are going through my inn right now. They're going to break my Steubens, Ava!"

She peered down at her unicorn as if it were a precious baby.

She took a deep breath before continuing, then sighed. "I'm sorry. I didn't mean to blame you."

"Let me go back up to the inn with you. I can handle Jordy."

Izzy slumped against the cash register counter. "It's not you I'm upset with. It's all of them. I can't take their squabbling anymore, Ava. I can't take their complaints about the choice of food or wine for dinner or lunch. They complain about my choice of music in the front hall. They complain about one another, mostly. But who cares! They're murderers and thieves."

She spun and left so fast she might have been a fairy riding out on her flying unicorn.

Cody said, "Wow. Maybe I should tell her that I said all those things to the sheriff, not you."

"No. Don't go up to the inn, Ranger. That's not a good idea."

I had a feeling this was going to be a very bad day.

Chapter 15

That Thursday wasn't all bad. I got so engrossed in the art of loafing fudge with one hand that time escaped me.

At ten that morning Destiny Hubbard and my grandfather walked down the pier. Both did a jig in the middle of the shop, which made Harbor leap from his bed of towels by the beer cooler. I was the only one there. Cody had gone to school, happily so with his new buzz cut. He said he was a "new man." I suspected he felt Bethany would love the look.

Gilpa crowed, "I'm a free man! Isn't Destiny great?"

Harbor had his paws on Destiny's shoulders before I could intervene. I couldn't do much with my bandaged arm but say, "Harbor, sit."

He did, his tail swishing the floor as he stared at me with his big brown orbs. I slipped him a piece of beef jerky.

Gilpa asked, "And who's this?"

I hugged my grandpa, explaining about Harbor being a stray, then asked Destiny, "How did you do it? Bail had to be enormous."

She was brushing dog hair off a red pantsuit that

made her cute as a Christmas elf. "I studied all the theories about Rainetta Johnson and convinced the authorities that with that much circumstantial evidence only and nothing concrete, they had to reduce the bail. Considerably."

Gilpa hauled an arm around Destiny's shoulders. "We got bail down to only this shop. They left my boat alone. I gotta go take a look at 'er and get myself ready for weekend tours."

I almost told him about the smoking engines, but didn't want to break his happy mood. He gathered tools, then hiked out. The bell clanked behind him. His footsteps faded on the wood pier.

Harbor watched him through the windows, then put his front paws up on the edge of the marble loafing table for a gander at my fudge.

"No, Harbor!" I raced to pull him down with one arm. "Sit."

He did. Then he snuck a lick of my hand.

I sighed. "At least he knows some tricks. Ranger found this mutt this morning. I have to call the Humane Society. And I have to wash my hands again. You want to come back while we talk?"

I headed to the kitchen.

Destiny's heels echoed on the floor. "Having a dog is good psychology. Maybe you should skip calling about him for a couple of days at least."

"Why?"

"Nobody looks guilty when they have a cute dog by their side. The press will be back when news leaks out about the Reeds and the other guests all possibly being arrested for a conspiracy. Nothing like this has ever happened in Wisconsin or maybe anywhere."

With the water running in the sink, I wasn't sure I'd heard her right. But when I asked her to repeat it as I dried my hands, the molecules in my body realigned. I thought of poor Izzy. "As much as I want publicity for my shop, there's a big downside to all this attention. It's stressful for everybody here in Fishers' Harbor."

"But you can't wish it away. You're going to have to deal with this for weeks to come."

I thought about the diamonds Pauline and I had left in Jeremy Stone's room. "Did they find anything yet?"

"Too early for me to know. And the sheriff isn't going to divulge anything until he feels like it. But because Gil Oosterling is my client, I'll of course stay vigilant and request anything that's public record."

My appreciation for this sharp slip of a young woman rose yet again. We headed back to the front just as Laura Rousseau surprised me by walking in with a huge box cradled in her arms. She was struggling to carry it because of her huge pregnancy bump and because Harbor kept leaping into the air to try to look in the box.

I introduced Laura to Harbor, and Destiny to the owner of the Luscious Ladle Bakery and Cooking School in Sister Bay. Cinnamon fragrance swirled around our heads, intoxicating us.

"Don't tell me you brought cinnamon rolls?" I helped her set the big box down on the register counter and tucked away the thought of developing cinnamon-bun-flavored fudge.

"Made with wheat from Washington Island," Laura said. Washington Island was off the northernmost tip of Door County. The wheat was famously used now in Wisconsin beers as well as baked goods. "We talked about doing an exchange to help cross-promote each other, so here I am. I'll leave my rolls here for sale if you'll give me Cinderella Pink Fudge for sale at my shop."

"And maybe you can convince Al Johnson's Restaurant to give out samples since you deliver bread to them." I was feeling on top of things again. Grandma was right; I just had to commit to something. My fudge had to be my priority. And it was going to suffice for a relationship for now. Although it might please Grandma, I couldn't encourage Sam. Besides, it was proven that eating chocolate increased brain activity and your heart rate more than passionate kissing did.

Laura agreed to the deal just as the back door banged. It was Isabelle again.

This time she was dressed in designer jeans and a V-necked, white cotton sweater. Her face had been scrubbed. She had a sheepish demeanor. Harbor seemed to sense something was amiss and lay down in a furry puddle in the middle of the floor.

Izzy already knew Laura, but I introduced her to Destiny. They were close to the same height, a matched pair of cuteness and chicness.

Izzy said, "Cody's the real reason the sheriff turned my world upside down today."

I sucked in my breath, ready for a fight in front of me, but Izzy laughed. "I came down to apologize, Ava. I'm stressed out from this murder. It's an awful thing when that happens in your own house."

"All is forgiven," I said, rushing to wrap her in a hug.

"I want to make it up to you. I was thinking about having another party that would feature your fudge. Maybe we could introduce a second new flavor, to make the party special."

This puzzled me. "Are you sure you're ready for another party?"

"No, but it wouldn't be at my place," she said.

Harbor came over to sniff her, then sat next to me and leaned against my legs while Izzy continued. "Since the party was supposed to be a fund-raiser to refurbish that old mansion that the village inherited, maybe we could find a way to have the party there?"

A candlelike glow popped to life inside me. "Have you been talking to Cody Fjelstad?"

"No, why?"

I told the women about Cody's wish for holding a prom party in the mansion. Prom was only a week from Saturday, unfortunately.

"Not much time at all." Izzy worried a lip with her teeth for only a moment. "But we can do it. I'll contribute cleaning supplies and round up the cleaning ladies I hired last fall when I took over the Blue Heron."

Laura volunteered to provide balloons. "I keep tons of them on hand for my baking school parties for kids. And I can bake bread bowls for special dips and special cupcakes. What's the color scheme?"

"It has to be pink," I said. "Cody said Bethany's favorite color is pink, and he's already planning to give her pink carnations."

Izzy said, "And of course your fudge is pink."

We laughed at how quickly we put together a prom party. Harbor barked, making us laugh harder.

"He's volunteering, too," Destiny said. "What can I do?"

I asked, "Can you look into our village codes? We might need permits fast. Our village president is all of nineteen. He might need guidance."

"Nineteen?" Destiny struck a modeling pose. "This is a cinch. I'll stop by to talk with him before I drive back to Sturgeon Bay."

I told her where Erik Gustafson lived, and then Destiny took off. Laura left right after her.

I headed back to finish loafing my fudge at the front of the store, Harbor following and settling at my feet, so close that I feared he'd trip me.

Isabelle shook her head. "He sure sticks by you, for some reason. Maybe he's afraid of me."

"I doubt that, Izzy. Maybe it's that perfume you're wearing. What is it?"

Isabelle flushed.

Kneading the silken dough under my hand, I said, "Don't tell me. It's Rainetta's?"

"What use was she going to get out of it? Her manager would have just tossed it."

What she said made sense, though her taking things from a dead woman was starting to feel unsettling. Maybe I was just too sensitive and not being practical. But then there was my trust issue. I trusted Izzy. She had a good heart, after all, and was being put through hell right now, what with the sheriff rifling through her things and questioning her guests again. Izzy had to feel adrift; she was in need of true friends. "Thanks, Izzy, for the party idea. I hope we can get that place in shape within nine days. It's a mess. Have you seen it lately?"

"I've never been inside. Too busy with my own place."

I told her about my sojourn there with Pauline two days ago and confessed about being pushed down the stairs.

She gasped. "My gosh. I really have been distracted.

Did you always have that wrist bandaged? I never noticed it until now."

I held up my left wrist. "I only started bandaging it yesterday. It was Cody's idea, and it feels better with the support. He thinks the Reeds are responsible. Or at least, I think that."

"Will and Hannah are always nervous, and they are constantly arguing."

"Cody thinks the Reeds tried to push him down the back stairs in your place, and I'm thinking that maybe they were in that mansion and tried to do the same to me."

"Do you suppose they were trying to hide diamonds over there?"

"Or other things from your place, too. Have you done an inventory lately?"

"No, but I did notice a couple of the glass paperweights missing, but I assume my guests are using them on their desks or something. I'm sure they're still at the inn. I'm always there, and so are the Reeds."

"Are you sure? What if they've been sneaking down your back stairs? Hannah came through the back door of my fudge shop on Tuesday to make a purchase of some kind, then left the same way."

"But they'd have to go through Jeremy Stone's room."

"He's never around. They'd have no problem stealing and sneaking things out."

Izzy got a horrified look. "Maybe we *should* look around that abandoned mansion."

"I don't know if that's wise, not without the sheriff with us." I suddenly didn't want to go back to the place for fear of finding all manner of stolen goods from Izzy's inn.

"But all the suspects are with the sheriff right now at my inn. This could be a perfect time to check out the mansion for the party. And if we find diamonds or my paperweights, that's a bonus."

Izzy appeared to be her old self again, and her plea sounded too adventurous to pass up. I said, "Help me put this fudge in a cooling pan. Then we'll go."

Moose Lindstrom walked in just then, banging the door all the way back to where it clanged the cowbell against the wall under the big picture window. He glanced at all the pink stuff on the shelves on my side, shuddered, then said, "Did ya know your grandfather's trying to blow himself up?"

Gilpa had an engine casing off. He appeared to be rewiring old, frazzled wires that were likely the reason for us smoking all the way back in the boat yesterday. Izzy and I stood safely on the pier with Moose.

I called over to Gilpa, "What're you doing? Moose says you're trying to kill yourself."

Gilpa didn't look up. "Tell Moose to mind his own business because I've got a business of my own to run."

It was heading toward ten thirty, which made me look up at Moose, who was standing between Izzy and me. I asked, "Aren't you usually out with a fishing tour at this time?"

Thursdays were pretty busy days for Moose and Gilpa because people started four-day fishing weekends then. A lot of Chicago people came up to Door County on Thursdays.

Moose harrumphed. "Coast Guard had us stay in this morning. Something about inspecting all vessels for illegal cargo. Wouldn't surprise me if it was about those diamonds in your fudge. Wouldn't take much to run a batch of fudge in my boat to a buyer out on the water." He chuckled. "Imagine hauling fudge as if it were some pirate's booty."

"Moose, that's exactly how I want people to feel about my fudge."

Gilpa called over, "You tell 'im, Ava Mathilde! Chocolate doubloons!"

Izzy tugged at my elbow. "Everybody's all right here. Let's get to the mansion before I have to go back to the surly lineup of guests I'm babysitting."

"They might need to be in a lineup soon," I said, following her up the pier and past my shop.

The shop building looked worn out today; I was seeing it through new eyes. Grandma's words from last night were resonating with me. She was right about setting priorities. If I were going to thrive here, I had to do something about our old building. Gilpa and I were just too cramped in it. But I also knew that Door County didn't let you destroy the historical integrity of buildings, such as remodeling too much or razing them to build something bigger. I didn't have enough money to move anywhere else, though. Harbor put his paws up on the inside windowsill as I passed the shop, emphasizing that the shop was no bigger than a giant dog house.

Izzy and I made our way down the dock area, past the parking lot, and across the street and past the back sides of condos and shops. We headed for the corner. We had one block after that to reach Main Street.

Izzy asked, "Do you suppose they'd really check boats for something like those stolen diamonds?"

"I suppose they could. But I think Moose was just spinning a fish tale of sorts."

"But they haven't found all the diamonds."

"How do you know that?" I asked cautiously, wondering if she'd heard about the stash in Jeremy Stone's room.

"Why else would the sheriff and his deputy be searching my place again?"

"For evidence on who strangled Rainetta. Is he searching her room again?"

"Yes."

"See. That's what they're after. Evidence."

It struck me that Izzy didn't know all that much about the crime, considering she was living among a bunch of weird guests who were blaming one another and her. But maybe she had a good policy—stay out of the fracas and thus be able to sleep. Jeremy Stone had told Pauline and me quite a bit about Rainetta's odd connection to the New York diamond heist. I felt that if Izzy knew about it, she'd be spilling her guts to me right now. But she wasn't. And I wasn't about to divulge what I'd been told because it would then compromise us all. Having my own secrets seemed like a safe thing at the moment. Izzy and I thought alike on that score. Keep your secrets; keep yourself safe.

As we walked up Main Street, heading east, one car went by. From the distance I heard the faint, melodic sound of kids laughing on the playground at school. The town was serene. All that had happened didn't seem possible for little Fishers' Harbor.

When we crossed the street, we stopped to stare for a moment at the mansion. The front window that Pauline had broken with her purse and tree branch to get in to help me was still uncovered.

"There're probably animals inside," I said.

Izzy said, "Maybe this wasn't such a good idea."

"We're here. Might as well take a quick look to see what we'll need to fix besides the window in order to hold the party."

Izzy followed me up the rickety front steps and onto the porch. A couple of slats of yellow siding rattled in the wind next to the front door. I lifted the loose siding to peek under it.

"It's brick. This isn't the original siding."

"If the brick is in such bad shape that they had to cover it, this place may need to be torn down. Maybe we should just leave."

"But this was your idea."

"I know. I've changed my mind. I don't like spooky places."

But we ventured inside. The dust on the floor still retained the imprints from Pauline and me. And there were small animal tracks, probably those of a squirrel.

The mustiness made me sneeze. The space was bigger even than Izzy's foyer and entrance hall. Hers was taken up by a central staircase; here the staircase was much smaller and off to the right wall.

Because it was so dim, I looked around for a light switch in the vague hope there might be electricity. Izzy found a switch first, but when she flipped the toggle no bulbs popped on in the lights overhead or in the sconces next to a double door ahead of us.

She said, "Maybe there's a circuit breaker box or fuses in the basement that just need to be turned on."

I laughed then. "And you're expecting me to go down there alone."

"That would be nice." Hope scored her face.

"Chicken. It's just a basement." I looked about. "Now, where to find the door?"

"Mine's in my kitchen," she suggested.

We went through the double doors straight ahead, which opened to a large room that had to have once been a dining hall that I estimated could easily seat thirty people. The entire Oosterlings' Live Bait, Bobbers & Belgian Fudge could fit inside the room. Beyond that, we entered the kitchen and found the basement door. When I opened it I realized I had no flashlight, but light filtered in below, obviously from the basement window I'd seen from the outside on Tuesday. I made my way down the wooden steps.

Izzy waited at the top of the stairs.

My work boots made a heavy *clunk* with each step, which spooked me out.

I finally made it to the bottom, then felt better right away because the meager light from the cloudy basement window revealed a decent enough floor made of expensive but old green, white, and black tiles of the kind I'd seen in the old-style bathroom at my manager's house in Los Angeles. At least this wasn't some old root cellar, though those often existed in Door County under anything built prior to refrigeration, which this was.

Not seeing a breaker box anywhere ahead of me or to the right, I took a left turn around a post next to the staircase to head into the darker maw of the basement. What I saw sent a shrill scream spewing from me.

I raced back up the stairs two at a time. I bowled over Izzy.

We both went sprawling across the linoleum, sliding right up to the cabinets on the far side of the room. I didn't even feel my bad wrist because of the adrenaline shooting through me. "Izzy, there's a body down there!"

"What?"

"A body!"

"Oh my God! Are you sure?"

Disbelieving myself, I ventured back down the stairs, faster this time, my boots clunking louder. Izzy came after me, sucked up against my back.

When we got to the bottom of the staircase and then turned, there he was. Sprawled across the tiles. A big spot next to his head. Dried blood?

"We'd better call Jordy," I said.

Izzy ventured around me for a closer look. "I think I know this person." She stepped back toward me, her hand over her heart. "I do know him."

"Who is he?"

"Rainetta Johnson's manager."

A feeling akin to a sudden flu overwhelmed me. "Cody," I whispered with dread.

"Cody what?" Isabelle asked.

"He . . . He said he was here the other night . . ."

"Oh no." Izzy groaned. "You think . . . Cody did it?"

Chapter 16

The main show by noon that Thursday was the mansion on Main Street in Fishers' Harbor. Gusty winds frustrated three news vans that were trying to set up their satellite dishes along the street. Camera people braced themselves against the cold May breezes. The sun was out, but the temperature was in the fifties. Jackets flapped on everybody, and a couple of women reporters were constantly removing their coiffed hair from their mouths as they talked to unknown millions. I saw a network's peacock logo on a microphone.

Isabelle and I had run back to our respective places after finding the body. I'd called 911 on my cell, but the sheriff was at the Blue Heron Inn already so everything happened quickly. The medical examiner was inside the mansion now. Izzy and I stood on the porch, me in my red jacket and her in a stylish cobalt blue trench coat. We were a "Mutt and Jeff" team adrift between the camera people on the lawn and the sheriff and ME in the house. Jordy had asked us to come back to the place with him to retrace our steps.

I'd also called Sam Peterson. He was wending his way through the growing crowd on the lawn, where spooky shadows were made by the noon sun being blocked by the limbs of craggy oak trees. Once Sam finally reached the porch, I fell into his arms.

"Oh, Sam," I whispered. "There's a connection to Cody again."

"He's not a murderer."

Izzy whispered, "But he was here."

With grave concern casting a shadow over Sam's face, he asked me, "When was he here? Just now?"

"No," I said, my teeth chattering more from nervousness than the cold. "A couple of days ago." My brain could barely process the horror of it. "No, three days ago now. He said he was here Monday afternoon and heard noises in the basement. It spooked him out so much he said he didn't want to live here after all."

"But he was thrilled that the prom party would be held here."

"Probably because I volunteered to chaperone it. He knew there'd be others around. This place wouldn't be scary because he wouldn't be alone."

"Where is he now?"

"I assume at school. He was excited about showing Bethany his new haircut." Tears stung my eyes. "Do you think he could have harmed Rainetta and this man and not realize he killed them? They were accidents? Maybe he was stealing something and they tried to stop him and he panicked?"

"Stop talking, Ava. Trust me. He's not capable of these things." But his Adam's apple bobbed. He'd swallowed hard, as if he wasn't so sure about Cody anymore. "I'll go inform his parents right now before they get another call from the sheriff's department. Arlene and Tom are going to want to move away after this." Sam gave me another hug. "Hang in there, Ava. Cody didn't murder this guy. Or Rainetta. Cody needs you to believe in him, even if he changes his story to suit the day of the week. That's just him. Okay?"

"Thanks, Sam."

After he left, Isabelle and I stood with our arms around each other, visibly vibrating with our shivers, waiting for the sheriff to come out. I stared at the broken window, realizing now that a dead man had been lying in the basement when I'd fallen down the stairs on Tuesday.

The front door of the mansion creaked open. The sheriff's deputy held open the door. Volunteer EMTs Nancy and Ronny Jenks were on each end of the stretcher, which carried a body bag. We moved aside, then watched them navigate the few steps to the lawn. The ambulance was only a few feet away, parked on the meager spring grass. Within a minute, Ronny and Nancy steered the vehicle through the quiet crowd, finally wending around the news vans to get back onto Main Street.

But as soon as the ambulance disappeared, the newspeople crushed up the porch steps toward Sheriff Tollefson, Isabelle Boone, and me.

The reporter who'd called me a fudge "sculptor" days ago, yelled out, "Was your fudge involved this time, Miss Oosterling? Was fatal fudge found in the basement?"

So much for being my friend. Sheriff Tollefson herded Izzy and me inside the mansion and closed the door.

Izzy gasped, "Did you hear her?"

"Fickle-faced," I said, "and it's too bad Pauline isn't here. She would have loved the 'fatal fudge found' question." I noticed Sheriff Tollefson acting oddly. "Don't tell me my fudge was found down there?"

"Unfortunately for you, it was."

*   *   *

I couldn't believe it. Cinderella Pink Fudge was found in Conrad Webb's jacket pockets. He had two pieces, both with diamonds in them.

After Sheriff Tollefson mollified the news hounds by speaking to them on the front porch, he escorted me back to Oosterlings' Live Bait, Bobbers & Belgian Fudge. Isabelle hurried back to the Blue Heron Inn to face her angry guests.

Harbor was gone, which made me panic until I rushed back outside to look down the pier. He was with Gilpa in *Sophie's Journey*. I heard lots of cursing, which Harbor seemed to like. He was wagging his fluffy puppy tail rapidly.

When I ducked back inside, I couldn't think. Not with the sheriff standing there in his uniform and shiny star, hanging on to his hat in his hands and with his gun on his belt. So I grabbed a fresh apron for myself and tossed another to Jordy.

"What's this?" he stammered, catching it with one hand.

"I'm making fudge before you take all my ingredients again."

"I won't be doing that this time."

"Why not?"

"The fudge he had was old, likely from the batch you made for Sunday."

I was curious. "Did you taste it?"

"Now, why would I put evidence in my mouth?"

With a sigh, I said smoothly, "I was hoping to know what kind of shelf life it had, which could help you pinpoint the time of the murder. Working with cocoa butter and cream is tricky. White chocolate is made mostly from cocoa butter and it melts easier. But white chocolate holds flavors longer, and it coats the mouth more than dark chocolate. The taste sensation is more intense with white chocolate. The ten thousand taste buds inside your mouth send a big flag to the anterior cingulate in your brain, and this explosion creates emotions and your mood, Jordy. Are you in a white chocolate mood today or a dark chocolate mood? That's why infusing taste sensations into white chocolate is like nuclear science. The whole thing is either perfect or it blows up. Do you want me to draw you pictures again?"

"No!" He was sweating. "Stop it."

"You weren't good with science in school, were you?"

Jordy shook his head in derision that tickled something inside me. He said, "No more diagrams of chemical formulas. This is a murder case, not kindergarten drawing time and not science class."

"Cody didn't murder those people. And neither did I."

"Everybody's a suspect until I hear a confession."

"Did you get anything close to that earlier today from Will and Hannah Reed?"

"Well, no."

"You didn't try hard enough. This murder case is all about simple crystals—diamonds or fudge. Let me show you what it takes to make fudge. Maybe if you understand the process, it'll help you see how ridiculous it would be for me, Cody, or Gilpa to be involved with a murder using fudge. But maybe we can come up with some angle on the diamonds that will help us."

"Us?"

"Jordy, the diamonds were found here in my fudge, so come into my 'science lab.' You have no choice if you and I want to solve this case."

I led Jordy back to my kitchen and pantry. I held up my wrapped arm. He got the picture—I needed help. He collected the cream, butter, and the kilos of white chocolate bars that had come in yesterday. I was used to working with chocolate in the form of chips or coins, but I liked the bars better.

"They look like bars of gold," he said.

"I like to think my fudge is that valuable. Have you checked the commodities market recently for the price of gold?"

He looked afraid of my facts again, so I added, "Gold bars are worth thousands of dollars."

"We're here to talk about diamonds."

"And people like the Reeds and Earlywines who might be in the market for such things."

By now he had his arms filled with "gold" bars, pounds of butter, and containers of cream.

"Where do you get all this stuff?" Jordy asked. "There's still a chance that your suppliers had something to do with the diamonds."

"The dairy products are from our farm, Jordy. Mom and Dad aren't getting diamonds out of those udders. This chocolate came straight from Belgium in five-kilo boxes containing foil-wrapped bars—like gold. The luster dust came from France, not New York where the heist was."

"I know."

"You do?"

"We've been tracing the paper trail and Internet trail of the deliveries coming here."

"Looking for a connection to the diamonds? I'm impressed, Jordy."

He heaved a shoulder up in a shrug, which told me he

hadn't found a connection yet. I continued on with the analysis of my fudge ingredients.

I had also ordered glucose in big jugs, which is like corn syrup. I pointed out to Jordy, "It's harder to hide small diamonds in liquid glucose. It's a super-refined sugar." Glucose was commonly used in fancy candies. I was ready to experiment with using a Belgian candy chocolate glaze on top of my fudge, which was paintable.

Jordy was impressed with all the gadgets like my Felchlin chocolate warmer, my induction burners, which slid out on a tray from under a cabinet and didn't use any flame, and my industrial microwave that could handle stainless-steel pans inside of it. He took a look at the framed pieces of paper on the wall that showed I was certified in safe food handling. That made me nervous.

"Mercy must have been sad to see those," Jordy mused. "Foiled her attempt to shut you down but good."

Jordy didn't realize I didn't yet have a license to operate. I had just up and started making fudge two weeks ago when I arrived and moved in. Somehow Mercy had missed that lack of an operator's license, too, in her ardor to find my place unclean and unsafe.

"Do you know why she hates me so much?"

"She doesn't hate anybody. She's probably jealous of you and wishes you could be friends."

I scoffed. "Jealous?"

We headed to the front as Jordy said, "She's lonely, Ava. She got voted out of office, and now she has no purpose. You have a purpose with your shop. Mercy's always been a common laborer, worked in factories and been a truck driver most of her life before she got elected."

"I didn't know that." He was certainly making my

head spin in a new direction about Mercy, but I still didn't trust her. "Her nastiness seems to be a symptom of something deeper going on, Jordy."

"She lacks a lot of self-confidence maybe. She never went to college, like some people around here who've scratched out a living just fine without it."

The blood drained from my body to pool in my feet, making me feel hollow. I remembered spouting my snarky "college sorority girl" remark at Mercy right in front of the reporters, and Mercy getting madder after that. I'd been cruel, though unintentionally, of course. But still, I felt bad about my treatment of Mercy.

I said to Jordy, "I've found out recently from Cody that she's really on our side in all this murder investigation. She's been sniffing around on her own. She thinks the Reeds are your culprits."

"What else has she found out?"

"You'll have to ask her. And Cody, man to man this time, not sheriff to perpetrator. To Mercy's credit, she probably respected Cody more than the rest of us and made Cody her deputy of sorts, and that's why he got suckered into doing things that are wrong. I'm not sure those things were even Mercy's fault. Cody's impulsive by nature and just does things his way. The only thing that kid wants more than anything is to wear a badge."

"That puts a new spin on things for me. Thanks, Ava."

Jordy put down all the supplies on my cash register counter. With the apron covering up his badge and his boyish brown hair, Jordy was far less intimidating, though his pistol holster still stuck out from his side. He helped me pour ingredients into the boiler next to the copper kettles.

He said, "Not much for customers today."

"Well, besides you telling all the newspeople we wouldn't be talking for a couple of days until the ME's report comes out, there's the issue of 'pink.'"

"Pink?"

As I handed him the four-foot wooden stir ladle, I nodded toward the pink paper on the cash register counter, pink ribbons for tying up fudge gifts, and over on the shelving units, pink accessories for girls and women, including pink coin purses and teacups for both moms and daughters. "It seems in my quest to draw women down to the docks, I've also kept the men away."

"Then come up with manly fudge."

"The church ladies have tried that. They made a few flavors with nuts. Still didn't do much."

Jordy chuckled. "Men like grease and dirt under their nails. Think of a flavor for that."

"The flavor of dirt? Grease?"

He shrugged as he stirred. "You're the fudge expert. I'm only the expert on figuring out who murdered Rainetta Johnson and Conrad Webb."

"And neither one of us is doing all that well, are we?"

"At the moment, no."

It was a huge thing for Jordy to admit defeat. I felt sorry for him. But not too sorry. I was still scared that I was a silver bracelet away from being hauled off to jail. How had my fudge ended up with Conrad Webb? There was also Gilpa being under suspicion for stealing Rainetta's necklace and diamonds. And unfortunately, I'd hidden those things on his boat, so now we could easily be accused of smuggling them out to other boats on Lake Michigan. I could see that some high-powered New York attorney wouldn't have much to do to blame us and get a murderer off scot-free. Destiny Hubbard wouldn't have a chance. She was smart, but inexperienced.

As I watched Jordy stir the creamy confection goo over the heat, I asked, "Did you find any more diamonds at the Blue Heron Inn this morning?"

"Not a damn one," he said.

What had happened to those diamonds Pauline and I had hidden in Jeremy's room? Maybe Pauline hid them too well. I hadn't even thought to ask her where she'd hidden them. Or had Jeremy or somebody else found them already and taken them off the property? That could be, but where? I promised myself to inspect every inch of my entire shop again soon.

"Moose said he thought the Coast Guard was inspecting boats for stolen goods. Do you know what that's about?"

Jordy stopped stirring. "Our office is working with them, yes. And, yes, we're wondering if there's more than just the smuggling of diamonds going on. Don't tell the media."

My heartbeat sped up. "So it's true. You're looking for pirates."

"I wouldn't say that." He took off his apron and handed it to me.

I laid the apron on the counter, and with my throat so dry, I could hardly swallow, I ventured into treacherous waters. "Pauline Mertens and I saw the Earlywines the other day with a pouch of diamonds."

That made him pause in his step and put on his official hat. "A pouch? Full of diamonds?"

"Yes. I have to assume they stole them or got handed them by somebody at the inn. I thought at first they stole them from Rainetta Johnson, but I'm not sure anymore.

I don't think Rainetta knew that this was all swirling around her."

"What about her manager?"

"Jordy, there's a possibility he was behind it all. Rainetta's Q Score in Hollywood tanked a long time ago, so maybe he wasn't doing well financially. He also likely knew about the family feud over the diamonds."

"And how did you know about her connection to that feud? How'd you know she was part of that family?"

"Jeremy Stone."

"I'll have another talk with him."

I ached to suggest that Jordy inspect Jeremy's room for hidden diamonds, but something stopped me. I guessed it was trust. I trusted Jeremy Stone to have told me the truth. I couldn't blow that trust and get him arrested, even if I didn't like the guy. Besides, with my luck Pauline would confess and point the finger at me and I'd be behind bars in the blink of an eye.

I had a bigger challenge in front of me. What flavor of fudge would entice men back to the bait shop? Jordy said dirt and grease would work. All of us ate a certain amount of "grease" or cooking oil when we enjoyed our fried cheese curds, but cooking oil didn't belong in fudge. As for dirt, I'd just read a foodie blog about Europeans and Japanese chefs putting dirt in their dishes. But I wasn't about to toss some of our Door County sand and clay into my fudge. But as I stirred the bubbling ingredients with the wooden ladle while staring at the bobbers, bait, and snacks over on Gilpa's side of the shop, ideas began to pop into my head.

Chapter 17

I started a second batch of fudge, this one with extra-dark Belgian chocolate. Now I had a white batch with vanilla but no cherries cooling in one copper kettle and the boiler cooking up a dark batch. I realized I needed somebody to whip the fudge mixture in the copper kettles. My wrist still wasn't up to the task. I hadn't heard from Sam yet, or Cody, and I didn't dare call. I knew I'd hear any bad news soon enough. With the sheriff just up the hill at the Blue Heron Inn, the bad news was bound to run down the hill, inundating me again like a flooding river.

I tromped down the pier to *Sophie's Journey*. Gilpa was covered in oil again, and even worse, so was Harbor. The once cinnamon-colored, curly dog now looked like he'd been used to clean out a chimney.

"Gilpa, what in the world happened?"

"I had a bucket of rusty bolts sitting in a can of oil, and he tripped over it. And then he rolled in it before I could stop him."

"I'm sorry. I'm sure he'll be back with his owner within the day." I called the animal shelter on the spot to report our odd dog. Then I got back to business. "I was wondering if you could help me whip the fudge, but I can see that's a bad idea at the moment."

"Why not ask your grandma?"

"Her leg won't let her stand."

"Perch her on a tall stool. She's bored watching all that TV. She told me, too, she didn't much like her church-lady friends taking over your store like they did. She didn't mean for that to happen."

"I know. But that was my fault. I'm in charge now. Because of Grandma." The memory of her lecture made me feel taller and prouder. "I'll go ask her right now if she'll come over."

Grandma Sophie acted like I'd just given her the biggest honor in her life. I helped her hobble on her crutches across the street, then mince her way over the threshold of the back door. She hobbled with my help to the front shop area, where she took over stirring bubbling dark chocolate that was about ready to whip in the copper kettles. She smiled as she sniffed approval. "The cows are being fed good hay. That fudge smells like the clover and alfalfa blossoms in the cream."

"Ah, just like we're making fine wine," I said. "The wasps and flowers imbue the Door County grapes with unique flavors of our region."

"And the Oosterling cows and the Oosterling hay made on our Door County land make the best fudge anywhere. Just like grass-fed cows makes the best cheese. What's in the earth ends up in your fudge."

"We should be able to taste the minerals from the soil that grows the alfalfa that the cows eat and turn into the rich milk that makes my fudge."

She laughed. "And if we can taste the soil of Door County, then we can taste the rain that leeched through the dirt and was sucked up by the alfalfa to make the blossoms that the cows ate to make the cream that's in this batch of fudge." She pointed down at the batch of hot, dark, creamy chocolate fudge steaming in the boiler.

Grandma and I loved these nature games. She was scientifically minded like I was.

"Food fit for finicky fairies," I said, doing my Pauline Mertens impression.

As I crossed over to Gilpa's aisles in search of the one tall stool we owned so that Grandma could sit on a perch, I said, "Jordy was here earlier, and he said that I should have dirt as a fudge flavor. He said I'd get men buying fudge with that."

"Of course, nobody would actually eat dirt."

"Some chefs have tried it."

Her eyebrows rose.

I laughed. "It's true! Don't worry. No dirt in my fudge." I dragged the tall stool next to a copper kettle.

Grandma said, "Dirt holds its own secret codes. You can think up your own secret code of men, with something other than dirt. Let's think about what men love to eat and drink. Some flavor has to pop into our heads for your fudge."

A secret code. The phrase sparked an idea about the murder. I had to catch up with Jordy Tollefson and Jeremy Stone. The reason all the guests at the inn seemed to be involved with the diamonds was probably that they were. They all shared some secret. I was taking a chance by tipping my hand with a reporter like Jeremy Stone, but I had to try. The answer to who committed the murder lurked at the outer edges of my brain, like the fog off Lake Michigan rolling in and hanging around at the docks but not quite reaching my fudge shop door.

"Grandma, I have to go up to the inn right away and see Jordy."

I helped Grandma pour the mixture into the kettle for cooling. She had two kettles to tend now, one with white chocolate and the other with dark. I figured if nothing turned into fudge, I'd take it up to the Luscious Ladle and Laura could use it for topping on a cake. I gave Grandma the long-handled, stainless-steel spatula and the walnut one, with directions about how to use them.

She asked, "But what new kind of fudge flavor am I making?"

I looked around the bait shop area. Crazy ideas came to my brain, and I didn't even stop to analyze my science. I scribbled some quick instructions on a piece of paper. "Here's our next flavor. It's the secret code of men, Grandma, and we'll also make another flavor that's the secret code flavor for little boys."

She squinted at my hasty diagram. "Oh my, this is over the top. You sure you want to try this with fudge?"

"Grandma, if that doesn't attract men, nothing will."

Then I took off, my head swirling with clues going back to the party on Sunday.

I was huffing and puffing by the time I travailed the steep grade to the Blue Heron Inn. The Reeds' arguing drifted to the outdoors. I didn't bother knocking or ringing the bell. I walked in to find the husband and wife practically stalking each other, barely missing the Steuben glass pieces. Other guests were in the front hall, too.

Boyd Earlywine halted when he saw me. He had a beer in hand. "You! You and that sheriff are keeping us hostage in this miserable house. I want to go home. I can't believe you almost killed a man this afternoon." He guzzled his beer as he trooped up the blue stairs.

John Schultz trotted out next from the dining room, carrying a beer. "I need to get back to Milwaukee by tomorrow for a convention."

They must have drank all of Izzy's wine by now and had moved on to any beer she had in her refrigerator. I pleaded, "What am I supposed to do about any of your lives?"

"Stop making fudge!" Hannah Reed said.

John said, "I heard they found more fudge killed the guy. The same fudge that was here on Sunday, so now we're in lockdown again while they look for more hot pink fudge."

I could see why Isabelle was going out of her mind with these people. I said to John, "I doubt you have to be anywhere by tomorrow. You're probably lying about having any job, just like you lied about being out on the boat with my grandfather on Sunday."

He sputtered beer off his lips.

"Yes," I said, punctuating my words by stabbing his chest with my index finger, "you're a big fat liar. How dare you? My friend even likes you."

"She does? I can offer her discount tickets to the Brewers games."

"Oh, stop it, you big fake. You're no travel agent or tour guide. You just say that so you can get into places for free. Shame on you." I stepped around him and marched up the stairs.

The Earlywines were in their room talking loudly again. I was tempted to stop and listen, but moved on down the hall. The sheriff was inside Jeremy Stone's room with Jeremy and Isabelle, the door ajar. I stepped inside, then closed the door. "They're all in it together. Maybe you're in it with them, Jeremy. Are you? They're splitting up the diamonds so none of them are caught with the whole treasure chest."

"Slow down," Jordy said, rising to offer his space on this end of the love seat.

Isabelle was looking up in wide-eyed wonder at me from the other end of the love seat. I sat down in Jordy's spot. My body hummed with nervous energy. My theory could solve the case. I hoped.

Jordy stood between the couches, his arms crossed. "Now what's got your undies in a bunch?"

"Jordy, you're letting them all get away with murder. I think they know who did it, but aren't saying because they're all packing diamonds to take home."

"We haven't found any on them," he said.

"Not yet. Because mostly you've found them hidden in my shop or in my fudge." I ached to ask where the diamonds were in this room to prove my theory. I gave Jeremy a stern look that made his crooked nose twitch. I couldn't tell if he was only nervous or guilty. I forced myself to still trust him, so I didn't say a word. Instead, I said to Jordy, "You've hauled in me and my grandfather for the crimes, and my employee, Cody, but you haven't arrested any of these yahoos. If you arrest any of them, they'll start spilling one another's secrets."

"Tattle on one another?" Jordy asked, crossing his arms while blocking the door.

"Exactly," I said. "They're on the verge of doing it now. The other day I overheard the Earlywines say they came here for something valuable. They're professors who should still be teaching. The semester isn't over, so isn't it odd they drove up from Madison to come here? And the Reeds came all the way from New York before the tourist season opens, when it's still chilly. Even Taylor

Chin-Chavez is a mystery, but we know she could probably use some money. We don't know her exact connection to the rest of them, but if you arrested her, I suspect she'd begin to spill her secrets, too."

"Arrest them all? You seem to have forgotten that I need cause to do that. I can't just arrest people."

"I'm the one who had diamonds put in my fudge. Somebody wants to pin this on me. No, all of them want to do that. It's a true conspiracy, Jordy."

"This isn't your television show where we can just make up things as we go along."

Now, that made me really mad. "Writing a TV script takes weeks of hard work. You have to gather the ideas together in the staff room, toss them into the middle of the table, then cook up the outline. From there, you stir, revise, see if it's tasty, revise again, and then make sure the story and dialogue pass muster with the actors."

"So writing for TV is like making your Fairy Tale Fudge," Jordy said with a sigh. "And speaking of actors, Rainetta and her manager weren't pleased with your fudge. You're still not entirely cleared of suspicion by the DA. We found your fingerprints all over Rainetta's room, a note card from you to her, and six messages on her phone from you practically begging her to invest in your fudge. Something about her helping you promote your fudge for the swag bags?"

My stomach acid did a big flip-flop. "Those are the gift bags given to all the nominees at the Oscars and Emmy Awards."

"I know that. I'm not an idiot. My point is that you have a lot of interest in this woman who's dead. Why were you in her room, as in all over it with your fingers? And did you meet up with the manager at the mansion, too? I heard you were over there. We'll likely find your fingerprints all over that place as well. This is beginning to look more than circumstantial."

My blood pressure was zooming. Jordy had turned on me.

I explained, "I did sneak into her room a couple of times." I gave a sheepish look at Isabelle. "Sorry, Izzy, but I snuck in on Friday night and left the note in Rainetta's room when you were at the fish boil. And I looked around again after she was murdered because I wanted to help solve this fast because it marred our reputations."

I pleaded with Jordy, "But that's all it was, me trying to help you. I didn't want to go to jail. I didn't murder anybody. Trust me. And how can I possibly trust you when you sneak things out of my kitchen. What did you find, Jordy?"

His face burned red. "Nothing."

"You took something."

"Your measuring spoon set. My deputy missed it. I'm having it tested and fingerprinted."

"Tested? Fingerprinted? Why? You think I used it to spoon poison into my fudge?"

"It's a common tool used to measure all kinds of things, from illegal drugs to diamonds. Somebody could've used it recently for all sorts of things."

"Somebody like the crazies staying in Izzy's inn."

Izzy held up a hand. "I like her notion of them all be-ing in cahoots."

Jeremy leaned forward. "Arrest everybody? Clean out the inn? Can I get the exclusive on this?"

Izzy said, "If you arrest them all at once, they'd clam up with their lawyers. What if you could take all of them out for a boat tour together? They could relax, start talking about things, maybe divulge a secret or two, and they can't get away unless they fall overboard and drown."

I blinked at her perfect solution. "Pauline and I will go along to stir things up."

"You're damn good at that," Jordy said, again niggling my blood pressure. He opened the door, ready to leave. "I'd advise you to stop interfering, Ava, in this investigation. Putting yourself in the middle of Lake Michigan with a bunch of possible suspects could get you into more trouble than you already have."

He closed the door behind him with a loud *thunk* to punctuate his words.

Jeremy, Izzy, and I glanced at one another.

Izzy said, "The idea of getting out for some fresh air on Lake Michigan sounds good, no matter what the real purpose."

"Relaxing is the real purpose," I said. "At least the one we'll tell them. Jeremy can take notes."

He said, "You heard the sheriff. He warned you. And they're not going to say anything with me taking notes."

"Well," I said, swallowing hard, "maybe tell them you found diamonds hidden in your room so they feel like you're one of them."

His nose twitched. He paled. It was obvious to me that Jeremy had found the pouch of diamonds Pauline had hidden in this room. He finally said, "I suppose I could plant a small lie like that. Just to stir things up, as you put it."

Isabelle said, "Is there any chance Gil's boat is ready now? I'm desperate to find some peace again."

We could hear the Reeds still going at it downstairs, and now John Schultz's voice rose, too. A young woman's voice—Taylor's probably—said something like, "Shut up, maggots!"

Feeling the urgency, I offered, "I'll go ask Gilpa right now. You don't mind if I go down the back stairs?"

As the arguing crescendoed downstairs, I left via the quiet safety of the back stairs leading from Jeremy's room.

To my shock, when I got to the pier, I found that Gilpa had the steering mechanism pulled apart in his boat. My body fizzed with frustration.

"Gilpa, we need your boat. Now."

"It'll be ready by tomorrow."

"That won't do. Isabelle needs you to take her guests on tour now. Before they bust up her place. We're on a mission."

"Do tell. Huh."

He was still covered in grease. Harbor was, too. He panted, plunking his big fuzzy puppy paws on the edge of the boat, about to leap off to get to me.

I backed up enough to discourage Harbor from jumping out at me in my white shirt.

Gilpa said, with the steering wheel in his hands, "Tomorrow is soon enough."

"You don't understand. If we don't figure out who killed Rainetta and her manager, you and I could be headed for jail or at least some very big trouble. The sheriff's got my fingerprints and other things that might put me in a poor light."

"Do tell?" His shoulders sagged.

"I'm sorry. I'll explain it all later. I've just been trying to help. We need your boat."

"We have Destiny."

"She's no match for a half dozen lawyers from New York firms coming after us. If all these people leave, we're up a creek. Jordy can hold them here for only so long before all their lawyers start complaining. A week is a reasonable time, and most of them have been here since last Thursday or Friday. Tomorrow is Friday, Gilpa. We need a boat. Now."

I paused to catch my breath. I wasn't used to such speeches. It dawned on me that maybe I would have been more successful on staff at my TV show if I'd spoken up like this. I told Gilpa about Isabelle's plan. "You're easy to talk to. You get things out of people. That's why it'd be good if you took them on a tour. You can figure this out with me."

He plopped his tall, wiry frame down on an overturned bucket with the steering wheel in his hands. Harbor chewed on it instantly as if it were his toy. "The boat's not going to be ready."

Gilpa looked so sad that I couldn't bear it. "What do you mean?" I asked.

"There's something wrong in the wiring. I haven't figured it out yet."

I hopped aboard, letting Harbor rub his oily dog hair on my jeans as he leaned against me while wagging his tail.

"Gilpa, maybe it's time to make a change. The wiring is shot. Beyond repair. Why do you insist on nursing this decrepit boat like you do?"

"Honey, why did you stick it out in Los Angeles all those years with that TV show?"

His brown eyes peered at me with something like the luster dust I used for the fairy sparkles on my fudge. He already knew my answer.

But I confessed. "Because I was stubborn. I wanted it to work out for me. Too much pride."

"And I'm a cheapskate, too."

"No, you're Belgian."

That brought a smile to his lips. His brown eyes twinkled.

I got braver. Or more desperate. "What if we try something new today? Like a new boat?"

"Can you conjure a boat with your fairy fudge dust?" He looked about the docks and small marina in the cove; then his gaze caught mine looking over at the *Super Catch I*. "Oh no. Not that. We're not renting that today. We can't afford it."

"We're not going to have to pay for it. Your attorney, Destiny Hubbard, will rent it for us. Put it on our tab. When Destiny sues the murderers for all the damages to my business and yours, Destiny will have the other side's lawyers arrange for payment for it."

Gilpa smiled. "That's a right smart plan. But are you sure the sheriff would be okay with us all going out for a tour?"

Jordy's warning to stay out of trouble echoed inside my head, but he hadn't barred the Blue Heron Inn's guests from leaving the inn. "He's asked the guests to stay in Fishers' Harbor, and we plan to return to Fishers' Harbor after our sojourn on the water. I don't see how Jordy can object to that. Besides, I think you'd look debonair, Gilpa, behind the controls of the *Super Catch I*."

By three o'clock that Thursday afternoon, Gilpa was at the helm of the *Super Catch I*. On board were me, Pauline Mertens, the Reeds, the Earlywines, Taylor Chin-Chavez, John Schultz, and Jeremy Stone. Isabelle stayed behind. I called Sam to see if Cody could come over to the shop to watch Harbor and help Grandma. I brought along the batch of Cinderella Pink Fudge I'd made yesterday, just to keep the murder theme in front of everybody.

It didn't take us long to stir up more than the cold waters on Lake Michigan.

Chapter 18

Pauline didn't seem to mind that John Schultz was a liar; she was so excited about the prospect of being with him on a boat tour that she was littering my cottage's floor with alliterative lettering dropping out of her mouth. I'd gone to my cottage to get a sweatshirt and jacket; we'd frozen yesterday in our journcy to find Cody. Pauline now wore a heavy Scandinavian sweater she'd bought years ago at the gift shop of Al Johnson's Restaurant in Sister Bay. She also had on grubby rubber shoes, much better for getting wet than her fancy pumps.

"Those pumps were perfect before you popped me in the pool," she said, still upset. "It was the first time I was a fashionista at school, if only for five minutes when I changed clothes, but as always when I'm with you, the flying fickle finger of fate finished me."

We were aboard the *Super Catch I* at three o'clock with Gilpa beaming at the helm. He'd showered off most of the grease and oil, though some lingered in his hair. If you got close enough to him, you smelled WD-40 instead of Old Spice. But man oh man was he happy, grinning from ear to ear, a kid in a candy store, as the saying goes.

At first, the guests of Isabelle Boone's Blue Heron Inn came aboard in polite wonder, too. They'd been told that the tour was a gift of the townspeople. But Jeremy Stone, Gilpa, and I knew the truth. We hoped to net information—if not confessions—out of this school of diamond filchers and murderers.

The boat was a thirty-two-foot Grady-White, big as a house around here. When Gilpa started her up and backed off the pier, his face opened in admiration for the quiet, smoke-free engines. His instrument panel was a luxury for him, too, with its state-of-the-art electronics. The boat had radar, sonar, 3-D lake-bottom mapping, GPS, VHF radios, weather and sea conditions sent through a Sirius satellite system.

"Heck," he said, "this thing has autopilot. I don't have to drop anchor to drop trow in the toilet."

The restroom, or head, was something to behold, too, with its fancy pedestal sink and faucet and sleekly tiled shower. Hannah Reed said, "It's practically as big as what we have at the Blue Heron Inn. I can't wait to leave that dump."

Pauline said, "If you can't say something nice, don't say anything at all."

The teacher in her was coming out, but it made me smile to see Hannah toddle off to the back of the boat, which was outside. At any moment, when Gilpa engaged the four-stroke engines to top speed, Hannah would get drenched with spray. But to my dismay, this big boat was so smooth that nothing happened. It was like we were in a flying living room. We even had a flat-screen TV, stereo CD/iPod system, and the kitchen area was replete with all the appliances and loads of snacks, wine, and my fudge.

At first, our plan to make them spill their guts looked like it'd backfired. John Schultz announced he was going to fish, probably so he could keep busy and thus ward off his seasickness. The men took over the fishing rods at the back of the boat. They appeared to be getting along, which disappointed me. I figured fighting could push them into spilling secrets.

Taylor Chin-Chavez began pouring wine. This was a brilliant idea for loosening tongues, so I helped her with heavy pours for everybody. We had a crisp apple wine and a Cabernet, both made in Door County.

"Taylor, have you found a lighthouse you like yet?"

Her scowl said it all. She flipped her silky black hair over a shoulder. "Unfortunately, I haven't been able to take the tour yet, and our visit to Chambers Island was a bust."

Gilpa spoke up. "I can take you there now, if you like. This boat is seaworthy for any kind of waves and storm. I guarantee it."

He was already sounding as if it were his boat.

Hannah, who was lounging on the tufted couch with her glass of Cabernet, said, "I'd love to see something. We haven't gotten to see anything here much at all."

I said, "But you're newlyweds. I'd think you wouldn't care if you saw anything."

Her cockeyed, chopped hairdo went even more cock-eyed with a twist of her head in reaction to my words. "You have no appreciation for what I've been through. Or any of us."

I was standing at the bar, which allowed me to look down on Hannah, which gave me a tiny thrill. "Oh, I think I do. Somebody with plenty of time on their hands hid their diamonds in my sugar."

"You think I did it?" She slammed back a swallow of her red wine. "You might try that lady over there."

Her gaze flickered to the couch on the other side of the boat where Ryann Earlywine, dressed in a leather jacket and cowgirl boots, sat munching on a piece of my fudge. Ryann laughed, her mouth working like a cement mixer. "I had nothing to do with diamonds being stolen or going into any fudge. This is good, by the way."

Her compliment still didn't make me miss the fact that she'd just lied to everybody, and she'd done it knowing I'd taken the pouch of diamonds from her and her husband on Tuesday evening. A bold move on Ryann's part.

"I'll package up some more fudge for you to take home with you. Maybe with an extra sparkle in them." I winked, which made her scowl and turn white. "I have a new batch cooling right now back at my shop. Do you want fairy wings and glitter, too?"

"Please. My daughter will love it."

Taylor sat down next to Ryann with a glass of the apple wine and a piece of my fudge. She looked quizzically at the pale pink cherry-vanilla confection. "I've sculpted with almost every medium but fudge. Pieces of this could be used to construct replicas of buildings in Door County."

Pauline said, "Like sand castles made with fudge. My kids use gumdrops to create houses and igloos."

The idea so excited me that I bubbled at Taylor, "Replicas of the lighthouses you love!"

Taylor said, "Maybe you could hold a contest for the best fudge lighthouse."

"Maybe you could sculpt a replica out of clay for the prize," I said.

"Chambers Island Lighthouse could be the theme of the first contest. We didn't get to go inside it on Sunday because of the storm, so I'm looking forward to stopping there. We can make notes on its exact architecture." Taylor got up, all excited, stuffing my fudge in her mouth. She mumbled, "This is ambrosia."

I said, "Food of the gods and goddesses? High praise from an artist. Thanks."

We women voted for the lighthouse tour, so with Gilpa at the helm and happy to make a big, beautiful turn in Lake Michigan, we headed westerly to Chambers Island.

The waters were choppy, but our floating house handled them well. It was cold, though, all of forty degrees out on the water. That kept the women inside the cabin, where Gilpa was whistling while playing with all his radar and sonar gadgets. The men stayed outside, huddled up, stoic against the elements, trolling for trout and salmon. I didn't have much hope that Jeremy Stone was getting any new information from them. They were bonding into fast friends as they fished and drank beer. The boat was equipped with cup holders along the back rail, and every one of them held a can of beer. But I couldn't judge, not when we women were becoming experts at pairing wines with my fabulous fudge fit for goddesses.

As we disembarked at the private marina, I had a feeling of déjà vu, really more of a creepy feeling that we'd missed something yesterday about the island and the lighthouse. It was no stretch to wonder if this were a rendezvous point for stolen goods.

Pauline had the feeling, too, she said as we walked along the path toward the lighthouse. The others were ahead of us. Gilpa stayed with the boat. Pauline said, "If this were in a movie you'd written, I'd swear that this was where the pirates buried their treasure."

I stopped her on the path. "Three of them were here on Sunday, when Gilpa got stranded. Do you suppose one or all of them on that boat took advantage of that and made a connection here with another boat? They probably got out to stretch their legs while my grandpa worked on the boat."

"And they hid diamonds at the lighthouse for pickup later?"

"It's usually locked," I said.

"But it wasn't when we came yesterday."

"But we know Cody had unlocked it."

"Or had he?" Pauline asked. "But either way, we might be able to think back and figure out who's the culprit. Who appeared to be the most eager to get on this boat or go to the lighthouse?"

"Taylor," I said.

"Indeed. But Hannah and Ryann were just as excited to get out of the inn."

"And Hannah was strangely poking around my shop."

"Using the church ladies like a cover," Pauline said, smirking. "Looking for jewels or diamonds to pick up or plant."

I sighed. "But like Jordy said, excitement over an idea doesn't make it true or have the force of the law behind it. Not until we hear a confession. Though Hannah and Ryann trying to accuse each other of something on the boat was mighty close to one."

"Ryann was out here on Sunday with your grandfather, and Hannah was back at the Blue Heron. Do you think they planned it that way? Maybe they were scouting for a way to smuggle the diamonds away from the Blue Heron and onto a boat?"

"Possibly. Along with a few Steuben statues and anything else they could get out of the Blue Heron without Isabelle noticing. That collection has to be worth a million or more. These people wouldn't all be scrambling for the action if it were much less."

Our shipmates' voices rose above the lap of the nearby water and wind whooshing through the pines. That made me grin. At last Jeremy Stone and I were getting somewhere with our little plan.

"Come on, Pauline. We might have solved a murder case."

Screams rent the air then, though. Pauline and I turned on our inner juice and ran full force like we used to do across a basketball court chasing down a ball that meant the game.

Hannah Reed was standing at the railing from her perch atop the lighthouse, waving her hands at us. "Help! Hurry! My husband's in the water! He's drowning!"

By the time I got to the water's edge below the knoll of the lighthouse grounds, everybody including Hannah was looking out at the water. John Schultz was swimming back in with a lifeless body under an arm.

As he was coming within wading depth, Pauline and I shed our boots and splashed in. She also knew CPR, something the school district asked all the teachers to learn. We grabbed at Will Reed and relieved John of him. A sharp pain lanced up my arm, but I gritted through it. John collapsed out of breath onshore while Pauline began working on Will. I called the Coast Guard.

Boyd flung his jacket over Will's bottom half to keep him warm.

"What happened?" I asked.

Boyd Earlywine offered, "We don't know. We were looking around the place. I was inside."

"Me too," said Ryann.

"I was in the tower," Taylor said.

Hannah was crying, bent over her husband's head on the ground. He was not opening his eyes, but Pauline was giving him CPR.

Hannah screamed, "Somebody tried to kill him! You bastards."

Pauline pushed Hannah back so we could turn Will over. I knelt down to help, saying to them all, "This is somebody's doing. The man didn't just leap in the water for no good reason."

"He went in because of me," Jeremy Stone said as he trotted up to us.

Echoes of "You?" went up around me as I stayed in my crouch to help Will. But I looked up to excoriate Jeremy with my scorn.

His nose was twitching. "He and I went up to the top of the lighthouse tower for a look. I showed him the pouch I had. Told him I had the diamonds he was looking for."

Everybody gasped. A few repeated, "Diamonds? You have the diamonds?"

Ryann Earlywine said, "What'd you do with the diamonds?"

Boyd Earlywine grabbed Jeremy's jacket front in an ominous way. "You had the diamonds?"

John Schultz hauled Boyd off Jeremy. "Those were the diamonds in Taylor's room."

"I don't know how they got there. I swear," Taylor said, pleading for my help.

While Pauline was thumping Will's back to drain him of water in his lungs, I thought I heard another thumping sound. I stood up in time to spot a Coast Guard helicopter coming up the bay from the west.

I asked Jeremy, "Did you really throw that pouch into Lake Michigan?"

"Yes," he said. "I flashed the pouch in his face; then he chased me down the staircase and out here. When I got to the beach, I used my best baseball throw."

"Are you nuts?" I said, rhetorically.

"Wasn't it our plan to figure out who stole the diamonds and murdered Rainetta and her manager?"

"Our plan was for you to talk about the diamonds, yes, but not to throw the evidence in the lake!"

Our saying that so loudly wasn't good. The guests began talking at once and accusing me of being the vilest person alive. One person even said my I should rename my Cinderella fudge "Fickle Fudge" because that was what I was. And those were their nicest "F" words.

The Coast Guard landed at the airstrip within a minute. John Schultz and Jeremy Stone hustled Will up the knoll, and then the helicopter crew met us and took over. They had a stretcher and all the right equipment. Within only another minute, they'd loaded Will for the ride to the Sturgeon Bay hospital.

Gilpa hadn't been part of the unfortunate mishap. He didn't know the plan that had gone awry. Poor man tried to be his cheerful self but got an earful as we boarded. He pressed the *Super Catch I* into full throttle for Hannah's sake. She was wailing.

Pauline and I huddled in our chairs near Gilpa—away from the others who wanted to toss us overboard like their precious diamonds. While sitting there, I thought about how weird the mishap was. We'd all gone out in the boat according to plan, which was good, and then we'd got into trouble, which was bad—but that was my pattern. Everybody expected I'd get into trouble. So who needed the "expected" trouble? Did Jeremy Stone? I suspected already he hadn't thrown real diamonds in the drink. Or did somebody at home want us out of the way so they could sneak into the Blue Heron Inn and abscond with diamonds and more?

"Mercy Fogg," I muttered as Gilpa eased the *Super Catch I* into its slip at Fishers' Harbor. A shiver of realization like none other gripped me. I felt as if I'd been the one half-drowned in the icy lake. I had discovered who the murderer was. But could I be sure?

Pauline asked, "What about Mercy?"

"We have to find Mercy and ask her some questions."

"I knew she did it! Mercy the murderer."

"No, Pauline, I don't think so. I need to get her help in putting some pieces together."

"You'll have to go it alone. I've got to meet some other teachers tonight to go over the upcoming field trip regulations."

"Shoot. But I'll meet up with Cody at the shop as soon as we disembark. It's about time he began telling me about his deputy duties with Mercy."

But when I got to the shop, Cody wasn't there. Neither was my grandmother. It wasn't like either of them to abandon the shop. Only Harbor was there, sleeping on his towels. I untied him, then called my grandmother.

"I'm sorry, honey," she said. "When I left, Cody said he was going to be in charge of the shop until you got back. I thought it'd be okay."

I didn't want to worry her. "It's very okay. He probably had to go with Sam to see Jordy again."

But a phone call to them didn't unearth Cody. I broke down and called his parents, Arlene and Tom. They hadn't seen him. They asked me if I thought he could kill somebody. I made the mistake of choking and they hung up on me. I swallowed the lump in my throat, then hugged Harbor. He whined, as if in sympathy.

Or maybe he was just hungry. I tossed him some of the last of Gilpa's beef jerky treats from a sales shelf and a package of cheese curds out of the cooler.

It was going on six o'clock, the dinner hour at the Blue Heron Inn. The guests would probably take a full hour to wash up after our harrowing trip, and Hannah Reed would be driving down to Sturgeon Bay to see her husband, Will.

I decided that the best thing to do next was to close up my shop and head up the hill to fill in Isabelle on my version of what had transpired. I was sure that the gang of guests would offer their own various versions, all of them not true. I still couldn't fathom Jeremy Stone tossing those diamonds away like that. If he truly had done it, his action served those greedy people right. By now that pouch had probably washed out several hundreds of yards into Lake Michigan, lost forever like the many ships that had gone down with their booty aboard, never to be found.

I sneaked a peek at the fudge cooling in pans set out on the white marble table. Grandma had laid a dish towel over the top. I pulled it off gingerly. She had followed my diagram to a T. This introductory flavor of Fisherman's Catch Fudge was going to dazzle the guys. She'd also made a flavor for little boys. The rich, extra-dark Belgian chocolate in both batches smelled divine. But it was the secret ingredients that I whiffed and spied that had me smiling. My mouth was watering. But tasting had to wait. I put the cloth back over the special new fudge flavors.

But now I was hungry. I hoped Izzy was making a luscious dinner; I'd invite myself to join them. I'd probably clear the place out; none of those people would want to sit with me. Especially once I announced who the murderer was.

Harbor followed me to the kitchen. I halted so fast at the sight before me that Harbor's nose and head smashed into my backside.

Sacks of sugar had been busted open. Sugar had showered the floor.

Harbor was lapping at it fast with his tongue.

My new jugs of glucose and inverse sugar—like honey—were upside down over strainers in the sink. Every kilo bar of chocolate had been opened, as if somebody suspected those of being gold bars. But I knew what they'd been looking for—those darn diamonds.

This was Mercy's doing. I suspected she was trying to throw me off a bit so she could apprehend the murderers herself. The real murderers wouldn't risk taking the time to do this.

Gilpa startled me by walking in. "What in the Sam Hill—?"

"Somebody looking for more hot ice, Gilpa. This'll take me a while to clean up."

"You could just let that dog lick it all up. Or I can take care of this, Ava honey."

"No, Gilpa. You've had a long day. And Grandma needs you, I'm sure. She made some wonderful fudge for me today. I'm sure she's tired."

"Where's Cody? He can help with this."

"That's just the oddest thing. He's not here."

"You think he did this?"

"No. I think he's off worrying about prom. That's how he is lately—flighty." That gave me an idea. "Would you mind going over to the old mansion? He might be there. That'll let me go up to the inn and connect with Izzy and her guests about this."

"They were all out with us. They didn't do it."

"Yes," I admitted with a sigh. "It appears they didn't."

"You don't suppose Cody's parents would do this? I know they're not happy with you or me lately."

It had occurred to me, too, that they were suspects. The revelation had thrown all my theories into the air. I had to draw new diagrams in my head to figure out the physics of all the clues and connections of people to the clues. But Cody's parents needed a lot of money to keep Cody healthy and provide him with services—even a home—for now and in the future. They fit a profile of people who might need to steal diamonds and glass Steubens.

Ironically, this new angle gave me clarity. I was beginning to figure out the jigsaw puzzle of the murders.

"Thanks, Gilpa."

"For what, Ava dear?"

"For being you." I gave him a huge, long hug before taking off up the hill.

I was hoping to find Izzy fast and fill her in on my theory. Izzy wasn't at the inn, however. John Schultz came down the stairs with a beer in his hand and said,

"There was a note in the kitchen that said she'd be back later, that we were to help ourselves to salad fixings for dinner."

He and I eyed each other as if we were in a kickboxing cage ready to fly at each other. I said, "Listen, John, whoever you are, if you killed two people I'll, I'll . . ." I scrutinized this guy in his Hawaiian shirt under a hooded, zippered sweatshirt, baggy shorts despite the weather, and huarache sandals, and all the wind went out of me. "You're not a killer, are you?"

"No."

"But you're also not a trip organizer, either. What do you do?"

"I really am a trip organizer." He filched into a pocket, then handed me a card. "Look me up on the Internet. You haven't done that yet?"

His card showed all his social network addresses. My face grew hot. "I was *that* wrong?"

He nodded, then went on his way. I felt so foolish. Some detective I was. This made me wonder if I was wrong about Mercy again. I'd just assumed she was innocent, but what if that was her plan all along?

I was about to turn around and leave when the stairs beckoned me. Mercy had been up there on Sunday. I also realized Jeremy Stone was probably upstairs working on a story. I needed to talk to him about his possible headline for me: "Fatal Fudge Femme Fatale Flubs Foolishly." Pauline would use my story to teach a social studies unit to her kindergartners. I could hear her voice now. "Now, kids, don't grow up to be like Ava Mathilde Oosterling."

As I passed by the Earlywines' room, I heard only subdued talking this time. Taylor's room was open; she wasn't there. It looked like she'd packed. She was probably downstairs, hoping to get early permission to leave. By now somebody had likely called Sheriff Tollefson.

I decided to take one last look at Rainetta Johnson's room. Part of me wondered if Cody were hiding there, too. He wasn't. The closet and the room were pristine clean, ready for the next guest.

An inspection again under the bed and mattress yielded nothing new.

The dresser drawers were clear. I realized I'd never looked behind the dresser and mirror. To my surprise, the mirror was so tall that it hid a door that allowed access to the community bathroom. If Izzy moved the dresser and mirror over toward the window wall, this room could become a suite with its own private bath.

My whole body froze.

That was how *it* happened.

That was how Rainetta Johnson was murdered. Somebody had gone in through the bathroom, then moved the dresser into place later.

I got down on my knees to look at the wood floor under the dresser and in the path of the wheels. The antique wheels were also made of wood. They wouldn't scratch much if the dresser was rolled carefully, but if one was in a hurry and shoved the wheels sideways and thus not let them turn . . . one would find the scratches I did a few feet to the right of the dresser, along the bare wall closer to the chair and window. The scratches were slight. But they were evidence somebody had moved the dresser to and from that spot—to hide the door to the bathroom, the escape route for a killer. The killer had to be quick. The person had to have strangled Rainetta Johnson, ducked through the bathroom, then snuck back in the room to roll the dresser and mirror back into place.

My brain ticked off the suspects. Mercy, Sam, Cody, the Reeds, and John Schultz. And Jeremy Stone. All of them were here, and all were strong enough to move this empty dresser and mirror. Strong enough to commit murder.

I considered what Gilpa had said about the Fjelstads. I would have heard if they'd been at the party on Sunday, and since I hadn't, did that mean they'd been sneaking around there, too, like Cody? They were still suspects of sabotage at my fudge shop. Were they capable of killing for diamonds to support their son? I didn't want to believe this theory, but what about a friend of his who was only a year older—village president Erik Gustafson? Erik lured us all to the dining room for wine on Sunday, but maybe that was part of a plan to perhaps get Rainetta tipsy. Was Erik using Cody? Their plan hadn't worked so well because the diamonds got in my pink fudge and shocked Rainetta, so she hurried upstairs. But she then discovered Cody—or somebody else—wanting to rob her. Since I knew Cody wasn't capable of wrongdoing, a picture of that "somebody else" was flowering in my brain.

That awful feeling like the flu came over me again. My ten thousand taste buds detected sour skullduggery for fame and fortune.

This time, I knew for sure who had killed Rainetta Johnson.

My knees went weak. I had to focus for a moment to steady myself before I ventured out of Rainetta's room. My list of suspects was mighty long by design—by design of the killer who had been like a conductor of an orchestra of suspects. The wiliness of it scared me. This person was dangerous. But I had no solid proof. I had to come up with a plan.

Chapter 19

I eased from Rainetta's room, listening for others in the Blue Heron Inn. Only my pounding heart interrupted the quiet. I treaded lightly to Jeremy Stone's door to peek in. He wasn't there.

Back in the main hall, I entered the common bathroom. Down in the backyard, Jeremy and John were starting the grill. Salad fixings rarely sufficed for a meal for men in this region. My phone said it was six thirty.

I went to the blue-carpeted stairway, but paused, thinking about my next move, yet again mesmerized by the way the Steuben glass statues sparkled. From this angle high above the room below, I could see why Isabelle loved these amorphous crystals. There was magic in them. Her fond memory of picking up the diamond with her mother in the Arkansas field came to me. For Isabelle Boone, the Steubens were more than just pieces of nostalgia. This glass surrounding her probably felt like one of our Door County Belgian hugs. Sadness overwhelmed me. I'd been too busy to realize she might be lonely here.

Isabelle wasn't back yet, so I decided to leave her a personal note, and not one for all to see in the kitchen. I went to her living quarters, hoping to find it unlocked like everything else in the Blue Heron Inn. But it wasn't. She was probably fearful of her crazy guests. I jiggled the doorknob hard, risking being heard. The lock popped. I slipped inside.

As I was writing a note for her to call me when she got back, my phone rang. It was my grandmother.

"Honey, I haven't heard from your grandfather. Is he at the shop still?"

"No, Grandma. Neither of us is there. I closed up. I'm up at the Blue Heron Inn. I asked him to see if Cody was at the mansion. We can't seem to locate Cody again."

"Oh dear. I'm fine, but that man must be draggin' butt by now. Send the old coot home."

I decided to go over to the mansion myself and get the "old coot." I was heading down the hill when Mercy Fogg marched toward me, her dyed blond curls bouncing with every heavy step. She barked out, "Where's my Cody?"

"I was about to ask you that." Her possessiveness made me shiver, despite Jordy's odd tenderness toward her. "You've been using Cody to play detective. Have you come to any conclusions about who the murderer is? Or who you'd like to blame it on?"

"I'm not sharing my theories with you. Now, please excuse me, Ava."

She began marching past me. "Isabelle's not home and Cody's not here either."

"Oh." She stopped, then turned around. "Isabelle told me Bethany wanted Cody to meet her at the mansion earlier to look at the place for the party. I guess Isabelle must've gone over there, too."

"My grandfather's there now, so maybe they'll all come trooping back here soon."

"I hope so. I have to talk with her right away."

"What about?" I asked, curiosity prickling up my back as I took in Mercy's worried face.

She marched up to Isabelle's front porch and then inside as if she owned the inn. I followed, knowing instinctively that Mercy knew something important. My insides felt like a California trembler had started. I repeated, "What do you need to talk to Isabelle about?"

We stood in the foyer amid the Steubens. In my imagination, I forced a movie to play out of Mercy ripping the sacks open at my shop, her hiding the necklace, and her moving a dresser after choking Rainetta Johnson and stuffing my fudge in her mouth. The images didn't fit. This woman of almost sixty drove a snowplow in winter and a school bus year-round. This was a flag-waver woman. Jordy's instincts were right. As much as I wanted her to be guilty, Mercy Fogg wouldn't do things that could send her to jail. I wondered now if her constant pestering of me had somehow helped protect me from the killer. Was Mercy being protective of me? What did Mercy know?

She kept perusing all the glass statues, as if counting them, so I asked, "Is there something about the statues that Isabelle needs to know?"

"Yes. Somebody has been trying to steal these. Maybe they already have stolen a few right out from under Isabelle. I want to warn her that I think somebody might try to murder her next."

I gasped. "You're sure? How?" I could feel Mercy and myself converging on the same conclusion as to the murderer's identity.

"Like Rainetta, she's too trusting. This place has no

locks that work. I begged Rainetta to stay with me." Her bottom lip trembled.

This made me swallow. But I couldn't bring myself to ask her about her relationship with Rainetta Johnson.

"Mercy, I need to go find my grandfather. He's over at the mansion with Cody, and my grandma wants him to come home. I left a note for Isabelle for her to call me when she gets back. I'll call you when I see her if you don't want to hang around."

"Thanks, Ava. Maybe they're late because they've found treasure in the basement, or more dead bodies." She chuckled, but I could see she was struggling to keep her composure.

She hurried out.

Expecting Isabelle to come back at any moment, I decided to wait a few more minutes at the Blue Heron Inn. Why would somebody want to murder her? I sat on the bottom step of the staircase, staring up at the Steubens. Maybe only thirty seconds went by before the sparkling glass throughout the room seemed to chime loud warnings at me. Mercy's words rushed back to terrify me. *They've found treasure in the basement, or more dead bodies.*

Treasure? Bodies? Cody said he'd heard something from the basement the other day. I'd been thrown down the stairs. A body had been found in the basement. Why was I sitting here? They were in danger! But so was I. Somebody had wanted me dead then. What about now? Could somebody be watching me, just waiting to get me alone? I flipped my head back and forth. I saw nobody in the foyer, but my heart was racing.

I looked around for a weapon. Nothing in the foyer

would do. There were just amorphous artwork crystals. But then I remembered a *certain* alignment of crystals that could serve as a weapon.

I raced into Isabelle's private quarters and to her fireplace. I grabbed the poker with my good hand. That would be unwieldy to use with only one hand. I set it back down, then grabbed a solid hunk of glass that I could throw better—the glass unicorn.

I took a moment to call Jordy, but got the lady officer at the front desk.

She said, "He's across the peninsula with some traffic accident."

"Send anybody. Now! I've just solved the fudge felonies, but I've got people in danger of losing their lives at the mansion." I gave her the address.

Then I raced down the hill, the unicorn weighing heavily in the crook of my arm and against my sweatshirt.

Cradling the unicorn in my good arm, I burst into the mansion. "Hello? Gilpa? Cody?"

There wasn't a sound except wind gusts rattling loose siding outside. Because it was going on seven o'clock, the sun was west of the house. The interior was now in sepia tones. I needed a flashlight—that was what I hadn't grabbed at Isabelle's place. I couldn't believe how stupid I was. But I prayed the unicorn would bring me luck and the dangerous peril here was only my imagination gone awry.

I thought briefly of going upstairs because the person had been there before. But my gut told me that I'd find my grandfather and Cody in the basement. I was icy cold all over, even under my sweatshirt and after running all the way here from the Blue Heron Inn.

"Hello?" I called again, holding my breath to listen.

After no response, I hurried to the kitchen. The basement door was open. Fright sent the atoms making up my body cells into a frenzied overdrive. I hid the Steuben unicorn weapon under my sweatshirt, hugging my wrapped left wrist to myself to make the statue's bulge look less obvious. I took a deep breath, then put a boot on the first step.

Then another boot.

A shuffling emanated from the bowels of the basement.

"Grandpa? Cody? Isabelle?"

Had the worst happened? I feared descending any farther into the half-light down there at the bottom of the stairs. My hands grew sweaty. Perspiration was popping out on my face, too, prickling my forehead and upper lip.

Maybe I'd heard only mice running around. I waited, listening. A truck lumbered by out on Main Street. My mind remembered Conrad Webb sprawled across the floor. Had the sheriff's office done a chalk outline? What was down there now? Maybe I was being crazy and Gilpa and Cody had left. Maybe Bethany had wanted to go out for burgers and a malt. Isabelle was likely back at the Blue Heron by now; we'd missed each other on the street somehow.

I went down all the way for a quick and reassuring look.

I saw nothing on the floor. No chalk line. Then I spotted light limning the seams of a door across the basement, maybe thirty feet away. Swallowing against my dry throat, I ventured over. Maybe the sheriff's people had left the light on by mistake.

"Hello?" I called.

My hand went to the doorknob, but it burst at me before I could turn it.

I yelped as I stumbled back a few steps.

Isabelle stared at me, looking ghostly. She held a pistol in one hand.

Stupidly, I asked, "What's that in your hand?"

She smiled, then lowered the pistol. "I just wanted to be sure the place was safe for the prom party next week."

The room behind her was maybe eight by eight feet, big enough for me to stretch out in if I lay on its dirt floor. It had rock walls. It had to be an old root cellar. But there was an opening beyond in the opposite wall with a short wall of about a foot high. Was that mystery room an old coal bin? The short wall would hold the coal that was dumped into the cavity from the outside and the surface above. It was a pitch-black maw, though, and any old trapdoor to the outside had long ago been boarded up and sodded over. My brain banged about in my skull in warning.

I managed to croak out, "Are you hiding more things you've taken from Rainetta Johnson?"

A flicker in Isabelle's gamine dark eyes told me everything I needed to know. "Yes," she admitted, to my surprise. Her shoulders eased. "I can't trust any of my guests anymore. But you know that."

"Mercy Fogg doesn't trust them either. She thinks you could be in danger." I cradled my bandaged arm with my good hand, hoping I wasn't going to accidentally drop the unicorn in my terror.

"And what do you think?"

"Izzy, let's go back to the inn and talk."

A shuffling sound behind her drew my attention. A moan rose from the black cave.

Isabelle shifted slightly, pulling the pistol back up into place.

My gaze darted past her to the short wall and the floor, where I spied several glass paperweights of various sizes, some the size of baseballs. They'd be heavy. Especially if they hit you on the head. I swallowed a whine in my throat.

"Izzy, your paperweights were never missing or borrowed by your guests at all, were they? You brought them here to use as weapons." The whine in my throat turned into a maddening scream of anger. "What have you done to my grandpa? To Cody?"

I moved to get past her, but her pistol popped and a bullet zinged past me into the basement. The bullet pinged and ricocheted onto something with a *thwack*, then rattled across the tile floor until its movement died.

I stared wide-eyed at my friend. My former friend. She was short, petite, cute—and totally crazy.

"How can you do this, Izzy? Please, just let them go."

"I can't. Cody was always snooping. He knows everything I've been doing. And your grandfather, I'm sorry about him, but he came and I had no choice."

"Where's Bethany?" After she just stared at me, I said, "You made that up to get Cody here. You made up a lot of things, didn't you?"

She didn't respond. I feared she was trying to squirrel up her courage to shoot me dead. Maybe she was pausing because I had meant something to her.

I willed tears to stay out of my eyes so she could see how furious I was as I looked down at her and her pistol.

"So what did you do? Shoot them? Let me get them to the doctor. You can run, Izzy. Just run now."

"There's no need to run. You're going to join them, and then I'll brick you all in."

That was when I noticed she'd prepared for this. Bricks and instant-mix concrete were in a corner. She even had jugs of water.

"This is what you were going to do with Conrad Webb. You almost got away with his murder."

"I still plan to do so. I can get away with them all."

"Maybe you can throw the blame on other people easy enough for Rainetta's death, but people will want to know where I disappeared to."

"I doubt it," Isabelle said, her gamine face taking on color again. "They'll think you ran back to Los Angeles."

A sickly realization curled in my innards because she was right. Nobody believed I really wanted to stick around little Fishers' Harbor. "And by the time they find out the truth, where will you be?"

"Right here. With my Steuben collection. I might need to expand to another space, though. And this house looks like a good bet. It's half again the size of the Blue Heron with twice the basement space."

The thought of her living here with my body and the bodies of my grandfather and Cody in the basement horrified me. My throat burned with the names I wanted to call her. Instead, I tried another tack.

"I could help you, Isabelle. We could go into business together. You likely need a partner. Now that the manager is gone."

"I don't need help."

"Conrad Webb knew all about the diamonds, didn't he? I bet Rainetta told him about them sometime in the past, and about her family's feud, and then you and Conrad talked and got to know each other. Conrad Webb found out you loved Steubens, and it wasn't a stretch to realize quiet little Fishers' Harbor in Door County might be the best place to fence a lot of diamonds. I bet Rainetta had them in her luggage and she didn't even know about them because Conrad took care of her transportation. But somehow on Sunday she found out what you two were up to. Then you had to get rid of her."

"Like I have to get rid of you now," she said, the pistol steady in her hand as she backed away to keep her distance from me.

The pistol was pointed right at my belly, right where the Steuben lay hidden under my sweatshirt and sprained wrist.

"Go ahead and shoot me, Isabelle, because if you do, you'll break this."

I withdrew the unicorn from its hiding place.

A whine whipped from her throat. Wrinkles scored her pale forehead. Her pistol wavered for a flicker of a moment. "What're you doing with my unicorn? Give me that."

I held it up high with my right hand, way above her head or ability to jump up and get it. Being tall was one of my few weapons at the moment.

I said, "On the day of the party, you told me this was your favorite piece. You said unicorns and fairy tales belong together. Your mother gave you this, I bet, when you were a little girl listening to her tell you fairy tales. It's your first Steuben, not the vase. The vase was a gift to your mother in the hospital, but this unicorn is really when the glitter in your eyes started for you. It's precious, for many reasons. Isn't it?"

Her chin quivered. "Stop this."

"Your mother loved you. Very much. But she refused to let you pick all the diamonds you wanted in the field, and you never forgot that. So now that's all you want. Riches. Sparkly diamonds to get back at her, to make up for what a horrible mother she was."

"She wasn't horrible. Stop saying that. She died of cancer."

"And you were poor. So poor until you began to mull over how much money these sorts of gifts from rich people can bring. I suspect some of these weren't gifts at all. You stole some of the Steubens. What was the connection? Did your mother somehow know Rainetta's rich relatives?"

A twitch at the corner of her mouth confirmed that.

I said, "Your mother was a maid for them sometime, wasn't she? It was easy enough for you to get inside their homes. And then you met tired old has-been movie star Rainetta Johnson and her manager at some point, and you saw a perfect partner in him. Am I close with my theory? How many homes did you manage to burglarize? Breaking into places is easy for you, isn't it?"

"Please, stop it. You and I are friends." Her eyes were fiery now, like the core of molten meteors that had created the very diamonds she lusted after. She flexed her fingers on the gun.

I flexed mine around the glass unicorn I held high in the air, hoping I could trust my instincts enough to save myself and Gilpa and Cody. "My hand is getting tired, Isabelle. I need to switch hands, but that means I have to hold the unicorn with my weak hand, the hand you sprained for me when you tripped me down the stairs.

Wouldn't it be a shame if I dropped the gift your mother gave you all *because* of you?"

"Stop it!"

I juggled the glass figurine between my hands in the air above my head. My hands were slippery with sweat, but I managed to hold on to the unicorn with both hands. My shoulders were getting tired, though. I wasn't sure how much longer I could continue this ruse. There had to be a way to subdue Isabelle. Maybe I just needed to be more direct.

"Drop the pistol, Izzy, or I drop the last remnant of your mother in your life. Dropping this unicorn will be like killing your mother all over again. It'll be worse than her cancer. She's looking down at you now, Izzy. Your mother is hurting. She gave you this. It's your last connection to her. It's like she's alive within the light that shines in this glass."

She stared up at the precious unicorn.

My arms and shoulders were killing me from holding the position.

Finally, she lowered the pistol.

When I stepped forward, though, she snapped the pistol up. In a reflex motion, I slammed the unicorn down. I heard the gun's retort echoing as my body crumpled.

Chapter 20

Shards of glass exploded between Isabelle and me. My back slammed onto the hard dirt floor, my head just missing the doorjamb.

I wriggled up on my elbows in a scramble to run, then paused in shock. Not a yard from me, Isabelle lay bleeding with a big chunk of broken glass unicorn stuck in her neck.

The bullet had evidently hit the unicorn, shattering it, sending parts sailing.

I kicked the dropped pistol out of the room and heard it skitter in circles across the basement's tiled floor.

I was prepared to have to sit on Isabelle to subdue her, but she was in so much panic waving her arms over the chunk of glass in her neck that all I had to do was say, "If you move, it'll slice your jugular."

She whimpered, immobilized.

In the coal bin, Grandpa lay covered in soot, tied up, and gagged. He had a good welt on his forehead, and blood had caked on his face. Cody's condition was the same. As I was helping them get out of the coal bin and past Isabelle, who was prone on the hard dirt floor, the sheriff and his deputy clomped down the basement steps.

The deputy hustled over to Isabelle while Jordy called for an ambulance.

As soon as he ended his call, he hugged me in a fierce way that went way beyond perfunctory, saying, "Ava, are you all right?"

He was squeezing me so much, I couldn't breathe. "Jordy, let go. I'm alive. And you're killing my bad wrist. Ow."

"Sorry." He let go to help my grandfather to the stairs, where Jordy sat him down. "Wait here for the EMTs."

Gilpa's gash had reopened. Blood gushed down his face. He swiped at it with a hand, looking at the red streaks across his fingers. "At least it's not oil. Your grandmother's tired of me coming home all oily."

I gave his shoulder a gingerly squeeze to show him I loved him, then went to help steady Cody. He was woozy, wavering in his stance but insisting he had to go back inside the coal bin.

I ventured in for him, and found a pink gift bag. "What's this?"

"Cinderella Pink Fudge. I wrapped up several pieces for Bethany." He reached in and made the cellophane crinkle for me. "I thought I was meeting her here. Do you think I should still try to give these to her?"

I gave him a really big hug so that he was sure to feel the good oxytocin kick in. "I think so. Just not tonight, okay?"

"Okay. How's Harbor?"

"Just fine. Guarding the fudge and minnows."

"We should've brought him along. Dogs make people calm. Isabelle wasn't being calm."

I sighed. "You're right. As always."

*　　*　　*

This time when we all met with Sheriff Tollefson at the Sturgeon Bay justice building offices, he had to have us meet in an even bigger room. It was the next morning, Friday, at ten o'clock, after the milking was done on the farm. My whole family was there, plus Cody and his parents and Pauline Mertens. My one true friend had called in for a substitute teacher that day in order to be with us. Our clan was represented by Destiny Hubbard. She sat at the end of the table next to me.

Gilpa and I hadn't even opened our shop that morning because we saw the caravan of news vehicles arriving at the docks at five o'clock. We were actually in our shop because we hadn't been able to sleep. I was making fudge at four in the morning. Gilpa was restocking shelves after I'd used some of his snacks to make the new fudge flavors I was going to introduce later today.

At first I thought I'd just bring in the fishermen coming for Moose's tours and let them taste test the new flavor for guys, but with the news media there, I had bigger plans. But they and my new fudge flavors had to wait.

Cody had brought the pink bag of Cinderella Pink Fudge from last night with him. While we waited for the sheriff, Cody announced he was putting a cellophane-wrapped piece of "famous fudge evidence" in front of every chair.

Sheriff Tollefson walked in with a female detective he introduced as Emily Remington. They took their seats at the other end of the table, next to my parents. Emily was a fifty-five-ish retired cop they'd rehired to help with this case, which Jordy said had gotten "complicated." I liked the sound of that. We were important. My fudge was a star.

Jordy said, "We're here today so that you folks can help us piece together what happened."

I said, "Isabelle hasn't confessed?"

"No. She insists her guests were in a conspiracy to steal her blind."

"Well, she's right," I said. "She wanted them fighting over diamonds so they could be blamed for the murder of Rainetta Johnson and Conrad Webb."

The detective woman was looking over information on an iPad in front of her. "Are those the diamonds that were thrown in Lake Michigan, or the diamonds that were in your fudge?"

"I'm not sure diamonds were thrown in the lake."

"Who has the diamonds?" she asked.

"Moose Lindstrom," I said.

All heads swiveled to look at me.

"Jeremy Stone likely faked throwing them in the water. He probably just tossed a bunch of rocks away. But he's not the kind of guy who'd want to keep the diamonds on him. He's a reporter, a really good one. He probably stowed them on the *Super Catch I*."

Gilpa raised his hand. His face sported a sheepish look. "I took those diamonds. I saw him dumping something in an empty beer can. While everybody was off the boat, I tidied up. I put the diamonds in an empty fudge wrapper. The wrapper is back at the shop, under my cash register."

I panicked and asked Emily Remington, "Gilpa won't be arrested again, will he?"

Destiny's hand snaked out to touch my arm, stopping me from saying anything more. "No, he's not going to be in trouble." She appeared calm. She wore a royal blue suit with a shimmery white shell underneath and killer drop earrings in the shape of American flags that flapped with her every move. "We have to get the whole truth out on the table now."

And we did. My theory about Isabelle's mother being a maid for the Kruppenmeiers or Alpanelps in New York didn't pan out entirely, but the detective said that Benton Alpanelp admitted to dating Isabelle Boone for a short time. It was true, though, that the people Isabelle's mother had worked for all thought highly of her and thus welcomed Isabelle to their parties over the years.

Jordy said, "We think she's like a black widow, just not marrying them. We're looking into some deaths of other people of considerable means."

"Were all the Steubens stolen?" I asked.

The detective said, "We're not sure about all of them yet. Benton Alpanelp said he'd given her some as gifts, which she requested instead of payments for helping him with parties. She had a shrewd eye, it seems, for investment. Steubens are no longer made, so the collection she has risen in value every day."

My grandmother asked, "What will happen to the collection?"

"We don't know," Emily said. "For now, it has to sit in the Blue Heron Inn under lock and key."

"Make sure they're new locks," I said.

Jordy shot me a burning gaze. "And don't be taking down my police tape this time. That's how all your trouble started. You making fudge when you weren't supposed to."

I promised him I would never again bust through police tape at a crime scene. Pauline snickered next to me.

We quickly sorted out what had happened, according to our version of the story. Isabelle had received the diamonds in Rainetta's luggage the moment it arrived. The diamond collection was so vast, though, that it probably surprised even Isabelle. She panicked and wanted it off her property so she wouldn't get caught. Since she was in and out of my place all the time for our shared deliveries, she thought she could hide the diamonds overnight until Conrad Webb figured out how to make his connection to a boater on Lake Michigan and sell them. Since my shop was right on the docks, they thought this would be easy. And, of course, they thought if I were caught with the diamonds, I'd go to jail but nobody would tumble to Isabelle Boone being the thief.

I told the sheriff and detective I remembered that Isabelle had turned up the music in the inn on Sunday before going up the stairs. Now we could assume she did that because she planned to go up and argue with Rainetta.

"I think they both simultaneously recognized that diamonds were in the fudge. That's why they hurried up the stairs. To figure out what was going on," I said.

Cody raised his hand. "I saw them, but not together. Miss Boone went to the bathroom. I was hiding in Miss Chin-Chavez's room because I wasn't supposed to be there. And then I saw Sam, but he left. I followed him, then got pushed down the stairs."

Mild frustration racked me. "Cody, why didn't you tell us this before about hiding in her room? And seeing Sam leave?" I felt awful about ever thinking Sam might be a party to the murder somehow.

Cody said, "It's not polite to talk about bathroom stuff. They tell us that at school all the time. Don't they, Miss Mertens?" He was trying his sarcasm lessons on us again.

Pauline nodded.

"So it was Miss Boone who pushed me down the

stairs?" Cody asked, but it was in a perfunctory way that told me Cody was sharp and had figured a lot of this out ahead of most of us.

"Yes," I said. "And she did the same to me." I held up my wrapped wrist.

The rest of the details spun out of us. Isabelle had gone up earlier to pull the dresser back away from the door so she'd have access. She was already fearful that Rainetta Johnson was onto her and Conrad Webb. This made it look premeditated, though that was tricky to prove, Destiny told us. But the sheriff confirmed that there were marks on Rainetta's neck that fit the size of Isabelle Boone's hands and fingers. She strangled the movie star, stuffed my fudge down her throat as far as it would go, then shoved the woman into the hallway. She went back through Rainetta's inner doorway to the bathroom so she could come out and look innocent to everybody in the hallway. In our rush to revive Rainetta, none of us noticed when Isabelle sneaked back into the room to move the dresser and mirror back in front of the door. We also hadn't noticed that Isabelle stole the necklace, which she'd later hidden in the cookie jar in my shop, to be picked up later by her or some contact.

I was curious, though, as to exactly what was at stake for Isabelle. "How much are those diamonds worth?"

Detective Remington punched up a new screen on her iPad. "Altogether, more than ten million."

Cody whistled, then said to his parents, "See what my fudge was worth? I have a good job. I bet every piece of that fudge was worth a whole million dollars."

Everybody laughed. But then I remembered my fudge and the newspeople staking out the dock and Oosterlings' Live Bait, Bobbers & Belgian Fudge. Since it was going on noon already, I asked that we be excused. Jordy and the detective agreed. Destiny set up another date for further interviews with Detective Remington.

Destiny said to all of us with a huge smile, "This is going to be a trial that will put y'all in the spotlight for a while. Think you can handle it?"

While everybody else wasn't sure, I wore a big smile. I muttered to Pauline, "My fudge will end up in the swag bags yet."

In my yellow truck and on Highway 42 going back to Fishers' Harbor, Pauline said to me, "I feel sorry for Sam. Everybody's going to know he had a fling with Rainetta Johnson."

"Sam will be fine."

"If he has you as a friend," Pauline said.

"We can't be friends. I jilted him. We have a tainted history."

"Oh please," she said with polite disdain. "You married Dillon Rivers, who happened to have at least two other wives at the same time in Nantucket and Biloxi, and you didn't even get a good vacation to those places out of the deal. That was Dillon's fault, not Sam's. Sam is the forgiving kind."

The memory of my running away with Dillon came back to me. It was an August Friday, brilliant sunshine on the cornfields. Sam and my immediate family were inside the Catholic church in the countryside near Brussels in Door County for our wedding rehearsal. My wedding to Sam would actually be the following week on that Saturday. Everybody in Door County, it seemed to me anyway, had been invited to the wedding and reception that would follow. Distant relatives were due to arrive from Belgium, too. On that rehearsal Friday night, Sam had gone inside the church to wait with his groomsmen at the altar. They were getting instructions from the priest. I was waiting outside, watching the sunset, ready to practice my entrance and march down the aisle. Music was playing inside the church.

I'd just graduated college; Sam had graduated two years before and had been part of the Green Bay Packers practice squad for two years, but now he'd just gotten his first job as a social worker. His dream. We were going to settle into the farmhouse with my parents until some refurbishing was finished on the house that Sam had bought. We'd be taking the bedroom where my grandparents used to sleep when they lived there. My mom had already been talking about converting the spare bedroom she used as a sewing room to a nursery so she could babysit her grandchild after he or she was born.

Then Dillon Rivers drove up in a brand-new shiny Porsche convertible.

He was dressed in a tuxedo, of all things. He hopped out of the car, then took me in his arms and kissed me thoroughly, the kind of kiss that makes women lose their minds. All of the good times we'd had together over the years bubbled inside of me, fizzylike, as if I were already sipping champagne and celebrating a special event in my life.

And then he said to me, "Is this how you want your life to end?"

To end? He said it in such a way that it made me look around at the dry leaves of late summer coming down off the trees. Instead of the vibrant fields and the sunset splashing a pink tinge around us, I noticed all the dead, dull brown leaves on the ground—a harbinger of fall and winter to come. I felt dead and dull in that moment. Suddenly, marrying Sam was all wrong. The prospect of living on the farm with him and under my parents' roof, then moving to the little cottage later, felt like a backward step in life. I panicked. Immature, yes, but that was how you were in your early twenties. At least I was. I got in Dillon's car.

We eloped. Yup, we went to Las Vegas, where Dillon had a comedy gig nights at an aging resort hotel just off the Strip. I knew it couldn't be long before such a funny, talented heartthrob would be a headliner at the Mirage or Bellagio. Instead, weeks later, in late September, a woman from out East called me. Then a woman from down South. I had loved Dillon for his partying ways, but it was too much for me to handle if he'd somehow ended up getting married and didn't even remember it. Later I found out that he'd been defrauded by at least one of the women who claimed he'd promised her a good life and lots of money. These things happen to people in show business now and then, but I got my divorce and hightailed it in humiliating fashion to Los Angeles. It took me a year to get over being mad. It helped to write it into a script for *The Topsy-Turvy Girls*.

Now, driving along familiar old Highway 42 in my preowned yellow Chevy truck, I harrumphed at Pauline. "Maybe I do need a vacation to places like Nantucket and Biloxi, but it's hard to leave Door County. You know, it's pretty fun driving my truck around our hilly, winding roads."

"I'll call up John Schultz and ask him to set up a winery tour here, and you and I will go on it. It'll be a nice break."

"I'm not sure I want to go with him if drinking's involved."

"Don't be hard on John. You were wrong about him, too. You're not a very good judge of men when it comes down to it."

"You remember what Dillon was like. Do you blame me?"

"Yeah. I remember. I stood up for you when you eloped with that tall drink of water who made us laugh all the time. Chestnut hair like an Adonis stallion, chocolate-fudge-colored eyes, a killer smile." Her voice had grown lusty soft. "He had a cute butt and walked with a swagger."

We went silent for a few moments. Because we were hot just thinking about the guy. Now, there was a man who would put my new fudge flavor to the test.

The news media fell in love with the new flavors for the guys. The reporters crowded into my crappy little shop that I loved, and this time I asked Gilpa and Grandma to help me show off the brand-spankin'-new Belgian Beer Fudge for guys and a flavor for boys that Cody assured me they'd love called Worms-in-Dirt Fudge made with gummy worms in Oreo cookie "dirt" on top and layered in the middle of the chocolate fudge.

For the men, we packaged and sold the beer fudge in six-pack beer cartons. The fudge had two layers: dark on the bottom and a white fudge on top to look like beer foam.

Using beer in fudge reduced the shelf life to only two days at most because the yeast in the beer grew and bacteria could form, but I figured with this flavor, and with it looking manly in the six-packs, the men would buy it almost blindly and scarf it down fast anyway.

And they did. I let Cody explain the recipe for Belgian Beer Fudge; he made it sound like a geology class lesson about sedimentary layers. My scientifically bent self swelled with pride.

After about two hours, the news media left. I used my phone to text Jeremy Stone to get his take on it all. He texted back, "Belgian Beer Fudge all over Internet. Same for Worms-in-Dirt. You ready for monster orders?"

My reflex reaction was to say, "No." I realized, though, that the person I hadn't learned to trust most of all was myself. I texted back instead: "In Hollywood, stars have their own groups and 'peeps.' But I have church ladies. We're ready for fame and fortune Door County style."

We shared an LOL.

As the day wore on, it was just me, Pauline, Cody, and Harbor in the shop. I was exhausted. It was around five in the afternoon. I slumped against my white marble table near the window in time to see Jordy coming up the dock.

The bell clanged on the door as he sauntered in, his badge glinting at us. "I almost forgot to collect those diamonds."

I headed for Gilpa's cash register counter. But I didn't find anything underneath.

"Cody, did you put the diamonds somewhere? They were in a pink wrapper with a pink ribbon."

He rushed over from wrapping pieces of Cinderella Pink Fudge. He took a wrapper out of his pocket. "I found this on the floor."

"Where on the floor?"

"Back by Harbor's bed, by the beer cooler."

Pauline and I looked at each other. I rushed back to Harbor. The cinnamon-bear-like puppy peered up at me from his sleep with soulful eyes.

Pauline shrugged at me. "Just like pop beads or pearls. They'll eventually come out."

Cody said, "Holy cow. That's one expensive dog right now. What's he worth? About two million?"

I laughed. "Yup. Something like that."

"Wait until I tell Bethany."

Jordy shook his head in derision at us. But on his way out the door, he winked at me and said, "I guess we have a date in the morning to walk a dog together."

That weekend Oosterlings' Live Bait, Bobbers & Belgian Fudge was the center of the universe and a huge success. The church ladies came on Mother's Day, but the men didn't seem to mind all the frilly stuff they had for sale. We sold the Belgian Beer Fudge in its beer six-packs on Gilpa's side as part of our new line of Fisherman's Catch Tall Tale Fudge. Kids were loving their gummy worms in fudge, too. Gilpa was racking up huge sales of everything, especially after he told the fishermen that his minnows smelled extra good to big fish because the minnows had been fed a steady diet of my fudge. Fishermen believed any tall tale if they thought it would catch a big coho salmon or trout.

On Sunday night my manager called, to my shock. I realized I hadn't even thought much of my old job in Los Angeles for several days. .

"Didn't think you'd make something of yourself back there," he said, joking with me. He continued. "Just talked with the producers over at *The Topsy-Turvy Girls*. They want you back."

"I find that hard to believe. They were doing just fine without me mostly."

"Actually, the two stars on the show heard you weren't

coming back possibly and they balked at resigning for next season. Seems they want more of a woman's voice in the storylines. And they liked your fudge."

A smile curved my lips up fast. I had never thought the actresses on the show might notice me. Or care.

"They want me back?" Something akin to a warm, spring breeze blew through me.

"How soon can you get here? I called your agent, and she's got your new contract ready for signing." He went on to explain some pretty generous terms—everything I'd ever wanted.

With the phone in my hand and my manager still jabbering his gibberish, I wandered through my shop, past the copper kettles, past the white marble table at the window. If I truly wanted to, I was sure I could keep the fudge shop going in my absence with Cody's help and that of the church ladies.

I stepped outside, taking in the chilly, dank and damp air coming off Lake Michigan. It'd be down in the forties tonight; in Los Angeles it would be in the seventies or eighties probably and perfectly sublime for May. I stared at the phone. With the salary my manager had scored for me, I could fly back and forth. Maybe I could have both worlds at once.

But when I turned to go back inside, I noticed the sign above the door. The sign that my grandpa had re-done two weeks ago—going on three weeks now. He'd moved the apostrophe over. Instead of "his" shop, Oosterling's, it was now "our" shop, Oosterlings'. He'd taken down the word "Beer" in Oosterling's Live Bait, Bobbers & Beer and had put up Oosterlings' Live Bait, Bobbers & Belgian Fudge. I realized I wasn't done yet with the sign.

I said to my manager, whom I'd kept waiting on the phone, "Marc, thanks, but I pass."

"You can't pass."

"I just did. Tell them I'm working on a screenplay about pink fudge and a dog pooping out diamonds. And it's going to be worth millions."

"Are you nuts?"

"Yes. And very happy."

We said good-bye.

I smiled up at the sign. Then I went inside, hunting up the missing piece to the sign, the part that Gilpa and I had taken down. I got the tall stool, the hammer and a nail from Gilpa's toolbox, then brought them outside. With a little nailing and a little paint to help things along, we now had Oosterlings' Live Bait, Bobbers & Belgian Fudge & Beer.

I had a feeling that my Gilpa and I were going to be very, very busy from now on.

And we were. The next week tested me. Sales went crazy, like dandelions turning park lawns, medians in highways, and sidewalk cracks yellow all at once. I made fudge day and night with the help of my church-lady "peeps," whom I was training now with the four-foot wood paddles and spatulas and the copper kettle cooking—the only major copper kettle operation in all of Door County.

We had a lot of pink fudge to make—both for the upcoming prom on Saturday and for the Sunday Booyah Bash, where my fudge would be raffled off to help pay for restorations for the historic Saint Mary of the Snows church in Namur, near Brussels.

More than making fudge occupied my mind that

week. My future was filled with puzzles to solve. I wondered what would become of the places where the murders had taken place—the Blue Heron Inn above me on the steep hill and the abandoned mansion on Main Street where my grandfather could have been killed, too. I thought it was time Gilpa got the new boat he deserved, but how could we possibly afford such a thing? We needed more dogs pooping out diamonds to make that happen.

I suspected Fishers' Harbor would now pop for a new stoplight, what with all the traffic. Mercy Fogg would be happy. For a while. I had a feeling she would find something else to fuss over in the future. Maybe me. My heart said I needed to apologize to her for my nasty comments toward her and my misconceptions about her; my head said trying to get close to Mercy would bring on more trouble from her somehow.

Finally, I wondered what would become of Sam and me. And Jordy seemed to stop by a lot now, too, always with some excuse about needing details for the "case" that felt lame to me. Could I possibly trust my heart enough to just let nature take its course with Jordy and Sam?

Somehow, despite interruptions by the press, the church ladies and I made it to prom night with loads of Cinderella Pink Fudge. With Pauline's help, we turned the entire Fishers' Harbor docks into the prom location. We tied pink and Green Bay Packer green balloons on all the tire bumpers on all the piers. The Packer stuff was Sam's idea. I'd learned my lesson; too much pink didn't work for men. But anything belonging to the Packers did, Sam reminded me.

Since Gilpa's boat wasn't working, we used that for

taking photos of the couples. Bethany decided to be Cody's date after all. He had become something of a hero. He looked like a hero, too, with his buzz-cut red hair and tuxedo.

Jordy came as a chaperone, but he had another agenda. In front of the entire crowd dancing on the docks, he gave Cody a special badge—a star for his chest that said, "Star Citizen." It was a good citizenship award that the sheriff's department bestowed rarely enough to make it special. Jordy thanked Cody for his bravery and role in solving the murder case. The crowd went wild. It was pretty sweet. I even saw tears roll from Mercy Fogg's eyes. Cody's parents apologized to me and even thanked me for the role I played in Cody's changes.

Most everybody had gone home by midnight. I returned to my shop to tidy up.

Cody, with Bethany in tow, popped his head in. "There's some guy down the docks looking for Oosterlings'. He says he's lookin' for his dog." Cody bit his lower lip, clearly worried.

I must have had the same look because Cody added, "We could take Harbor and make a run for it out your back door."

At the mention of his name, Harbor bounced up from his sleep, then slammed into my legs, wagging his big brush of a tail. He sat his butt on my feet, then stared up at me with big brown eyes, his shaggy, cinnamon-colored ears like inverted V's, questioning me. A lump lodged in my throat. Surely my feelings were about Gilpa and Cody growing to like the dog. I couldn't possibly want this dog.

Cody said, "Do we have to give him up? I like telling people we have a dog that poops diamonds."

I had to sigh. "Life isn't all as sweet and satisfying as our fudge recipes, Cody."

"But we can make our life what we want it to be. We can have a 'homemade' life. Isn't that why you're staying in Door County? It's a homemade place to live."

"Homemade?"

"Yeah, Miss Oosterling. It's filled with homemade goodness here." He swung Bethany's hand, which he'd been holding. They smiled at each other.

Rainbows bloomed in my heart for them. I said, "Time for you and Bethany to go home now, and for Harbor, too, I'm afraid."

Cody and Bethany left.

I gave Harbor a pat on the head. "Hey, big fella—" My voice broke. "I guess your daddy's comin' for ya."

The cowbell clanged on the front door.

I looked up, then almost fainted dead away. "Dillon?"

The Origin of Fudge in the United States

Fudge was popularized in the United States in 1888 when students at Vassar College made fudge for a senior class auction. Emelyn Battersby Hartridge (Class of 1892) attributed the recipe to a classmate's cousin, who ran a Baltimore, Maryland, grocery store, where the fudge sold for forty cents a pound. Emelyn's letter discussing the auction is the first instance of documentation of the recipe for fudge in this country, according to Vassar College's Web site. Two other women's colleges, Smith College and Wellesley College, created their own recipes soon after the appearance of the Vassar fudge.

Vassar College Fudge Recipe

Before you cook: Prepare an 8x8-inch pan. Line with wax paper that covers the edges and then spray the paper with nonstick vegetable oil so that the fudge can be easily removed later for cutting.

  2 cups granulated white sugar
  1 cup cream
  2 ounces unsweetened Baker's chocolate, chopped
  1 tablespoon butter (melted)

In a heavy-bottomed pan, heat sugar and cream until hot, stirring constantly. Add in chocolate. Keep stirring constantly and cook until mixture reaches the soft-ball stage (238 degrees Fahrenheit). This will take 20 to 25 minutes. Remove from heat and add butter. As it cools, keep stirring or "whipping" fudge until it starts to thicken. This will take about 10 minutes; the fudge will become thick and glassy-looking. Pour into an 8x8 pan.

Note from Christine DeSmet: This is a simple, slightly grainier fudge like "what my mom or grandma made." I let this fudge sit in its pan overnight on my counter before cutting it. When you're ready to cut it, lift it out of the pan in one piece and onto a cutting board, slicing into one-inch squares, or any size of your choosing, with a long, smooth blade. Serving this fudge to my coworkers had them swooning and swapping stories about the fudge they remembered from "when they were little."

Cinderella Pink Fudge (with Diamonds) Recipe

This easy microwave recipe for a cherry-vanilla fudge is a favorite with my friends and coworkers. They like the "diamonds" they find in the fudge. (Leave out the diamonds if you don't like the crunchy surprises in the texture.)

Before you cook: Prepare an 8x8-inch pan by lining it with wax paper so that the wax paper comes over the edges. Spray the paper lightly with nonstick vegetable cooking spray.

> 2 cups white chocolate chips
> 14-ounce can sweetened condensed milk
> 1 teaspoon vanilla extract
> 1 cup dried cherries (or canned whole tart cherries, chopped)
> Red food coloring
> ½ cup edible white or clear glitter (large size) for "diamonds"
> Pink or white luster dust (optional)

Mix chips and milk together and melt at medium power in the microwave for about 5 minutes. Stir and return to microwave until fully melted. Stir in vanilla and four or five (or more) drops of red food coloring to turn it pink. Just before pouring it into the pan, blend in the cherries and 1/4 cup of the glitter if you want diamonds *inside* the fudge. Then pour it into the pan. Sprinkle the top of the fudge with the rest of the "diamond" glitter.

Optional: Before you sprinkle on the diamond glitter, first brush on luster dust, which is a very fine glittery edible powder you can buy in various colors. It's best to apply luster dust with a small artist's brush so that you don't waste it; don't try to shake it directly from its container onto your fudge or use your fingers. Sprinkle the rest of the "diamond" glitter on top of the luster dust.

Let your fudge sit for a few hours or overnight. When ready to cut, transfer it from its pan to a cutting board. Use a knife with a smooth blade or a fudge cutter. Cut into one-inch squares or any size you prefer.

Worms-in-Dirt Fudge Recipe

This is an easy microwave recipe for fudge that's especially popular with kids and guys who love gummy worms.

Before you cook: Prepare an 8x8-inch pan by lining it with wax paper so that the wax paper comes over the edges. Spray the paper lightly with nonstick vegetable cooking spray.

    12-ounce package semisweet chocolate chips
    1 cup milk chocolate chips
    14-ounce can sweetened condensed milk
    2 tablespoons butter
    12 Oreo (or similar chocolate) cookies, grated
    Gummy worms

Melt chocolate chips in microwave with sweetened condensed milk and butter on medium heat for 3 or 4 minutes. Stir and return to microwave as needed until melted and smooth.

To "bury" gummy worms in "dirt" in the middle of your fudge, first pour half the fudge mixture into the prepared pan. Next, sprinkle in a light layer of cookie dirt across the entire pan. Lay as many gummy worms as you wish in the dirt—about 10 worms will be enough. Sprinkle more dirt on top of them. Pour the remainder of your fudge on top. If you wish, sprinkle more dirt on top, or add more gummy worms.

Let cool without a cover for a few minutes; if covered, it might steam and melt your gummy worms on top. Ironically, the gummy worms in the middle of the cookie dirt inside the fudge stay intact without melting much. You can also choose to skip putting the gummy worms inside the fudge and just layer them and the dirt on top. You might need to push the gummy worms into the fudge slightly on top before cutting the fudge.

This yields a chewy fudge—expect a gummy worm in every bite.

Ackowledgments

Many thanks go to John Talbot of Talbot Fortune Agency and Danielle Perez, executive editor, New American Library/Penguin Group, for their creative ideas, expertise, and hard work.

Thank you to my colleagues for their support: Bridget Birdsall, Marshall Cook, Laura Kahl, Laurie Scheer, and Laurel Yourke. Thanks also to other colleagues at University of Wisconsin–Madison Continuing Studies who taste-tested fudge recipes and who provided me with fudge recipes and tips.

Thank you to my fellow Sisters in Crime members, including Deb Baker, Kathleen Ernst, and M. J. Williams, for their support, as well as Karen Wiesner, who read every word of the manuscript for me. Thanks to Mystery Writers of America member and critique partner, Jerol Anderson, too.

Much appreciation goes to my research team: Darlene and Jerry Kronschnabel of DePere, Wisconsin; Theresa and Al Alexander of the Belgian Club in Door County, Wisconsin; and Alyssa Haskins, head of research and development for DB Infusion Chocolates, Madison, Wisconsin.

Each of us needs a true cheering section. My cheering section included the fine new novelists from my summer Write-by-the-Lake Writer's Retreat: Barbara Belford,

Cheryl Hanson, Julie Holmes, Blair Hull, Lisa Kusko, and Roi Solberg.

Finally, thanks to my family! And a big thanks to the man in my life, who has to "suffer" through all the fudge recipes I try—Bob Boetzer.

Thanks, everybody!

Don't miss the next novel in the
Fudge Shop Mystery series

HOT FUDGE FRAME-UP

by Christine DeSmet
Coming from Obsidian in Summer 2014.

Chapter 1

Everything and everyone has a purpose in life and a place, my grandmother Sophie says. "And everyone and everything can be good and then go bad. Lloyd Mueller is like beer fudge. Enjoy it now because it has a shelf life of only about three days."

I shivered at what she'd just insinuated. But nobody contradicts my Belgian grandmother. Especially when she's upset. Yet I plunged in like a ninny. "Grandma, Lloyd is a good landlord. Or was. At least he's giving me a refund for having to move out of his rental cabin early. He's bringing the check to the meeting at the fudge shop. And please don't talk about him having a shelf life." My skin rippled again, this time with big goose bumps. "You make it sound like somebody will do him in for making me move."

"Bah and booyah! Maybe he should watch out! You're moving out of this lovely cabin and then moving into the storage room of your fudge shop? Whoever heard of living in a fudge shop! This is going to be trouble for you and worse for Lloyd!" Exclamation points spat out of her mouth as my grandmother splashed suds about the fudge utensils in my cabin's kitchen sink.

My cabin is one of several rentals along the three-block length of Duck Marsh Street in Fishers' Harbor, a tourist town on peninsular Door County, Wisconsin, which juts into Lake Michigan. Our county is known as the Cape Cod of the Midwest. In the summer, when the condos and summer homes fill with vacationers from Chicago and beyond, our village's population of two hundred swells to a couple of thousand in the immediate area.

"I don't like it," Grandma said, persisting. We Belgians are like that, the old "dog on a bone," never giving up. "He's up to no good."

I had to admit I felt the same way. Everybody knew everybody's business here. Lloyd was the richest man in town by far. All we knew was that he intended to buy the Blue Heron Inn, but he wasn't telling anybody his intentions for it except to say it wouldn't be an inn. People all over town were nervous about the secrecy. Even Lloyd's ex-wife, Libby—who got along with him fine—had told my grandma she was worried about the mysterious surprise he had cooking for Fishers' Harbor. Libby said he wouldn't even tell her. What did that mean? That he's up to no good, as Grandma says?

It was hard for me to worry too much about this big secret at the moment. I was in the living room area packing books in a hurry in sticky July humidity. It was Friday morning after the Fourth, and I'd told Lloyd I'd be out by Sunday. The early-morning fog was being steamed by the sun, steeping me like a tea bag. My long brown hair, in a twist atop my head, was coming undone on my damp neck, and my trademark pink blouse was beginning to stick to my back.

I'd been up since five, the water had been cut off in

my fudge shop today, and the bird-call clock over the sink had just cardinal-chirped eight o'clock, which panicked me. I had to meet up with the fudge contest judges and confectioner chef contestants at my shop in a half hour. Fortunately, Oosterlings' Live Bait, Bobbers & Belgian Fudge & Beer was only about thirty feet across my backyard. It sat on the docks of our Lake Michigan harbor.

Grandma said, amid pans rattling in the sink, "I don't see why you can't live in our sunporch for now."

Grandma and Grandpa Oosterling lived across the way, in one of only two cabins on this street not owned by Lloyd Mueller, an old high school buddy of Grandpa's. Moving in with my grandma Sophie and grandpa Gil would be convenient, but I was thirty-two, and I'd heard too many jokes about thirtysomethings moving back in with family to be comfortable with the invitation.

"Grandma, I'll be fine. I need to worry about settling on a new fudge flavor for next week's contest." I tossed more cookbooks and scriptwriting books into the next empty box sitting next to me on the floor by the couch.

"You like Brussels sprouts."

"Sprout fudge?" I swallowed down my gag reflex, then heard her squelch a giggle. My grandma was like that, always keeping me on my toes. "What fairy tale is that based on?" From the start of my business, I had decided that all my fudge flavors for women and girls had to be named for a fairy tale.

Grandma said, "The story of the Three Bears. Porridge fudge."

Smiling at that flavor, I countered, "Maybe a Goldilocks flavor, something in gold? I'm not sure what flavor that could be, but it needs to be as nice as my cherry-vanilla Cinderella Pink Fudge." The Cinderella fudge had become an instant hit with the tourists. "I want something gal pals will savor with a fine Door County wine or that their little girls will find cute and fun for their tea parties. I'm starting to panic."

"Ah, the sweet success of your first fudge flavor is pressuring you." Grandma Sophie wrestled a big stainless-steel mixer bowl into the sink. "Come over for dinner tonight and we'll brainstorm. And move your stuff into our cabin. Whoever heard of living in a storage room amid milk, cream, and mice!"

"There are no mice in my fudge shop, Grandma. There's only Titus here in the cabin, in the bottom cupboard."

"I can't believe you named a mouse. Bah."

"Well, he wouldn't climb into my traps for cheese or even peanut butter, so I figured I'd give him a name and then just call him out of hiding."

"Booyah to you." The word "booyah" refers to a traditional Belgian celebration stew made with chicken and vegetables, but now the word is used all the time as a cheer word. Grandma continued as she swished suds around the bowl. "That mouse will have more living space than you. And moving now is the worst possible time to do it in your life. Lloyd should be ashamed of himself for telling the new owner you'd be gone by Sunday sometime. Who do you suppose he sold these cabins to?"

"Maybe Libby's learned more. I'll ask her. I have to stop over at the lighthouse later with her batch of fudge anyway." I sneezed from the books as I packed another box on the floor. I hadn't dusted anything since I'd arrived in town in late April. Opening and operating the fudge shop had kept me too busy. "Grandma, maybe we should just be happy that Lloyd isn't letting the inn sit empty and become a home for Titus's relations."

"I suppose you're right. Not many people want to move into a place where a murder happened."

I shivered all over again for the umpteenth time just thinking about my involvement. Back in May my fudge had been stuck down the throat of an actress who'd been choked to death. The killer had tried to pin it all on the newbie back in town—me. I wondered now if some relative of the murdered woman had bought my cabin in order to be close to her spirit. Was my landlord afraid I'd be freaked out? Try to stop the sale?

But I had more important worries. The annual Fishers' Harbor Arts Festival was being held a week from tomorrow—Saturday. Back in May, I'd been conned into sponsoring a fudge contest by my best friend's new boyfriend. John Schultz was a tourism and tour promoter out of Milwaukee who looked for any angle to bring himself up to Door County to visit Pauline Mertens. John had convinced me that a fudge contest was my way of participating in the arts festival, thus helping me look like a good member of the business community—while making amends for drawing bad karma to Fishers' Harbor with the murder involving my fudge. The taste-off next Saturday afternoon would be followed that evening by an adult prom dance on the docks outside the fudge shop. The prom was also hatched by John, with Pauline's blessing. I couldn't say no to Pauline. She felt sorry for me. I'd never been to a prom because as a teenager I'd been a too-tall, athletic nerd farm girl whom the boys passed in the hallway as if I were invisible.

Unfortunately, things were already going wrong. The guest celebrity chef contestants who had arrived this past Monday for a two-week stay had taken over the six copper kettles in my shop—as in *not sharing* them with me at all. And I couldn't seem to come up with a new fudge flavor that would knock everybody's socks off. What's more, I had to come up with a prom dress—something that wouldn't reveal how much fudge I'd eaten in the past couple of months. My excited and desperate gal pals Pauline and Laura Rousseau were coming over later this morning with yet another set of fabric swatches and dress patterns.

Rapid-fire knocking on my front door was followed by my young red-haired shop assistant, Cody Fjelstad, yelling through the screen, "Miss Oosterling! Come quick!"

My mother was with him. She hollered from behind Cody, "Ava honey, your shop's being destroyed!"

"What?" The nonsensical news kept me rooted on the floor for just a second.

Cody opened the screen door, then waved frantically. "Get a move on, Miss Oosterling. Your chefs are chasing each other around the shop with fudge cutters. They keep saying they're going to kill each other."

My fudge shop and all my freshly made fudge were being held hostage by two chefs with circular knives.

When I rushed in through the back door of my shop, Kelsey King, a petite blonde from Portland, Oregon, and Piers Molinsky, a portly giant from Chicago, were wielding fudge cutters from their stances on both ends of my white marble-slab table. My freshly made Cinderella Pink Fudge lay hostage in its pans between them. Kelsey and Piers had fudge cutters poised over the pans.

Fudge cutters look like pizza cutters—round, sharp

disks. Kelsey held up the one with one disk, while Piers had one with multiple disks, which could cause a lot of quick damage if tossed at Kelsey.

I stood in shock behind my old-fashioned cash register, thinking I might need it as protection.

My mom muttered behind my back, "I forgot to tell you about the smell, too."

The grab bag of aromas in the place made me pause. What had the chefs been up to in only a few minutes' time this morning? I'd left the place just an hour ago, and nobody had been here but my grandpa Gil and a few fishermen. It had smelled of the strong fresh coffee we always had on hand and my new batch of cherry-vanilla pink perfection fudge. Now the bait and fudge shop smelled of bacon, of all things, and a heady, earthy mix of spices such as nutmeg, cinnamon, ginger, maybe some anise and orange peel tossed in.

I called out from behind my small fortress, "What's wrong with you two? Stop!"

Piers, his chubby face red, his furry brown eyebrows pinched together, kept his gaze lasered on his enemy across the marble table as he picked up a pan of my fudge.

My heart rate accelerated. "Put the fudge down, Piers."

Piers ignored me, growling at Kelsey, "You do not belong in this contest. This is what fudge looks like." He waved my pan of Cinderella Pink Fudge in the air.

Behind me, my mother whined in panic or disgust or both.

Kelsey snatched up the other pan of my fudge, waving her fudge cutter over it as she glared at Piers. "You see this fudge? This is your face!"

She slashed at my pretty pink fudge.

My mother screamed, nearly turning me deaf. I gasped, stunned for a moment, waiting for my hearing to come back.

Cody, whose dream was to be a law officer or park ranger, grabbed one of my four-foot spatulas from a nearby copper kettle. "I'll stop 'em, Miss Oosterling."

"No, Ranger, don't. Stand back." Cody liked being called "Ranger," especially after he'd helped me solve the murder a couple of months ago and our county sheriff awarded him a good citizenship star.

I could've used the sheriff's help at the moment. Ordinarily, my popular pink fudge sat in front of the big bay window to cure and entice tourists. Now, there was nobody outside, just the view of Lake Michigan lapping up against the boats rocking at their moorings. Any customers there to buy fudge or bait had scattered to save their lives. Even if I called Sheriff Tollefson or a deputy, the sheriff's office was a half hour's drive away in Sturgeon Bay.

I glanced to the bait shop side of the place. "Gilpa?" The word came out strangled in my tight throat. Since I'd been a little girl, I'd called Grandpa Gil the shortcut name of "Gilpa."

Ranger said, "He took a fisherman out just as I got here."

I appealed again to the chefs. "This is silly. It's going to be a beautiful day. Why start it out with a fight?"

Neither looked at me. Instead, they started a volley of words while shaking the fudge cutters and my fudge all about in the air. The glass in the bay window within inches of them was vibrating from the intensity.

I hesitated going over to the two on my own. Kelsey's blond cuteness and petite frame rendered her deceivingly harmless-looking. But she was a fitness guru who ran a health spa. She knew karate and ate the bark off trees. I was probably smelling bark cooking in the aromas floating about us. Piers, whose bulk reflected his love of the muffin tops he'd made famous in Chicago, growled like a bear at Kelsey.

Piers used his fudge cutter to gouge out and flick a good-sized portion of my precious pink confection onto the floor. He smashed it with the heel of one boot. "This is your face."

We all cried out in pain—me, Cody, my mom, and two customers who popped up from behind a shelving unit filled with handmade Cinderella Pink dolls, purses, and teacups. I recognized the ladies from my grandmother's church group. They rushed out screaming something about "saints and sinners." The cowbell on the door clanged. A teacup fell to the floor in their wake and broke.

Those ladies would spread the gossip fast, so I had to take action. I used the weapon that always worked. "There could be *TV cameras* on you, for all you know. I think that's John coming down the docks right now."

My mother whimpered, "Oh no."

John Schultz had been videotaping us every spare moment of his time. To keep things manageable for his videotaping, John wanted just three contestants—me and these two trying to kill each other. He'd scoured his universe of contacts in the travel industry and had come up with Piers and Kelsey. I'm sad to say I approved them. Shows my talent for judging people. John had insisted that he tape the fudge contest activities this week and next with the hopes of ending up on a cable channel. He'd get a show of his own, he said, and I'd get fudge fame. But John wasn't coming down the docks right now; I'd lied.

Fortunately, my lie worked like a hose on two fighting cats. Kelsey broke into tears, dropping her fudge cutter on the marble slab. She looked around for the camera on her. It was pitiful. I almost wished John were here. Piers whipped off his white apron, then used it to swab my ruined pink fudge off the floor. He, too, looked about for the camera, smiling, which galled me.

"Were you two faking? Practicing?" I asked. "You gave my mother a heart attack."

"I'm so sorry," Piers said, turning into a teddy bear. "Please forgive me, Ava. You were so kind to invite me, and yet I did this to you. Sorry."

His words were stilted, obviously an act for the non-existent camera. At least he was being polite again to me and my fudge.

Kelsey, though, slapped a hand on the marble table. "Sorry? That's all you've got to say for cheating? He was hogging the copper kettles again for his hog that he's cooking." Her shoulders hunched up to her earlobes in a shudder. "He's putting hog bits into the fudge."

"Hog bits?" I asked.

"Bacon," Piers said, pulling his shoulders back in pride. "I'm experimenting with bacon fudge."

Kelsey sniped, "He took over four of the kettles; then he put bacon in one of my kettles of boiling ingredients so I'd have to throw it out. After I did, I looked away for just a moment and he'd tossed more bacon—meat—into my kettle. Yewww."

My mother touched my arm. "Honey, I have to finish making deliveries. Maybe you should come with me and let them cool down."

Kelsey said with big fake smile, "That cow truck you drive is just the cutest thing, Florine."

Mom—Florine, never Flo—drove a black-and-white cow motif minivan around the county delivering our farm's organic cream, cheeses, milk, and butter to various restaurants and to my fudge shop each day. When I'd contacted Kelsey King weeks ago in Portland, where she had a fledgling TV show featuring organics, she'd been thrilled to hear about our farm's organic nature. She agreed instantly to the adventure of being a contestant in a fudge contest and arts festival in Door County. I tried to use that modicum of respect to quell the fight now.

"Kelsey, my mother can replace all of your ingredients with fresh ones right now. And maybe the bacon falling into your fudge mix was a mistake."

"No, it wasn't." Her fake smile stiffened.

I turned to look up at Piers. "Why do you need four kettles? You were each assigned two to use. Two for each of you, with two left for me."

That's when the smells in the place became a warning along with the odd sounds of audible gulps, lapping, and growls. I looked at the north wall area behind our short counter and glass shelving where the six kettles sat over their open-flame heating units. "Oh my gosh!"

Two copper kettles had bubbled over, oozing sugar and mystery ingredients—and bite-sized bacon pieces—onto the floor. A troublemaking furry brown dog belonging to my ex-husband—the infamous bigamist—leaped about in the middle of canine nirvana, slurping up bacon bits as fast as his long, pink tongue could operate. We were lucky the dog hadn't knocked over the open flames and caused a fire. Ironically, my ex had named the dog "Lucky" after his gambling prowess—my ex's prowess, not the dog's.

Since my ex had come back to town for utility construction business in May, the dog seemed to get loose and show up in my shop just about every other day. I glanced toward the door now with my heartbeat racing a bit in nervous trepidation. The dog's rogue appearances usually brought Dillon Rivers through the door soon after.

Ranger dashed over to turn off the burners. He grabbed the gangly water spaniel who was now rolling in the bacon goop on the floor. "Harbor, no! Come with me." Cody had dubbed the dog Harbor the first day he had sneaked into our shop because the gregarious animal loved to fling himself in the harbor water outside our front door.

The dog with two names was always a mess unless he was secured with a leash. Lucky Harbor also loved to steal fudge if I didn't watch him. Chocolate isn't good for dogs; it can be fatal. I dashed over to Gilpa's side of the shop for a piece of twine. Lucky Harbor began barking so loudly in protest over having to leave his puddle of bacon that everybody in the shop had their hands clamped over their ears.

"Please take him into the back somewhere for now, Ranger. Tie him to a doorknob or something."

Piers said, "At least the dog shows good taste."

Piers found a spoon, then began ladling up the mess on the floor. "You weren't using your kettles, Ava, so I took them over, thinking I was doing you a favor. You weren't here when I arrived. You didn't see Kelsey sabotaging the ingredients."

Kelsey yelped, "You liar." She grabbed the fudge cutter again to wave at him. "You're the one sabotaging me, you sausage hick from Chicago!"

At that moment, the fudge judges arrived, two of

them through the front door: my landlord, Lloyd Mueller; and a local cookbook author, Professor Alex Faust.

My grandmother—the third judge—came in through the back door, finally catching up with us. "What's that smell?"

"Bacon," I said.

"No, the other smell. Like dirt cooking."

Kelsey seethed at Piers. "That's the smell of my ruined fudge."

Piers snapped, "It's real dirt. She's passing off black dirt as chocolate fudge!"

Kelsey flew at Piers with a karate kick, which he caught in his beefy hands, but he slipped on the oozing syrup and bacon fat on the floor. They slid out from behind my glass counter loaded with various fudges, landing on their backs in the goo. I rushed to help, but Kelsey got up fast to push me away so she could go at Piers again. I grabbed her in an armlock to break it up—

Just as Dillon Rivers charged through the door. The cowbell clanged against the wall. "Whoa, are we puttin' bets down on who wins this wrestling match? I've got five bucks on the fudge lady."

I let go of Kelsey.

My tall, killer-handsome ex swept off his hard hat, combing his chestnut-colored hair with his fingers. His muscular chest was bare and glistening already from morning exertion. Both my heart and my stomach did a flippity-flop.

My mother groaned. She did not like Dillon. She said to me, "I'll call the sheriff." She was dialing her phone as she said it.

Grandma said, "I'll buzz Gil." She dug in her jeans for her phone.

Professor Faust, a genial, sixtysomething, gray-haired guy in a blue shirt and tan pants, stood wide-eyed. He was carrying a stack of his latest cookbook. "Perhaps this isn't a good time for a meeting? Where can I leave my books? They're all signed."

Everybody ignored Professor Faust because that's what happens when Dillon is in a room, especially with his shirt off.

"Hey there," Dillon said, with a look that said he knew exactly what he was doing to me. He slipped on a neon yellow T-shirt with his construction company logo on it, which he'd had shoved in a back pocket. "Anybody see my dog? And what's this I hear about the fudge shop closing and the contest being canceled?"

Ugh, Grandma's gossipy church-lady friends must have met him on the docks.

I said to Dillon, "We're in the middle of something. Your dog's in the back. You'll need to take him for a swim before you let him in your truck."

Dillon chuckled as he looked me up and down. "Maybe you'd like to go for a swim, too." He sniffed at me. "You smell like bacon. I better ask you to the prom before other guys get a whiff of you."

"Very funny," I said.

My mother rushed between us, clicking off her phone. "Honey, come with me to the lighthouse. Now."

At first, her urgency was lost on me. Kelsey and Piers were arguing again while cleaning up the slippery floor, and the dog was barking from the back. Cody had come back into the main shop to boss Kelsey and Piers; Cody obsessed about germs and cleanliness in the fudge shop.

Lloyd, with his salt-and-pepper mustache wiggling,

rubbed his bald head with one hand in confusion held up an envelope in the other hand. It had to be my rent reimbursement. "Should I hang on to this check and come back another time? This doesn't look like a good time for a meeting."

Grandma was on him like flies on fish left too long in the sun. Shaking a finger under his nose, almost touching his mustache, she said, "This is your fault, Lloyd. You're ruining my granddaughter's life. Why?"

Dillon said, "Hold on there, Sophie. The man's an upstanding citizen."

My grandmother muttered Belgian words under her breath as she advanced on Dillon.

My mother and I hustled Grandma Sophie out the door before another fight started. I felt bad that my ex was such an object of scorn because he was a decent enough guy; he'd just been too eager to fall in love when he was too young to handle the concept. Me, too. But Florine and Sophie blamed Dillon for whisking me away to Las Vegas eight years ago to marry him in one of those youthful, stupid indiscretions that, looking back on it, not even I can believe I did.

I put thoughts of Dillon aside as Mom was driving erratically ten miles over the speed limit through the back streets of Fishers' Harbor and then even faster on Highway 42 outside of the village. We were heading southwest, with glimpses of Lake Michigan going by like flipped pages in a book.

"Mom, slow down. There are tourists all over the place." Tourists often stopped their vehicles at the oddest times to gawk at the spectacular scenery of the lake or to find the quaint art shops tucked away in the woodlands.

Grandma gasped when Mom hit the horn and swerved around a slowing car ahead of us on the two-lane highway. "Florine, what the hell—?"

Mom veered into the entrance to Peninsula State Park. We went through the park gates, then headed down Shore Road, which went to the Eagle Bluff Lighthouse.

I told Mom, "I forgot Libby's fudge."

Mom barely missed a hen turkey and her poults, which were strutting across the blacktop. Before I could complain again, I noticed the sheriff's car with its red and blue lights swirling in front of the lighthouse.

The lighthouse was made of Cream City brick with a red roof on top of its main house and atop the cupola tower. In the morning sun, the four-story tower had a yellow glow but with red and blue striations.

"What's going on, Mom?"

Her knuckles were white on the steering wheel. "The sheriff said Libby found something that he wants you to look at."

"Me? Why didn't you tell me?" I knew why. My mother did not handle stress or my adventurous life very well.

We parked next to the cruiser. Before we got out, my mother had a shaky hand on my arm. "Honey, are you in some kind of trouble again?"

"No," I said, though I always seemed to be in trouble and not know it. I searched my brain for something that would require a sheriff but came up with nothing. The fighting confectioner chefs was the only issue that came close to needing law enforcement interference as of late. "Is Libby all right?"

She paled. "I forgot to ask. When I called the sheriff, he just said something had happened out here and he needed you."

By then Sheriff Jordy Tollefson had come out to greet us. He was about six feet, four inches tall; he had six inches on me. Jordy was in his early forties, lean, a runner, with the demeanor of a Marine—perfection and precision. He escorted us inside, into the small room that served as the gift shop. A window had been busted.

Libby was sitting on a stool by the register counter, sniffling into a tissue. When she saw us, she rushed over to hug Grandma.

"Oh, Sophie, I'm so glad you're here. And I'm so sorry it has to involve your granddaughter."

A tiny bomb went off inside my stomach. I looked up at Jordy's stern face and steady brown eyes and said, "What happened?"

Jordy picked up a Baggie off the counter. It held a rock. "Somebody sent this through the window."

Then he picked up another Baggie with a piece of ruled paper in it. In perfect orange crayon, the note said, *Somebody will die if you don't convince Lloyd to throw the contest. Miss Oosterling must not win.*

Blood drained from my head. I looked at Libby wrapped in my grandmother's arms and said, "Who would do such a thing? It's a silly fudge contest. I'm so sorry, Libby. Somebody's threatening you and Lloyd?"

My mother said to me, "Honey, you don't seem to get it. Somebody's threatening *you*."